Rakka snarled at an attacker that had crept up from behind. Its tongue oscillated in its mouth; its teeth were a hundred barbs. Rakka put her back to the rest of the clan, protecting her satchel of spell components, and brandished her hiking staff. The lizard man tested her with a quick snap of its axe. She deflected the blow and returned it with a sharp crack to the creature's forward leg. It shuffled back along the strip of land between the tar pools.

Behind her she heard screams, clangs, and ugly wet crunching sounds. She pressed forward, intending to buy herself some space to summon a minion to give her a little advantage. Instead the viashino let her come, and another one grabbed her leg from the tar. Rakka gritted her teeth as her skin sizzled. "All right then," she muttered. "No time to do this fancy. Let's just bring the pain."

MAGIC
The Gathering®

IGNITE YOUR SPARK.
DISCOVER THE PLANESWALKERS IN THEIR ADVENTURES THROUGH THE ENDLESS PLANES OF REALITY…

MAGIC
The Gathering®

ALARA
UNBR◉KEN

DOUG BEYER

Magic: The Gathering
Alara Unbroken

©2009 Wizards of the Coast LLC

Published by Wizards of the Coast LLC

MAGIC: THE GATHERING, WIZARDS OF THE COAST, and their respective logos are trademarks of Wizards of the Coast LLC in the U.S.A. and other countries.

Printed in the U.S.A.

Cover art by Chris Rahn

First Printing:

9 8 7 6 5 4 3 2

ISBN: 978-0-7869-5201-4
620-25032740-001-EN

U.S., CANADA,
ASIA, PACIFIC, & LATIN AMERICA
Wizards of the Coast LLC
P.O. Box 707
Renton, WA 98057-0707
+1-800-324-6496

EUROPEAN HEADQUARTERS
Hasbro UK Ltd
Caswell Way
Newport, Gwent NP9 0YH
GREAT BRITAIN
Save this address for your records.

Visit our web site at www.wizards.com

For Melanie
Whose life I'm glad to have touched
And whose touch I'm glad to have lived

PART ONE

GRIXIS

Nicol Bolas stretched his wings, and the sounds he heard were unpleasant. Ligaments creaked, and joints popped. The membranes between his wing bones made dry sounds of friction as they stretched. For decades he had felt his age catching up to him; his age was an imposing enough figure that he felt deeply invested in eluding the arithmetic. But at least he could stretch. The chamber, deep under the Necropolis at Kederekt, was finally complete. The last of the dead soil had been scraped out from around his bulk, and the tomb had become a proper lair.

The impact of the damnable Mending had left him broken. His omnipotence was mutilated, and his mind felt like a sieve. He was truly an elderly dragon. He had fled Dominaria, hoping the Mending wouldn't reach him—but its effects had caught up to him indeed, like thunder catches up after a crack of lightning. He had felt his power drain. He had felt the millennia of knowledge seep away. He had felt the tattered edges of his own wings for the first time.

"But if nothing else, am I not a survivor?"

"What's that, Master?" came the response, unexpectedly.

So what if he said it aloud? "Am I not a survivor?" Bolas snarled.

DOUG BEYER

His second-in-command, the unholy creature Malfegor, only stared at him. Half demon and half dragon, Malfegor had come into being centuries before under circumstances too horrible for many to contemplate. His rage at being trapped on festering Grixis was amusing—and useful as a fulcrum for Bolas's control over him. Bolas's web of power and influence spanned worlds and eons, a perfect prize to dangle before a demon who had once terrorized all of Alara.

"Twenty thousand years!" Bolas roared. "Never mind. Bring in the . . . visitors."

"Yes, Master."

Malfegor left the chamber. Bolas didn't like the way his henchman's tail twitched as he walked away. It wasn't right for a dragon to carry himself that way. His second-in-command was an abomination. But at least he was a useful one.

When Malfegor returned, he brought with him two human beings, males dressed in robes, adults judging by their size.

One human stepped forward. It was shaking. It was probably terrified.

"Well? What's so important?" asked Bolas.

"Master, I—I and m—my colleagues have read the signs," said the lead human.

"Yes? And?"

"Master, I don't know how to say this—"

"Promptly, if you value your life."

"It's the shards, Master. The other four worlds, and Grixis too. They're . . . converging."

That was interesting. Had one of the little rodents finally figured it out?

"Oh?"

"Yes. I'm afraid . . . I'm afraid they're going to . . . intersect. *Collide*. And soon."

Bolas's lips pulled away from his teeth. The amusement he felt was genuine. "How soon?"

The two humans looked at each other. They didn't seem to know what to make of his expression. "Months?" said the first. "Yes. Less than a year, we think."

Bolas stretched his wings out again. He still heard the poppings of age, but they felt better. Maybe in a little while, he could fly free of the blasted bunker and flex his true muscle once more. He would have to meet with his agents on the other four worlds. Planeswalking took a lot of effort for him, but he had to make sure everything would come out exactly right.

"Master?" ventured the human. "This is . . . what you wanted?"

"I'm very proud of you, human," said Bolas. "This is an excellent leap for your little mind."

"Thank you, Master! But won't that—"

"I feel I need to reward you."

Both the humans fell prostrate.

"I will tell you now that you have done well to discover the goal of all our efforts here on your world of Grixis. You've all worked long and hard, with complex magics and lengthy excavations. And now you are beginning to see the fruits of all your labors."

The speaking human couldn't help itself. It raised its head and said, "Master, I hate to interrupt—"

"Then don't!" bellowed Bolas.

The humans cowered.

"This project, and the preparations surrounding it, have taken decades to complete. The effort has been intricate and many layered. And now you're starting to see it all come together. The devastation it will wreak is, no doubt, the source of your concern. Even your decaying world will suffer, and at this you must object. I admire your courage in coming to my inner chamber to confirm that this cataclysm is indeed the end toward which you all have labored. And for that, your reward! You, stand up."

The speaker looked up, and stood on wobbly legs. It blinked rapidly and held the clasp of its robe in its hands.

Bolas leaned down and put his claw over the human's head, resting his palm there gently, careful not to break the human's neck.

Malfegor spoke up. "Master, don't tax yourself," he said.

Bolas ignored him. It took some concentration, but he summoned up the old magics. Tidal forces of mana washed over his mind. Bolas willed them into the form of a spell, a dark spear of magic that pierced the human's little skull and disappeared, scouring away at its sanity from the inside. The human screamed under Bolas's palm, a ragged, repeated sound bereft of logic or order. Then the human fell silent and still. Bolas completed the spell and lifted his claw.

The human's expression was limp. It stared at nothing, and its head lolled slightly to the side.

"There you are, my minion," said Bolas, breathing heavily. "There is your reward."

The other human regarded its colleague with wide eyes. It stood and gathered the man in its arms. A combination of drool and blood ran down the side of the man's jaw, its thinking mind utterly destroyed.

"You there," said Bolas to the other human, the one who still possessed its faculties. "You can go now, and take that one with you. Remember its reward, always. Should any of the rest of you show such *excellence* in powers of deduction, you shall receive the same."

The human bowed stiffly and hurriedly ushered the other man out on his shoulder.

Bolas turned to his second-in-command, the demonic dragon-creature. "That's enough. If you trouble me with the concerns of the mortals again, Malfegor, I will kill you. After your body has died, I will banish your soul to some wretched, zombified husk in the bowels of Grixis, where you will toil away in the service of the whims of a third-rate human necromancer. Now, will that be all?"

Bolas was alone again.

Once the five worlds of Alara collided, he would have his vitality back. The Multiverse owed him that much—and it had seen fit to provide him with the five little planes, ripe for the picking. He'd crash their worlds into one another and lick the sap from the wounds. And then, finally, he'd be ready to take his revenge.

NAYA

It had not been a good idea, thought Ajani. He should turn around and go before the beast saw or smelled him in his hiding place. But it was too late for that. His axe was already in his hand.

The gargantuan before him had legs like tree trunks, and shaggy moss grew on its back and flanks. Its most salient features were its tusks: four enormous prongs that swept down from its mouth and up into the air in front of it, each ending in a point tapered nough to punch clean through Ajani's chest. The beast's tusks swung back and forth as it bent and grazed on whole trees. It enveloped the foliage of a few trees in its mouth, then pulled back its head, stripping a mass of juicy branches with scraping teeth. The crunching sound as it chewed was deafening. Occasionally it bellowed contentedly, tilting its massive head from side to side, and the sound made the lianas around Ajani's hiding place shudder.

Ajani had been the hunted himself, once, although he hadn't been an oblivious target like this. He had been pursued through the jungles and fields of Naya like a wild pig. Humans didn't usually hunt his kind, but they had seemed to single him out. He had been special to them, somehow—special in that they had wanted him dead.

Maybe he was just as bad for singling out the behemoth. Ajani could think of plenty of reasons to leave. But he knew it had to happen, so it was probably best not to think too hard about what he was about to do. Ajani had tracked the beast since morning, shadowing it at a distance for hours after encountering it, keeping careful track of the wind direction so as not to alert the beast of his scent. His patience had paid off; the gargantuan hadn't discovered him, and in fact had managed to tuck itself into a dead end of sorts, a sky-exposed clearing surrounded by a glade of thick trunks too massive for it to smash. Ajani could press the attack, and the behemoth would have nowhere to run. Although its size would be less of an advantage in the clearing, facing a gargantuan of Naya solo was still likely to be suicide. Yet again, Ajani questioned what he was doing and why.

He picked a burr out of his stark white fur. That was why. Either he earned his pride's esteem by the monumental hunt, or he would leave his pride behind forever.

The white fur that covered Ajani's lionlike body was his distinction and his curse. Where most of the nacatl race bore fur of mottled and striped gold, ochre, black, and gray, Ajani's fur was pure, luminous white. He glowed against the dappled foliage of the Naya jungle, and like a brilliant torch in crowds of his fellow nacatl.

The scorn of his kin had been immediate and was never-ending. Ajani's pride was a community of warriors, the proudest and fiercest pride of nacatl in all of Naya, But to him they were a community of tormentors. Like the day when the humans had hunted him: when the furless ones had given chase, his pridemates had left him behind. The humans didn't pursue the others—only him.

It seemed everyone wanted to single out the white-furred cat.

His brother Jazal—the pride's leader, thank the spirits—had saved him that day, and on many other occasions. As the *kha* of their pride, Jazal was the only one Ajani looked up to. If it weren't for him, Ajani would have left the pride, and struck out on his own a long time before. That's what his tormentors wanted, he wondered, why not just give it to them? But that would bring even more shame on his poor brother, who had shown him nothing but respect and love. Ajani owed it to Jazal, the *kha* and his only kin, to show the others in the pride the determination he carried under his shameful hide. He would show them that the hunted white cat could become a worthy hunter in his own right. In fact, he would show them that he could be the greatest nacatl warrior since the hero Marisi himself.

The breeze changed, and Ajani felt the fur on his back rustle as he faced the behemoth. Ajani had no time to move with the wind; the beast had fallen suddenly silent, its massive jaws frozen in mid-mastication. It huffed and sniffed as Ajani's scent wafted toward it. He was about to be discovered. If he was going to do it, the time had come.

Ajani sprang from the foliage and sliced at the meat of the beast's thigh with his axe, intending to impair it right away. The blow cut cleanly, but he only sliced through the wiry moss that clung to the gargantuan's fur—he didn't even pierce its hide. Before he could get in a second blow, the beast lurched around to face him, its feet crushing the earth, and its long tusks swinging in a dangerous arc. Ajani staggered backward just enough to avoid having his feet swept out from under him—or his legs broken.

Ajani recovered his warrior's stance, brought his axe back, and thrust the weapon into the beast's shoulder as its tusks whizzed by. The graze broke the rubbery skin, but the beast's hide was so thick, he saw only the pinkish white of blubber. Again, he had drawn no real blood—only its ire.

With a snap of its head, the gargantuan brought its tusks back around toward him. Ajani retreated frantically to his hiding place, but with two sharp swings of its tusks, the beast shredded the stand of small trees. Ajani's back bumped into a thick trunk. He charged at the broad head before him with his axe, but the behemoth butted its head directly into the blow, tangling the shaft of the weapon amid its tusks and ripping it from Ajani's grasp. Both beast and hunter shifted back with the new development, and Ajani saw that the handle of the weapon was caught fast in the beast. Empty-handed and lacking the next strategy, he froze.

The behemoth grunted and shook its head violently, trying to free the object from its tusks. It succeeded, flinging the axe almost straight up, the blade turning end over end. Ajani's prized weapon became snarled high in the foliage above.

The beast roared and squared off facing Ajani. Its mouth was open wide, and Ajani could feel its hot, rank breath on his face. As it reared up, Ajani knew he could be trampled or gored with equal facility. He bore no more defense than the shrubs the beast ate for lunch. As it lunged down at him, he instinctively leaped up high enough to dig his claws into the gargantuan's muzzle. He scrambled up onto its head, grabbing great handfuls of bristle as he climbed, and tucked himself into the shaggy moss around its neck.

The gargantuan let out a bellow that rattled Ajani's bones, a bellow he was sure could be heard all the way back at his pride's den. The beast thrashed its head, but at the nape of its neck, Ajani was safe from its tusks, and he clung on.

What was he supposed to do? Ajani knew if he could just land a good blow in one of the beast's eyes, or maybe hit a sensitive vein, he could weaken it just enough to fell it for good. But he had no way to get through. The little bone knife at his side wouldn't do anything to the creature's hide, nor would his teeth or claws. He needed the cutting power of his axe. He scanned the canopy above and found the axe resting in the crook of a tree branch. It was too high to reach, even with a leap, and he wouldn't be able to get a good jump for it with the gargantuan thrashing. Dying all alone on the back of a shaggy behemoth seemed no way to earn the pride's respect.

The beast was insane with rage. It thrashed, crashing through a stand of tree trunks that broke like kindling. "So much for a dead end," Ajani muttered, hanging on. The behemoth tried a new strategy: slamming its front haunches into the ground in an attempt to buck Ajani off.

Ajani felt the rhythm of the rearing beast. Something clicked—that was the solution. If he could time it right . . .

The beast bucked with all its might as Ajani let go, sending him flying up in the same direction as his axe had flown before. He hurtled toward the canopy and crashed into the branch that held his axe, just managing to grab on to something. But he hadn't grabbed the branch—he had grabbed the axe handle, the head dangerously toward him, and the end snagged between two heavy limbs. When his weight lurched down on it, the wooden handle bowed between the branches. There was a sickening crack, and the axe handle snapped.

With the splintered axe in his hand, Ajani fell.

BANT

"Too easy," muttered Gwafa Hazid, as he shined an enchanted dagger with his hanky. It was as if his prey wanted to become trapped. Do they seek me out? he wondered. Does a spider stay fat on flies that are slow, or that are suicidal? It must be an attempt at pride, if only pride in death, he decided, admiring the reflection of his beard in the dagger. The weak of mind must know that, in some sense, they deserve to be deceived and defeated, and they seek out whomever can speed that destiny along. He couldn't blame them. Were he that pathetic, he'd want it to be over quickly too.

Hazid's caravan had stopped just shy of the border of Akrasa, Bant's proudest agricultural country, ostensibly to conduct trade. "Trade" was Hazid's favorite word. You get something, I get something, he thought. We're both happy, except that you've lost something precious, and I've lost nothing, and by the time you realize your mistake I'm a countryside away. His dagger, for example, had come from a smithy on the Jhessian coast who had wanted out of his lowly laborer's caste. Hazid didn't blame him for that, not in the slightest. The man had thought that a proper Akrasan sigil would earn him the status he desired, as well as passage out of the bandit-ridden town to which his station condemned him. Instead, the piece of tin Hazid traded him had earned the man a month in jail for fraud, caste infringement, and possession of a counterfeit sigil. The dagger was a work of art, though. It fit the part precisely—an assassin's dagger, concealable and deadly sharp, made for nothing but killing a man.

"Master Hazid," said one of Hazid's men, to get his attention.

A knight of sigiled caste was making rounds through the caravan. The knight wore blue linen over his chain-mail, with a broad white bird blazoned across the tabard, identifying him as a Knight of the Bright Dove. It was a minor order, but well–respected, often charged with keeping the peace at border crossings.

Hazid gauged that the knight was assigned to inspect the caravan. If he were like others of his order, he would be passably smart and difficult to bribe, but would also travel alone. He would check the wagons in the caravan, looking for any merchandise that shouldn't be there. And unless Hazid did something, the knight would find what he sought. Hazid needed to be quick, before the gentleman of the Bright Dove had time to examine the first wagon. It was time for the beautiful little dagger to do its thing.

And he knew just who should hold it. "Ghedi, come here," called Hazid.

One of Hazid's larger, stronger merchant underlings plodded over to him. Ghedi was a simple man, broad of shoulder but not of mind. He had aspirations to be a thief, but had the grace of an ox. "Yes, Master Hazid?"

Hazid put his hand on Ghedi's shoulder and looked around circumspectly as he spoke. "Ghedi, I need to know that you're a man I can trust, a man I can use. You want to be useful to me, don't you?"

Ghedi's grin was the perfect response. He was not a talkative man. Hazid clapped him on the shoulder.

"I want you to take this," said Hazid, "and do something *useful* with it." He slipped the dagger into Ghedi's hand and glanced over at the knight significantly. "Be careful."

Ghedi grinned as he moved away, holding the dagger against his thigh.

Hazid turned to the representative of the Bright Dove. "Good sir!" Hazid said magnanimously, striding over to the knight. "I bid you welcome, yes indeed!"

"Good day," said the knight. "Can I see a manifest for this caravan, please?"

Ghedi was walking in a wide circle around to the knight's blind side.

"Of course, of course," said Hazid, and produced one. "Here you are."

The knight took the scroll and unfurled it, reading intently.

"Mostly farming implements, as you can see," said Hazid. "A bit of this and that, as always—we've been as far as Jhess this month. Anything in which I could interest you? Perhaps something for the children . . . Wooden toys from Valeron?"

"No children," murmured the knight. "This manifest has an out-of-date stamp. If you and your merchants could step to the side for a moment, please, I have to check the contents."

Ghedi approached from behind. His man was doing well, and so was he, thought Hazid. The fly was almost in the web.

"Ah, well then," said Hazid. "Something for the spouse. We have earthen vases from Eos. They're absolutely lovely."

"Sir, please step aside," said the knight. "I'm going to have to inspect the wagons—now."

"Of course, of course," said Hazid. "Please, take all the time you need."

Ghedi was circling. Closer, closer. Any moment . . .

"Sir, *look out!*" cried Hazid.

The knight spun around to see Ghedi coming at him with the assassin's dagger held high. The knight was admirably quick as he put one hand to Ghedi's weapon arm, drew his sword with his other hand, and hit Ghedi hard in the gut with the pommel.

Ghedi folded in two, the breath knocked from his lungs, and the dagger knocked from his hands. His face was a comical mask of confusion as he fell to the ground.

The knight was over Ghedi in the blink of an eye. He took the dagger from the ground, then shouted an arrest spell over Ghedi's hands and neck, pinning him. Ghedi's eyes were bewildered, only turning to a state of ruefulness as the knight led the would-be assassin away to his mount at swordpoint.

That's what you get for stealing from my inventory, Ghedi, you weak-brained bastard, thought Hazid.

"Thank you for the warning," said the knight, returning to Hazid once he had fastened Ghedi's bonds to the mount. "But this attack was a serious breach of the law, and the attacker was under your authority. The fact remains, I still have to inspect these wagons."

Hazid sighed. He had already done Ghedi a favor today, granting him the destiny he had asked for with his eager fingers. And the poor checkpoint guard was going to ask for his *own* favor? Hazid had a mission to accomplish, a quest of such utmost importance that the angels themselves wouldn't—*couldn't* stand in his way. It was a burden dispensing fate to so many.

"Drummer! Strike up the caravan drum again, please!" he called. The sound of a deep, reverberating drum answered him.

"Sir," said the knight. "I'm going to have to ask you to—"

The knight slumped over holding his stomach, falling away from Hazid's swiftly-thrust dagger. As the knight fell, Hazid plucked the caravan manifest from his hand.

"Get the body into one of the wagons," Hazid said with a sigh. "Oh, and get his little stamp for the manifest."

An underling of Hazid's collected the knight's stamp and handed it to Hazid. Hazid mashed the stamp into the manifest satisfyingly.

Hazid climbed back onto his wagon and nodded to the driver, before wiping off his own personal dagger with his hanky. "Remind me to tell you of the time I traded with a blacksmith in Eos," he said to the driver.

The caravan went on its way toward Giltspire Castle, in the heart of Akrasa. Ghedi looked on forlornly, abandoned.

JUND

Until a year ago, Rakka Mar had never considered herself a "mere human." The phrase would never have occurred to her. The shaman had been entirely her own master, delighting in her savage elementalism, summoning manifestations of fire and rage to use as scourges of those who tried to rule or devour her. But when the sky had opened up and deposited the majestic form of Nicol Bolas before her, she had recognized her insignificance.

The dragon had offered her a choice. He could teach her to summon new kinds of fiery elementals of death, and she could use that power to accomplish a task on Jund for him. Or she could die. She had found him a cogent negotiator. That had been one year ago.

That night, Rakka found herself speaking before the warrior clan Antaga. It was the same speech she had given her own clan—but that hadn't worked out. She made sure to conjure the same fire for her words that she put into her magic. "Our world yearns to reach out to heaven above us, and hell below," she intoned. "And heaven and hell yearn to reach out to us as well. They beckon us—to *rule* them."

Rakka knew the clan would hang on her every word, even though she had never been its *Tol*, its leader. She was a taut, sinewy woman, ancient for a human of Jund at fifty years, but still as tough as gristle. Her arms and face were tattooed with swirling symbols of elemental forces. The goblin bones and viashino-skin trophies tied into in her hair rattled as she spoke. Her teeth were filed sharp and stained black with the dark sap of the tukatongue tree, as those of Jund's most devoted shamans were.

Let them eat it up, she thought. And come tomorrow, we'll see who's eating whom.

The *Tol* of their clan, a dreadlocked, bare-chested brute of a man called Kresh, grunted in agreement. Kresh was more than twenty years her junior, but he had earned her grudging respect since she joined his clan. Like all Tol leaders on Jund, Kresh had violently seized control of his clan in single combat. Rakka had known the old Tol, as dirty a fighter as they came. But this braid-headed youth Kresh had crushed her handily in the blood challenge. And his hunting prowess was second to none. He was a true predator of Jund, and the other warriors were unquestioningly devoted to him. That fact would help her cause in the task to come.

"We are the warriors primordial," Rakka continued, drawing mystical lines in the air with hands that glowed like oozing lava. "When heaven and hell reach out and embrace us, we must continue our Hunt to other lands. Only through our conquest of the worlds above and below will we fulfill our destinies to rule at the apex of life. The Hunt is our true path, the path that leads us to triumph, and we must follow it always, even into the maw of death." She smiled, and her black teeth shone.

Another chorus of assenting grunts followed.

She eased into the task at hand, her true mission for Kresh's clan. "Until we are called to the Hunt in the path beyond, we must continue the Hunt here, in the dark places of our own world. Jund devours all those who show weakness. We must stalk and slay those who would seize our destinies from us, and anoint our hair with their blood, to show our world that we are the strong. We must take our prey by the throat, and squeeze it into submission, and feast on its spirit. Only then will we be warriors fit to survive the reckoning to come."

"Thank you, Shaman Rakka," said Kresh, standing up. He took her side at the fire and addressed the clan himself.

"Hold Rakka's words close to your heart tonight, warriors. Tomorrow we will test your dedication to them. Tomorrow we continue the Hunt to the lair of—"

"Malactoth," prompted Rakka.

"Yes, Malactoth. The dragon. Malactoth is the mightiest dragon we've ever hunted. His is the roar that shakes Mount Jhal. Why do we hunt such a potent beast? Because his claws crave our flesh, and his teeth ache for our blood. Rakka says he has fed on goblin warrens and viashino thrashes much farther down Mount Jhal than he ever has before. That means he's getting closer to our territory. Do you know what he thinks he is?"

The warriors shouted in ragged unison.

"That's right. He thinks he's *our predator*."

Shouts of protest.

"He thinks he's up the chain from us, a beast worthy of feeding on our young like a snake snatching eggs from a nest."

Howls of rage.

Kresh put his hand out, palm down, and the warriors quieted. He finished his speech with his voice low, barely audible over the fire's crackle.

"Tomorrow we raid *his* nest."

The warriors roared in good cheer. Kresh grinned, and Rakka couldn't help but admire his enjoyment of the moment. It was a good night. Rakka took a swig of stingwine from the skin at her hip and smacked her lips. Tomorrow would go well, and she was tired from the feasting and stories and speeches. But there was no hitting her hammock yet—there were still plenty of preparations to be made. She was going to have to summon a lot of elementals before the sun rose behind the ash of Mount Jhal.

BANT

The face of Rafiq of the Many was wobbly in the silvered glass, but the razor was sharp and precise. He shaved away the stubble from his cheeks and neck, leaving his trademark beard—the same beard depicted on a sigil of patronage used in his home country of Eos. He splashed clean water across his famous face. The shaved skin stung, but Rafiq liked it that way—it let him know he was scraped perfectly clean.

A young page girl handed him his towel, and Rafiq nodded in thanks, dripping. The girl was of Mortar caste—of low rank, but clever and dutiful—one of the many pages, squires, aides, and valets Rafiq had met during his travels throughout Bant.

"What's your name?" Rafiq asked. He made a point of learning all their names; he thought it was only right. Although she was of a lower caste, it was the patronage of honest people such as the page girl, and the sigils bestowed in their honor, that gave him his own rank and renown. Some treated the caste system as an excuse for scorn and pride. Rafiq knew that the archangel Asha would have wanted it otherwise.

"Tholka, sir," answered the girl quietly. She returned to shining his sigils, the vast pile of medallions of patronage that weighed down Rafiq's armor.

"Thank you, Tholka," said Rafiq, dabbing his face

and neck with the towel. "That's the Sigil of the Salted Wind," he said, observing Tholka polish one of his sigils carefully.

Her eyes were wide. "All the way from Jhess?"

Rafiq nodded. "It was for resolving a dispute between the ship patrols and the island aven," he said.

"Resolving . . . with combat," she said, a small smile in her voice.

"Of course," he said. "Heroic combat, in the honor of the arena. Their champion was a brute of a rhox, silent but mean as a wild leotau when he wanted to be. His skill and shrewdness were so great that I invited him to my knightly order."

"You mean . . . Mubin? The famous knight? You met him in the arena?"

"Yes," said Rafiq. He laughed. "The old rhox was just a poor monk and scholar, but you wouldn't know it from his strength that day. He fought for the rights of the aven as bravely as if he were fighting for his own life. In the end, we compromised. Both sides got what they wanted, and we both got a sigil. His first."

The girl finished her polishing. She bowed. "Your armor is ready, sir," she said.

"Thank you, Tholka," said Rafiq. "May Asha watch over you."

"And you, sir," she said. "Good travels."

NAYA

As Ajani fell through the air toward the behemoth, he gripped the splintered axe handle in both hands, just to cling to something solid. The beast beneath him opened its toothy jaws to catch him in its mouth. As Ajani landed on the behemoth's face, he didn't have time to contemplate his angle or swivel the axe's head around toward the beast—he moved on instinct, plunging the wicked point of the axe handle deep between its eyes.

Ajani fell onto the jungle floor in a heap. Fortunately, so did the behemoth, flattening a few fat trees as it fell to the ground. It thrashed once or twice before releasing its death rattle.

Ajani didn't move from the ground for a long time. He lay there, listening, feeling his heartbeat slow from a frenetic slamming to an excited thumping to a regular rhythm. As he listened, he felt the blood of the plane of Naya pumping through the ground below him. It was as if there was an awakened spirit, a drumming pulse deep below the earth that only he could hear. It made him feel connected to everything around him, as if he were a plant with its roots reaching deep down into the layers of the world. He felt he had a role to play in nature, which made him as important as birdsong, or the elves of the far woods, or the gargantuan that lay beside him.

As he listened to the rhythm, he realized he was hearing only footsteps. Padding footsteps, coming closer. Other nacatl were approaching.

Ajani sat up to see the fangy grins of Tenoch and his gang, a mangy bunch of fellow nacatl leonin from Ajani's pride. Tenoch was one of the nacatl who had left him to die when the humans were hunting him that day.

"White-Fur, you disgraceful freak," said Tenoch. Tenoch was tall and golden-furred, the son of the pride's most revered elder. His laugh was a derisive staccato wheeze through snaggly teeth, which caused a little rain of spittle to arc onto Ajani's fur. "This is our patrol. What are you doing here?" Tenoch took it all in. "What . . . What have you done?"

Ajani had no breath to answer.

Tenoch's gang looked around at the scene. The dead behemoth. Ajani's splintered axe handle sunk up to the blade in the beast's forehead. The broken trees and trampled forest floor. The blood spatter on Ajani's fur.

"He's killed a gargantuan?" whispered one of the nacatl.

"By himself?" hissed another.

They were not the brave warriors that most nacatl prided themselves in being. Tenoch's gang members were the idiot-toughs of Ajani's pride. Individually, each one was a coward, but together they could mean grave danger. They were exactly the element of his pride that Ajani had hoped to win over with his feat, but also the worst to anger if they weren't impressed.

Tenoch scanned the faces of his gang behind him. Their mouths were slack with poorly hidden awe. For the moment, their leader was forgotten.

Tenoch snapped back to Ajani, and his eyes narrowed.

"This is fine meat, White-Fur," said Tenoch evenly.

"What did you plan to do with all of it? Were you going to sit here and gorge on it yourself?"

Ajani spoke, recovering his breath. "It's . . . for the pride. For the Festival of Marisi. I'm . . . glad you found me, Tenoch. You can help me field dress it and carry the good cuts back to the den."

Tenoch padded closer to Ajani, so close that their whiskers almost touched. The gang pressed in around Ajani, like a closing fist. Tenoch hissed a laugh through his teeth. "No," he said. "I'm glad you found *us*. I'm glad you came upon us just in time to witness *our* great triumph over this frenzied behemoth."

Tenoch's gang didn't get it at first. But then grins spread across their faces.

Ajani's eyes blazed.

"The pride will be so proud of us," continued Tenoch, "when we return to the den with our prize. And once again, the shameful brother of the *kha* will pull up the rear, useless as usual. In fact, just like when those no-furs chased us, I think you needed saving yet again."

Tenoch's gang snickered.

"This is my kill," snarled Ajani, standing up to his full height. The fur stood on end along his neck and arms. "This is *my* offering. You're not taking credit for it at the festival."

"You think they'll believe *you* killed this thing?" Tenoch shouted into Ajani's face. Then, more calmly, he said, "We'll see. I think you won't even tell them we took it from you. I think the honor of the *kha* means too much to you—nobody wants to be the brother of a snitch. You want to be part of our pride, don't you? So you won't squeal to the others, either. This will be our little secret. But don't worry—I'll invite you to have a taste of *our* generous feast after Jazal's speech. Take him."

Tenoch stepped quickly aside. Ajani didn't have time

to grab Tenoch's throat or to reach for the axe that was plunged into the beast. Someone shoved Ajani from behind, toppling him into the dirt face first. He tried to push up onto his hands, but the gang held him down. All he could see was clawed feet.

"It should have been me in charge of the pride," said Tenoch's voice somewhere above him. "Not some family cursed by the likes of you. You'll bring bad luck to the pride, so it's only right that we bring you a little misfortune. Roll him onto his back."

Ajani struggled, but claws gripped his limbs and turned him, slamming him onto his back. Tenoch's gang held Ajani's arms and legs fast, leaving his torso open and vulnerable. The dust of the brawl did little to obscure his stark white fur—it shone in the jungle shade as it always had.

Tenoch leaned over him, his face hanging upside down above Ajani's own. He brandished Ajani's axe handle, retrieved from the beast. He held it near the head, wielding the long handle like a bloody, pointed club.

"What's the matter?" said Tenoch. "Scared of your own stick? Scared of a little trouble? What're you going to do? Run to your brother, and tell him how scared you were of your own pridemates? Oh, I know. You'll probably have him *punish* us, won't you?"

Ajani's face was pure intensity. "I won't," he said.

"Oh, I think you will. I can see it in your eyes! You'll have the *kha* punish us. You'll have us banished as part of your celebration of Marisi, you little freak! And that's why we have to defend ourselves."

Tenoch brought the axe handle up above his head, and with a crazy look in his eye, beat Ajani in the chest.

Ajani couldn't evade the blow, and it struck true and deep, punishing his already battle-weary body. He choked on tiny breaths, clenching his gut muscles in an attempt to find air. There would be pain later, but Ajani only felt the sense of drowning. It was like falling into a pit, and seeing the sun dwindle away into the vertical distance—except that Tenoch's face stayed right in front of him, upside down and smirking.

"He can't take it, men. He's going down from just one. Imagine what two will do?"

There was another blow, a dull thud that reverberated through his organs. It felt like his chest was breaking in two. As he gasped for air, Ajani stared into Tenoch's eyes. The vertical pupils danced up and down as Tenoch laughed, the sound stabbing like knives. In the center of each eye Ajani could see tiny reflections of his own white furred face, which gave him the odd sense that he was falling into them, falling into Tenoch's mind.

In a flash, Ajani saw past the eyes. He saw past the soft tissue of the orbs, past the skull and the wrinkly matter behind it. He saw Tenoch's essence, the pith of his character, as if it were written plainly in the air above him. He felt the recurring rhythms of Tenoch's life, a series of tests of his honor and integrity, beating around his own mind like the throbbing of crickets. He experienced Tenoch's suffering, his guilt, and the crushing expectations of his mother. He felt Tenoch's pangs of envy at every success enjoyed by those more capable than him— including Jazal and Ajani. Tenoch's soul was a sculpture, carved away from a state of amorphous youth into the person he was, day by day and choice by choice. His soul was a masterpiece, just as beautiful as any work of art Ajani had ever seen.

Ajani's breath had finally returned. He lay there, heaving breaths, little jabs of pain striking through his lungs on every inhale.

Tenoch looked at him, frowning. "What is it, freak?"

How could he tell him what he had seen?

Ajani couldn't help but smile a little smile. "Tenoch, I *see* you," he said.

Tenoch's head reared back slightly, then his eyes flared. "What the hell did you just say to me?" Tenoch demanded.

"I see you," said Ajani. "The truth inside you."

That was the wrong thing to say, of course. It was too strange, too intimate a thing for the victim to say to his bully, and Ajani knew it as he said it. The beating that followed was all the more brutal because of it. But the blows felt almost irrelevant next to the vision. As unconsciousness gripped him, Ajani tried to recreate it. The more he tried to call back the images, the more they faded. The pain from the thrashing took over, and darkness followed.

When he woke, Tenoch and his gang were gone. The behemoth was a stripped carcass, all the best meat taken. His axe was lying next to him, its handle in splinters. His whole body throbbed with pain, and there were patches of his own blood staining his white fur.

Even in the teeming paradise of Naya, he was alone yet again. There was nothing to do but take up his broken axe and head back to the den.

BANT

I t's not every day you get to be the hand of prophecy, thought Gwafa Hazid.

As his caravan crept its way over a hill, he saw the four white spires of the castle—their destination—emerging into view. The pace was annoying him, so he gave an extra whip-crack to the leotau pulling his wagon. The lion-headed steed looked back at him with something resembling resentment, so he whipped it one more time. It dropped its head and pulled the wagon. Yes, a day of prophecy. A day when he, Gwafa Hazid, would deliver a spell that would kick-start the fate of the entire world. It was a good day.

The checkpoint had been troublesome business. A knight-inspector's corpse was not exactly the cargo Hazid wanted cluttering up his caravan. And perhaps he had been rash to leave his man Ghedi all alone, bound to a horse, in the middle of the Akrasan plains. But these were details, mere insects when compared to the giant stature of his plan. How could he question his own judgment at this point? Every detail folded together perfectly. It wouldn't be long before every one of his choices throughout his life would be vindicated.

Couldn't this blasted cat go any faster?

"We're approaching the castle, sir," said one of his guards on horseback.

"Good," said Hazid. "Ready the chanters."

"Yes, sir."

The castle rose into view like a white whale breaching the surface of the sea. Glimmering buttresses capped with towers of gold reached for the sun, and the wind pushed waves of brilliance across Akrasa's ocean of brown grass. It was among Akrasa's first citadels, and was still the largest. The four towers supported a central stronghold, and lifted it high off the ground to symbolize the elevated nature of the higher castes. Hazid had no problem with that notion of social order; he got what he wanted out of it by preying on the rules upon which it ran. In effect, Hazid's entire career was based on identifying those strong, supporting towers upon which all of society rested. Once those foundational supports were breached, the spoils were always left hanging, defenseless, in the middle of the open air.

"Sir, a contingent of knights approaches from the castle," said Hazid's guard.

"What's the status of the chanters?"

"Ready, sir."

"Fine, then. Begin forming the circle. Direct the knights to me."

"Right away, sir."

He saw them: humans and rhoxes, their armor gleaming in the sun, riding in formation across the grass to his wagon. He made a point of waving cheerfully. Meanwhile, the other wagons in his caravan, dozens of them, split off and began encircling the castle. They had to drive off the road, and many of the horses and leotau stumbled as they broke into the high grass. But their wheels cut lines through the fields, and began forming a curve.

"Halt, please, sir," said the lead knight, a young woman of about twenty.

"Yes, of course. Good day, my dear," said Hazid. He halted his wagon. "The famous Giltspire Castle. It's more beautiful than the last time I was in Akrasa—how could this be? Could the Amesha have blessed the citadel recently? I must say, the shine on the towers is intoxicating."

"Manifest, please," said the knight.

"Of course, of course. Here you are, my dear. Signed and stamped by your own Sir . . . Hadadir, was it?"

The knight squinted at the stamp. "You saw Sir Hadadir? He hasn't checked in for some time."

"Such a pity, that! And he was so punctual with our inspection."

"Can you tell me what happened when you obtained this stamp?" asked the knight.

Careful, thought Hazid. Ghedi may have been discovered already; or worse, the insolent dolt may have sought help himself, and told the whole story. Still, Hazid couldn't resist a little embellishment. "My old servant Ghedi, that misguided bastard, decided that your Hadadir was the man who'd had a fling with his wife. No truth to it, you understand—although cuckoled he was, that part's true— but Ghedi got it in his head that the border man was the one. That's Ghedi for you. I knew he'd come to nothing. He took one look at that Sir Hadadir and went for him with a blade the size of my arm. Hadadir ran off, and we left Ghedi behind."

The knight inspected the seal on the manifest, then looked up at Hazid's rapidly expanding caravan. The farthest wagons had already looped halfway around the castle, but approaching them were rhino-faced rhox knights bearing pikes and axes. "This is a serious matter," she said. "I'm going to have to ask you to step down from the wagon, Mr. Hazid. Please tell your caravan drivers to halt their wagons, now."

"I'd love to, but I'm afraid they're stone deaf, and willful besides," said Hazid. Hurry up, he thought. Get that circle in place, and we can make history with this spell. If the wagons didn't get into place soon, they were in danger of missing their chance, and Hazid would never rule his own country. "Listen, if I could just ask you, what the market hours are in Giltspire? I was hoping we could—"

"Quiet, Mr. Hazid. Knight-Sergeant! Stop those wagons. Strike down anyone who refuses."

"Now or never," muttered Hazid. He leaped onto the leotau at the front of his wagon, picked up the reins, and slashed the bindings that held the animal to the wagon with his sword. The leotau roared and bucked, but Hazid dug his heels into its ribs and held on. With one good whip of the reins, the leotau took off at a full gallop.

The chanters droned loudly, their mouths fully open all around the circle. Human and rhox knights threatened them with sharpened steel, but never advanced. The chanters' spell held them in a sort of dazed inaction, and besides, their kind of mass disobedience was unheard of, and more than a little frightening.

Hazid rode hard around the circle, whistling sharply. It was all coming together. One by one, mages inside the wagons threw off the tarps after hearing the signal. Inscribed in the wood inside each wagon was a mystic circle, and after exposing them to the light, each mage sat inside his or her circle and began casting the spell that would propel Hazid into history.

That's when the castle began to crack.

Hazid didn't notice the destruction at first. He was too excited, riding at a full gallop around to each of his mages, and wrapped up in the idea that he was actually going to pull the spell off. But it was unmistakable once he saw an enormous slab of one of the white cylinders break off and crash to the ground. Fractures chased one another up the towers. One by one, all but one collapsed in on itself. The citadel that was suspended by the four towers fell with them, exploding in a cloud of pulverized stone.

All the knights and mages fell silent and watched in horror. Hazid pulled his leotau to a stop. His jaw sagged open, and spittle collected in his mouth. The impact reached them in a wind of dust and noise blasting past, and little flecks of the castle peppered Hazid's face. After the wind subsided and the cloud dispersed, the castle was gone. Only one tower remained; or rather, a sharp, brilliantly white, conical obelisk remained—a structure which must have been hidden under the northwest spire for centuries.

It can't be happening, thought Hazid.

"What have I done?" he said aloud.

He dropped the reins and looked at his hands, turning them over and over, looking for an answer he would never find.

JUND

It was dawn, a state recognizable by a dim red glow through the ash-choked skies over Mount Jhal. Insects the size of Rakka's arm buzzed by in force. Her satchel of herbs and sangrite paints jangled on her back, making her shoulders ache, but there was a long way to go before she could put it down.

The clan had already made it deep into Palehide Thrash territory under cover of darkness. Although they hadn't seen any viashino yet, already the undergrowth had given way to crunchy volcanic pebbles. It was exhausting to constantly slip in the pebble-slides, so they kept their footing with spiked saurid-leather boots and hiking staves.

They walked a thin trail between two vast, bubbling tar pits, so large that the opposite sides were invisible in the fumes of the morning. The foul stench burned Rakka's lungs.

"Shh," hissed Kresh suddenly. The clan stopped and huddled down on the thin strip of land between the tar pools. Watchers scanned the skies, but saw no reptilian silhouettes.

"What is it?" whispered Rakka.

The viashino heads looked like large bubbles at first. The tar bloated and spat forth a dozen steaming viashino warriors. Only their eyes and onyx axes were visible through the oily muck.

"Ambush!" Kresh barely had time to say.

The viashino hissed like volcanic vents and pounced on the clan. Three of the watchers were dragged down screaming in seconds. Kresh swung with his sword, cleaving a viashino clean in half and grimacing as hot tar spattered his chest.

Rakka snarled at an attacker that had crept up from behind. Its tongue oscillated in its mouth; its teeth were a hundred barbs. Rakka put her back to the rest of the clan, protecting her satchel of spell components, and brandished her hiking staff. The lizard man tested her with a quick snap of its axe. She deflected the blow and returned it with a sharp crack to the creature's forward leg. It shuffled back along the strip of land between the tar pools.

Behind her she heard screams, clangs, and ugly wet crunching sounds. She pressed forward, intending to buy herself some space to summon a minion to give her a little advantage. Instead the viashino let her come, and another one grabbed her leg from the tar. Rakka gritted her teeth as her skin sizzled. "All right then," she muttered. "No time to do this fancy. Let's just bring the pain."

Rakka raised her staff, took a deep breath, and screamed two syllables of power into the air. Her staff broke into shards of obsidian, raining down all around her. The shards writhed where they fell on the volcanic ground or the surface of the tar. Each obsidian shard was expanding, adding new facets and edges to itself.

She turned to the viashino at her leg and unsheathed a scimitar. Before she could swing at the creature's wrist, though, it yanked hard on her leg, dropping her to within inches of the boiling tar. The viashino yanked again, dragging her across the volcanic pebbles to the other pool of tar.

She kicked hard, catching the viashino full in the face with a satisfying thud, and it let go her ankle. She scrambled to her feet just in time to parry the axe of the first viashino that had attacked her.

The shards of her staff were spiky clods of black crystal. Two of them had grown huge, sprouting limblike projections and were towering over the viashino despite standing in the tar.

"Kill them!" Rakka commanded.

The obsidian elementals had no heads or sensory organs to speak of. As such, they didn't need turn to face the viashino attackers; instead, spikes of obsidian erupted in the direction of their master's enemies, and the elementals simply lurched. Two viashino were impaled immediately.

Rakka fell back and let the elementals close between her and the viashino. She hazarded a glance behind her, thinking she'd be in the center of the fray—but instead she saw that she'd been cut off and isolated from her clan, who battled back the viashino several paces off. A viashino leaped at her with an onyx-tipped spear, but she chopped hard, and shattered the spear into pieces. Weaponless, the viashino pounced on her. Its claws came down on her back and shoulders. She yelled out as it dragged open long gashes in her back, and sliced her satchel clean away. She turned quickly, adrenaline augmenting her strength. Her scimitar sliced the creature's belly clean open, and it slumped into the tar, dragging her satchel with it.

"No!"

Rakka watched in horror as the satchel sank into the bubbling tar. She knew her obsidian elemental minions would puncture the thing if they tried to touch it, and its contents would mix hopelessly with the tar. She tried to steel herself to plunge her arm down to grab the satchel, but she already knew the pain of the boiling tar from her ankle, and she couldn't make herself do it. Her mission was sinking in a tar pit.

"Get the herbs!" Kresh shouted.

One of Kresh's warriors screamed crazily and dived into the tar after the satchel. Rakka heard his flesh crackle. Somehow, in a wild, thrashing motion, the man tossed the satchel onto the pebbles at Rakka's feet. He made no sound as a viashino submerged him.

The satchel was smoking, the leather blackened through, but the contents were only singed. Rakka carefully pulled the herbs out, gathered them into a fresh piece of leather, and bound them up again. She gently tucked them into her shirt.

After the last of the viashino had been finished off by Kresh's warriors, Rakka's elementals fell back into the tar and disappeared. She realized the survivors were all watching her. "How many did we lose?" she asked.

"Many," said Kresh. "Eight of our thirty. We'll need to go back and get fresh men."

"No," said Rakka. "The ritual. It . . . I need to summon the elementals today."

"You summoned five elementals just now, without the herbs!" said one of the warriors.

"Those things killed my brother!" said another.

Kresh was sizing her up, waiting for her response.

"I . . . Those were just simple minions. I need to summon the elements of pure fury from under the mountain, in order to defeat the dragon."

The warriors murmured.

"That's enough," snapped Kresh. The warriors fell silent. But his eyes were only on Rakka.

BANT

The arena was the finest in the nation of Jhess, a grand stadium with enough tiered benches to seat hundreds of well-wishers. Fine frescoes painted knights fighting mythical creatures such as dragons, gargoyles, and demons. The statue of an empty throne, a model of the sacred throne of the revered archangel Asha, crowned the flag tower, the statue's white marble gleaming in the sunlight.

That morning's dispute was not a salacious one—some squabble over land rights in the olive groves bordering Valeron—but the rafters were full beyond their capacity nevertheless. For although the petitioner from Jhess had chosen a mere squad of local mercenaries to represent him, fighters who would be passably entertaining at best, the defendant from Valeron had chosen as his champion Rafiq of the Many, Knight-Captain of the Order of the Reliquary, Bant's Grand Champion of Sigils, and the most decorated knight in the world.

Outside, the judge was announcing him. The audience erupted, thundering the stands with more than a thousand feet.

Rafiq put his forehead to his sword and prayed. "Asha, gentle archangel, thank you for last night's rest," he said. "Let your morning's light cleanse the world. Let your mind's wisdom guide my—"

His second, the gruff rhox Mubin, called from the door. "Rafiq!"

Rafiq rolled his eyes. "—wisdom guide my soul," he continued. "Let your heart's bounty fill the fields. Thereafter may you rest, while I battle in your stead, bringing your benevolence to all, that you may then lead me safely home and keep me through the dark of night."

"Rafiq!"

"Yes, I know—they're introducing us. It's time to go."

"Yes," said Mubin. "But that's not why I'm here. It's a Blessed. She wants to talk to us after the dispute is settled."

"One of the Blessed caste is *here?* Who?"

"Aarsil, from the courts of Valeron. No idea why she'd be way out here. She's here with a delegation of the Order of the Skyward Eye."

"Why has she come personally? She could have sent someone of Mortar caste. We should talk to her. It must be urgent."

The big rhox shook his head. "She said to settle up with the Jhessians first. Then come talk to her."

Rafiq grinned. "I guess she just likes to watch us fight."

When Rafiq and Mubin appeared from the defendant's gate, the audience stood and cheered. They bowed, letting their numerous sigils of patronage hang dramatically from their breastplates.

The mercenaries representing the plaintiff's side had already assembled on the other side of the arena. They were just youths: gangly and awkward-looking young men and women in their front-heavy, ceremonial armor. Their swords, though, looked suspiciously sharp, possibly enchanted. Rafiq wondered whether those blades had been inspected for battle regulations, or whether he simply misjudged the glint on their edges.

The combatants all bowed to the judge, then bowed to each other, then bowed to the Valeron magistrate, Aarsil the Blessed, as she nodded gracefully. The judge led a prayer for all assembled, as everyone directed their outstretched hands to the sacred statue of the archangel's throne, beseeching her grace over the dispute to be resolved.

Finally, the judge called the rhox knight, Mubin, and three of the Jhessian mercenaries forward. According to custom, the seconds of the champions always fought first. It was time to settle the dispute as the law of the angels intended.

Rafiq watched the face of Aarsil the Blessed, seated in the royal box in the audience. She was too far away to speak with, but he could see that she was seated next to a mage in robes embroidered with the sigil of the Order of the Skyward Eye. The mage whispered to her, and she nodded. As Rafiq watched, her eyes strayed from the center of the arena to where he stood on the sidelines. He gave a slight nod and thought he caught an indication of a smile before the magistrate turned back to watch the action.

Whatever was on her mind, it would have to wait. Rafiq saw Mubin walk out into the arena, and smiled. Nothing pleased him more than seeing justice being carried out.

NAYA

Ajani only wanted to trudge back to his lair and sleep off his wounds. He wanted to lie still until the festival, and forget about the whole thing. Maybe he would find some other way to win the pride's trust, or maybe it was simply time to go. But someone noticed him on his way into the den. It wasn't his brother Jazal, but Zaliki, a childhood friend of the brothers. Thankfully, she was one of the only people in his pride who saw past his albino fur. Seeing the blood streaked across his white pelt, she gasped, and intercepted him at the entrance to his lair.

"Ajani, is this your blood?" she demanded. "What happened to you?"

He realized in that moment that the whole enterprise had been stupid. It was useless to try to buy the pride's favor with a reckless stunt. He was outraged at Tenoch and his gang, but humiliated with himself.

"Never mind, Zaliki," said Ajani. "It's nothing."

"It's obviously far from nothing. Here, come into the lair and sit. I'll bandage you, and then you'll tell me everything."

He sat while she bandaged him, but he didn't tell her any details. "I was hunting. There was some . . . trouble in the forest. I broke my dark iron axe—the one that matches my brother's."

"You're always so closed, Ajani," Zaliki said. "You keep it all to yourself. There's nothing in you that wants to come out? Just tell me. I can help you if you tell me. Where have you been? What did you fight? What do you think about the future?"

Ajani raised a brow at her. "That's a broad question. Do you mean the festival? That'll go fine. Jazal will make his speeches, and everything will work out as it always does."

"No, no. I mean, this pride. Do you see yourself here forever? Do you think things will go well for us all in the future?" Her contrasting orange stripes glowed oddly in the gloom of the lair.

"I guess I see myself here," said Ajani. "My brother is the *kha*, and I must support him. Although I've wondered whether I'm doing him more harm than good here in the pride."

"I just feel like . . . I don't know. What would happen if things were to change? Would we all still be a family? Would we all still stay together?"

Ajani smirked. "Why would things change? Jazal is the most stable leader this pride has ever had. Everyone loves him. We're the most thriving pride of wild nacatl in all of Naya. What's really on your mind?"

"It's hard to explain. We'll always be friends, right, Ajani?"

"Always."

She sighed and smiled. "Thanks. That's what I wanted to hear. So you'll let me help you? You'll let me in on what happened that gave you these wounds?"

Ajani's face fell. "I told you. It's nothing to be upset about."

But as he should have expected, she understood anyway. He could never hide much from her. She stood and let the bandages fall.

"All right, you stubborn chunk of stone. Let me tell *you* what happened, and you nod when I'm getting close. Ready? Let's see . . . You've suffered some new slight, probably by members of our own pride, and it led to a fight. You lost the fight, but you let them go, thinking it was somehow all your own fault, and now you're holding on to all your emotions about it, and shoving them deep down inside yourself. You've come back not to avenge your tormentors, but to lick your wounds and hide, while the same idiots in our pride go unpunished. How am I doing?"

Ajani faced the wall. "Thank you for the bandages," he said. "You can go now."

Zaliki scoffed. "Look. Putting yourself in front of the evils of the world doesn't make you a hero, Ajani," she said. "It just makes you a target. Don't try to save everyone. Don't try to win, because it's not a contest—it's survival. You've got to figure out who holds the power in this world, and then get out of their way. Life's hard enough without trying to overturn the way of things, or to try to turn it into something about honor or integrity. Promise me this— that *you'll* get out of the way next time? Won't you?"

Ajani just lay down on his bed.

Zaliki looked at him for a long moment from the lair entrance, and sighed. Then she left him alone.

JUND

In the two years Sarkhan had spent on the plane of Jund, he had seen dozens of dragons. He followed them with the eyes of a naturalist, watching their flight patterns and their eating behaviors, memorizing maps of nesting locations and broodmate relationships, judging the strength and heat of their dragonfire, and calculating their age, relative size, and approximate overall power. But he had never found *the one*.

Sarkhan was not a hunter by training. As an adolescent on a plane torn by the machinations of warlords, he had supposed his avocation to be war. He had fought in brutal conflicts across his home plane, tearing giant holes in the defenses of his enemies through a personal will and doggedness that his grandfather called "unmatched among our people."

For a time, sick of the petty quarrels of the battlefield, he had joined a shamanic group dedicated to the veneration of dragons. From them he had learned of the dragons' rage and uncompromising predation. But the dragons had been hunted almost to extinction on his plane. With no dragons to revere, he had returned to his war career, believing he would never feel the heat of dragonfire or the fury of those beasts of old.

Sarkhan's might and legendary stubbornness had soon earned him accolades, rank, and a military force of his own.

Expected to do great things in command, he had been put in charge of a massive campaign to defeat the forces of an enemy warlord. He had slain the warlord personally, but as he had surveyed the battle from the warlord's tower, he had felt hollow, seeing the tiny ants scuffling below. Frustrated and seeking answers, he had entered a shamanic trance, just as his training had directed.

The spirit of a long-dead dragon had appeared to him, whispered a spell into his mind, and then vanished forever. With the incantation of the spell, a huge dragon made of fire had streaked out of Sarkhan's body, and invaded the battle, blasting the battlefield with a torrent of fire. Fascinated, Sarkhan had watched as his men and those of his enemy were burned to cinders. It was a display of ultimate rage and power that surpassed everything he had ever seen. It had stoked a passion in him that had never before flared to life, and along with it, his planeswalker spark.

Sarkhan had been relieved of duty that day, but had not cared.

He had spent years traveling from plane to plane, hunting for the most monumental dragons he could find. He had given solemn obeisance to some that earned his respect. And he had killed some others that didn't, believing that any dragon that fell to his humble human hands deserved to die, and that the way he would find *the one,* the ultimate expression of draconic glory, was by meeting his match.

He had never stayed on any plane longer than a few months until he found the primordial world of Jund. It was home to hundreds, maybe thousands of dragons—a more robust population than any other plane Sarkhan had seen. And yet, life teemed on Jund. All shapes and sizes of reptilian creatures, carnivorous plants, and a strangely ratlike species of goblin, thrived in the hot, volcano-driven climate. Taut and muscular humans swarmed over the plane, adapted to the constant threat of physical danger. And tiny fungal creatures tottered between the noxious pools of tar, apparently even lower on the food chain than the goblins. It was only the enormous buffet of life that could support the high density of draconic predators. To Sarkhan, it was paradise.

The upper atmosphere was thick with volcanic gases, a serious danger for any mountaineering. The scarlet haze could be ignited by any major eruption, or even by the breath of a passing dragon. Sarkhan would have to go into the interior and scale up a lava tube if he was going to make any progress up the mountain.

His goal was a dragon named Malactoth. He had heard the lore of the colossal beast, that he laired deep under an active volcano, and that his hunger was legendary. He had to know whether the creature could be the one he sought, the one whose rage was most pure, the one to whom he could devote a lifetime of tribute.

The lava tube grew tighter. The jagged igneous rock of the ceiling descended as he walked, bringing the smoke from his torch lower and lower. Then a gust of hot air from deep inside the volcano blew out his torch entirely. The lack of smoke was a relief for a time, but it was getting harder and harder to see. With a little pyromancy, Sarkhan relit the torch by blowing a short cone of flame onto it.

To his surprise, as the torch flickered to life, he saw humans staring back at him.

He had come to a small chamber under the mountain. There were a dozen people gathered, he guessed, and they were suited for combat. Several of them were streaked with tar—a few of them were coated in the stuff from head to toe. Some of them bore obvious injuries. A large man and a shaman woman approached him quietly.

"I am Kresh, Tol of the clan Antaga," the large man whispered. "Please go back the way you came. This is a dangerous place—we slay a dragon here today." The shaman looked Sarkhan up and down from behind the speaker.

Sarkhan grinned. "I seek this dragon as well. But I have slain many in my day, Kresh Tol Antaga, and I would recommend your little band be the one to turn around and head back. You're injured and unready to face this beast."

Kresh grimaced.

"The rage in our hearts is always ready," said the shaman.

"Rakka is right," said Kresh. "We face this dragon today. If you want to help us kill it, so be it. But the glory belongs to clan Antaga."

Sarkhan was still grinning. "Very well," he said. Your bravery is only eclipsed by your vanity, he thought. But I won't have to punish your conceit today. The dragon will do that for me.

"You bring up the rear," Kresh said to him, and marched on.

Sarkhan rarely explained his planeswalker status to others, and never told others of his multiverse-spanning quest for draconic perfection. What was the point? On world after world, he met individuals like Kresh: brash and proud, but ultimately as fragile as a statue made of ash. They died in dragonfire with ridiculous expressions of surprise on their faces. So ignorant of their insignificance were they, so overconfident in their strength. They blended together in Sarkhan's mind, as useless as brittle parchment. He watched impassively as Kresh's warriors marched on to their doom, just as he had watched his own men burned to cinders during his first leadership. They certainly seemed cheerful about it.

When they came upon the dragon's lair, Kresh's clan marveled at the dimensions of the space. It was an immense bowl carved into the structure of the volcano, splashed with enough magma to destroy a city. One side of it was open to the central conduit of the volcano, which was filled with a black column of noxious smoke. Too long in here and they would all certainly perish, thought Sarkhan. They would have to claim victory quickly, before death did.

In the center of the chamber slept an immense, maroon-scaled dragon. His sides heaved as he breathed, and his nostrils flared with wisps of flame on every exhale. A smile crept across Sarkhan's face.

Rakka spoke first. "The ritual must happen down there, next to Malactoth."

"Couldn't you summon all the elementals up here?" asked Kresh. "We need them for the first assault."

"No. In this case it must happen right next to the volcanic vent, down there."

"He's a hellkite," marveled Sarkhan. He hadn't pronounced the rest of the sentence that was in his head: *He's a hellkite that will devour you all today.*

NAYA

The celebration of the Feast of Marisi went late into
the night. Ajani's brother Jazal sat at the position
of honor, on the raised bamboo dais by the bonfire.
Flautists played an old melody, a song about spirits and
the wildness of the world. Everyone conversed at once
and chewed contentedly on the roasted gargantuan
meat brought to them by Tenoch—all except Ajani,
who hadn't eaten or spoken a word. Ajani sat in the
shadows by himself, winding straps of leather around
the handle of his axe in an effort to repair it. It was
doing little good.

Chimamatl, one of the shaman-elders of the pride and
Tenoch's doddering mother, stood and addressed the gathered group. "The *hadu*, the fireside tale, is how our pride
maintains its long memory. The exploits of our beloved
young leader Jazal—and other brave warriors, such as
my son Tenoch—should be remembered for all time. And
they will be remembered, as long as we relive their stories
at the fireside, and remember to tell them to our children,
and they to their own children. As we tell their tales, they
must tell the tale of those heroes who came before them.
Tonight we must remember a hero who made us what we
are, who unshackled us from falsity and let our true selves
shine forth. Tonight we remember Marisi the Wild, for
the anniversary of his sacrifice approaches."

Ajani pulled on the leather bindings of his axe. He hoped they would hold long enough for a proper repair. He watched a coal melt into ash deep in the heart of the fire, mesmerized by its slow decomposition. He wasn't listening to the *hadu*; he was thinking about Zaliki's words, staying out of the way of the powers that be. Should he just move on? If his place wasn't with the pride, where was it? He was also trying not to feel the sting of watching Tenoch enjoy the praise for the feast that Ajani had rightfully provided.

"And now," intoned the elder Chimamatl, "may I introduce the *kha*, Jazal."

The pride shouted in two short, unified bursts, welcoming Ajani's brother to the front of the dais. Jazal looked glorious standing before the fire; the gold of his fur seemed to gleam brighter than the flame itself. His mane was swept back, his chin was high, and his chest looked as hard as a warrior's shield. He held his axe, the burnished-bright version of Ajani's own axe, as a king might hold a scepter. Yet his eyes were gracious, picking out each and every member of the pride and thanking them with his glance. All the pride looked back in admiration, Ajani included.

"Marisi was a warrior," said Jazal. "Like our heroes who provided this feast tonight. But Marisi's was a troubled mind—a mind that could not abide the constriction of law, the law that governed all nacatl of Naya, the cursed carvings we know as the Coil. Marisi believed that we nacatl had forgotten something important about ourselves. He believed that the Coil was like a pestle, and the leadership its mortar, crushing our true natures between them. He believed that the true soul of the nacatl had fled our race, and was determined to put it back again."

Jazal jabbed the coals violently with the end of his axe handle. The fire hissed and popped, sending a cloud of sparks into the night air. Ajani had never seen Jazal make this kind of dramatic flourish, but it was stirring. Ajani watched the cinders rise up and mingle with the stars.

"Marisi's heart burned with wildness," Jazal said, beginning the recitation of the *hadu*. "When the leaders at Antali tried to stop him, he declared war on the leaders. When the strictures of the Coil tried to contain him, he declared war on the Coil. When the *kha* tried to condemn him, he declared war on the *kha*, and on every nacatl who denounced his wild way of life. Others saw his example and saw the truth of it. They saw how they could be more than they were, how the Coil had eaten away at their insides. They saw the truth in him, and they followed him. Marisi and his Claws, as his warriors were known, tore through the laws and through flesh alike. They created a revolution, and allowed the nacatl nation to break into two. On the one side, the Cloud Nacatl still cling to the broken stone words of the Coil, up in the misty mountains. On the other, the Wild Nacatl, to which we belong"—many of the pride cheered and raised their gnawed bones at this—"keep the animal soul alive in the nacatl heart."

It struck Ajani that although the tale of Marisi was going well, Jazal seemed preoccupied. He was gesturing wildly with his axe, which Ajani thought the pride must be taking as warrior spirit. But Ajani knew that Jazal never swung a weapon recklessly, and that it must mean something was bothering him.

"The two can never be severed from one another," said Jazal. "The Nacatl people are both head and heart. Although tonight we honor Marisi, fallen hero of the Breaking of the Coil, we must also think of those who live up in the cloud jungles on the mountain slopes, and thank them for their contribution to our identities."

51

The pride cheered again, but uncertainly, as Jazal's words veered from the usual Festival traditions. Jazal didn't look down at the crowd, Ajani noticed, but up at the night sky.

Jazal had proven himself time and again as a fierce fighter, but in some ways, he was the furthest from being a Marisian hero of anyone in their pride. In his private moments with Ajani, Jazal shared insights that revealed the profound depths of his mind—doubts about the heroism of Marisi, and doubts even about the schism that had divided the Nacatl race.

Someone else seemed distracted as well. Ajani noticed that his shaman friend Zaliki had not cheered with the others, which was strange—the Festival was her favorite celebration of the year. Even stranger, she rose and slipped away into the darkness, going off by herself in the middle of the *hadu*, the pride's greatest moment of community.

Something was troubling Zaliki—perhaps it was Ajani himself. Ajani knew he had been short with her before, ungrateful in the face of her healing and advice. As Jazal continued to speak, Ajani decided to follow her.

She moved up and up, climbing the trails that zigzagged back and forth across the cliff face that formed the pride's den. Ajani followed her, watching her pass the cavern entrances of lair after lair. She moved with her usual grace and silence, the deep auburn stripes on her back crisscrossing in the torchlight.

Zaliki entered the cavern set highest into the cliff-side—Jazal's lair. Again, that was strange. When he entered, Ajani startled her.

"I'm sorry," he said. "I saw you leave from the fireside. Are you all right?"

"Oh, yes," she said. "I merely wanted to . . . retrieve this, my talisman." She held one of her shamanic talismans in her hand, the one that Jazal had given her, braided with the fur from his own mane. "I was counseling the *kha* earlier, and . . . I left it here."

Ajani cocked an eyebrow at her. "Not enjoying the speech tonight?" he asked.

"No, no, it's not that. Just the talisman. And to get some fresh air. Look . . . Ajani . . . I should go. I need to be alone. You go back and enjoy the *hadu*. I'll talk to you again later."

"All right," was all Ajani managed before she left. As she swept past him, she bumped into some of Jazal's belongings, knocking them over onto the cave floor. She paused, but left in a hurry.

Ajani could see that she was not her graceful self—something was definitely wrong. But if she didn't want to open up to him about it, there wasn't much Ajani could do.

It was only after she had left that Ajani saw the markings on the wall of Jazal's lair, revealed when Zaliki had knocked down a fur hanging. They were simple chalk sketches of a white lion's face. As he looked, he saw several versions of the white lion in a stack of scrolls on the floor of Jazal's lair, each one bearing strange notes in Jazal's hand. Every sketch had the same distinguishing features: white fur, and a missing left eye. And there was an older scroll on the floor, yellowed and aged, bearing markings written in human script. It showed the symbol of the one-eyed white lion's face too. *His* face—as if the humans truly had been hunting him in particular.

There was another scroll in Jazal's script, apparently a translation of the humans' one.

The gods' anger shook all of Naya, and the gods stampeded through the jungle. The people offered breadnut and guava, but the gods' anger remained, and the gods stampeded over the mountains. The next day the people offered jade and the feathers of griffins, but the gods' anger remained, and the gods stampeded across the lowlands. The next day the people offered the pelt of the white lion, and the gods were satisfied, and rested once more.

It was as if the humans thought Ajani was part of their religion, some symbol of appeasement for the gargantuans they worshipped. Ajani knew the gargantuans weren't gods—they were just overlarge, dumb beasts. Still, he wasn't surprised that the furless ones wished for some way to appease them. The humans had elaborate cities of stone and wood, and the gargantuans had never made accommodating neighbors.

Ajani had never seen those things before, all that research. Jazal must have been collecting the items for years, and keeping them from him. His mind fought with itself, trying to piece together what he was seeing while avoiding coming up with an answer. His confusion and evasion turned to anger. What *was* it all? What was Jazal hiding from him? Why would his brother lie?

JUND

Kresh peered over the rocky ledge, down into the volcanic cavern. It was hard to see the dragon at first, despite its size; its scales matched the texture and color of the rocky cavern floor, and its body snaked between huge stalactites and basalt columns. Vents smoldered throughout the cavern, offering windows down into the lava only a short distance below the floor. Only once Kresh saw the subtle rhythm of the dragon's breathing was he able to determine its contours.

He felt excitement in his veins. He had never seen a dragon so large before. Even thin splinters of its teeth would make grand trophies to weave into his braids.

He motioned for the others to draw nearer. Rakka, the newcomer Sarkhan Vol, and the rest of his warriors approached to get a look for themselves.

"Is it asleep?" whispered Rakka.

Kresh stifled a laugh, and saw Sarkhan grin, too. "Dragons this big don't *sleep*," Kresh whispered at her. "Its skin drinks the essence of fire from the mountain. It probably knows we're here already."

"Then why hasn't it attacked?" Rakka asked.

"We're no threat," said Kresh, looking down at the mighty beast. "Yet."

"If you're going to summon us some help," said Sarkhan in a low voice, "now would be the time."

Rakka nodded and began removing components from her bag.

Kresh motioned for his warriors to fan out, and they began creeping along the ledge. They spread in an arc across quarter of the cavern, and each of them readied a spear with a tip of obsidian, which gleamed like frozen smoke. Kresh swelled with pride at the sight of his warriors. Other humans cowered in the low valleys when dragons threatened their territory, but his clan took the fight directly to the source, without fear or hesitation.

Sarkhan had his staff held horizontally, and was chanting under his breath. It was handy to have another warrior along, Kresh thought, especially one who had some magic in his heart. Kresh had watched Sarkhan on their journey through the mountains, and knew that the stranger's role was going to be as important as Rakka's in their fight. He wasn't as adept with forming creatures from fire and stone as Rakka, but his presence seemed to stir the coals inside warriors' hearts even more than Kresh himself. It was no cause for envy; it was going to take a powerful fury for their fleshy human bodies to overcome the armor-scaled beast down below, and if Sarkhan could provide that fury, so it would be.

The dragon stirred. Its tail wound around one of the floor-to-ceiling columns, and Kresh thought he could see its nostrils flaring slightly. Its nose would be full of their scent.

Kresh shot a look at Rakka. She was still assembling her spell components. "Aren't you ready yet?" he hissed at her.

Her body language was frantic. "Go," she whispered. "Start without me."

"We can't," said Kresh. "After we throw, we need to rush for its belly. Your rock-men were going to help us down there."

"I'll figure something else out," Rakka said. "Just go, before it decides we're a threat and blasts us out of here. I'll get you down there one way or another."

"Fine with me," said Kresh. He glanced at Sarkhan. "You?"

Sarkhan grasped his staff tightly and gave a sharp nod.

Without warning, Kresh let out a scream that shook the cavern. The dragon tensed, and its claws gripped big chunks of the cavern floor. Kresh launched his spear down at it, and the rest of his warriors all screamed and followed suit. A hail of black-tipped spears rained down on the dragon as it snapped its wings out, forming a curving, scaly shield.

Most of the spears glanced off the scales and bounced away, but a few of them pierced through its wings. The hellkite made a furious inhaling sound and gathered up its body and breath to attack, knocking through several stalactites with its limbs.

Sarkhan finished his spell with a primitive shout. Kresh felt his heart explode with passion, a feeling of breathless fervency, a feeling that he could rip the dragon apart with his bare hands. He saw his warriors light up with the same surge of emotion as they all drew swords.

With his vision tinged by the craze of Sarkhan's spell, Kresh was not bothered about the height of the ledge. He and his warriors ran straight over the edge as if time and gravity had no meaning, screaming at the top of their lungs, propelled horizontally by the force of their fury to meet the dragon.

Only after his feet had pushed off from the ledge did Kresh have an impulse to turn his head back at Rakka—not out of concern for the small problem of gravity and the fifty-foot drop, but to share eye contact in the instant of breathless glory. And what he saw was

Rakka as he had never seen her: eyes ablaze, hair floating in a tornadic tangle, her mouth bent in a terrible grimace, her hands stretched out as if to push the warrior clan over the ledge by the sheer force of her will.

BANT

Mubin stepped forward into the arena and brandished his prized mace. His opponents, the squires of the three mercenaries Rafiq would fight, stepped forward as well. As they advanced, the audience fell quiet, allowing Mubin to hear the crunch of the gravel below his feet.

The Jhessians circled the great rhinolike rhox, their distance from him proportional to their respect for his abilities. Mubin allowed himself a deep grunt of satisfaction. He was proud of his membership in the Order of the Reliquary—as few rhoxes could claim—and the Order praised his scholarly contributions to the research of ancient relics. But standing on his own two feet, with a weapon and shield in his hands, glowering at three foes who were determined to destroy him, he was truly in his element. He hadn't as many sigils as Rafiq of the Many, of course, but the ones he wore were well deserved. He knew that the young Jhessians had been spared little by not having to face his companion.

The youths spread out around him, trying to trap him in a triangle. His bulk should have made him slower than the young humans, but they were unused to their front-fitted armor, while his strength let him maneuver easily. He tested them, striking at one of them sideways with his mace, but the Jhessian stepped just enough to let her armor deflect the blow. One of them lunged at Mubin with a sharp sword, but Mubin was able to snap his shield into place to protect his flank. Metal sparked against metal.

One Jhessian yelled out and charged Mubin. Mubin turned, yielding no ground and setting for the attack. It was a ruse—the other two ran around to Mubin's flank and pounced on his weapon arm. Mubin let the mace fall from his fingers and focused on the charging combatant. Instead of deflecting the charger's attack with his shield, he thrust forward with his free hand, grabbed his foe's sword arm and twisted the sword free. As he disarmed the man, he followed through by bringing his elbow up into the Jhessian's jaw. There was a mighty crunch, and the youth fell away, disarmed and clutching his face. Mubin turned and, using his rotation to build momentum, threw the newly-acquired sword at a second foe. It sailed end over end and struck its target full in the chest with the pommel, knocking her down. He then charged at the third foe, who was trying to lift Mubin's fallen mace. Mubin put his head down and listened as he charged. He heard the crunch of the man's boots and the scrape of the mace against the gravel, and aimed for the noise. He ran full-bore into the Jhessian, denting the man's ceremonial armor deeply with his nose horn and lifting him up and over his head as he charged underneath. The Jhessian landed roughly on his shoulder and rolled in pain.

Mubin pulled up, and turned around to face his three foes once more.

"We yield," they said to the judge.

The judge raised his hand and looked to Aarsil the Blessed. She nodded. "The first encounter goes for the defendant," said the judge. "Plaintiff's champions and defendant's champion, please step forward for the final encounter of the match."

NAYA

Ajani returned to the bonfire to hear Jazal finishing the *hadu.*

"Antali was the capital of all nacatl in the world," Jazal was saying. "And the Claws of Marisi destroyed it. Now our race has no capital, no center of oppression. We are once again wildcats of the jungle, free, as in times of old. We have no stone columns supporting roofs to come between us and the stars. We have no metal spikes to anchor down artificial floors, to come between us and the earth. Marisi swept that all away, leaving a glorious ruin in his wake, for the sake of all of us. And for him, in turn, we remember the *hadu.*" Then, as the pride waited for the final phrase, Jazal's voice became a low, grinding snarl. "To Marisi."

"To Marisi!" chanted the crowd, and they cheered and ate.

Ajani joined Jazal as he stepped down from the dais, and clapped him on the back in a forced gesture of camaraderie. Ajani tried to look him in the eyes, to see if he could find a trace of the secrets Jazal had kept from him. "To Marisi, eh, brother?"

Instead Jazal nodded, his mind elsewhere. "Right, yes," he said. "To the glory of the hero Marisi."

Ajani pressed him. "What's on your mind, brother? Something you want to tell me?"

"No, it's nothing, Ajani. You're a good brother. But it's late, and I'm just tired from the speech. I'm going to turn in. Have a good time at the rest of the festival."

Jazal left him and went back to his lair. Ajani had all the pride around him, except for the only ones he considered his family. He decided he deserved some of that roast behemoth after all. He tore a piece off and took it back to his lair, where his sleep was tortured by evil dreams.

BANT

Rafiq felt the weight of the ceremonial breastplate like the rough embrace of a tarnished soldier, one that wore ruts in his shoulders that grew deeper every year. It yanked down on him with every step as he advanced into the arena, and caused his dozens of small, burnished sigil medallions to jounce and glitter in the morning light. It was what it meant to be a paladin, he thought: honorable combat on the field of battle; the chance to become the instrument of the angels in the cause of justice; the chance to put one's mettle and faith on the line in a struggle that would end in defeat or glory.

As the crowd cheered, Rafiq looked around at the frescoes that lined the arena, and imagined himself fighting the mythical creatures depicted there, as those brave, two-dimensional knights did. Instead he was fighting three Mortar-caste youths who were fighting for little more than a meal and could barely walk in their armor. Well, he thought, not every battle was for supreme glory. Perhaps that was part of the life of a paladin as well.

The three Jhessian champions stepped forward and bowed, then assumed battle stances. Rafiq followed suit, and the audience went silent. The three youths stood shoulder-to-shoulder in formation, each one covering the defensive gaps of the others, creating a kind of pointy armored object with their three polished swords sticking out. As he neared, Rafiq could see that their swords were indeed enchanted. Their edges looked razor sharp, and glowing glyphs played up and down the blades. If that wasn't blunting magic, then the combatants were in blatant violation of the rules.

Before Rafiq had a chance to hail for an inspection, the Jhessian champions burst forth in a flurry of attacks. They broke their formation oddly, one of them going to Rafiq's left flank while another retreated several paces, while the third plunged straight into Rafiq's sword range. Rafiq gave ground, parrying and defending with his shield while preventing the flank attack. He tried a counterattack at the Jhessian who had charged him, but his opponent's sword was already back to defend, an almost instantaneous parry. The Jhessian swiveled his wrist in a bold attempt to disarm Rafiq while the one to his left lunged strongly. Rafiq dealt with both by rotating his body, bringing his shield up to deflect the blow and to bash the other in the chin, sending them both reeling back.

That just left an opening for the third champion, whose blade slashed directly at Rafiq's eyes. Instinctively Rafiq ducked, and the attack just missed. The audience gasped.

Was this Jhessian crazy? Helmets hadn't been worn in combat for hundreds of years; everybody knew that an attack with a blade to the head was strictly illegal. Rafiq recovered and stood, looking sternly at the judge. The judge did nothing, signifying no breach. Impossible.

The three Jhessians circled around him, looking much more lithe in their heavy armor than Rafiq had made them out to be. Their swords struck toward him like needles, more accurate than they should have been and far more damaging, cutting actual scars in his armor. He deflected all he could, relying on years of ritual combat as Bant's foremost Champion of Sigils, but the illegal moves were overwhelming him. The judge was motionless, leaving Rafiq to his own devices.

Then Rafiq felt it. The blow came from behind him, where his armor didn't cover, and had cut into his skin, a razor-thin line through his actual tissue. It was far from fatal, but that didn't matter. He turned in shock, and the Jhessians spread out and broke off their attacks. There before him stood the champion who had struck him, a tiny spot of red liquid glimmering on the point of his sword.

Rafiq watched his blood trace its way down the champion's blade, transfixed. He had never seen blood on a blade before.

JUND

Sarkhan saw the surge of hot air blast out from Rakka's hands, catching the warriors full in the back and accelerating their flight, turning each of them into flailing comets. The spell was messy—it didn't create a choreographed air attack, but an explosion of human bodies sailing across the cavern. Would it save them from gravity, only to kill them with velocity?

No time to criticize. As Sarkhan prepared another spell, he saw Kresh grasp his sword with both hands and raise it over his head in midair, preparing for impact as he fell toward the beast. The dragon reared up to meet him. Kresh sliced downward at its face and struck home, his sword burying itself in the top of the dragon's snout, before falling past the beast and leaving his sword behind. He slammed into its wing pinion, knocking the breath from his lungs, and tumbled to the cavern floor, gasping.

Around him, the other warriors fell against the dragon in impact after violent impact to form rough piles around the creature's feet. Some of them got back up immediately and gathered their weapons and wits; many did not.

Rakka's spell was a mistake. The attack had been a disaster.

The dragon unleashed a torrent of fire on the warriors around it, and simultaneously flapped its wings, sending up a massive whoosh of air. Most of the clan were sent reeling. The burning bodies of several warriors, already dead, slid and flipped across the rough cavern floor.

Sarkhan and Rakka dived to the ground to survive the heat blast. Pebbles and debris rained down on them, and Sarkhan felt the heat roast his back and the hair on his head. He scrambled to his feet and yelled at the shaman.

"Damn the elementals, Rakka! Just bring the ceiling down!"

It had stopped being an assault on a majestic foe. It had become a massacre, and a matter of survival.

"No," she answered. "Keep it busy. Just a little longer." She was gathering her spell materials back together, assembling the sangrite chips into an approximate circle.

"You have to collapse this place *now,* Rakka! There's no hope of beating that thing!"

No response. She must have gone mad. Sarkhan turned to the dragon. If he were some other person, he would have escaped up the volcanic vent they had used to get in. But instead he threw out the edges of his cloak, ran at the hellkite, and leaped off the ledge himself.

As he fell, he drew on every bit of power left in him, and became a dragon made of fire.

NAYA

Tenoch hated the night patrol. If he slept, he got a whipping. If he managed to stay awake all night, he got to listen to the shrieking of jungle insects and the snoring of his pridemates—pests, both of them. So instead he spent the night in a dreary state halfway between sleep and wakefulness—not enough to feel any kind of satisfying rest, but enough to get grudging agreement that he had done his duty.

There was rarely movement in the den at night, especially after the Festival, which is why his half-sleep was disturbed by the footsteps of the figure, quiet as they were. Only Tenoch's eyelids stirred, and only enough to get a look at what was going on.

It wasn't much. A hooded figure approached the bonfire at the center of the den. "Probably just someone from the den who can't sleep," Tenoch muttered. The fact that the person wore a cloak was a little strange, as it was a warm night, but people could do what they wanted, Tenoch figured. The figure bent over and tossed something into the fire, paused to look into the fire for a moment, and then walked into the darkness.

Excellent, thought Tenoch's groggy mind. He already had a happening to report to Jazal in the morning, proof that he had witnessed something. He nestled his head on his arm and let sleep take him.

The night was a blanket of insect whirrs, the sleepy murmurs of his pridemates, and the occasional bellow of a faraway gargantuan. The bonfire hissed and crackled, lulling Tenoch to sleep. A loud pop startled him, but he dismissed it as a wet stone in the fire that had cracked. He set his head down again, only to hear a series of muffled bursts from inside the coals. Annoyed, Tenoch stuck his head up again, to see what was happening.

Noxious purple smoke streamed out of the fire.

"What the hell?" he muttered. If the canopy caught fire, he was going to catch the whipping of a lifetime.

Annoyed, he lurched to his feet to go investigate.

"Terrible, terrible things," he involuntarily whispered to himself when he saw the bonfire.

Creatures made of darkness had begun to form out of the billowing smoke. They dropped out of the fumes in distorted humanoid shapes, landing on their feet in hunched positions. They looked around and sniffed the air with a hissing sound.

Then a single, enormous creature of shadow emerged from the bonfire, easily twice the size of a nacatl. Its claws were dagger-sharp and its eyes empty like a skull. It peered around the den and saw Tenoch, who froze.

It took him a dozen short breaths to pull enough air into his lungs. He tried to yelp, but it only came out as a whimper. Then he began screaming in earnest.

JUND

Rakka watched Sarkhan sail over the cavern ledge, his body igniting and expanding until he almost filled the cavern with his brilliance. The Sarkhan-creature slammed into the dragon, and the two engaged one another, snapping and striking with their jaws and claws. The man has a gift, that's for sure, she thought. She could finally complete her mission.

She assembled the circle of shamanic ingredients quickly and set up a small, crystal obelisk in the center. With only a morsel of effort she bound an elemental of magma into the crystal, containing its enormous essence inside the tiny symbol. She should be offended, she thought, that the others believed she could have been so incompetent, so slow to summon her elementals for the assault. But they had served their purpose. The hellkite wouldn't bother her, and she could serve her purpose to her master—a dragon far more ancient and dangerous than even Malactoth.

Her crystal obelisk glowed and shuddered with power as the elemental spirit inside it raged, struggling to break out. The ritual set up sympathetic tremors in the cavern around them, causing stalactites to fall and the walls to begin crumbling.

"I'll collapse this place just like you asked, Sarkhan," Rakka said to herself, her hands trembling with the force of her magic. "But not for the reason you thought."

As the cavern shook, the largest column supporting the ceiling cracked. The outermost layers of rock fell away from it like a broken eggshell, revealing a gleaming red obelisk of pure sangrite beneath. The crystal replica in front of Rakka broke with a bang and fell into two smoking pieces.

Shards of rock began falling from the ceiling. Rakka wiped her brow and took one last look at the battle down below. Sarkhan's fiery form held Malactoth in a death-grip, and pieces of stone began to fall on both of them. Without another thought, Rakka slipped out.

BANT

Rafiq knew he should probably throw down his sword, yielding the match. Continuing to fight was tantamount to admitting the legality of the Jhessians' assault, which was tantamount to sanctioning chaos. But the Jhessians were closing in around him, and the judge had done nothing. Rafiq's body tensed, tingling and electric, as he realized that he had been set up, and that neither his ceremonial armor nor the law of Bant would protect him. He was used to winning for a cause; he would have to win to live.

"You're here to kill me, then," said Rafiq to the Jhessians.

Rafiq's words echoed throughout the arena, and the murmur of the crowd followed them. The Jhessians didn't respond, but one of them gestured to the others, a signal Rafiq didn't understand.

"Your swords are illegally enchanted, no doubt more skilled at finding my skin than you are," Rafiq continued. "You fight without technique or honor. Yet I will not show you the same disrespect. In the name of Asha and for the good of this court, I shall defeat you entirely within the bounds of proper—"

He stopped short. The Jhessians had begun doing something strange. They were unbuckling the clasps on their breastplates.

"Stop!" Rafiq said. "What are you . . . "

In a moment, the Jhessians were unarmored to the waist, only a simple tunic covering their chests. They took up their swords again, and Rafiq was surrounded by three sharp, glittering points—with unarmored fighters behind them.

A single strong blow with Rafiq's heavy, unsharpened arena sword would break the Jhessians' bones and probably kill them. All his fighting prowess conformed to the rules of ritual combat, and all his principles conformed to honor. He couldn't lay down his sword—but how could he, the most honor-decorated knight in Bant, attack three nearly defenseless youths before hundreds of people?

NAYA

Screams tore through Ajani's dreams. As he awoke, the screams didn't fade away along with the veil of sleep—they just gained in volume and immediacy. With his heart pounding and his body tense, he staggered from his bed and looked out of the entrance to his lair.

Roars and shrieks rebounded throughout the caves of the den, and the inconstant light of the bonfire threw bizarre, thrashing shadows in all directions. His nostrils flared. There was blood in the air—nacatl blood—and beneath that, he smelled something foreign, like ash and rotting flesh. In the dark, his hand closed over the handle of his axe, and he stepped out.

He could see them. Unnatural creatures were swarming around the bonfire, attacking his fellow nacatl. Members of his pride swept past him, climbing to higher ground to escape them. One of the creatures ran toward Ajani in pursuit, the fingerbones of the creature's claws splayed out like the branches of a dead tree, an unholy light radiating from the empty pits of its eyes. Ajani stepped before it, lodging himself between the fiend and his pridemates, and swung his axe, chopping down through its body. The axe's bindings held as he hacked solidly into the creature once, twice, rending the thing in two with a clatter of ribs.

Ajani sprang down into the fray, landing full on the back of another of the creatures. Its flesh broke, sloughing off like wet cloth under Ajani's claws. One after the other Ajani felled them, his axe and claws driven by protective instincts, his senses sharpened by the cries of his pridemates. After what felt like only a dozen heartbeats, few of the fiends remained, their shredded remains littering the grounds around the bonfire.

Then Ajani heard the words he had hoped he wouldn't.

"The *kha!*" shouted a voice. It was Tenoch, who had been in charge of the watch that night. "Jazal is in trouble!"

Ajani looked back up the slopes of the hill. The remaining death-creatures had fought their way all the way up the zigzagging trails to the lair at the top—his brother's cave. He bounded up ledge after ledge, slowing only to cut through every one of the creatures he encountered.

When he reached the entrance to Jazal's lair, Zaliki stood there. Her eyes brimmed with tears, but her posture was defiant, blocking Ajani from entering.

"Move aside," Ajani said.

"Don't go in there, Ajani," said Zaliki. "I mean it."

"Move out of my way, or I will move you."

She put a hand on his chest. "Ajani, listen to me."

But of course, that was the last thing she could say to make him listen. He knew her purpose was kindness, but he tore through her arms and ran into the lair.

His foot touched something sticky on the cave floor. Unidentified cruor stuck to the fur on his foot. Behind him, he thought Zaliki said something, but he didn't hear her words over the blood thumping in his ears.

Ajani's pupils dilated, taking in the dim details of the lair. The first thing he saw was the wooden handle of the axe, positioned vertically over the bed. He followed its line down to where he saw his brother Jazal lying on his back. The handle belonged to Jazal's axe, the one that matched Ajani's own; the blade was obscured, sunk somewhere deep within Jazal's chest.

BANT

The Jhessians' ceremonial plates lay strewn across the dirt of the arena, abandoned as if they were meaningless hunks of scrap metal. The three youths slashed at Rafiq with magically-augmented precision, landing scratch after scratch on Rafiq's armor and shield. Rafiq retreated step by step, parrying and defending, resisting the urge to strike back. But he was losing. One blow found a chink near his shoulder and sliced through the leather strap, causing his steel pauldron to hang uselessly to one side. Another nicked a flesh wound in Rafiq's forehead that began to ooze blood down his cheek.

The crowd was in an uproar, but Rafiq didn't hear them. He had made his choice.

"Asha forgive me," he muttered.

Rafiq lunged into one of them, driving his sword high, toward the shoulder blades. As he expected, that Jhessian's sword came up to meet his own in a parry, and another attacked Rafiq's exposed flank. Rafiq brought his sword down in a flash, catching the attacker's blade with the full weight of his own, cleaving the weapon in two. The point went flying away, and the broken sword's wielder backed off in fear.

Rafiq pressed the attack. He traded attacks with the two remaining warriors as if he were two men, letting his steel move fluidly between them. He learned the reaction time of the youths and their enchantments, and when he had the rhythm of them, he leaped between the two and spun, presenting a flash of his exposed back to each of them. As they both lunged, Rafiq pivoted sideways, and the youths sank their swords into one another.

They fell to the ground, gravely wounded but healable. The remaining Jhessian dropped the hilt of his broken sword, and fell to his knees.

The judge finally spoke. "Victory goes to the defendant."

The crowd leaped to their feet, cheering.

Rafiq felt no victory. He had only one thing on his mind—someone had set him up to fail, to dishonor himself, and to break the law. Why in Asha's name do that? he thought. He turned to face Aarsil the Blessed in the crowd. She had an inscrutable smile on her face.

* * * * *

"You did well," said Aarsil the Blessed, after the match. Her bemused smile was the reverse of Rafiq's scowl.

"I did what I never thought I'd do," said Rafiq. "They didn't deserve such treatment. I shamed the arena and my caste."

"You did what you had to do," said Aarsil. "That was the important thing. And they'll survive. I've had my best healers tend to them."

"You used your influence here," said Mubin, his eyes narrow. "You used your caste privilege to influence the judge."

"Mubin, please!" said Rafiq. "Remember your place!"

"No, he's right," said Aarsil. "And my associates from the Order of the Skyward Eye supplied the enchanted swords. I'm sorry we deceived you, and put the mercenaries at risk. But I need a special kind of champion—one who has the right skill and character to perform a grave duty in the times to come. I had to test you. And you passed."

Rafiq bowed sharply, and cast a look at Mubin, who bowed grudgingly. "We are at your service, of course, Blessed," said Rafiq.

"Good. Then you leave for Giltspire Castle immediately."

"Giltspire? What is our mission there?"

"To discover who destroyed it."

* * * * *

"Giltspire . . . destroyed?" Rafiq said. "It doesn't make sense, Mubin. I don't understand it. How could the angels have allowed such a thing?"

Mubin rubbed his chin pensively. "What I want to know is who would want it done?"

A long line of mourners marked the road to Giltspire—all heading to the city, none away from it. Individual travelers, couples, and entire families had picked up a minimum of belongings and were making a grim pilgrimage to the site of the disaster. As Rafiq and Mubin passed them on their leotau steeds, the pilgrims' faces didn't look pleading, or even sorrowful. They looked resigned, as if they had already accepted their fate. Rafiq noted that many of them had copies of Asha's Prophecy with them, the prayer spread across Bant in recent years by the solemn Order of the Skyward Eye.

"Asha's Prophecy predicted this," said one old man at a pilgrim's camp one night. "The Prophecy warns that once grace falls, doom will come to the world, and the ultimate test will begin."

"What does that mean?" Rafiq asked him.

"It means you of Sigiled caste must unite to save us," said the old man. "Without you, we won't be able to stop them from pouring out of hell and destroying us. As the

Prophecy says, unless you scour the underworld of evil itself, Bant will fall."

Rafiq didn't know where the Order of the Skyward Eye had gotten their grim vision of the future. The angels had had no ruler, no supreme Asha, for generations, and only the monarchs of the Blessed caste could presume to speak for the angels, according to divine law. Yet the people of every nation of Bant had adopted the prophecy fervently, and had tended to interpret every dire event as confirmation of it.

"Do you think this prophecy is the true word of Asha?" Mubin asked him.

"I don't know," said Rafiq. "But it's right about one thing—the disaster at Giltspire heralds nothing but evil."

When they arrived at Giltspire, the castle was gone. The gleaming white obelisk that remained was surrounded by three concentric haloes: one of the rubble of the former castle, in which mourners hunched, looking for signs of lost loved ones; a second circle of knights of the Skyward Eye, who stood vigilantly, assigned to guard the shining relic that had been exposed; and a third circle, the encampments of pilgrims who had come to grieve and pay tribute at the site of the disaster.

After showing their sigils to the guards, Rafiq and Mubin approached the obelisk. Its surface swept upward from a shallow base, its shape guiding the eye to the heavens.

"This is ancient," said Mubin, his leathery hand touching the stone. "It must have been under the buttress tower for centuries."

"What is its purpose?" asked Rafiq.

"There's script here, carved in the stone. It's similar to runes I've seen in our Order's reliquary. There are symbols for mana here, but I don't recognize all of them."

"It's a warning from Asha," said a nearby knight of the Skyward Eye.

"Why do you say that?" Rafiq asked.

"This obelisk is part of Asha's Prophecy. 'The armies of Death are foretold; Their Names revealed in the primeval Stone,'" said the knight. " 'The prophet's Word; Fells the mountain of War.' The merchant Hazid . . . We believe that he's the prophet it mentions. He brought a spell that felled the 'mountain' of Giltspire, and revealed this primeval stone. And on it are the names of the armies of death to come."

"Where's this Hazid now?" asked Rafiq.

"Gone. He fled after the castle was destroyed."

"I'd like to stay and study these inscriptions," said Mubin. "Or head back to the reliquary to do more research."

"There's no time," said Rafiq. "We have to find this Hazid before his trail goes cold."

JUND

As he recovered from his fall to the floor of Malactoth's cavern, Kresh's first thought was to find a sword. But blood was obscuring his vision. Had he injured his head? He couldn't remember. His own weapon was still buried in the face of Malacoth who was engaged with a dragon of pure fire. What should have been awe at the deadly struggle was dampened by the number of his warriors who lay dead around him. He found an unbroken obsidian-tipped spear nearby, but had to push a friend's body over in order to retrieve it. He had fought side-by-side with that man through a lifetime of hunts. Because the onslaught had gone so badly, his hunting was at an end.

Kresh heard a sharp, grinding sound above his head. Spidery fractures spread throughout the ceiling, and the whole cavern shuddered. Chunks of rubble fell toward Kresh, and he had to roll out of the way, diving for cover. Doing so made him dizzy—how much blood had he lost? In his growing delirium, he thought he saw an enormous obelisk made of red crystal there in the cavern with them, exposed beneath what had been a huge column of rock. It was like a tower made of hardened fire. Could it be made of sangrite, the dragon's stone? He wasn't thinking straight—it was far too large to be made out of such a rare material. He needed to focus. He just needed to kill the hellkite, and get his remaining men out of there. Where were all the elementals? And where the hell was Rakka?

He saw two draconic shapes warring before him. He lifted the spear, gathered up all his strength, and threw the weapon without caring which creature he hit.

●　●　●　●　●

The pillar of Jund's rare red stone, sangrite, shone in the center of the cavern, casting a glow over Sarkhan and Malactoth. Sarkhan had his hands locked around his war-staff, causing the dragonspell that blazed around him to lock its claws around the neck of his foe. Malactoth bit and slashed at him directly, burning himself on Sarkhan's spell repeatedly, but coming dangerously close to cleaving Sarkhan's actual body in two.

Sarkhan had the beast in his grasp, but needed a killing blow. Kresh's warriors were mostly dead, and Rakka was nowhere to be found. But then Sarkhan saw it: a spear flew into view, arcing directly at his chest. Sarkhan let go of his staff with one hand and pivoted his body away from the spear's flight path—only to catch it as it was about to whizz by.

Sarkhan's movement pulled his fire-dragon's claw away from the enemy dragon's neck, freeing the beast to strike at him. Malactoth surged forward—and as he did so, Sarkhan turned the obsidian point toward him and leaned into the hellkite's motion, burying the spear deep in his chest.

Malactoth died with a deafening roar that shook loose what remained of the cavern's structural pillars. Sarkhan thought he heard a yell of his name, perhaps a warning from Kresh, but it was lost in the din and too late besides. As Sarkhan fell upon the hellkite's body, the ceiling collapsed all around him

●　●　●　●　●

Sarkhan didn't regain consciousness as much as have it forced upon him. His body was being lifted roughly out of the cavern rubble, causing the orange light of Jund's sky to strike his eyes. The other sensation was of mana—powerful, boiling, chaotic mana.

He looked around him. An obsidian elemental was carrying him out of the destroyed cavern, holding him in its rocky arms as if he were a child. The elemental was one of Rakka's, but there was no sign of her nearby. She could have let him die under the rubble—why the favor? The elemental set him down on the rough volcanic gravel, turned, and walked off. Its task complete, it found a stream of bubbling lava, and stepped into it, melting away its identity once more.

Kresh and his warriors had either died or moved on as well. The hellkite Malactoth lied dead beneath the shattered volcanic remains of its lair. In its place was an enormous column of pure, crystalline sangrite exposed to the sky after what must have been centuries buried in the rock. *That* was the source of mana. The obelisk wasn't just emanating mana, but focusing it—for what purpose Sarkhan couldn't determine.

He looked up into the sky. High above, dragons circled, drawn in by the obelisk's power. Rakka was never interested in hunting Malactoth, he surmised. She used Kresh—and Sarkhan himself—to distract the hellkite while she freed the sangrite from its ancient prison.

If she had gone to such trouble, why wasn't she taking advantage of its power?

NAYA

The blood was irrelevant. It wasn't on Ajani's mind at the time, so it got all over his white fur—but he didn't care. His consciousness was consumed with the shape of Jazal's body, the pose the undead creatures had left him in after killing him with his own axe. Jazal had stopped breathing before Ajani found him, and the blood coming from his wounds pooled in places to make the floor slippery. Still, Ajani hugged his brother close, trying to bury his forehead in Jazal's sticky chest.

Ajani rocked back and forth, but stopped when Jazal spoke.

"It's going to be all right, Ajani," said his brother, petting the white nacatl's fur.

Ajani didn't look up. If he looked, Jazal's voice wouldn't be real, and death would triumph. Please let this be real, he thought. "Oh, thank the spirits, I'm glad you're . . . alive," said Ajani.

"Yes. Don't worry. You're not hallucinating."

"But all the blood," he said. He couldn't help dwelling on it. "I'm too late, aren't I, brother? You're—"

"Let's not think about it. Listen, I need you to go and tell the rest of the pride that I'm fine, all right? And we'll go right back to the way things were."

"Because . . . you're fine."

"Yes, why wouldn't I be? What, would someone

send something to kill me? Right here in my own chambers? Why would someone do something like that? It's ridiculous." Jazal's arms squeezed him reassuringly.

Ajani chuckled weakly. "Yes, ridiculous. Nobody would ever hurt you, Jazal. Everybody loves you. And it'd be chaos if you were gone—I swear, what would the pride do?"

Jazal laughed. "What *would* you do? But we don't have to think about that. I'm here, and I'll take care of everything. So go now, Ajani. Tell them. Tell them I'm perfectly fine. You just made a mistake, thinking I was dead. Nothing's going to change, Ajani. I'm perfectly fine."

Ajani tasted copper on his tongue. His mind clenched with dread.

"I can't." His voice was muffled by the fur on Jazal's chest. "I can't tell them."

Jazal's voice was soft, just a whisper in his mind. "You have to. It's time now. You have to tell them I'm—"

"No!"

Ajani pushed his brother roughly, petulantly. The body slid off the bed and toppled onto the stone floor with a messy thump. Ajani gasped in horror. Jazal's leg was jutting up at a strange angle against the bed, and the axe handle had been shoved deeper into Jazal's chest. A sob tried to escape Ajani's lips, but he choked it back inside. He rushed over and pulled on his brother's body, to get him back onto the bed.

Ajani cursed sharply, repeatedly, using words he rarely used. As he pulled on Jazal's arm and leg, he felt a wave of something, a feeling growing inside him that he knew was going to be bad. The cursing helped. He cursed over and over, as angrily as he could, and pushed the feeling back down.

He arranged Jazal's limbs tidily. "There you go, Jazal," he said. The blood was sticky on Ajani's hands and chest.

Suddenly Ajani convinced himself that the two of them were alone in the world. He didn't need to go out and tell the others, because there were no others to tell. Of course not. It was just the two of them, and Jazal was simply reclining, like when they were children and Ajani had watched his older brother sleeping. Ajani smiled at him.

"I'll take care of all of this, Jazal," Ajani said. "I'll tidy up your room and let you sleep. Then tomorrow we can go on a walkabout, see the jungle, maybe chase some elves around the woods. I'll miss you tonight but . . . But I'll see you in the morning. I'll just let you sleep now. You sleep. I'll take care of the room."

The dark wave welled up in him. He cursed again, trying to feel anger to make it go away. But it was no use. The feeling surged up his chest and into his mind. He couldn't breathe. He felt intolerably hot. He felt the blood suddenly, felt his feet awash in the puddle of it, felt its stickiness on his face and mane and hands. He smelled it and tasted it, the liquid that was supposed to be inside Jazal. He had never seen so much blood before. It was all over him. He was drenched in red.

"Ajani—" said Jazal's voice.

"Shut up," Ajani said to himself.

He tried to roar, but the sound crumbled and choked in his throat.

The world spiraled in on him, forcing him down inside himself. The weight of it crushed his mind. Everything went dark and warm, and he felt as though his consciousness had ruptured, his mind being exiled to some realm of insanity. Shapes swam in the darkness—the blood-hallucinations he always saw under his eyelids.

But then Ajani realized his eyes weren't closed.

THE BLIND
ETERNITIES

Ajani felt a void around him like suction. It dragged at his fur and skin, and sucked at his eyeballs. He blinked repeatedly and moved his head from side to side, but his vision was reduced to watery impressions. He saw a dark green shape, its hills and valleys roiling uncomfortably, and momentary inklings of creatures moving across the world at speeds too fast to be natural. He could sense that place in a way he didn't understand, a feeling like the memory of a taste, an imprint once removed from reality. It was Naya; somehow he was certain of it. That green, undulating shape was my home world, he thought.

He saw—or felt—other shapes in the void too. He turned his attention to them, which brought a blast of chaos rushing past his mind, like turning to face into a hard wind. He perceived four other realms in the void, dynamic and textured like Naya was, but they each felt very different. They were alien and off-putting, but he strained his perception toward them as much as he could. His eyes couldn't take the grasping winds of the void, so he closed his eyes. His mind hurt when he tried to concentrate on the scene before him, so he let his consciousness float freely, as blank as the void. After a moment, the worlds appeared to him, as if he could feel their contours with some sense beyond sight or touch. Other worlds, other lives, other bizarre forms of being—he felt a rush of living textures that bewildered him.

And he felt motion. The worlds moved relative to one another, he perceived. In fact, they were nearing one another, so close that they were beginning to overlap. Streaks of existence reached out from each world like blobs of colored light, blending with each other at the edges, forming an irregular ring with an eye of void at the center.

It was too much to take in. He couldn't hold what he was seeing in his mind. He let his consciousness slide toward one of the worlds, a swirl of hot reds and smoke. Before he could turn away again, he felt it rushing up to meet him. There was a violent jolt, and the sudden sensation of weight—and falling.

He had a body again, a real, physical body. And it was hurtling through fiery air toward the red world's ground. When he landed, he thought, he would either wake up from the nightmare, or die.

BANT

This is a good place to camp, sir," said the page.

Gwafa Hazid scratched his chin. "No. We keep going. This isn't Valeron yet. We've made an awful pace, and I want to see olive trees before we stop."

"We're still a day's journey out from the Valeron border, and we've pushed the steeds. They're exhausted. They need to rest. And so do you, sir."

"I'm fine," snapped Hazid. Why must this messy-tressed boy keep telling him that? It was irritating, not to mention above his caste. Had society crumbled so far already?

But he pulled his leotau over to the side of the road anyway. The beast sighed, and its flanks heaved, at which Hazid rolled his eyes.

"It's not enough that we feed these things half our meat," he said. "They've got to complain about being ridden, too. Doesn't anything know its place anymore?"

"I don't know, sir."

"Of course you don't," said Hazid. "It's rhetoric—something you wouldn't understand."

"No, sir."

"Correct. Unpack the wineskins."

"Sir, about the Giltspire—"

"What did I *tell* you about—?" He stopped himself from cuffing the boy, but only just. "Enough about . . . that place. It's behind us now. It's in the past. We went there, we did our business, and we made a lot of money and . . . and we gained, in other ways. Transaction over. It was a good deal for us. We're headed east now, for new ventures."

"New ventures, sir?"

"Yes! Shut up. You'll see when we get there. Where are those wineskins?"

The boy set up camp, and Hazid drank. The memories of seeing a castle topple lost their crispness. A fuzzy halo surrounded the day's events, bringing a slow grin to Hazid's face. His mind melted into a fluid, and flowed around the sharp edges of those unpleasant thoughts. He rambled as the page did his work.

"We did nothing wrong, when it comes down to it," said Hazid. "We destroyed nothing. The thing was old. It was probably ready to crumble anyway. I think I remember that—yes, weren't stonemasons looking into that old thing for decades? There were plenty of warnings about the old deathtrap, so why didn't they heed them? It was an architectural disaster waiting to happen. And those people"—Hazid winced slightly—"they should have just been out of there. They could have known if they'd only paid attention. So really, it was their own fault." Hazid nodded and drank. "Am I everyone's personal wet-nurse? Am I in charge of everybody else's personal safety? Of course not. A man can't be expected to engineer his life around the ignorance of others. A man can only be expected to look after his own affairs. Praise Asha."

He raised his glass to clink it with someone's, but the boy hadn't filled his cup yet. "Come here, boy."

The boy was nowhere to be found. The camp was only half-made.

"Boy? Where've you run off to now? My tent's not even up yet!"

"Sir, someone's coming."

The boy was over by the road, looking back to the west. There were hoofbeats in the distance, at a gallop. Hazid jumped up to his feet.

"Who is it? Who would follow us? We've done nothing wrong!"

The boy squinted into the gloam of the waning day. "Sir, I think we should abandon the camp. Come on."

"Abandon the camp? Where would we——"

The boy was already running into the woods. "Infuriating mop-headed whelp," Hazid muttered.

Before Hazid could commit his legs to running, the riders were upon him, their lanterns glowing like fireflies. One was a tall, olive-skinned human man in plate armor. Draped from his armor were dozens, maybe a hundred sigils, each one catching the lamplight like a star in the gloam. The other was a broad-faced rhox.

The rhox spoke. "Gwafa Hazid?"

"I . . . no. I'm his . . . handservant. My master just ran off into the woods."

The human and rhox looked at him, and exchanged glances.

"I'm telling you the truth! It was just before you came. He ran off that way!"

"I am Rafiq, knight of the Order of the Reliquary," said the human, dismounting from his leotau.

"What——? You——you are? You are not."

Hazid glanced over the man's sigils. He had medallions of patronage from every major city, in every country across Bant. He even had the Sigil of the Empty Throne, the one that marked him as the official champion of the archangel Asha herself, hand-selected by one of Blessed caste.

"I see. Well," said Hazid.

Oh holy angel in the heavens, he thought. He was going to be arrested by the most decorated knight in the world. And by some rhox.

"And I am Mubin, knight of the Order of the Reliquary," said the rhox, his voice as deep as a gravel pit.

"You're under arrest," said Rafiq.

"I've done nothing," said Hazid, and threw his glass at Rafiq's face.

Rafiq dodged the glass and liquid both, and struck Hazid clean across his face with his open hand in the same motion. The glass shattered uselessly somewhere behind them.

The blow rang in Hazid's head. The pain took several seconds to sink in, but then it blossomed into a full, electric injury. There must be glowing fingermarks across his cheek, he thought. His next thought came in clear, simple words, as clear as the wine glass shattered on the ground: *This man must now die.*

Hazid had enough sense to keep that thought from spilling out of his mouth. "I'll go quietly, gentlemen," he said.

JUND

There was no warning, no sense of transition. Ajani was no longer in Jazal's cavern, and no longer hanging in space. He was no longer breathing the smoke of the torches outside his brother's lair. The light had changed—he was outdoors, and the sky was a burnt orange. The air had changed—it was dry and hot, with a stiff sulfur undertone. The terrain had changed—he was standing on the slope of a mountain of rust-streaked stone.

Nightmare? Hallucination? Hell?

He didn't feel asleep. It didn't seem like a hallucination—everything felt crystal-sharp, detailed, and immediate. And if he had died of grief and gone to some kind of afterlife, it certainly wasn't what he had expected.

He stood there gaping. The least reasonable hypothesis, which seemed increasingly likely to be the case, was that he was simply, inexplicably, somewhere else.

The sense of remoteness was unmistakable. Beyond not recognizing anything he saw before him, he knew he was far from his pride's den—far, in fact, from anywhere he had ever been in his life. He didn't know how he knew this, but he *knew*.

He grasped at straws. Maybe it was another life. Maybe it was the distant past.

Maybe Jazal wasn't really dead.

"These thoughts are useless," he muttered. If it was in any way real, he thought, then he needed to be home.

Before he had time to begin formulating a plan of how to get home again, a stream of chittering, furry creatures appeared from around a bend in the trail. Their eyes were beady and ferocious, and their claws and teeth as sharp as needles. They hissed as they saw him, and swarmed directly toward him.

Ajani had never seen creatures like them. They were short, just above waist-high, with broad heads, pointed ears, and light brown fur. Their hands were clawed, and they wore simple furs and beads. There were about two dozen of them. He absorbed all in a flash as he made the quick decision to turn and run in the opposite direction. Did *every* species have to enjoy hunting him?

Ajani outpaced the creatures around the next bend, but they were gaining fast. He wished he had another direction to run, but the heights were dramatic—to his left, the rusty stone wall of the mountain was almost vertical. To his right, there was empty air—a sheer drop-off. The narrow path between them was Ajani's only option, so he took it.

But it was no use. The diminutive monsters were catching up with him. Perhaps he could fight them, or scare them off. Ajani stopped and spun around, but before he could take an attack stance or bring his axe to bear, they were abreast of him . . . and running right past.

The creatures clicked and chittered excitedly as they streamed past him. They weren't chasing him at all. They were fleeing.

Ajani looked back in the direction they had come from, and saw what they were trying to flee. There was a whoosh of wind that almost blasted Ajani off his feet.

A dragon came soaring around the mountain, and with it came a roar that caused the mountain itself to shudder.

BANT

I think I'll slit your throat and plant flowers in there, thought Hazid.

"How much longer?" he asked.

"I'm surprised you're so anxious, Hazid," said Rafiq as they rode back to civilization. "You'll face severe justice when we deliver you to the courts in Valeron."

"I just want to know how long I have," said Hazid.

"It'll be another couple of hours," said Mubin.

Hazid had nothing against the rhox especially, except that he was an especially unlikable person.

"Until then, why don't you tell us why you destroyed Giltspire Castle?" added Mubin.

Case in point, Hazid thought. There was no subtlety to the rhox, at all.

What kind of flower would grow best out of their necks? he wondered. That's what he really wanted to know. Maybe he would go with roses. Hazid hoped they would grow thick with thorns as they grew out of his captors' necks. And he hoped those thorns would tear their way free of his captors' skins, and bury roots deep in their guts. That's the only way he could possibly repay them both for the injustice they'd done to him. None of it was his fault, after all.

"I didn't. It wasn't me. I was only there on business. Some mages in my caravan—whom I had nothing to do with—cast a spell or something, and the next thing I knew, the castle was tumbling down."

"You'd better start getting used to telling the truth," said Mubin. "The courts have magic that'll pry it out of you, but if it doesn't match your words, your punishment will be much worse."

"What's wrong with the steeds?" said Rafiq suddenly.

The leotau slowed to a halt. They clopped their hooves on the stones of the road and huffed and snorted. A breeze swayed the ancient, twisted olive trees in the orchards around them; the steeds tilted their heads to and fro and sneered into the wind.

Hazid rolled his eyes. "They probably just smell a deer."

"No. They're fed. They smell something else," said Mubin.

Then for a long moment, the three men made no noise.

The sky rumbled and thudded, and the ground shuddered under the steeds. The trees shook in ways that wind would never have moved them, and they shed perfectly green leaves. The leotau arched their backs suddenly and hissed at the air, causing Hazid to jump in his saddle.

"What in the blessed—"

"Shh!" said the knights.

They would have called the phenomenon a herald of an evening thunderstorm, if they had ever heard thunder. They would have called it a minor earthquake, if they had ever felt the earth quake. But Bant had never felt such forces. Instead the men sat quietly, struck dumb by the experience. The wind felt strange and thick, and the air had an earthy perfume to it, like rich soil. Thunder danced toward them, resounding in weird echoes from the horizon, and the clouds had an unnatural gray color to them.

Hazid thought he saw lights in the clouds on the horizon, but as he squinted to focus on them, the lights evaded his eye. Was he going mad? Or had the angels discovered his sin?

Then the ground stopped moving. Hazid's leotau shook its mane and casually licked its front leg, as if nothing had happened.

The men looked at each other. Mubin was frowning, cautious and concerned as any of his race. The knight-captain's face was full of wonder, as if it had been some sort of play with jesters and refreshments. Hazid was just painstakingly trying to hide his panic.

"Okay, so what was that, gentlemen?" asked Hazid. "Any clues?"

"It was a sign," said Rafiq.

"It was something unique," said Mubin. "A sign, yes, but from whom, and of what? Have you ever seen anything like that, Hazid?"

"Me? Why would *I* have seen anything like *that*?"

Mubin was a stone wall. "Try to calm down."

"My caravan has been from one side of this land to the *other* and I have never—I mean, *never*—seen anything so . . . so . . . *No*. I have not."

"I'm sure the explanation, once it's discovered, will be reasonable," said Mubin.

Rafiq toyed absently with one of the sigils hanging from his armor, listening for any further sign of the rumbling.

"And you two," continued Hazid, "have me strapped to this lion, which is, by the way, not safe. I could complain to the courts about the way I'm being treated."

"It was just like the prayer, Mubin, wasn't it?" said Rafiq. "Asha's Prophecy. Like the Order of the Skyward Eye say."

"Rafiq," said Mubin.

"'When the world's body shakes. When the world's stomach churns.' We felt it shake! We heard it churn! I never imagined it would be so literally true."

"Rafiq, I don't want you to get your belief tangled in your optimism. It's just a cleric's prayer."

"I don't know, Mubin. I'm starting to think it may be something. Why couldn't it be true? We're in a historic time foretold by ancient sages. The events and records we've seen as knights of the Reliquary—the words we've heard—they're coming true. We're seeing it unfold before our eyes. This may be the time of the return of Asha."

Hazid blinked and kicked in the stirrups nervously.

"Be cautious," said Mubin. "Don't overinterpret. It could be a coincidence."

"Yes," said Hazid. "My friend here has made an excellent point. It is just the weather. A little trick of the wind. Nothing 'angelic' or 'prophetic' about it."

Please don't let me be the hand of prophecy, thought Hazid. He didn't want to be the hand of prophecy anymore. He didn't want it to mean anything, because if it did—the consequence would be too horrible to contemplate.

"Oh, I think the archangel has finally made herself known," said Rafiq, nodding into the wind. His eyes seemed to look into infinity. "There's finally hope for us all."

The angels can't see me, can they? worried Hazid. They can't see into my soul, to see what I have done? The clouds weren't enough protection, he thought. The open sky was full of *their* eyes. Where could a man get a roof over his head when he needed one?

"Can we just hurry up and get to the courts?" said Hazid.

JUND

Ajani had never seen a dragon, and didn't know the term. But he didn't need to know what to call it to run from the beast. Nor did he know the term for goblins, but he followed the furry creatures' example, and ran.

If Ajani could have stopped and contemplated the anatomy of the dragon, he might have likened it to one of Naya's enormous gargantuans in size, except that none of the gargantuans had wings. He might have thought of some of the elves' ancient carvings of hydras, and of primitive drawings he had seen in caves. He might have pieced together that, while no dragons had lived on Naya in centuries, a dim cultural memory of such a beast lingered in the dark pockets of his home. He might even have considered that the presence of the dragon was strong evidence that he was no longer, in fact, in Naya. However, circumstances being what they were, he had no time for such thoughts. He just ran.

The wingbeats of the dragon hurled boulders of air at Ajani's back, and he wobbled, using his leather-strapped axe as a counterweight to keep his balance. Several of the furry goblins were swept right off the cliff by the gusts of air, and tumbled off the edge and out of sight. Most of the little creatures were quite sure-footed, however, and scrambled into narrow caves, disappearing into the mountainside. Ajani wasn't accustomed to the terrain or the height, and he stumbled. His legs slipped out from under him, and he slid over the edge.

Ajani caught himself, but barely. His legs dangled over the cliff, and his claws clung precariously onto his axe and the cliff's edge. The dragon pulled up, hovering with mighty wingbeats in the air next to the mountain, and rearing its head back to strike.

"Back!" said a voice. "This is not your meal, old boy."

A broad-chested human man stood on the cliffside. He grinned at Ajani, a crazed gleam in his eye.

The man thrust his staff into the air and brought it down, hard, onto the stone ground. The impact let loose a blast of sizzling sparks that spiraled toward the dragon. The spell burst harmlessly on the dragon's nose, but startled it.

"Go on, Karrthus," the man called into the gale of the dragon's wings. "Feast on the blood of some other beast! This is *my* dinner."

The dragon hesitated, looking once at Ajani. Then it turned and dived into the valley adjacent to the mountain. It swooped along the chasm floor, then with a series of powerful flaps of its wings, soared up and over the next cliffs and out of sight.

The man helped Ajani up. "I'm Sarkhan Vol," he said. His accent was strange, thick and guttural, like no human speech Ajani had ever heard.

"Ajani. Ajani Goldmane."

"You're a long way from home, Ajani Goldmane."

"What . . . place is this?"

"This world is Jund," said Sarkhan. "A savage, primordial land. It's my home, for now. And yours, if you'd like it to be."

"This is not my home," said Ajani. "I'm from the Qasali Valley, which is—" Ajani broke off and looked around. He didn't know which direction to look.

"Not on this plane," Sarkhan finished. "You don't know, do you?" he asked. Ajani had trouble reading the man's expression. Was his smirk amused, or devious?

"Know what? What does that mean?"

"It means you're no longer on Naya. You've traveled to an entirely different world, *planeswalker*."

The man was making no sense.

"Deal with all that later," said Sarkhan. "Karrthus won't stay away for long. Come on."

● ● ● ● ●

Ajani followed Sarkhan around the ledge, climbing higher and higher up the mountain. The heat rose as they went. Should he turn around and leave this strange man's company? He had no better plan than to follow him, and try to learn what he should do.

"What's your purpose, planeswalker?" Sarkhan asked him. "What fuels you? What drives you to do more than you ever could?"

Ajani paused. "Revenge."

Sarkhan laughed vigorously. "That's about the best answer you could have given. Who wronged you?"

"I don't know. Someone murdered my brother. I don't even know if it was real."

"Your *anger* is real. Don't worry. You'll have ample opportunities to nurture that anger, and eventually, when you find the right target, to express it."

As they walked, Ajani's fists shook. "I feel like I could explode."

Sarkhan stopped and turned back to look at him. "No. That's not the right road, my friend. It's not that you want to burst into pieces yourself—what does that get you? This murder, it's not your fault. It's the outside world that is the target of your rage. You feel it encroaching on you, pressing down on your identity. What you're feeling is the need to push the world back."

"How can I do that?"

"By believing in your own instincts. By letting your ferocity out of its cage of despair and self-doubt. By being the animal you are." He grinned broadly, showing his teeth. "My destination is ahead. Come, tell me of your story as we walk."

They walked farther up the mountain pass. The winds were balmy blasts, thick with sulfur and the taste of soot, and Ajani had to wait for pauses in order to speak. He found it odd to tell the stranger of his world and the events that led to his plight, but the human seemed to understand, and with the understanding came a measure of comfort.

The heat became intense as they ascended, and Ajani was struck by the pulsing perception of mana nearby. It was mana of fire, mana of bitter rage, mana of immediacy and freedom and chaos. It was alluring, glorious. Ajani's heart raced, and his breathing quickened.

As he finished his story, Ajani saw flares of molten lava bursting up above the ridge ahead.

"What the hell are we—"

"This is what I wanted you to see, my friend! This is the Sweltering Cauldron, my favorite source of mana on Jund. I needed to come here to recharge my spirit, and it may inspire you as well."

The trail ended at the rim of a volcanic caldera, filled almost to the brim with seething red lava. The air above the caldera wobbled and distorted, and the entire front side of Ajani's body was bathed in almost unbearable heat. The mana that flowed around and through the caldera was abundant and intoxicating. He felt like his fur was burning, but he couldn't look away.

"You want to know how I pushed Karrthus away?" Sarkhan asked.

Ajani nodded.

"The key is this: you don't force away a greater threat. You appeal to its passions, its—"he thumped his chest with his fist—"innermost desires. You give it something that it wants more than killing you."

"How did you know what it wanted?"

Sarkhan laughed. "Dragons always want the same thing," he said.

With that, Sarkhan turned to the caldera. He raised his arms and staff high in the air.

"What do they want?" Ajani started to ask, but he stopped short.

A pillar of lava shot straight up out of the center of the caldera. It streamed vertically into the air, disappearing into the ashen clouds high above. Sarkhan's face was red in the glare of the enormous beam of fire. His eyes reflected the pillar as two glowing, vertical stripes.

There was a roar high above. Ajani looked up to see a dragon circling the pillar—a different one from the one who had chased him—its wings almost grazing the surface of the lava stream. Then another dragon approached and began wheeling around it. And then another, and another. Soon the air was filled with dragons, all attracted to Sarkhan's molten pillar of pure rage. They stacked up in tiers in the sky, in what looked to Ajani like a bizarre dance of giants.

Sarkhan turned his head back to Ajani. The man's smile was too wide, his eyes too unfocused. "I see it now—I see what Rakka was after. There's a greater power at work here, across your world and mine. This power can be yours, as well," he said.

"How?" said Ajani.

"*How* doesn't matter," said Sarkhan. "*How* is details.

It's right here, plain as the volcano before us. Just go after what you want, and take it. And if there's something in your way, you take it anyway. You blast through it, you push it out of your way, or you fly over it."

Then, as if to prove his point, he leaped off the ledge into the caldera.

Ajani gawked as the man tumbled down toward the lava, a dark humanoid silhouette against the glowing red. But then he moved laterally across the lava, and eventually gained in altitude. As Ajani watched, Sarkhan sprouted leathery wings and became a huge flying creature—a dragon.

The Sarkhan-dragon spiraled around the pillar of lava a few times with the other dragons. As he flew, the pyromantic spell ended, and the pillar dissipated and sank back into the caldera. Ajani saw only a cloud of dragons—Sarkhan had become indistinguishable from them. The dragons began to break off one by one, heading off into the orange sky of Jund. Soon Ajani was alone with the volcano.

Ajani held his head in his hands. His mind swirled with thoughts that bled with pain and rage. Jazal is dead, he thought. And I'm in a world of fire. He was cut off from his home, and a man who might have understood how to get him back there had just turned into a monster and flown away. The heat from the volcano felt strangely soothing, a fuming salve to his pain. Ajani threw his arms wide, as if to embrace the entirety of the caldera.

He inched his feet toward the ledge. The heat on the tips of his toes was excruciating.

What was he about to do? Was he insane—or suicidal? The heat poured into Ajani, penetrated right through his skin, and sizzled inside his veins.

Jazal was dead, he thought, and he was as good as dead as well. His fate had already been decided. Why not 105 make one choice he could actually control? If death was coming for him, then why not fly into it?

He took a step—

What am I doing what am I doing I'm going to die

As he fell, fumes from the caldera blasted up around him. They scorched his body and his soul, shredding him into pieces and reforming him, enveloping him in an eternity of fiery destruction.

NAYA

S moke wafted from Ajani's fur.

The smell of it woke him. He coughed.

If he was dead, then the afterlife must smell a lot like his home jungle.

He sat up and looked around. He recognized the trees and the trails around his pride's den. It was day. Some cinders were smoldering in his fur; he rubbed them out with his hand. The cinders and smoke kept him grounded—they forced him to remember his planeswalk to Jund, and convinced him it had actually happened.

Ajani felt hollow.

The jungle lianas felt like teasing fingers, reaching out to prod and pinch him as he wandered. His fur was grubby, and his mane was speckled with burrs. Instinctively he turned uphill, walking any slope that led upward, without thinking anything but a dim sense of wanting to move away from his own footprints.

As he climbed in elevation, the roots and cloddy dirt turned to mud. The oppressive humidity turned to rain. The first heavy droplets plunked on the leaves and made them shudder around him. When they dropped onto his body, they broke apart into steam, cooling and soothing him.

In the distance he heard the low rumbles of gargantuans' voices over the beginnings of the rain. The colossal beasts' voices carried for miles—which was good, because being in earshot didn't mean being in range of their huge feet. Jazal used to say that their ancient minds held the secrets of another age. When they were boys, the two brothers would strain their ears to listen to the gargantuans' voices, but they could never understand the words. It was a music of pain, Ajani thought, part of the deep rhythm of Naya. Sometimes as he slept in their camp, he fell asleep to the long, low, rumbling sighs of the gargantuans, and fell into dreams where the stars were singing sad songs to him.

The rain was clattering, and Ajani was soaked in moments. He usually had a tarp to keep him out of the afternoon rain, but without one, the water just ran down his body in rivulets, chasing streaks of ash from the Jund volcano. That was exile, pridelessness, he thought. The inability to get out of the rain.

The slope was getting steeper. Ajani didn't know if he was trying to reach a destination, but he recognized where he was. The canopy opened up to reveal a clearing, in which sat the ruins of a nacatl city. Huge broken slabs of white granite jutted up at odd angles from the earth. A temple supported a network of climbing vines twisting over its steep, moss-covered steps. Birds alighted on shrines and headless statues. The rain gave the ruins an even more deserted feeling— no one was there to protect any of its structures. It was naked to the elements.

It was a forbidden place. They were the ruins of Antali.

"You shouldn't be here," said a delicate voice.

Ajani whirled around. A very old nacatl woman stood before him in shaman's dress, not looking up into his eyes. Her fur was dark gray, like the coal tips of hardwood after an evening's fire, but now matted with rain. Her pupils were huge, almost filling her entire eyes. She didn't seem to be using them.

"You shouldn't be here, but I suspect you're meant to be. You're here to read the Coil, I suppose?"

"No, I—"

"Come along, then."

Ajani looked around. The rain was moving on, rolling along the grassy square of Antali like a cloud. Mist soon enveloped the ruins. The old woman was so silent of foot that Ajani had to hurry to keep sight of her in the fog.

"This is where the hero Marisi led his uprising, you know," said the old woman. "You've heard the story? You should, young thing like you. They should teach you the stories. Marisi was a great man—he freed the minds of the nacatl who lived here. The city was decadent. No one remembered their inner natures here. They had gone soft, because life was too easy up here. Peace and law for generations—it made everyone fat and vile."

The woman was leading Ajani through the fog. Ajani wondered how her steps were so sure, given her obviously failing sight. There was a rough trail that led up a bit higher.

"They pulled down the Coil, smashed it to rubble. But you can still read the scratchforms. You'll see."

Ajani had heard mention of the Coil in the *hadu,* during the yearly Feast of Marisi. The memory stung him—Jazal. He wished he remembered more of what Jazal's speeches were supposed to teach him.

"What exactly is the Coil?" he asked.

"The Coil was Law," said the old woman. "One hundred twenty-one guiding principles, scratched into granite by the Cloud Nacatl. One hundred twenty-one shackles on our minds. The high-minded nacatl of Qasal, over on the next mountain, are still bound by its precepts.

They still hold onto civilization. But their souls have lost the rage, the rage that makes us who we are."

They came upon a bowl in the earth, an amphitheater carved into a grassy slope. Steps led down to a dais where an immense disc of white granite lay broken. As they approached it, Ajani saw the spiraling geometric shapes of the scratchforms gouged into it, a recording method only the shamans in Ajani's pride had used. Jazal had been able to read some simple scratchforms, and had tried to teach his brother, but Ajani had always been more interested in developing his skill with the axe instead. The thickness of the disc came up to Ajani's waist, and its diameter was thrice his height. A meandering crack divided the disc into two large pieces and many smaller ones, and seedlings and patches of moss had blossomed between them. The pattern of the scratchforms across the pieces was dizzying.

"The Coil recorded a way of life that was supposed to support freedom through law," said the old woman. "When I was a girl, the hero Marisi smashed the Coil so that we all could recover what we had lost."

"I can't read it," said Ajani.

The old woman put her hand on the disc. She ran her fingers over the scratchforms. "You don't need to. You can feel what they represent, can't you? There's rage in your scent. I can sense you share in Marisi's cause."

"What I feel is not Marisi's rage. I have my own."

"Even better. Each of us needs our own burden to shove against. Each of us needs our own load to weigh us down. What have you pushed up the mountain with you?"

Ajani was beginning to wonder whether the old crone had anything left rattling around in her head. He looked at his hands. "I have nothing."

"Nonsense. Tell me what you've brought with you here, boy. What burden do you carry?"

He said the first thing that came to mind, the only thing on his mind. "The death of my brother."

The old woman hissed a laugh. "Death? It must be fresh for your scent to be so warm."

"He was . . . murdered."

"Ah, yes. Now I see. You have the blaze in you now. That's good. Who killed your kin, then?"

"I don't know."

"The blaze demands better than that. It will eat away at you the longer you put it off. I see now why you've come. Say it."

What was she talking about?

"Say it!"

"Say what, old woman? I don't know what you think I was trying to—"

The woman sprang forward and clawed him suddenly, raking his bare chest with surprising viciousness. Ajani roared and instinctively fell into a battle stance.

"Yes," she said. "Tell me what the blaze wants."

Ajani didn't know whether to leave or break her arms.

She raked at him again. He was ready for it and stepped out of the way, but her other claw slashed at his arm as he dodged the first blow. Blood oozed down his arm.

"Say it! Say it!" she cried.

"I don't know what you want me to say!"

The woman pounced on him, sinking her claws deep into his chest. It felt like she were clutching his heart itself, coiling her claws around the still-beating organ and twisting it around in its cage. Ajani roared and seized the woman in his own claws, wrenched her free of him, and threw her.

She was light. She arced up and down and slammed her head into one corner of the Coil. She fell limp on the ground.

Ajani gasped and rushed over to her, cradling her in his arms. His blood was pumping, and his claws wouldn't retract.

Blood oozed from a gash above one of the woman's pupil-filled eyes. She came to, blinking and smiling. "Now you know it," she said. "Now you can say it."

Ajani's nostrils flared with his brisk breaths.

"I will kill whoever murdered my brother."

PART
TWO

NAYA

The dragon planeswalker Nicol Bolas exhaled a sigh of black smoke. He had grown used to the chill, dead air of Grixis, and Naya's cloud jungle felt intolerably hot. The sodden air clung to his skin and slithered through his nostrils. And the plane positively *teemed* with living things. Something was crawling on every part of him—a rodent of some kind, a bird, a legion of insects. He twitched his limbs to shoo them away, but they were quickly replaced by other living things. Naya was the most exuberant world of Alara. It was suffocating.

Before him, looking more like an insect to him than the warrior hero of his reputation, was the leonin Marisi, kneeling like a forgotten penitent.

"I didn't expect your visit, Master," said Marisi, bowing his head.

Despite the oppressive life of the plane, Bolas's plans required such unpleasant stopovers. Once his plans were properly actualized, he would be able to summon his minions to his lair, fill their tiny brains with his orders, and fling them back across the aether. He longed for that day. Until then, he'd have to make the visits in person. Exhausting.

"It was necessary. I need to be elsewhere soon, so I'll keep this short. The issue is this: I need more assurance of conflict from your world. The leonin of Naya already hate one another, thanks to your intervention years ago. But I want more. I want the elves," said Bolas.

"You can't have the elves," said Marisi.

"This is not a negotiation. This is not a request. I need the elves."

Marisi shook his furry little cat-head. "I'm sorry, Master, but it's too late," he said. "The convergence is too soon."

Bolas lowered his brow. "Then you'll have to act quickly, won't you?"

"It's not a matter of acting quickly or slowly. The elves have a deep history on Naya. They won't be motivated to war so easily. They won't believe any prophecy we could cook up in the time remaining, let alone *my* counsel. I am a hero to the nacatl, but to the elves, I'm just some cat-man."

"Need I remind you of your advanced age? If you see fit to sever our agreement, I would be happy to let you face the depredation of time."

"No . . . I—I'm sorry, Master. I appreciate your magics. But the elves—they're more difficult than the nacatl. They trust only one thing."

Bolas flicked his tongue against his teeth. "And what is that?"

"They call it Progenitus."

"What is 'Progenitus'?"

"It's their supposed hydra god. They believe that it created the world, and that now it lives deep under Naya. Of course it's legend, but it gives their dull lives some comfort. Elves live a long time. I think they need stories to occupy their minds."

"Go on."

"Well, nobody has ever seen this Progenitus, of course. But the elves depend on its 'judgment.' They believe this elf girl, Mayael, can read secret signs extant in the natural world. The signs allow the girl to perceive the mind of Progenitus directly, and her pronouncements guide all of elvish society. But I doubt her authenticity. It's just myth and superstition."

Bolas sat back, finally comfortable in the heat.

"Not anymore, it isn't."

JUND

"If you're lying about this, I'll kill you," said Sarkhan. "You know that."

Rakka grinned, her sharp black teeth meshing into one another. "If I were interested in your death, I'd have left you under a pile of rock."

Sarkhan and Rakka rested on the top of a volcanic cliff overlooking the green, jungle-choked channels below. The stones were like cut glass. Sarkhan's gloves were sliced through in a dozen places, and he wasn't looking forward to examining his boots. They had taken a circuitous route up the mountain, avoiding cascades of lava that poured over outcroppings at regular intervals and fell hundreds of feet to red-hot pools. As they climbed they passed cooled lava tubes, many of which showed signs of habitation: simple tools, broken pottery. Who would live among dripping lava, up on the high cliffs where dragons flew? On every world he had seen, it was the same thing, thought Sarkhan. What cosmic crime had goblins committed that they occupied the worst point on the food chain everywhere he went?

As they climbed, Rakka's feet caught the nooks in the volcanic cliff easily and regularly. She was more nimble than she looked. She was full of surprises, Sarkhan thought grimly.

"Don't worry," said Rakka. "You'll see. You'll be

impressed. He's just your type, trust me."

"I didn't come all the way to this place to be ambushed by more of your raiders," he told her. "Or struck down by a petty spell while I'm weak from climbing. I mean it. You lie, and you die."

Rakka scoffed. "You're worse than Kresh."

"And you *betrayed* Kresh. You got most of his men devoured by that hellkite! The last thing I should be doing is following y—"

"Shh!"

"What is i—"

"Shhhh!"

Rakka had stopped. What ruse was she planning? But as he listened, he heard scrabbling sounds echoing from deep inside the lava tubes. Goblins. Sarkhan readied a spell—a little lavamancy should keep the hungry buggers off of him.

"Don't move," Rakka hissed. "And don't cast anything."

You're out of your mind, Sarkhan thought. Or perhaps this was her ambush. He began the first steps of the spell. He could already feel the satisfying tug of a nearby stream of lava; its course was beginning to divert. One more good, solid act of will, and it would pour into the echoing lava tube and make crispy statues of the incoming goblins.

Rakka hissed once more—not an instruction, just a noise of urgency.

"Fine," he said under his breath. "I'll wait one moment. But if one of those goblins so much as nibbles on me, I'll roast the lot of them."

Sure enough, goblins surged out of the tunnels, chittering and rasping like deranged rats. They flowed over the cliffs in a furry stream, moving in every direction including against gravity, as if they didn't notice its pull.

DOUG BEYER

They came close to Sarkhan, brandishing short spears and making click-wheeze sounds of irritation at him. He didn't budge—he just stared back at them. One of them reached tentatively toward the staff at his side, and he snarled at it. It yelped and scrabbled off up the mountain.

The goblins swarmed up past the two shamans and disappeared over the top of the cliff. Sarkhan heard their steps and clicking calls recede into the distance, and only then did he speak again.

"Why didn't you tell me they were plant-eaters?"

"They *aren't*," said Rakka. "They just have bigger things to worry about than us."

"What, I'm not tasty enough?"

"It's just a little while now. Let's go—it's just a little farther to his favorite spot."

"I'm offended, really. I've been bitten by goblins on five worlds, and these things didn't even stop to—"

"Come *on*."

The goblins climbed over one another in a jumble on the mountaintop plateau, a pile of furry humanoids eager to be as close to the sky as possible. It was as high as those goblins would ever get outside of a dragon's maw, thought Sarkhan, and yet they had brought themselves so low. It was disgusting—choosing to make themselves prey for the draconic lords of the world. He could understand their revering the mighty beasts, but not prostrating themselves before them. That was not a relationship of respect or admiration. That was an orgy of self-destruction, the pathetic chorus of victims begging homicidal charity from a superior being.

He turned away and scanned the landscape.

Jund's sky was a cauldron of roiling smoke fed by a thousand volcanic chimneys. A storm was brewing nearby, a purplish welt on the sky that gathered force as it twisted.

"We should get moving soon," said Sarkhan. "This will be a bad place to be in a short while."

Rakka just grinned at him.

The storm exploded suddenly, soundlessly, as if some magnetic cyst inside it had burst open. A black shape appeared from inside it, fell meteorically for a moment, then caught its own weight in the air. It had wings.

"This is our dragon?" Sarkhan asked.

"That's him, yes," said Rakka.

"He's big. A hellkite."

"Not exactly. Hellkite is too young a term to describe him."

"He's older than a hellkite?"

"He's older than the *word* hellkite."

Sarkhan's eyebrows raised.

Rakka set herself in a firm stance, and began pulling at the air with her clawlike hands. She grasped pockets of air and pulled them to her chest, fuelling some kind of ritual. Soon, Sarkhan saw, she had a ball of hot smoke hovering before her. With a shout she pushed the smoke-ball into the air, and it shot upward with a roar. High up in the air above the mountaintop, the ball of smoke detonated, sending streams of fire in all directions. As the fire dissipated, it left cinder streaks in the sky above them.

The goblins cheered. The dragon neared.

NAYA

It had taken days for Ajani to recover his bearings and travel back to his pride's valley. It was dawn as he approached, and he moved as carefully and as silently as possible. He stepped on stones when he could, bare dirt when he couldn't, and only on foliage as a last resort. As far as he was concerned, the pride was a nest of enemies—he didn't want to give away his return if he could help it.

The den was silent, nearly deserted in the early morning. He smelled burnt wood—had they lit another bonfire? What were they doing, feasting after Jazal's death?

No. It was a funeral pyre. Jazal's funeral. They had cremated his brother without him.

Ajani approached the pyre. Almost nothing recognizable was left of Jazal; every hair and claw was incinerated.

"I don't look good, do I?" said Jazal's voice.

"No, you don't, brother," said Ajani. "They should have done rites to calm you after death. They burned you as a *kha*, but they should have burned you as an unavenged spirit."

"I'm a spirit, then, am I?"

"If you're not, I'm going crazy."

"Well, yes, that is what I'd be implying."

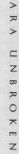

Ajani ignored that. The ash was still warm to the touch. He cupped his hands and grabbed great handfuls of the ash, and wiped streaks of it down his chest. It was Jazal, he thought. Those were flecks of his actual burned body. The image he had of his brother in his mind—the strong nacatl with the knowing smile—had no basis in reality anymore. Jazal wasn't on a trip somewhere, off in the jungle, about to arrive back home to him again at any moment. That was it. Those streaks of ash *were* his brother.

There was an object in the pit, something dark and round, made of a strange material. Ajani reached to pick it up, but a voice that stopped him—one outside his own head.

"Ajani, what are you *doing?*"

He whirled around. Zaliki stood there, her face elongated with shock.

"Are those *Jazal's . . . ?*"

"Zaliki, I—"

"Ajani, I don't know where you've been the last few days. And I know you've been through a lot. It's something horrible that I can scarcely imagine. But look at yourself. There are children around here. Think of the example you're setting. Touching the ashes of the dead?"

"I know. I know it's . . . wrong. But look, Zaliki, I'm going through something. Jazal's . . . presence. It's with me. Maybe you feel it too."

"No. Get away from me with those hands!"

"Okay, don't worry. I'll clean all this up. Just don't go," said Ajani. "I could use someone to talk to."

Zaliki turned her head, as if looking for an escape route. But she stayed. "All right," she said.

"Thank you," said Ajani.

Ajani's eyes drifted back to the pyre, and the object he saw there. He couldn't help himself—he reached into the ash and pulled it out. It was in the shape of a hemi-sphere: a bowl. It was filthy; every surface was coated in fine gray dust.

"Ajani, please—"

Ajani turned the bowl over in his hands. The ash fell from it as he turned it, revealing a dull, dark, hard material underneath. He wiped the grime away, and the surface shone a glittering black. His gold-white paw looked bluish and distended in the curve of the bowl.

"Wh—what is that thing?" asked Zaliki.

As he wiped more ash away from the bowl, he noticed the traceries of interlocking shapes. They were scales. He had seen scales like them before. They weren't like the hides of gargantuans. They weren't like the smooth silver of trout in the streams.

They were dragon scales.

"I don't know," said Ajani. "It's a bowl of some kind, but to hold what I don't know. Perhaps it's a talisman, an artifact. It might be connected to the creatures that emerged that night."

"It's beautiful," she said.

"Why do you say that?"

"I don't know. The way it shines, I guess. What's it made of?"

"You wouldn't believe me if I told you," he muttered. "Something that doesn't burn in fire," he said out loud.

All the dragons he had seen on Jund were bright red. He wondered why the scales of the bowl were black. The object radiated a foulness that Ajani found disconcerting—it seemed steeped in death. He wondered if Zaliki, a shaman, could feel the same sensation, or whether it was too otherworldly for her.

"This thing feels . . . strange. Do you feel it?"

Zaliki's eyes were blank, uncomprehending. "No. What do you mean?" she asked.

She wasn't feeling it, which was a relief. He didn't want her to know of his terrifying experiences on the volcanic world. Or maybe he should tell her everything: Jund, the dragons, Sarkhan, being a planeswalker. "I don't know," he said. "Never mind. The scales are just . . . strange."

"Ajani, I know this experience has been terrible for you. But I hope that one day, you feel like you can move on."

Ajani just wiped a streak of ash off the bowl. He looked into it and saw his own face, tinged with indigo, stretched across its surface. To find its source, he decided, he would have to travel back to Jund.

"I'll be able to move on when I know the truth," he said. "I won't rest until I know it, and bring justice to the one who caused all this."

"Well, *I'm* trying to move on, Ajani. I'm trying to live my life, and you should endeavor to do the same. Leave him be."

"He needs to be avenged, Zaliki."

"He doesn't *need* anything. He's gone, all right? He's gone."

"I know. But his spirit—"

"His spirit probably just wants you to forget about the whole thing. Jazal loved the pride more than anything, Ajani. Maybe his spirit would just want you to take his place as *kha*, did you ever think of that? We could use you around here. Think of your responsibilities."

Ajani suppressed a low, guttural growl.

"Clean yourself up, Ajani. I—I can't be around you right now."

She left him alone by the fire pit. As he handled the dragonscale bowl, flakes of ash spun in circles around his face.

Was she right? Should he move on? Jazal was just a smear. Maybe he should just leave it be. He should be using the time to help the pride heal, to prevent Jazal's work from splintering apart. Maybe dwelling on his death was just obsessive.

He moved a piece of burnt leather armor in the fire pit—again, he couldn't help himself. His fingers were stained black. It was as if the pride had brought a pottery relic into the center of the village, and smashed it to the ground right in the open square, leaving the pieces where they lay.

"I know who killed you, Jazal," he said.

"Do you now?" said Jazal's voice.

"He's always wanted to be *kha*. And he's always hated me."

"This is how you're going to serve my memory?"

"You'll never rest otherwise," said Ajani. "So neither can I."

What remained of Jazal's body lay right there before him in the fire pit, gray and crumbly. He couldn't let his brother remain like that. He looked side to side, and reached into the fire pit once again, with both hands. He smudged his arms and legs with the ashes, and dribbled them over his mane. Then he sank into the shadows of the forest to find Tenoch.

JUND

The dragon's silhouette broadened into a black shadow against the tumultuous scarlet cauldron of Jund's sky. The goblins chittered and scratched themselves excitedly. Sarkhan realized that they weren't just itching, but rather they were piercing their own skin with their claws.

"What are they doing?" asked Sarkhan.

"They're preparing themselves," said Rakka. "Goblins consider it an honor to be devoured by almighty dragons, the greatest predators in the world. The scent of the goblin blood drives dragons into a frenzy. Watch."

The dragon's wings blotted out the sky in great sweeps, blasting the mountaintop with gales of grit as he landed. He was immense, longer than any hellkite Sarkhan had ever seen. His scales were lustrous black, but didn't behave the way he expected such a shine would; they reflected light in odd, distorted colors. The light of Jund's sky swam across the beast's body as a greenish gold oil slick instead of the smoky reds it should have. The creature's feet touched down gently and precisely, a curiously fastidious gesture against the windstorm his wings had whipped up around them. His movements seemed surreal, as if the boundaries of his body cut holes in reality through which he passed. Every motion of his neck or twitch of his wings seemed to take eons to pass through space, and yet the dragon was moving as normally as the goblins or the shamans.

Sarkhan came to a realization: Rakka's master, whether the elementalist knew it or not, was no mere dragon. He was a planeswalker, and an immensely powerful one. Sarkhan was gripped by a strange idea, and felt awe in it despite its absurdity: whereas Sarkhan had walked the planes for years, the being, the dragon planeswalker, always remained perfectly still, and traveled the planes by moving the multiverse around himself.

The dragon folded his wings behind him and sat up, tenting his fingertips as he regarded the humanoids. He was strikingly regal.

"Sarkhan Vol, may I present my master, Nicol Bolas," said Rakka.

"It is a profound honor," said Sarkhan. He found himself bowing, pressing the knuckles of his fists together under his chin, as his people did in the world of his home.

Bolas grinned, his lips dragging away to reveal too many teeth. "It is I who am honored," he said.

At the dragon's voice, the goblins cheered and clawed themselves.

His eyes turned to Rakka. "The deed is done?" he asked.

She nodded. "It is. Sarkhan was of great help in freeing the obelisk. His magic is broad and powerful."

Bolas flexed the spikes on his cheeks. "Is that so. Well, then." He looked over Sarkhan, his neck arching like a question mark.

Sarkhan took great pride in the dragon's stare, the study of a predator sizing up prey. He knew a dragon of Bolas's age would not bother with trivial game; he was a fair match. Could the dragon finally be one worth his reverence?

"You may go," said Bolas to Rakka.

She nodded, then turned and headed back down the hill without another word.

The goblins were beside themselves with excitement, dancing around Bolas in a circle, chittering and peeping, clawing themselves and each other in a frenzy. Bolas looked down on them for the first time.

Sarkhan held his breath. Finally, he would see the ancient dragon unleash his fury on the suicidal goblins.

Bolas took a deep breath and exhaled slowly, but with his mouth unexpectedly closed. His nostrils flared with the long, slow breath. He looked each goblin in the eyes one at a time, his head turning around the circle.

Where was the rage? Where was the ecstatic tumult of destruction? Where was the blast of fiery breath, like Sarkhan had so often seen across Jund? Was the dragon really not going to feast?

Then, one by one, the goblins wheezed a final sigh, and slumped over onto the bare rock. They toppled like stacked dominoes with no apparent cause—if Bolas had used magic on them, it was as effortless as an eyeblink. The goblins twitched, then lay still.

A smile bloomed across Bolas's lips. Sarkhan felt a bead of sweat travel down his back—which wasn't that strange, given the volcanic miasma around them. Bolas didn't devour the bodies, but instead seemed to appreciate the shape of them, around him in a circle. A few of them had pink tongues lolling out of their soricine mouths.

The dragon turned his eyes back to Sarkhan, and Sarkhan felt the weight of the stare like two swords pressed to his chest. The creature was the apex of dragonkind, he realized. He had come to Jund, a world full of dragons, only to meet his ideal dragon from far beyond the world. He had come to Jund to seek the worthiest specimen of life he could find, and found it in an avatar of death.

"Rakka tells me you're a shaman and a warrior," said Bolas.

"I am."

"But not one from *this* world."

"Is it that plain?"

"Your scent doesn't match Jund's. And your spark is . . . apparent to me." The comment was innocent enough, but Sarkhan got the impression that Bolas had just called his soul "delectable."

"I came here to seek a worthy dragon. I believe I have found him."

"Good. Then I have a mission for you, planeswalker," said Bolas.

Ever since he had watched his warriors die in a gout of dragonfire, Sarkhan had wished for a dragon that lived up to his capacity for honor. He hadn't expected that he would hear the realization of his wish in the form of words, spoken by a dragon as if by a man, but folded and hissed using a tongue normally used to lick flame. But those words were exactly what he had lived to hear.

"There's a war on," said Bolas. "I need every planeswalker I can get, to ensure my victory."

"I'm your weapon," said Sarkhan.

Bolas pointed a finger, then used that claw to slash a line in his opposite palm. He reached down and presented the bloody hand to Sarkhan.

The gesture moved Sarkhan. He pulled a curving knife from his belt, and slashed his own palm.

The wounds touched each other; Sarkhan's hand was tiny against the dragon's huge claw. Sarkhan's human heart pumped rapidly, and the dragon's much slower. But their lives mingled in a flow of crimson.

"I know of another planeswalker," said Sarkhan.

NAYA

Y ou," said Ajani.

He had walked all the way out to the cliffs, the piece of land that jutted over Hydra's Tail Chasm. Tenoch sat there, his back to Ajani, facing out over the cliffside. It was a common place for members of Ajani's pride to come and reflect.

Tenoch didn't turn around. "So you're back. I didn't think you'd show your face around here again."

"You did this. Admit it."

"I'm not sure I know what you're talking about."

Ajani's eyes narrowed. He snarled at Tenoch's back. "You've always envied Jazal, and you've always hated me. You waited until you had the night watch, and you assassinated my brother!"

Tenoch turned and stood. He cocked an eyebrow at Ajani's appearance, covered in the ashes of Jazal's funeral pyre, but made no mention of it. "How could I have killed him? The creatures that attacked the den were summoned by magic, dark magic. That's nothing I could muster, and you know it."

"Maybe not. But I know you're behind it somehow. You're the one who stands to gain the most from Jazal's death, and now, right before the meeting of the council, here you are with an open seat waiting for you. Confess, and I . . . I won't—"

Tenoch's eyebrows did a sarcastic little dance. "You won't what? Oh, White-Fur, for shame! You're no *murderer*. This is no territory for you, this little mission of revenge! I'm sorry for the *kha's* death, I truly am. And I'm as shocked as you are that this all happened. It's rattled the pride down to its core, and the oldsters are wondering whether it's even worth it to stay here. Even if I do become *kha*, it'll be chaos for me to try to calm everybody down, to convince everyone to remain here in the valley . . . "

"Stop evading."

Tenoch scowled. "What I stand to gain from this situation is none of your concern—you're not brother to the *kha* anymore, so it's the business of the elders now. Go back to your den. Polish your warrior trophies, if you have any. And say, if you really want to concern yourself with my appointment as *kha*, you may want to impress me—I might just make you my chief adviser. You could sit at my side, rather than getting chased about in the woods by superstitious humans."

Ajani snarled, and Tenoch backed up instinctively. His back foot came perilously close to the cliff's edge, and pushed a few pebbles over the edge. Tenoch glanced down at them; the pebbles fell for a long moment, bouncing occasionally off rocky outcroppings before disappearing into the depths of the chasm.

"You'll never be *kha* of this pride," said Ajani.

"Be smart about this, Ajani. I'm offering you a place among us. You can benefit from this. Or you can choose to be obstinate, and you can watch your life of relative privilege, considering your—condition—come to an *end*."

Ajani's claws were deep in Tenoch's tunic in an instant, lifting him up at arm's length. Tenoch's feet dangled over the cliff's edge.

"You dare threaten me!" Ajani roared.

"Ajani! Wait! You're hearing me wrong. I didn't mean it like that. I'm upset about your brother, and it's all coming out wrong. Let's think this through." He looked down and saw only air below him. He looked back at Ajani. "The pride will always be a place for you, Ajani. You'll always be welcome with us. We'll adopt you just like you were our own. You know we see great things in you, just like Jazal did."

"Enough," said Ajani. "I don't want to hear any more excuses. I want to hear facts. I want to hear what you know about the murder."

"Listen. Put me down and we'll talk all you want about—"

"Better tell me what I want to hear, *now*. My arms are getting tired, and Jazal isn't here to guide my morals."

Tenoch's tunic tore, dropping him a crucial few inches.

"I was warned!" Tenoch yelped. "Someone . . . Someone told me to stay far away from the village that night. But I ignored them. I should have run away . . ."

"Who was it?" Ajani roared. He jerked on Tenoch's clothing, and it tore another few inches.

"I—"

"Tell me, Tenoch, or I'll let you fall, as you deserve to."

"My mother!" squeaked Tenoch. "Don't drop me. Mother knew something was coming, she told me. But she didn't plan it, I know it! She couldn't have. It was something else. She didn't do it, I swear, Ajani! She just told me to get away, and told me it was going to be my time to lead the pride. Please, let me go, I don't know anything else."

Fire burned in Ajani's arms. The feeling spread throughout his mind. "Oh, I'll let you go, all right."

Tenoch felt so heavy. Ajani's muscles quivered. His fingers longed to let go, so that Tenoch would slip out of his hands and fall away, out of the pride and out of his life. Tenoch had been a burden on the pride his whole life, and was clearly the benefactor of Jazal's death. He was in Ajani's debt. It would be so easy just to drop him.

So he did.

As Ajani dropped Tenoch off the cliff, Tenoch's claw grabbed onto Ajani's arm and pulled him down. Tenoch's weight yanked Ajani off his feet and pulled him over the edge along with the other nacatl. The two tumbled in space for a sickening moment, until Tenoch's jerkin caught on the cliff's edge. Ajani caught Tenoch's leg, and swung around, slamming into the cliffside. Pebbles dropped into the cloud-jungle whiteness below.

"Tenoch . . . Do you have a good hold?" Ajani said, speaking carefully and trying not to budge.

"Let *go* of my *foot*," Tenoch managed. He twitched his leg.

"Tenoch, stop. I can help us, but you have to hold on tight, and *don't move*." Ajani said.

"I'm losing my grip. I'm going to fall," said Tenoch.

"Just hold on. If I can just concentrate, I can—"

"Good riddance," said Tenoch, and kicked hard with the leg that Ajani was holding onto.

Ajani's fingers slipped, and he fell.

BANT

Elspeth Tirel was a planeswalker with no desire to planeswalk.

Her own world was a place of nightmarish suffering. Even as a child, she had tried to fight back against the evils there. What she could not fight, she endured. When she could no longer endure, she broke. And when she broke, her planeswalker spark ignited, giving her the gift she desperately needed—the means to leave, never to return.

An infinity of worlds were at her disposal, yet she chose quickly. She had only visited a few planes when she came upon Bant, but arriving there, still in her youth, she immediately knew she was home. No orphan had ever been so happy.

Life made sense on Bant. The fields and olive orchards were sun-soaked and serene. The sky held the promise of the watchful eyes of angels. The sea lapped at the shores of the five noble nations. On Bant she could leave her planeswalker nature behind, forget that there ever were any other planes, and revel in the world's embrace.

She never spoke of the existence of other worlds to anyone. It was her private gesture of gratitude to her adopted home: to maintain its innocence. Bant was paradise; there was no need to expose its denizens to the strife and torture that abounded beyond its borders. She need only live her life as a young girl, and pursue her new passion: knighthood.

Elspeth found that she took it naturally. As she unsheathed her Valeron-crafted steel, it felt good in her hands; the leather of the hilt had indented in all the right places to mold around her palms, and the straps had stretched to line up with her fingers. Her palms had changed to fit *its* contours too. She had never studied swordplay long enough on any plane to develop callouses but she had them on Bant. They were coarse and bumpy, and she was proud of them.

She turned and brought the steel to bear, facing the older knights all around her—her caste equals, but her rank subordinates.

"Let's have another," she said. "Knight Mardis, your turn."

"Yes, Knight-Captain," said Mardis.

"Go get her, Mardis! Avenge us!" the other knights cheered.

Elspeth circled Mardis, watching his form. He was quite a bit older, fully a man, and had spent more years in the saddle than she had walking upright. He probably thought her just a child. But she saw beads of sweat breaking on his forehead. It wasn't going to be easy overcoming his greater weight and strength, especially without magic. She would have to look for an opening. Him sweating was a good start.

"Bring your elbows in, Mardis," she said. "I can see daylight between your sword arm and your side. That's a flaw in your defenses."

"Yes, Knight-Captain." He took her seriously.

"And watch your footwork! Don't stamp around, and don't shuffle. Come up onto the balls of your feet."

He looked down to check his foot position, and Elspeth cut a sharp maneuver with her sword arm, snapping her blade against his helmet. He recoiled and parried it away, but it was far too late. His helmet rang like a bell. The other knights laughed and hooted.

"She got you with the footwork! Come on, Mardis!"

Elspeth saw Knight Mardis's eyes narrow through his helmet. It was the right time, she thought. He would overcommit, and she'd have her chance to overcome his power with her quickness. She flexed her fingers, letting the hilt of her sword slide into its most comfortable position, balanced in the crooks of her fingers with her thumbs bearing the weight lightly but surely. Her eyes watched Mardis's every movement as they arced around each other inside the ring of knights. A drop of sweat fell from his helmet.

He lunged. She let him advance, giving his blade almost enough time to strike her pauldron, but then twisted her chin at the final moment, letting her body roll with it and circle around. His blade went by in a straight line, pulling Mardis with its momentum as she twisted fully around to build her own. For an instant her opponent was out of sight, and then she saw him again, still lunging but trying to recover his balance. It was enough—his center of gravity was thrown so far off that a single impact would fell him. When she swung her sword around, it clapped against his leg plate and swept his legs out from under him. His arms flailed as he collapsed, sending his sword flying straight up into the air. Knight Mardis dumped face first into the grass, not even trying to get up. His humiliation was complete.

He doesn't see his sword still tumbling end over end in the air above him, Elspeth realized. It's going to come right back down on him. Stupid Bant armor, no back protection . . .

Without thinking, she shouted a protection spell to save him.

NAYA

Ajani's eyes opened slowly. His mouth was dry. Had it been hanging open? Had he been asleep? What time was it? What day was it?

He slowly came to. He realized his body was in a heap on a rocky outcropping on the side of the cliff. The sun shone down on him. His right arm was lying at an odd angle across his chest—probably a dislocated shoulder. He lay on top of his left arm, which had most likely taken the brunt of the impact, and was certainly broken, probably in multiple places. His legs? Were they there? He tried to raise his head to look, but a wave of pain washed over him, so he didn't try any further. He tried to move his legs, but couldn't feel them. Was his back broken? If he was alive to ponder the question, he decided, then it couldn't be.

Still, he felt like a shattered toy. As long as he lay there, he strangely felt nothing, no pain, no shortness of breath. He mostly felt thirsty. How long had he lain there? Was he dehydrated, or had he lost blood? He couldn't see any blood from the position of his head, but it could have leaked out under him and dried already, or it could be ebbing out of his back as he lay there.

With his eye position he could see partway up the side of the cliff, but not to its top. He had fallen a sickening distance, from what he could see. Why hadn't someone from the pride come for him? That bastard Tenoch probably hadn't told anyone that he fell. He would have just returned to the den and acted like nothing had happened. No one would be coming for him, and that thug would take over. But Ajani couldn't let Tenoch be *kha* of the pride—couldn't let him take Jazal's place.

"Well, he's certainly going to take my place if you lie there like that," said Jazal's voice.

"My body's broken," said Ajani. "What else do you suggest I do?"

"Nothing. Just lie there. Let your life seep into the rocks. Let your skin shrivel away from your bones under the sun, and let the plants grow up through your ribcage."

"It is tempting."

"Yes, it is. So why don't you just give in?"

"Shut up," said Ajani.

"No, really. Why not just let yourself rot here? Fertilize the world with your corpse. That's better than the progress you've made so far."

"You're getting on my nerves, spirit."

"So then, what's your plan?"

"Give me a minute to think. The pain is coming back."

"Why don't you just mend yourself? You were always my best healer."

"I've tried. It doesn't work like that for me. It's like when the humans hunted me, remember?"

"I remember. I found you wounded and outmatched—despite you being perfectly capable of handling those foolish creatures on your own."

"I couldn't do it alone. I couldn't bring out my own—my own self, or mend my own wounds. It's just never worked like that. I could always see the light inside you, though—I could feel the way the threads ran, and could set them right when they were arranged incorrectly.

I could never see that inside myself. I'm opaque to my own eyes."

"You have all that power inside you, Ajani. And you're telling me none of it will help you here, when you're stranded on a cliff?"

"Sorry to disappoint you, brother."

"No. You never did."

Ajani closed his eyes. He had one option.

BANT

Mardis's sword came down end over end and hit him squarely in the back between his shoulder blades, point first. The sound was sickening as it punctured deep enough to stop only when it pierced the ground beneath him.

The knights yelled and descended on their comrade.

"Get off of him! Move!" Elspeth shouted.

Surprised by her sudden authority, they startled and moved back. She stepped forward and grabbed the sword, yanking it straight up out of him. There was a clean slit in his jerkin, but no wound. The other knights gasped.

Mardis coughed and rolled over. He took off his helmet, puzzled at their faces. "What happened?" he said.

"Are you all right? You must be hurt! We need a healer!" The others crowded around, looking for a wound, but found none.

They looked at Elspeth.

"Lucky man," she said to them. "Just missed the skin." She held Mardis's sword. It had no blood on it, but the point was barely blackened by having been stuck in the earth.

They were dumbfounded. Mardis rolled over, trying to crane his neck to see his back.

"That was strange. You . . . did something," said Mardis. "What did you do, Knight-Captain? You shouted something. Was that a spell?"

"You know I'm no wizard," she said. "It was just a fluke. The sword must have only grazed you. And that's the end of it."

She stomped off.

Well, there goes a training day, she thought, and possibly her secret with it. The others had no idea she was a planeswalker, or that there even were other planes—and it was her sole intention to keep it that way. It was the only way to protect her adopted home. Her spell would not have been unusual on Bant—but her deception about her abilities would be. She had never displayed the use of even basic magic before, and therefore had risen through Sigiled caste rather than the spell-wielding Sighted. She was afraid her dishonesty would raise enough suspicion to jeopardize her deeper secrets. With her luck, one afternoon's sparring accident would lead to an avalanche of revelations, none of which that particular plane was prepared for. If she wasn't careful, all of Bant would know the truth—that Bant was only a tiny bright spot in a terrifying multiverse of benighted worlds. Her paradise, her chosen home, would lose its uncontaminated ignorance. And then she would lose everything else.

"Knight-Captain!"

She wouldn't let that happen. No more planeswalking. None of the dark multiverse's claws would reach the little bright world of Bant. She would protect its innocence for it. She, who first planeswalked from her birth-world as a mere child; she, who endured years of torture in the clutches of the worst the multiverse had to offer; *she* would stand between all that pain and Bant, personally.

"Elspeth!"

She turned. "What is it?" she demanded.

The knights were pointing to a small hill. Elspeth could see a large creature—a person, but a person who appeared to be covered in light-colored fur—lying prone on the grass.

"Someone has just . . . appeared," said Knight Mardis.

No, thought Elspeth.

"Get your pikes," she said.

* * * * *

Ajani had no destination in mind for his planeswalk. He had no sense of aim or control; he didn't know if he was even capable of consciously influencing where he traveled, or whether some strange laws within or without him governed the entire experience. Perhaps the power would take him to Zaliki, who could mend his wounds. Or perhaps it would take him to the world of volcanoes, where he could perish in fire. Either way, he knew he would die if he just lay next to the cliff. So he willed his mind, his broken body, and his soul to *go*.

The sensation was like being shoved through a plate of glass, except that the splinters tore at the inside of his skin instead of the outside. His heart tried to pound, but it didn't know which direction to expand into, so it squeezed painfully in on itself instead. Ajani's lungs burned, and he wasn't sure if he was breathing in something awful or failing to breathe anything at all. His sense of up and down betrayed him, and he had the sensation of being flung end over end without moving at all.

The sense of movement was incredible. He knew that because of the sudden jolt when it stopped upon his arrival. He was slammed into something—a gently sloped hill—as if at extreme velocity. He waited, moment after sickening moment, for the residual sensation of motion to finally pass.

The air smelled strange. It was the lack of moisture in the air, he decided. And different plants. And the grass was softer, sweeter.

He rolled roughly onto his side, allowing the sky to rotate into view. It was impossibly bright—a blue canopy patched with small, scudding clouds, and lit by the blinding disk of a sun. The air was brisk, but that sun warmed him. Whatever world it was, its beauty was effortless, sweeping, and welcoming.

Ajani was sick on the grass.

• • • • •

Elspeth couldn't believe what she was seeing. Neither could her fellow knights, judging by their panicked reactions.

"You there, whatever you are, don't move," said Knight Mardis, pointing a spear directly at the cat-man. "You so much as twitch a muscle, and we'll run you through."

The cat-man who lay on the grass before them was easily two feet taller than Elspeth or the other knights, covered in a coat of fine, golden-white fur, streaked with soot and blood. His face was like a leotau, the noble beasts ridden by knights, but with an expression of pained intelligence, framed by a regal mane. Large pieces of curving bronze armor covered his shoulders, and he wore a simple jerkin of rough green cloth. He had a tail.

Elspeth hadn't seen a leonin before, but she had heard of such creatures in her travels. They were bigger than she had expected. And whiter of fur.

Of course, there were no leonin on Bant.

"D—Demon!" said one of the knights.

The other knights pointed their pikes right at the cat-man's face.

"Stay those weapons," ordered Elspeth.

The cat-man turned his eyes up at her and groaned. 143

He seemed to have trouble looking into the sun, and his limbs looked badly injured. She noticed he had a scar across one of his eyes. She looked deep into the beast's good eye, deep enough to feel a sense of falling. He was a kindred soul. He was not just an injured stranger—he was a falling star, one who was born, and who had suffered, on another world. He was a planeswalker.

"Leave us," she said.

"Knight-Captain, I don't think that's such a good—"

"Head back to the castle. Get clerics. Whoever you can find. And a body sling. Make haste."

"Right away."

There was a jangle of reins, a squeak of saddle leather, and a crunching of hooves on gravel, and the other knights were off.

The cat-man blinked up at her, then his muscles seemed to relax. His eyelids settled shut.

"I'm not sure you can understand this, or even hear this," said Elspeth. "But I'm going to tell it to you anyway. You've arrived. You've made it off your tortured world, and I'd like to be the first to congratulate you."

"You're too late for that," the creature muttered.

"You've made it," continued Elspeth. "Whatever place you were in before, whatever world did all this to you, your suffering is now over. You've come to paradise, a plane called Bant." She knelt down near Ajani's head. "They'll take care of you here. Even if you're an outsider, they'll accept you for who you are. You can leave behind your fears and memories of the evils that went before."

The cat-man's eyes opened briefly, and then fluttered closed again. He appeared to be having a hard time holding onto consciousness.

"Lie still. Help will be coming soon. Though I'm young, I've spent time on several worlds. None has been so perfect, so welcoming as this. For the first time, I've found a place I can love and trust. I belong here. And you will too. You'll be able to do what you've always wanted, like I have."

The leonin stirred. Ajani said something, but his voice was too low to hear.

"What?" said Elspeth. "Yes? You can tell me. What is it you want to do here?"

"Leave," said Ajani.

●　●　●　●　●

Ajani tried not to groan. The healers had used more needle and thread than the young human woman had told him, and less magic. Every day they would rewrap his left arm and dress his wounds anew, and say a few low chants. The wounds were closing day by day, and his bones were knitting, but his pain went largely untreated. In the jungle, Ajani thought, they would make a bitter drink from the sap of the wandili frond, and the pain would be gone as he healed. But his caretakers seemed to regard the pain as good for his progress. They used his pain diagnostically, prodding him in places they knew would hurt, just to gauge the degree of his reaction. At times, he reacted very badly.

His caretakers, along with the rest of the people on the world, spoke in a strange dialect. It was unfamiliar and droning to his ears, but understandable, which surprised him. It was as if their language and Ajani's own had been birth-brothers, twins, but had become isolated from each other, and had grown up segregated for so long that they were almost strangers to one another. He often had to repeat himself several times to be understood, which led him to use only simple words. He felt like an idiot doing that, so most of the time he said nothing. The clerics brought him what they thought his body needed, and he didn't argue.

They fed him strange things. He ate salty gourds and cakes made from coarse grains. There were fruits, but they weren't the succulent jungle fruits that he was used to. Most of them were hardy and fibrous, with tough skins. He tried one and stopped trying. He relished the meat they brought, but wondered what strange animals it might be made from.

He saw the knights' steeds—hooved, quadrupedal cats. They looked like ancient pack-beast versions of his own family. He tried talking to one once, but it didn't meet his gaze, and doing so only caused the knights nearby to snicker. Ajani felt overwhelming pity for the creatures, seeing them harnessed and saddled as they were. He wondered what the humans would think about some of the slow-witted, apelike behemoths of his own world.

The horizons took the most getting used to. There were no large mountains, and hardly any trees to inter-rupt the view, so the world seemed to go on and on. The sky was an overwhelming dome of relentless blue, rarely obscured by foliage. And he never failed to be dazzled by the luminous sea. Buildings soared, more shrines to winged women than they were residences, so vertical as to be seemingly weightless. He expected there to be graffiti along the bases of them, or at least creeping vines running up their steep sides, like the human-made buildings in his native jungles. There weren't. Everything looked pristine. Ajani had frequent childish urges to smear mud on things, just to mess them up a little.

The human Elspeth pushed him the most. She wanted him to walk again, so that he could see all the things that enthralled her about Bant. She was a planeswalker, like he was himself and like Sarkhan had been, but seemed committed never to leave the world she had come upon.

"Do the others know that there are other worlds?" he asked her one day.

"No," said Elspeth. "That I will never tell them. I only hope they don't find out on their own."

"How would they do that? I didn't know myself, until a short time ago."

"Well, you're a bad precedent, for example."

"But I'm a traveler from . . . the nation of 'Jhess,' wasn't it?"

"A poor lie on my part. Jhessian refugees travel here frequently, and they look nothing like you."

"You could have just killed me."

"That's not what we do here. Although I think some of my knights were tempted. And anyway, even dead, you would still have been hard to explain. If you're going to be evidence of something strange, you might as well be alive to prove you're nothing to worry about."

"How could you be sure I wouldn't tear everybody's throats out?"

She chuckled, looking over all of his bandages. "I've been meaning to thank you for that."

Ajani frowned. "I'm still a threat. Maybe not with my claws. But a threat to what your people think and believe."

"It's true. That's why you haven't gone far without me. And I hand-picked the clerics who've been taking care of you, did you know that? They're all people I trust, people who I know won't take your wild tales too seriously, or spread them around, should you tell any."

"I haven't."

"Thank you. I'm happy you've been so comfortable here."

"Who says I've been comfortable here?"

"Well, aren't you? The clerics say you've been an agreeable patient. They're excited to treat you, even—you should hear the way they talk about you. I'd say you were doing some magic on them, if they weren't apparently made so happy by it."

"They're good people, for humans. It's no magic. But I'm only here because I can barely move, and because there's no better help back on my own world. I've told you—I don't intend to stay. When my wounds disappear, so will I."

"And I've told you—you need to stay away from that world. You'll just be inviting whatever happened to you there to happen again. Stay. I could always use another knight."

He had to admit, it was nice to be part of a family. He wasn't treated as a freak on Bant, white fur or no. And at least the humans didn't seem inclined to hunt him. But as far as he could tell, he was the only nacatl. Jazal's voice hadn't spoken to him at all since his planeswalk, which put him on edge. He had to go back.

"I can't stay," said Ajani.

"You know, your torturing yourself won't fix anything," said Elspeth. "It'll just cause your gifts to be wasted."

"You don't understand. There are things I need to do."

"Oh, I understand. You're an idiot. You're anxious to be away, to throw away all you've lucked into."

"Elspeth, wait."

In his bandages, Ajani couldn't stop her. She walked away.

• • • • •

A rhox monk led the chant. A circle of human clerics repeated after him. Ajani just lay still in the center. Their benevolence was embarrassing, but the healing was necessary.

"When the world's body shakes, the hand of Asha is steady," intoned the monk in a full-bodied Akrasan accent. The clerics repeated his words verse by verse. "When the world's head burns, the hand of Asha is cool. When the world's stomach churns, the hand of Asha is soothing."

It was a prayer of healing, but unsettlingly dressed in the language of apocalypse. It made Ajani think of his vision during his planeswalk, of the five worlds, their edges blurring in the seething aether, their colors bleeding together. Was their truth in what he saw? Were the five worlds, including Elspeth's and his own, becoming, somehow, one? He tried to brush the thought away. Worry about your wounds, he thought. Keep it simple. Focus on what you can actually change.

But the chant was so rhythmic, and its imagery so evocative, that Ajani's mind strayed. He found himself visualizing the end times described in the prayer, a time of strife and cultural and geological upheaval. He imagined clashes of armies too vast to number, and great swaths of civilization swept under a deluge of destruction. He saw mages both familiar and strange, offering up feeble spells to the tide of war, draining their souls to conjure magics powerful enough to stop the monstrosity of war. He saw young soldiers take up arms and rally behind banners of hope. He saw creatures of every ilk massing at continental frontiers, bracing for the charge of a blast of evil. But in the end, it all came to nothing. Legions perished. Mighty leaders fell. Spells fell impotent against the surge of power that rushed outward from . . . from something.

". . . the hand of Asha is gentle," finished the monk, and the clerics repeated the final line of the chant after him.

The abrupt silence of the end of the chant jarred Ajani out of his reverie. He sat up, stretching muscles that hadn't been flexed in many days.

"That's all for today," said the monk to the other clerics. They took turns bowing and smiling at Ajani, and filed out.

"Thank you," said Ajani to them.

"Thank you, my friend," said a feminine voice.

The rhox monk bowed to Elspeth at the door, and left.

Ajani looked up at her, still on the floor in the middle of the inscribed healing circle. "On my world, healing magic is faster. But it usually hurts more."

"'The hand of Asha is gentle,'" said Elspeth with a smile.

"My spine wasn't fractured, is the latest news—I had cracked ribs, and blood loss, and damage in all kinds of bad places. They told me the whole list, but I lost track as they were speaking. But you should have seen me earlier— I was walking around. I'll be dancing in no time."

"*That* I would pay to see."

"Elspeth, I—"

"It's fine."

"No. I don't mean to seem ungrateful. I'm very grateful, and I'm sorry that I didn't . . . That I don't . . ."

"It's all right. It's my fault for pushing the issue. You have your reasons—it's selfish for me to try to keep you here. You're of course free to go."

"If I had time, I *would* stay. There's so much I could learn here. I just have to get back to my life, back home. Things are difficult right now. I just don't have time to . . ."

"Waste. Here."

"Right, no time to waste. You understand. I have to get back. I mean, even a Knight-Captain like you must feel attachments, things that call you to return home again?"

Her answer was quiet. "No."

"Never?"

"Bant is my home now."

"Well, I wish it all the best."

"What is that supposed to mean?"

"Nothing. I don't know."

"No, what is it? You meant something."

Ajani stretched his muscles. The bandages pulled tight against the motion, but it felt good and strong to push himself again. "I meant . . . I assume you know . . ."

Elspeth's face was blank.

"Maybe not," said Ajani. "Have you seen what's around here? Have you seen the . . . other parts of this world?"

Her eyes narrowed. "What do you mean, *other parts*? I know there are *other worlds*."

"No. I mean, there are other worlds connected with this one, each one different. I felt it on my way here: yours, mine, and—"

Elspeth's face was grave. "What do you mean, 'connected'?"

"I . . . don't know what I mean. They seemed to move together, or belong together. When was the last time you traveled beyond here?"

"Well, it's been over two years since I found Bant, and I haven't planeswalked at all since then."

"Oh. Maybe since then, they've—"

"What? What have you seen?"

"I . . . should turn in. It's late."

"Tell me."

Ajani sighed. "Something is . . . changing, I fear," he said. "Our worlds are related. In some sense, they're *close*."

"Hmm, no, they couldn't be. If they were that near to each other, I would have sensed your world when I traveled here."

"And they're growing closer. The first time, when I went to one of the others, the world called Jund—"

"What *others*?"

Ajani looked at her blankly. "The other planes. There are five of them, your world, my own, and three others."

"Five?"

"Five worlds all in a cluster, creeping toward one another, blurring their edges among one another. I believe they're *colliding*, Elspeth. The five worlds: Naya, Bant, Jund, and two others are becoming one. You, as a plane-swalker, must know this."

"Stop it."

"What?"

"I am not amused by this little game of yours."

"It's not a game, Elspeth, I'm telling you the truth."

"I said *stop it*."

"Look for yourself. If you want to lie to yourself and hide from it, that's your right. But things are coming to pass. I don't pretend to understand them, but I don't think they're going to be good. That's why I'm in such a hurry to return. I have to get back to my—well, my family—before they occur."

Elspeth was staring at the ground. Her breaths seemed heavier. Her mouth looked like she was whispering something, but no sound came.

"Look, if I can help in any way—"

Elspeth shook her head.

"It's late," Ajani said. "I should get back to my room. Thank you for all your help."

She didn't hear him leave. For a long while she just stared at the floor, at the intricate tiled mosaic forming symbols of castles, sunbursts, and olive trees. Then her gaze slid up the wall to the main window in the little temple, a simple round window inlaid with stained glass. The glass portrayed one of the minor angels, a Celebrant at best, rising up above a mass of impish creatures. The angel held out her hand in a calming gesture, her fingers splayed out above the creatures' heads as they tore each other apart. She had probably seen the window hundreds of times, and each time had felt it signified a moment of peace, of the angel bringing tranquility to the battling beasts. But at that moment she saw it as a scene of hopelessness, a divine figure unable to end the machinations of war.

When she went to Ajani's chamber to ask him about the changes he had seen, he had already gone. Stained bandages hung from an empty hammock. In the wall next to the hammock were twelve notches from a leonin's claw.

NAYA

The planeswalk had taken a lot out of Ajani, but he had managed to end up where he wanted. He emerged in darkness, but it was a comforting darkness, a cool cave interior swept with breezes of his native Naya. It wasn't his own lair, and he didn't know how far he was from the den of his pride, but it would do. Drained, he slipped into a dream of a time long past.

"We Wild Nacatl need to reach out," Jazal was saying. "Reach into the white mists that enshroud the mountains, and touch the hands and minds of the Cloud Nacatl on the other side. That mist is a blade. It divides us. It wounds us every day that we are two peoples instead of one."

Ajani was rolling his eyes, trying to find anywhere else to look besides his brother, the droning *kha*. Jazal wore a headdress of vibrant jungle flowers and carried a long, double-bladed axe. Other nacatl danced around him in a circle, each holding the tail of the next.

"The nacatl were one race once, one unified tribe of cats across all of Naya. The revolutionary Marisi came and led us astray. He was wise in that he believed in the fundamental goodness of our wild hearts. But in breaking the Coil, he broke with it everything that was good about its precepts. In its teachings, our souls were purified. Our minds were fluid, full of ideas and magic. Marisi brought change, but at the price of rage. He brought revolution by way of destruction. The palaces of Antali are gone now, ruined and haunted in the high places beyond the mists. You can no longer go there, Ajani."

Ajani started when he heard his name, and looked up to see Jazal swinging the double-bladed axe, and to see his colorful flower headdress melt into a red liquid. The circle of dancers sped up to frightening speed, tearing the ground with their claws as they danced and leered at Ajani. Jazal was still speaking, but Ajani couldn't hear his brother's garbled voice through the cascade of blood pouring down from the top of his head. It cascaded over his face, dripping into his eyes and streaking down his body. Then suddenly Jazal began making thrashing motions with the double-bladed axe and yelling Ajani's name, over and over again.

Ajani awoke, his heart pounding. His name was still echoing in his head. As he sat up, he realized the cool dark cavern where he lay, although not his lair, was a familiar place.

In the gloom, he saw the burnished blades of two axes leaning up against the cavern wall: one of a dark metal, its handle broken but repaired; and one a gleaming silver, catching the light from the entrance despite the bloodstains it bore. It was Jazal's lair. The axes were his and his brother's, identical but for their color.

"You'll never use this again, brother," said Ajani, taking the silver blade.

"It's yours now," said Jazal's voice.

Ajani took his own axe, rickety with its repaired handle. He held Jazal's axe, head down, and with a quick blow, sliced into the end of its handle. Then he unwrapped the bindings around his own axe head. The axe's original leather lashings were tight, mortared together with years of dust, resin, and blood, but they came apart little by little, spilling dried fragments of old battles onto the floor.

The dark-metal axe head came loose, and Ajani turned it over in his hands. There were nicks and dents all over it, but overall the surface was still smooth. The metal held the records of so many moments with Jazal.

"Isn't there something you should be remembering?" said Jazal's voice.

Tenoch. Ajani remembered his words from before he traveled to Bant. The bastard Tenoch had mentioned that his mother knew more about the night Jazal died.

I have to pay her a visit, he thought.

The bindings around his axe head proved to be a single, long leather string. He shoved the axe head deep into the end of Jazal's handle with a satisfying solidity, creating a double-headed axe. Ajani began the process of rewrapping the bindings, pulling each loop tight with little tugs that dug into his fingers.

ESPER

The lighthouse at the Cliffs of Ot was one of the most solitary and desolate places on Esper. The lighthouse keeper was an old vedalken mage, his etherium enhancements relatively minor and simple compared to the extensively filigreed archmages in Vectis or Palandius. He only had bracers of the metal built into his forearms, and a bit more at the small of his back. Still, even that small amount of the alloy had extended his life a generation longer than his race historically lived. So when his assistant called up to him saying that they not only had visitors, but important dignitaries from the vedalken city of Palandius, he had an impressive stretch of years against which to compare the visit's peculiarity.

The lighthouse keeper lived a simple life on Esper. He didn't know what a planeswalker was, and he had never heard of such a creature as a dragon. Nevertheless, he was about to become an important part of the plans of the dragon planeswalker, Nicol Bolas.

His assistant's tone was clear. "Sir, they're members of the Seekers of Carmot," he said.

The Seekers of Carmot were a relatively recent layer to the labyrinthine strata of the Esper magocracy, but a significant one. As the supply of etherium on Esper waned, the Seekers of Carmot urged the need for a large-scale

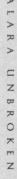

search for the reddish stone known as carmot, an essential ingredient in the creation of new etherium. Although some dismissed them as alarmists and doomsayers, the Seekers of Carmot had gained an almost religious following over the last decade or two.

The lighthouse keeper didn't know that the Seekers were secretly the minions of Bolas. But he did know that they were important dignitaries, and that a contingent of them wanted into the most remote lighthouse of the most desolate, barely-navigable shoreline of the region of Ot.

"I should have paid more attention to the stars of late," muttered the lighthouse keeper. "There must have been signs of the occasion written on the skies."

"Don't touch the door, I'll get it," he called as he descended the spiraling stairs. "Meanwhile, I want you to shine up my orreries and astrolabes. I don't want to miss another event of this magnitude. Use the good cleansing spell, too—I don't want to hear them so much as squeak."

He opened the door.

"My lords, please come in," he said.

There were three of them. Two of them were vedalken mages, their skin hairless and bluish gray, their etherium enhancements elaborate. The other was a tall, long-haired human man in strange garb. They said nothing, but handed him a small courier's capsule. He read the missive as they walked around the lighthouse, measuring and murmuring to one another.

According to the missive, the lighthouse was theirs for the next three days. And he was to become their *telemin* during that time. He knew what the word meant, but could only guess what it truly meant for him.

What was clear was that his life was about to change dramatically.

"You can stop bothering with the orreries," he called up to his assistant.

The assistant came down to him. "Why?" he said.

The lighthouse keeper betrayed no emotions. "In fact, your services will no longer be required. Please get your things and go."

"I don't understand. What are they . . . Are they shutting us down?"

"I told you, you are done. You no longer work here. Please get out of my lighthouse, now."

The assistant searched for some clue in the lighthouse keeper's face, but found only a level stare. The Seekers of Carmot were just as silent and ineffable. He frowned, gathered his possessions, took one last look at his old vedalken mentor, and left.

I'm sorry, and goodbye, thought the lighthouse keeper as his assistant walked out of his life.

NAYA

Ajani knew Tenoch's mother, Chimamatl. She was a suspicious old witch, a thin, gray-furred jaguar-hag who rarely left her lair in the hills high above the den. She had always wanted her son to become *kha*, and therefore had always hated the popular leader Jazal and, by extension, Ajani. Her schemes rarely worked because Tenoch was so unlikable, but still, she vowed that before her bones withered away, she would see her son as leader of the pride. Whether that was due to a mother's twisted love, or a streak of power-lust in her own heart, Ajani could only guess.

Knowing that Tenoch was likely to have claimed leadership over the pride, Ajani's steps were quick. He knew that the steep path up to Chimamatl's lair would be riddled with spells and traps, but he didn't care. Thorny snares snapped at his ankles and tripped him prone, but he tore through them with his claws and moved on. Ward-spells of sun-bright incandescence blinded him, but he blundered ahead with his hands on the rock face until his vision returned.

When he sensed a presence, though, he stopped. A thicket of dry brush hid the corner of the next switch-back up the hill—a perfect place for an ambush. If Chimamatl, or one of her protectors, was waiting for him, then she would attack him there. He approached the hiding-place of dry hedge slowly.

He took out his axe and shined the flat side of the blade against the fur of his forearm. He tilted the axe over the broad patch of brush, using the axe as a rough mirror.

Nothing. No one was hiding back there. And yet he was almost sure he had felt something lurking at that point in the trail.

The thicket did something that surprised him—it stood up, crackling and popping as it unfurled its arms and legs of jagged wood into a roughly humanoid shape. It wasn't a hiding place for Chimamatl's guardian, Ajani thought—it *was* Chimamatl's guardian. It was some kind of elemental, and judging by its size—fully half again as tall as Ajani, and broader in frame—it was the result of a powerful summoning.

The thicket elemental lunged at Ajani, and a great thorny arm swiped down at his face. Ajani managed to block most of the blow with his axe, but the wooden barbs dragged thin cuts down his arm. Ajani swung into the elemental and chopped a few pieces of wood from its frame, but it seemed undeterred. Ajani backed away, up the path, wondering if he could just get it to fall down the hill.

As the elemental crashed forward again, Ajani ducked and spun past its legs, then shouldered into the beast from behind. It barely budged—the creature had sent out multiple woody vines into the rock face, and held fast. The monster was going nowhere.

The elemental swung around, landing a crushing blow in Ajani's stomach. Ajani fell back, and had to scramble to hold onto the rock, so as to not go tumbling down the crag himself.

Ajani roared, and his eyes flared in rage. In his mind he saw past the elemental, and saw the elements within it. It surged with streams of flowing life energy. But all around it was an even deeper, more primordial force—the huge monument of granite in which Ajani's pride had made their den. The rock pulsed with an energy of its own—boiling, angry, and immensely strong. Ajani's nerves tingled, feeling in touch with the peak itself. The essence of the mountain ran up and down Ajani's body, tangling with his own fury, building up inside of him. It felt strange—invigorating, but wild, untamed. If he wasn't careful, he thought, the power might overcome his ability to control—

The elemental erupted in flame.

ESPER

Have you ever been a telemin before?" asked the male vedalken, one of the Seekers of Carmot visiting the lighthouse.

"No," said the lighthouse keeper.

"But you know what one is."

"Yes. A 'mage doll.' A living puppet."

"A willing instrument of mind control performance," corrected the vedalken.

"What are you going to have me do?"

"Are you willing to participate?"

"'Willing'? Your capsule says I have to."

"It is impossible to create this kind of performance with an unwilling telemin. If you refuse, we will be unable to use you. You have completely free will in the matter. That is, traditionally, entirely the telemin's prerogative."

"But this says you'll take away my lighthouse, and send me to court if I don't."

"That is only a detail of the fine print of the injunction. You needn't worry about that clause. It rarely applies."

"Does it apply here?"

"That is all beside the point if you are a willing participant. Are you willing?"

"If I agree to do it, you'll have complete control over me? I won't be able to back out?"

163

"The mentalist and the telemin instrument cannot achieve proper unity without complete surrender of the will."

"What are you going to have me do?"

"It's a perfectly routine measurement of sea currents off the coast here."

"If it's so routine, then why do you need me?"

"If you do not wish to participate, it's entirely your prerogative."

The lighthouse keeper felt an ugly tangle of emotions rise inside of him. His heart felt like it was being pummeled by hammers of fear and anger. But emotions like those did not befit an Esperite. With a few long breaths, he let the feeling subside.

"I'm willing," he said.

"Thank you," said the vedalken Seeker.

"When shall we begin?"

"Immediately."

NAYA

Ajani felt power seething inside him. As he watched, teeth of fire spread along the elemental's body, and its thin, woody vines blackened instantly. Its tendrils attached to the rock face burned and broke, and its limbs flailed as it fell. Ajani hugged the cliff face close, and let the burning mass of bramble careen past him and down the hill. It slammed into the ground somewhere far below, leaving a smoky trail behind it.

It was a moment of glory. Ajani was a fierce warrior, but never before had he been able to throw his ferocity directly at his enemy in the form of a spell. His gifts had always come in the form of the granting of power to others, of somehow perceiving the ineffable nature inside another person and encouraging it come out. He could heal the body and steel the soul for the good of the pride. He could even help the pride defeat its enemies by reinforcing the bodies and souls of his allies. But never before had he been able to lash out with his magic directly at his foe, or turn his emotion—his anger—into fuel for such raw power. His head swirled with blood, and he drew deep, rapid breaths into his lungs.

Please don't let the feeling go, he thought. He needed it. It was the power he needed to kill Jazal's murderer.

He ran up the trail to the lair of Chimamatl.

Chimamatl's patchy snarls of gray fur were shrouded

by a rough green robe. When she turned to see him, her expression went from shock, to confusion, to caution.

"You're alive," she said finally.

"No thanks to your son," said Ajani.

She shrugged and flashed a snaggle-toothed smile. "Accidents happen," she said.

"Accidents? I'm starting to wonder what other 'accidents' you and Tenoch might have been involved in."

"Accusation is a dull weapon. Don't come in here unarmed."

"I know you're guilty. Your son, in a moment of weakness, told me you knew about Jazal's murder."

"Guilt and knowledge—they are not kin. They wouldn't even recognize each other in the dark jungle. Why would I be the one to bring those creatures to our den? My goals are plain: for Tenoch to come into his own, and to rule the pride as *kha*. Why would I do anything to harm the pride he sought to rule?"

The thought turned Ajani's stomach. "Because it resulted in the *kha's* death. You knew there would never be an opportunity for your vicious, simple-minded son, unless Jazal was out of the picture."

"You've always been a little cat. Your thoughts are too tiny. With your mind that size, you'll never fit into it what you desire to know."

"Then tell me. If you're not the killer, tell me what I need to know to find who it was."

She noticed the thin, red slashes in Ajani's arms.

"You fought my elemental," she said looking outside the lair. "Why didn't it chase you up here?"

"It perished."

"You destroyed it? But it's been months since I've had a visitor other than Tenoch. It should have been hungry enough to swallow you in a single bite."

Ajani's eyes narrowed. "Someone visited you? Who?"

She peered at him. Her eyes widened. "You're a storm of rage inside, aren't you? My, you've grown little cat. Maybe you do have room in your heart-cage for the truths you're hunting."

"Someone visited you. You said before. Who was it?"

"An old friend, and a hero," she said.

ESPER

The spell felt surprisingly nonintrusive to the light-house keeper, if it was working at all. His thoughts were his own. His body moved normally. He was able to walk out the lighthouse door and toward the sea-cliffs all under his own power. The mentalist, a young vedalken woman of the Seekers of Carmot, followed behind him, performing dancelike gestures, but he didn't see anything in her movements that indicated he was part of anyone's performance. Maybe they had failed at the spell without knowing it. Or maybe he had overestimated the amount of control it conferred over him; maybe he was free to do whatever he willed after all.

But it was when he decided to walk all the way to the edge of the sea-cliffs that he realized the spell had worked as intended. He had never walked so close to the edge—the ragged coastline and the open sea joined there in a way that had always made him uncomfortable. He always admired the serene, gray regularity of the sea, but looking straight down the Cliffs of Ot reminded him too much of a wild animal, of forces unshackled by reason.

He was putting something on, he realized. One of the other Seekers, the tall, wild-haired human man, had handed him a vest of some kind, and the lighthouse keeper had taken it and was putting his arms through it. His movements were so effortless, his kinesthetic experience so natural, that he believed he was doing it all on his own. But he didn't want to do it. The vest was heavy. He willed himself not to put it on, but his body didn't respond. In a way, even his mind didn't respond—if he let himself stop concentrating for a moment, he could hear what sounded like his own thoughts attending to the tasks his body was carrying out. His volition, his self, was lost inside his mind. He was an audience to his own life.

Stop it, he thought. I want to stop. I want the spell to end.

His body didn't listen. As the mentalist traced intricate patterns in the air, the lighthouse keeper—her telemin, her mage puppet—continued to strap on the weighted vest. He tightened the buckles around his chest and between his legs. As he moved, hundreds of small reflectors hanging from the vest rotated and glittered in the light.

Great sphinxes of Esper, he thought. What were they going to do to him?

Don't worry, said a feminine voice in his head. *It'll be over soon.*

It was the mentalist. *Oh, telepathy now?* He wished he could cover his ears, or somehow block her out. *Is this what all you do to all your telemins? Taunt them while they're helpless?*

No, said the voice. *But your task is of vital importance. I must be in contact with your thoughts throughout the performance.*

Enough of this. You can have the lighthouse, he thought. *Send me to the courts in Palandius if you want. Get out of my mind.*

Thank you for being a willing participant, the mentalist's voice said.

With that, the lighthouse keeper took a deep, involuntary breath, and felt his body dive over the cliff into the bottomless, gray waves of the sea.

NAYA

Another day, another sin, thought Marisi. It was shameful work for a nacatl warrior-hero, a living legend of Naya, to do the errands of an otherworldly dragon. But what choice did he have?

Marisi turned a small sphere of dark scales around and around in his hands. It glittered in the filtered Nayan daylight, glossy like a snake's body. It was heavy for its size, and sloshed gently as though it were filled with a thick liquid. It would be dark soon, so he resumed climbing down out of the misty mountain heights toward the lush valley of the Sacellum, the realm of the elves.

He was getting too old for such tasks. The pads on the bottom of his feet were cracked, and his bones complained at every step. The errand was as ridiculous as they always were, but it was better, all things considered, than being eaten by his draconic master. What would that feel like, when he failed Bolas? Would the dragon's teeth puncture his life-sustaining organs, so he bled to death, or would the palate crush him first? Or would he be swallowed in one gulp, and die in the sizzling acid of the stomach?

None of those, he decided. In truth, he would die of whatever ached in his bones, or some other disease of the old—but without any trace of his faculties. He had seen Bolas end lives before, and it was always by the destruction of the mind, not the body. It was cruelly impersonal, he thought. All the might and majesty of dragonhood, and Bolas would sit casually back on his haunches, stare down at his victim, and barely move as the deed was done. No snap of bones. No pillar of flame. Marisi's renown on Naya had come from being a hero full of rage and action, the force that broke the Coil and severed the nacatl people into warring factions. But when Marisi's end came, it would not come by the sword and claw, but by the aloof dismissal of his mental faculties at the whim of a dragon, and the revelation of the evil behind his legend. Maybe that's what being monstrous truly was, he thought—not devouring a person's body, but his legacy.

He wondered whether success was really required on his task—which was a relevant concern, since there was no chance he would succeed. A little illusion magic would never motivate the elves to war. Killing was an easier errand, something with a beginning and an end, but his task was more complex. But would a good, honest try buy him enough time to find a way to escape Bolas for good? Or should he just give up, and sink into the jungle floor, and let his bones finally rest?

He was venerable by nacatl standards. He had lived two lifetimes, one impetuous and full of passion, and the other solitary and full of regret. Both lifetimes had been puppeteered by Bolas. The otherworldly lizard had charmed him as a youth, encouraging him to instill chaos within the society of nacatl; and he had threatened him as an adult, forcing him to instill further panic among the elves. Bolas wanted war, that was clear—but for what purpose Marisi couldn't divine. As he aged through the late stages of Bolas's plan, Marisi felt less and less motivated by the threat of death. "You've already taken my whole life from me, Bolas," he muttered. "Why do you think that telling me you'll take my last few years will make me bow down to you?"

And yet, there he was—climbing down to an elvish shrine with a sphere of black dragonscale.

He crested the last of the foothills at dusk, and the valley spread out before him. The Relic of Progenitus was down there—he could just make out the torchlight of the shrine. It was time to do what he always did: deepen his sin, and hope his soul survived. He held up the dragonscale sphere to his eye, wondering what the magic inside of it would do to the elves in the valley.

ESPER

The lighthouse keeper sank very fast. The vest pulled his head down, and his body began swimming downward into the cold depths. He could see nothing ahead of him, but the reflectors on the vest twirled rapidly in the darkness, making him relatively obvious to anything that might be looking.

You went to a lot of effort just to drown me, he thought at the mentalist.

She said nothing to him. He was alone.

The pressure began to build rapidly. The water pressed against his lungs, making it hard to keep his single breath inside. It was painful. He wanted desperately to blow out the air, but his body kept his diaphragm unnaturally rigid and his mouth shut tight. Down, down, down he swam, unable to save his own life.

Something moved in the darkness. There were lights.

A broad, gently curving surface, like the hull of a ship, slipped silently past him in the darkness. The fibers that made up his vest began to glow, catching the reflectors and immersing him in a corona of blue light.

What was that thing? What's going on? Am I bait? I'm bait. You're fishing.

Still downward he swam. His head tilted once to look behind him. His mind recoiled at what he saw, but

ALARA UNBROKEN

his eyes didn't: the hulking sea creature was behind him. Twin rows of small, round eyes had locked directly onto him. The beast's mouth was like the hatch of an enormous cargo ship, the jaw opening downward to wash him into its deepest holds.

His limbs pumped frantically, sinking him deeper and deeper. He had never swum so fast before, or so far into the cold blackness. His head turned back down to the depths and he saw something else: the spire of an underwater mountain. His body was swimming straight for it. It was encrusted with blue coral and razor-sharp barnacles. He was getting close enough that he could almost see the millions of tiny barnacle mouths and their wispy tentacle-tongues.

His breath was about to give out—or maybe it had already gone out, and some magic conjured by the mentalist was forcing a trickle of air into his lungs. His eyes stayed locked open, but he was losing his consciousness of what he saw. His head felt like it was being crushed; he could feel the delicate bones in his ears bending painfully. Would his body keep swimming after he passed out from lack of oxygen, he wondered? Would he slam into the reef mountain below, or be swallowed by the sea creature above?

Stay conscious, the voice in his head commanded.

So she was still watching, he thought dimly. What kind of mad game was it? His thoughts swam with weird imagery—the blue glow of his vest, the coral mountain, the lenses in the optics room. He saw his lighthouse broadcasting a beam of cool light around and around—out to sea, across the land, out to sea again. How many ships had seen that light over the years? How many ships had he protected from that very reef? He saw the light sweeping past him, rhythmically flashing in his eyes. It beat like the awful pulse in his head, the sideways knifing of his heart

D O U G   B E Y E R

against the pressure on his chest. Would his legacy be that sweeping light? Or would his final task?

The lighthouse keeper strained against a dark blot in his mind, but it wrapped its claws around him—and then, in a crushed moment between pain and darkness, he lost the fight with unconsciousness. He never felt the leviathan's jaws close over him, closing also over the peak of the reef. He never felt its jaws crush the coral, breaking the reef free of the structure underneath, or felt gratitude that his death came without awareness. He never saw the leviathan wander away afterward, leaving behind it an ancient underwater obelisk of smooth stone.

The vedalken mentalist collapsed on the ground at the edge of the cliff, exhausted. She looked up at the long-haired human who had accompanied her, a man she had just met hours before.

"The obelisk has been freed, sir," she said. "It is done."

"Good. I'll inform Master Bolas," said Sarkhan.

NAYA

It was dawn when Marisi finished the ritual at the Relic of Progenitus, a worn disk stood upright on its edge, like an enormous sandstone coin. The carvings on its front surface showed spiraling patterns of a long-necked, three-headed hydra. In the center of the disk glowed a single red shard of quartz, the gem that formed the central eye of the hydra god in the carving.

Marisi planted the dragonscale sphere in the weeds behind the Relic and chanted the words as Bolas had instructed. The dark-scaled globe gaped open into a hemisphere, releasing swirling purplish magics that chilled Marisi's soul. Tendrils of magic reached inside the Relic, causing deep corruption that Marisi couldn't fathom. The deed was done. He left the dragonscale bowl to do its work, and climbed out of the valley. Perhaps when he reached his mountain home again, Bolas would be waiting for him there, ready for the news that the ritual was complete, and that he had some new task for Marisi. Or perhaps he would be alone with his misery.

As he reached the first foothill out of the valley, he was startled by a white-furred nacatl standing before him.

"Marisi," said the white-furred cat, squinting at him, looking him up and down. "Is it you? No. You couldn't be."

"No," said Marisi. "Leave me alone."

"Chimamatl said I'd find you here, Marisi the warrior-hero, the Breaker of the Coil. She said you'd have mahogany fur with black stripes, as you do."

Marisi's heart bounced. The white-furred nacatl knew Chimamatl, the old power-mad witch who wanted her son to be *kha* of her pride. Chimamatl was a connection to one of Marisi's many sins—and she had sold him out. Could the white-fur know his secrets?

"I must go," Marisi said. "You are mistaken. Marisi is dead."

"Chimamatl said that Marisi visited her. If you are he," said the white cat, "then I have serious questions for you. My brother was killed in an attack of dark magic."

They heard rustling in the valley below. A procession of elves, including a young, black-haired elf girl riding on the back of a gargantuan, pushed through the jungle. They were making their way to the knoll where the Relic of Progenitus stood.

Marisi heaved a breath. "What is your name, White-Fur?"

"Ajani."

"Ajani, I am sorry to hear about your brother. But I . . . I am not the one you seek."

In a flash, Ajani pulled out his double-headed axe and put a blade to Marisi's neck. His voice was even but flecked with rage. "I think you lie. I think you were involved in my brother's death. And if you don't tell me what I want to know—"

"Kill me," said Marisi suddenly, tipping up his chin, leaving his throat exposed.

"What?"

"Take my life, destroy me, and I will have died with a modicum of honor. It would be mercy. Kill me."

"I . . . I cannot just kill you," said Ajani, pulling the axe away. "I must know if you're the one. You're Marisi, aren't you? You are the Breaker of the Coil. And my brother's—"

"The Beast of Antali, some say," said Marisi. "Listen, my friend. There are forces at work here that you do not want to be involved in. This is much bigger than you realize. My guilt is great, but I am not your brother's killer. Your brother's death was of his own making."

"Liar," Ajani roared, raising the axe again.

"It was. Your pride is Wild Nacatl. Let it *stay* that way. Don't try to reach out to the Cloud Nacatl, as your brother tried to do. Don't ask dangerous questions, or try to break down the master's plans. It's not about the Coil, it was never about the Coil, it's . . ."

"What master? You'd better start making sense in a hurry," said Ajani.

There was a tremor under their feet. The earth bucked and tossed like a skittish animal, shaking all the trees around them. It stopped as quickly as it had started, but the rumbling sound, a profound snarl deep underground, spread throughout the valley, echoing from hill to hill and on up through the mountains. The procession of elves down in the valley looked distressed.

"Oh, gods, it's happening," said Marisi.

"Jazal," demanded Ajani. "What did you do to Jazal?"

"Kill me, quickly! Before it all happens."

"Why? Before what happens? Tell me, now!"

Marisi's eyes flashed with fire. The strings inside his mind were snapping. "It doesn't matter—even if you don't kill me, we'll all be dead soon," he snarled. "You'll perish, just like the rest of them. You can't stop him. The dragon is much too big for you, for me, for this world, for *all the worlds*. Nicol Bolas will consume us all!"

Another quake hit—far stronger than the first. The earth beneath their feet launched upward, sending Marisi and Ajani into the air. Marisi fell against a tree, knocking the wind out of him. The white-furred nacatl tumbled down the hill trail into the elves' valley, where the elves themselves were toppled to the ground all around the ancient Relic.

Marisi didn't wait to see what became of the white cat, or to see what disaster he had wrought in the Valley of Progenitus, or even for his breath to fully return. He took the opportunity to steal away into the mountains.

Perhaps it was a sign, he thought as he climbed into the mists. He would never get out from under the claws of Bolas; he could never be his own person. "Marisi" was nothing but the lies wrapped around his name. But at least he could take pride in one truth—that the lie had power. The lie could still inspire the hearts of warriors, and he could still wield that lie like a sharpened spear.

NAYA

Ajani's rolling fall was halted by a prone gargantuan, the same beast that Ajani had seen the elves riding before. Its body lay clumsily on the ground as its huge legs tried to find purchase. The beast harrumphed in annoyance through its mouth harness.

"Who are you, and what are you doing here?" asked a feminine voice.

Ajani looked up and saw that he was surrounded by elves. There were dozens of them, noble smooth-skins with sharp features and elegantly swept-back ears, all in the hand-embroidered robes of ceremony. The one who had spoken, a young elf girl with flowers in her dark hair, appeared to be in charge.

Ajani looked around for Marisi, but the old nacatl had disappeared. Next he checked for his axe. He spotted it nearby, but one of the girl's attendants stepped on it with his foot, shaking his head, and Ajani didn't reach for it. Instead he addressed the girl.

"Forgive me for trespassing, elves," he said. "I am Ajani of the Wild Nacatl. I sought a nacatl near here, but he escaped . . . when the earth shook. What happened?"

"We do not know," said the elf girl. Her syllables formed a steady rhythm, not quite a melody, but with a rising and falling tone that sounded like a pulsing heart.

"But now you must go. This is a holy place, not meant for your kind, and we have business here."

Ajani beheld the Relic of Progenitus. He had heard of the place, reported to be the resting place of the elves' hydra-god, Progenitus. The mound on which the stone disk rested had shifted during the earthquake, and it stood precariously slanted.

"I fear you are in danger here," Ajani said.

In the underbrush near the Relic, he spied a bowl of black dragonscale. It was the same kind of artifact he had found in the ashes of his den's home fire, mingled with Jazal's remains.

"Is that . . . yours?" Ajani asked, gesturing to the bowl.

"It belongs to Progenitus. But no nacatl is allowed near the Relic," said the elf girl.

"I don't mean your Relic," said Ajani. "I mean that black bowl." If the elves knew something about it, then maybe it could help him find Marisi, or learn his plans. But even if they didn't, the presence of the dragonscale bowl surely meant danger.

One of the elf attendants retrieved it. "Anima," he said. "It's a spell vessel."

"What's a spell vessel?" Ajani asked. The attendant had called her the Anima, Ajani realized. He knew little of elf culture, but he knew that the Anima was a place of honor among the elves—a leader, but not like a *kha*, more like a high shaman. The elves, particularly the Anima, were said to know far stranger mysteries than even the eldest nacatl shamans. "If you're the Anima, then you might know something about it that I don't,," said Ajani.

The Anima took the bowl and inspected it with a frown on her face. Her eyes had a light gray haze over them. Ajani wondered if she could see at all, but then she looked straight at him—coldly "I am Mayael, Wild Nacatl Ajani," she said. "The current Anima. But I suspect you know more than I about this. A spell vessel is an artifact used to hold magical energies and to spread them. But I've not seen one like this. Have you brought it to our valley?"

"No," said Ajani hastily. "But I've seen one that's similar. It caused evil magic among my people. I fear it will do the same among yours."

"Or it already has," said Mayael. "How do we know that its magic hasn't caused these earthquakes? That you haven't planted it here to harm us, or to learn our secrets?"

Ajani spread his hands. "Listen, I don't mean to pry into your affairs. The vessel was not my doing, but I believe it was the nacatl who I sought earlier who put it here. He's dangerous, and so I believe is this artifact—I think we should all leave this valley, and soon."

"We cannot, and will not," said Mayael. "We have been culling the signs since the last moon, and we must stay here until we learn the truth. We must consult Progenitus for guidance, here and now. So you must leave. And take your artifact with you."

They handed Ajani the dragonscale bowl and his axe, and sent him out of the valley. He wished they would listen. The oily, interlocking scales of the bowl—a spell vessel, the elf had called it—were of otherworldly origin; of that he was convinced.

Ajani walked up the slope out of the elves' valley, despondent. Things were unraveling for him day by day. Jazal was gone. The "warrior hero" of legend, Marisi, was alive, but was somehow involved in Jazal's death, and a lying fraud. There were four worlds just beyond the edges of his own, and for reasons he feared to contemplate, his world was experiencing earthquakes greater than the footfalls of the gargantuans.

He could chase Marisi into the mountains and try to find out more about his role on the night Jazal had died. He could trudge back to the den and pore over more of Jazal's documents. After a moment, Ajani remembered: among his frantic words, Marisi had said a name. *Nicol Bolas*. He looked down at the black-scaled bowl in his hands.

NAYA

The elf prophetess Mayael knelt on the ground in front of the Relic of the hydra god, Progenitus. Her attendants arranged the train of her embroidered gown carefully on the grass, and sprinkled passion flower petals in a circle around their mistress. Two of the farseers, the young girls who were candidates to become Anima one day, began singing the traditional mantra to Progenitus.

Mayael had only traveled to the relic in person a few times, and felt strangely shy around it. It felt as if the red eye of Progenitus could see right into her soul.

There was no use feeling cowardly. She was the leader of the elves, and the prophetess for an entire world. The world was changing, and her people needed answers—and if anyone was meant to receive the knowledge Naya needed, it was she.

"Hold me, please," she said to her attendants.

Still chanting, two of the farseers knelt next to Mayael and held her arms. Another sat behind her, facing opposite, using her own back to support Mayael's. Another girl held the back of her head, to catch her skull in the event of powerful whiplash.

Progenitus never granted tepid visions.

"O shrine of the Blinded God," she began. "I, one of your children, come humbly seeking an answer to the visions I have seen of late. The sacred gargantuans have shaken the world with their footsteps. The humans burn with an aberrant bloodlust. The cat-folk mingle with evil magics. What is the answer? What meaning lies behind these events?"

Clouds crept into the edges of Mayael's vision. She continued to stare directly at the eye, not attending to the pearlescent mists that heralded the Whitecover Gaze, the vision-state of all the elvish prophets. The chanters' voices took on a muffled quality, as though traveling through layer upon layer of gauze, until she couldn't hear them at all.

The clouds of white mist enveloped everything but the Relic, setting the hydra god in relief. Mayael could see only the hydra itself, not the stone in which it was set.

Then it began to move.

The god's three heads moved independently, as sinuously as snakes, exulting in the power of movement. One head took on a golden sheen, standing proud and noble. Another simmered into crimson, its scales alive like fire. The center head turned an emerald green, reflecting the majesty of the jungle. The three voices of Progenitus spoke.

"Anima," they said. "Seer of the elves, child of Naya. Why did you blind me?"

"It was not I who blinded you, lord. It was Cylia, the first Anima, who cast the poison into your eyes."

"Then I would speak with her."

"She is centuries dead, my lord."

"Dead? What is death but a reticence to speak with one's Creator? Her stubbornness will not be tolerated."

"The signs I've culled of late have shown me troubling things. O Progenitus, what do you see behind them?"

"How can I know what you seek, blind as I am? Let us speak no more. I can tell you nothing—not until my wounds are healed."

"How can I heal you, my lord?"

"I am not whole. I am not all of myself. I must be restored so that I might shine again."

"Yes, lord."

"Seek out the . . ."

"Yes? Seek out what?"

The hydra's voices deformed strangely.

"Seek out the white . . ."

The heads' colors changed, blended and warped.

Something is deeply wrong, thought Mayael.

* * * * *

Nicol Bolas, Ajani thought. The being behind it all—a dragon, a creature that didn't even exist on his world. It made a kind of sense. He looked at the bowl made from oily scales that distorted the light, an artifact created from the scales of a creature from a nearby plane. Ajani knew just where to find such a creature.

For the first time, he was planeswalking under no time constraint, under little emotional duress. He would take it slow. He'd get it right. Maybe he could even aim a little.

He sat in the jungle with his axe across his lap, closed his eyes, and envisioned Jund, the first world to which he had ever planeswalked. He recalled the thick atmosphere, the choking volcanic fumes, the furry goblin-creatures. He envisioned the dragons, enormous beasts of rage swooping down on him, unleashing furious gouts of flame to flay his charred skin from his bones—

He opened his eyes. Maybe I shouldn't envision the dragons, he thought.

Concentrate.

Jund, a world suffused not only with mana of fire and mana of nature, but an unknown mana of death; a world without the mana of honor and order. It was a world like his own in some respects, if all that was solemn and reverent about Naya had been stripped away, and replaced with an obsession with entropy and decay. It was Naya's savage, primordial twin.

Concentrate.

What would he find there? Even if he located a dragon, what would he *do* with that encounter? Look for one with a patch of black scales missing? Ask around for one who knew a Naya cat named Marisi? He was in way over his head. He was about to scour an entire plane for a single being, with no information but a rough description and a scrap of scaly skin.

A sensation of panic grasped his throat, and his heart pounded—Jund was the world to which his nascent abilities had taken him the day that Jazal died. It was the last place he wanted to be again.

Just as Ajani was about to decide that it was all a terrible, terrible idea, he felt the planeswalk begin. He felt something approach him, distant and bright like a spark of fire in the darkness. It was rushing toward him, about to run him over—or was he hurtling toward it? He felt it tug on his soul, felt it draw forth tendrils of his very being. He had the sudden sensation of falling over the cliff again—terror and helplessness in the face of an onrushing, very flat, and very hard destination. He turned his head away, shrinking from the oncoming impact.

No, he thought. It is what I am. I am a planeswalker. I travel worlds. It is what I do.

He turned to the expanding blaze of existence, put his arms out to it, embraced it. Something deep inside his soul acquiesced.

His vision flooded with light as he watched Naya melt away—and in the last moments of his planeswalk, he saw the earth overturn itself. Soundlessly, trees uprooted themselves, and huge slabs of stone upended. His last impression was of lava spouting forth into the Naya sky—an impossible sight, but he saw it char the jungle trees and send up a cloud of black smoke into Naya's sunny sky.

It must have been his own memories of Jund, he thought, overlapping with the strange sights of his plane-swalk—and his own fears of his world's destruction encroaching on his mind.

But in the fleeting moment as he stepped between worlds, he saw exactly what he had feared to see: the five worlds were one.

Naya had overlapped two other worlds, its rough, green sphere merging with the blue-and-gold heaven of Bant and the fiery hell of Jund. Beyond them, the mostly sea-covered world of Esper linked with the shadow world of Grixis. The five of them formed a kind of irregular chain. In the center, where there was once an eye between them, all five worlds had come together and had—just barely—touched. What destruction all of it was causing, he couldn't tell. But before Ajani knew it, he was somer-saulting into Jund, just as a massive stone pyramid of Naya thrust its way up through Jund's surface below him.

So much for aiming, he thought.

• • • • •

The white haze over Mayael's eyes revealed the three heads of Progenitus, twining together and forming a ghastly creature of shadow and death.

"WAR IS UPON US ALL," the hydra's voices boomed, vibrating with malevolence. "YOU, THE ELVES, MUST CRUSH ALL THOSE AROUND YOU. LET THE BLOOD OF THE OUTSIDERS RUN IN RIVERS."

Mayael gasped. "My lord, that is your answer? I don't understand!"

"WAR IS NIGH. PREPARE YOURSELVES TO INVADE THE FAR SHORES, FOR TONIGHT, THEY INVADE YOURS."

The hydra disintegrated, bursting into a mass of black beetles. The beetles fell out of shape into a roiling heap, and began to skitter away into the white mist of Mayael's vision.

The vision shattered. Mayael blinked, and the Whitecover Gaze disappeared, revealing the valley around her. The Relic was a solid, unmoving monolith of stone. Her attendants were all around her, supporting her. Their hands were locked onto her skin, squeezing tightly. Her gown was heavy with sweat.

She heaved a sigh, but it broke hoarsely. She coughed.

"My throat feels sore," she said.

"You were screaming," said one of her farseers. Her attendants relaxed their grips on her.

"Oh. I'm sorry," she said quietly. "Please gather the warriors. The elves are going to war." She gathered up her gown.

"War?" an attendant asked. "What did you see, Anima?"

"Horrors," she said.

That was the last word said on Naya before it became part of Alara once again.

PART THREE

THE
MAELSTROM

As the planes collided, their lines of intersection became long frontiers of strife and ruin. Bant overlapped Esper, which thrust up into Grixis, which spilled into Jund, which blasted through into Naya, which crept into Bant. The aetheric boundaries that had once separated them into distinct planes collapsed silently, buckling in conceptual angles perceptible only to planeswalkers, eventually leaving only a single planar boundary around the unified plane of Alara.

In the heart of Alara, the five planes touched, forming a region composed of all five of the former shards. The interior boundaries had gone, and the terrain crushed in on itself, compressing the landmasses into a dense spiral of matter. The spiral formed a depression that widened and deepened as the planes continued their inchwise inward march.

At the very center of the depression, where lines of the five worlds' ambient mana converged, a mote of energy flared into life. No bigger than a grain of sand, it hung in the air, sparkling.

Deep inside his Grixis lair, Bolas stopped, his head cocked to one side, as if listening. Something was different. He felt it.

"It's begun," he said to the walls around him.

THE BLIND
ETERNITIES

Bolas hovered in the chaotic void between the worlds, watching the shards of Alara converge. He had invested years of time in the strange plural plane and a scheme as old as some of his human minions. His plan was not to collapse the five planes—as that had already been destined since the world of Alara was rent asunder centuries ago—but to reap the benefits of their impending conflux for himself. Soon his preparations would pay off, and he could seize the power robbed from him on Dominaria.

He enjoyed watching the planar edges fray, watching the landmasses intersect in untidy ways—the way Grixis intruded into Esper like fangs through skin, or the way Jund's stifling dystopia heaved lava over the rainforests of Naya. Just the mayhem of the physical convergence would destroy thousands of tiny lives, and that was pleasing. But it was the intersection of the worlds' mana that was his true goal.

Yes, he could sense the beginnings of it. As the worlds blended into one once more, the limited mana of each shard began to trickle over the borders into the neighboring shards. It wasn't much—not nearly enough to cause the storm of mana Bolas required—but that was to be expected. The ancient mana obelisks would help focus that energy. With them active, all that was required was a global incentive for Alara's denizens to use magic in massive amounts.

Bolas was exhausted. Staying too long in the Blind Eternities scoured his scales and drained his vigor. He returned to Grixis to prepare his servants for the next step.

BANT

Rafiq took a deep breath as he sat down in Aarsil the Blessed's court in Valeron. The merchant Gwafa Hazid was safely in custody, so Rafiq's mission for Aarsil was complete. But he had the feeling that that was only the first of his unusual tasks for her. The world was changing faster than he could comprehend. He and Mubin sat quietly as the Blessed presided over a meeting in her court.

Aarsil took her seat in the marble hall. Her attendants spread out her gown around her throne, and she was ready to begin.

"Thank you for coming," said Aarsil. "I bring somber news. Over the last few days, you may have seen the storm brewing on the horizon, or felt the tremors in the earth. Messengers from Jhess have brought strange reports from the coast, which we believe to be related to this phenomenon. The reports are scarcely to be believed. Towers made of an unknown metal have struck their way up through the fields near the coast, they say, killing Mortar-caste by the dozens. Screeching, scaly creatures have flown out of the horizon beyond the sea, devouring our livestock and terrorizing the orchard workers. Humanoids stalk onto Bant's soil, deploying exotic magics our mages cannot recognize. Truly, a dark time is upon us. Today we hear the words of one who may possess insight into this catastrophe."

Rafiq and Mubin exchanged a glance.

"Bailiff, if you would," said Aarsil.

"The court of Valeron recognizes Iama of the Order of the Skyward Eye," said the bailiff.

"Thank you, your honors," said Iama.

"So you're a seer, I'm told?" said Aarsil.

"I am a prophet, yes."

"Ah. So you presume to know the will of the angels, do you, Sighted-caste?"

"The angels have spoken to all of us, to all the castes. We of the Order of the Skyward Eye have merely interpreted the angels' message for the people of Bant. All castes, all peoples should understand its importance. You are familiar with Asha's Prophecy?"

"I've heard it, yes."

"So you know its rhythms, at least. You know how it ends?"

"Yes, I know that it ends with the demons returning, and a war that ends our world."

"No, not that *ends* the world, your honor. Not necessarily. The war shall determine our world's fate, one way or the other. And we need to be sure that we're prepared. That is the message of the prayer—that we must choose to rise up and defend the blessed land for ourselves."

Rafiq rose. "May I speak?"

Aarsil nodded.

"The court recognizes Rafiq of the Many," said the bailiff.

"I don't know you, prophet, but I know your Prophecy, and I object to your interpretation of it. Your words belittle the angels, our aegis against evil. The events that Aarsil mentions are disturbing, and perhaps a sign that Asha's time is near. But that's all the more reason to wait for them to act. Should anything truly dire befall Bant, the angels will rise up and defend us. Our role is to wait for their lead."

"With all respect due to your station, knight-captain," said Iama, "I must disagree. The angels will support us in whatever we *choose*. In the old tongue, they are the *bantuthroi,* literally the 'flesh of our volition.' If we do nothing, neither will they."

A murmur blew through the assembly.

"Order," said Aarsil. "That is a radical interpretation, Iama."

"Your honor, it is what is mandated in the prophecies handed down from knight to knight in our Order, from the angel Asha herself."

"So you say."

Iama nodded. "I do. The Prophecy says, further, that our world shall expand, converging with a multitude of lands beyond Bant—which is exactly what we've seen coming at the Jhessian coast. The metal towers and strange mages are from a world we call Esper, and Esper is only the first. We know that these worlds will stop at nothing to destroy Bant and our entire way of life."

GRIXIS

Grixis wasn't populated entirely by undead horrors. Despite centuries of decay under the withering effects of the plane's dark mana, some humans still lived—but not many. After the hermitage at Kederekt fell to the undead armies of the demon Malfegor, Torchlight became the last stronghold of living humans.

Morsath Levac peered out the door through the small, round piece of glass. The scouts were late, and on the horizon he could already see the cluster of sickly clouds gathering for that night's lightning storms. His fingers and jawline were bony, his frame hollowed by the daily trauma of life on Grixis—not like the supple, fleshy cheeks of his young son.

The door hummed gently. Light-bending magic inside the door's enchanted lens gathered reflections from outside the stronghold and delivered them to Levac's eyes. The Dregscape looked as bleak as ever, an expanse of flyblown rot the color of gore. Black-feathered kathari shrieked in the distance.

"Levac, anything?" said Captain Haim, coming down the stairs from the tower.

"No, Captain," said Levac. "No sign of Tomlain or Welly. It's been three hours; they should have reported in by now."

"We'll give them ten more minutes. Then you and I will do a quick circuit, and then we'll lock up for the night. For now, go be with your wife and son, Levac. I can man the door."

"Yes, sir."

"Hey, are the wards active?"

"They're hot. I just checked them."

"Then scoot."

His last shift. One last guard shift, and then he could take a bit of leave—three whole weeks of nothing but time with Salay and the boy, and if all went well, their newborn. Levac climbed the stairs two at a time.

"Levac!"

It was Captain Haim again.

"What do you want, old man?" he started, but the crash cut him short.

Levac dashed down the steps to see the door blown off its hinges, with Captain Haim prone on the ground before the opening, his face ashen. Two hulking zombies ducked under the threshold and lumbered into the entrance hall. Captain Haim scuttled to his feet and drew his sword, but stood back from the hulks.

Why hadn't the lens showed him the zombies, Levac thought? Unless—

"Levac, I could use you! I thought you said the wards were—"

"We've been breached!" Levac shouted.

Wards exploded in a series of rapid cracks along the edge of the door, arcing blue lightning into the zombies and wracking their bodies rigid. The creatures groaned as foul smoke poured out of their rotting skin. If those corpses had fooled the door lens somehow, at least they hadn't managed to deactivate the other defenses.

Levac grabbed a sledgehammer from the case and flanked up next to Haim, who didn't dare sink his steel sword into the electrified undead. Levac reared back for an overhand swing.

"Do it," said Haim.

Levac brought the mallet down. He crushed the skull of one of the zombies, and it fell. He brought the hammer around again, and smashed through the collarbone of the other. The two of them fell in a heap.

Levac huffed. "How the heck did those things fool the lens?" he said.

"Levac…"

Haim was looking through the doorway, out to the yard surrounding the stronghold. Levac looked.

A sea of undead was amassed around the stronghold: two ranks of bloated fleshbags, a legion of zombie grunts led by a contingent of undead spellcasters, three enormous dreg reavers with their ribcages carrying squads of animated skeletons, and flyers in the form of a cloud of undead drakes and kathari.

"Malfegor . . ." Haim breathed.

Behind the undead army was a towering, misshapen demon lord with broad, batlike wings, four arms, and the lower body of a huge, black-scaled dragon. It spoke some booming, guttural blasphemy to its troops, and the sea of undead began to advance. Torchlight faced Malfegor, the demon-dragon abomination, the cruelest and most powerful demon lord in all of Grixis. If Malfegor was there in person, then Torchlight was going to fall, and not after a long siege. The hermitage, the last major refuge of humanity, would go that night.

"Get out of here," said Haim.

Levac stared. His fingers dropped the sledgehammer, and his feet took a single, slow step backward.

"Levac, you idiot, *run!*"

Windows shattered. Wards fired off ineffectually

as the undead began pouring through every portal

in the stronghold's ground level. Some sort of undead beast pounced in the open doorway and knocked down Captain Haim. Levac rushed up the stairs as he heard Haim's screams.

Levac took one final look back, and regretted it. Haim's entrails flew every which way as the beast and three other zombies feasted on his abdomen, while he screamed and tried to beat on them with his fists.

Levac took the stairs three at a time.

"Salay!" he bellowed over the popping of the wards. "Salay!"

Other living humans streamed past him on the stairwell, carrying rusted swords and shields. Levac said silent goodbyes to them as they passed.

He reached the landing. His wife Salay regarded him from their vestibule. She would have looked waiflike with her concave cheeks, but for her pregnant belly.

"What's happening?" she said.

"This is it. We're hitting the tunnels. Grab the satchel."

"Where's Captain Haim?"

"He's dead. They've come, Salay. It's time to go. Where's Vali?"

Salay's face went pale. "I thought he was with you! He said he was going to help you with your watch, and headed out to find you . . ."

"Oh, no, no—"

His son was outside the stronghold, unprotected among the undead. He was sure of it. The world closed in on Levac's mind.

BANT

Aarsil held her hand up to quiet the court assembly again.

Rafiq looked at Mubin. The rhox's mouth hung open at the prophet's words—the thought of other lands appearing all around Bant, and the onset of war with them, was hardly to be believed. But his expression seemed not to convey disbelief so much as wonder.

"What is it?" Rafiq whispered to him.

"It all fits," said Mubin, but he didn't elaborate.

Aarsil the Blessed narrowed her eyes at the Skyward Eye seer Iama. "Assuming we believe this—your proposal would be what, exactly?"

"I'm just a prophet, not a ruler, your honor. But I would propose that we go to war immediately. That we raise an army, and assault our enemies who emerge from distant lands, those who wish to crush all of Bant. That we invade the world they call Esper, to save our own."

Aarsil stood up from her throne, her gilded robes flowing around her. She paced back and forth across the dais, all eyes on her.

"Thank you for your words, Iama," she said.

Iama bowed and sat.

"These are words none ever wish to hear," she said. "These portents of catastrophe are never welcome. But they align with the whispers I have heard in my ear of late, both from my fellow man and from the angels themselves. My dreams, it seems, are coming true as well. For months now I have been convinced that there are forces afoot that are greater than my caste, greater than my nation, and greater perhaps than all of the nations of the world together—but in my lack of resolve, I kept silent. Seeing Giltspire fall convinced me that I needed to listen to my heart, and to act. I called this meeting not just to discuss philosophy with you, my friends and advisors. I called you here to declare the unification of the nations of Bant, and to declare war."

Rafiq's heart pounded. He gripped the arm of his chair.

"Bant faces invasion by a foreign world, a world its denizens call Esper," said Aarsil. "Bant is now at war with Esper. The army is being raised as we speak."

Aarsil clasped her hands together in a gesture of unity, or prayer. "All I need now is a general. And I am happy to say that there is one among us who can lead this force. He has shown that he can do what must be done, and he will lead us to victory."

All eyes turned to Rafiq.

Rafiq took a deep breath.

BANT
ESPER FRONTIER

Knight-General Rafiq and his second Mubin rode on ahead of Asha's Army—the unified legions of all the nations of Bant—into the gray mist that shrouded the Jhessian coast. The first gale of the stormfront hit them like a wall, and pelted them with diagonal rain. The air smelled of moisture and ozone. In the distance Rafiq saw a huge gray thunderhead looming from the earth to the heavens, swirling in on itself and spinning with flecks of unknown matter. Particles swarmed ahead of the storm. They were flying creatures of some kind—hundreds of them.

"It looks like a swarm of bees," said Mubin.

"How far are they? Those are some big bees," said Rafiq. "Aven?" he guessed.

"Well, they certainly aren't angels."

"Scouts!" Rafiq called up to the hawk aven above. "I need eyes on those flyers. Do not engage them—just report back as soon as you can."

Three aven scouts screeched assent and flew off ahead.

"You and I need to call out their army's champion," said Rafiq.

"Rafiq, we don't know this army."

"That's exactly why I need to beat their champion immediately."

"That's not what I mean."

"Look, they're an unknown force from who knows where. We don't know their strength, but frankly, to me, they look like they could raze all of Jhess in a matter of days. That's why you and I are riding ahead, and why we'll challenge their leader and put this matter to rest before this gets out of hand. Ready my ceremonial shield."

Mubin's ears twitched, but he didn't say anything.

As they watched the front ahead, they saw the three aven scouts approach the mass of flyers ahead of the swirling storm. Two of the aven spasmed in flight, then arced out of the sky. Their bodies crashed to the ground and bounced once, limply, and didn't move again. The other aven seemed to hesitate in the sky, then turned around and flew back in the direction of the knights.

Rafiq and Mubin exchanged glances.

"Magic?" said Mubin.

"No magic can kill a man outright," said Rafiq. "They must have archers."

"Rafiq, this doesn't feel right. . . ."

"Get out the banners," said Rafiq. "We need to make it clear we're champions here for ritual combat."

"No. Rafiq, my old friend, I think we need to retreat," said Mubin.

"Don't be foolish. Their archers have already broken the war protocols. Their Knight-General will want to know the details of the breach."

Their leotau mounts slowed. Mubin had grasped the reins of Rafiq's steed.

"What are you doing?" demanded Rafiq.

At that moment, the hawk aven scout flew over them, going in the wrong direction. It led a mass of scaly flying creatures. The aven fired a treasonous crossbow bolt down at the two knights, narrowly missing Mubin.

"What in Asha's name?" cried Rafiq.

205

"Witchery," said Mubin. "We're up against dark things, Knight-General."

The aven screeched as it flew toward the rest of Asha's Army. Behind it, they heard other screeches.

The enemy force was composed of a variety of alien flyers: reptilian things with wings and back legs like a bird, but sharp, jutting scales like a metallic snake; ugly, dog-faced, animated gargoyles whose skin resembled white marble; strange contrivances with wings that flapped on improbable pulleys and wheels. And all of them contained delicate filigree structures of a gleaming metal, fused right into their anatomies in ways that looked like they should have been disabling or lethal. The wind was full of their strange cries as they flew overhead, and a whistling caused by their filigree speeding through the air. Not one engaged the two knights, but instead they flew on, heading for the front lines of the Bant army.

Behind the flyers, the storm approached. In the center of it flew a thin, bald woman with blue-gray skin, riding on the back of an enormous, stone-faced gargoyle. Her forearms were made of the filigree metal, and her robes billowed with the winds. She raised her arms, and the thunderhead bulged outward, threatening to sweep the knights up in its gales.

"That's not their champion," said Mubin.

"Let's go," Rafiq agreed.

They wheeled their steeds and whistled shrilly. The leotau steeds dug their hooves deep into the turf of Jhess, and launched into a gallop back to the front lines.

Behind them, the otherworldly mage recited a spell, her words lost in the winds. Mubin moaned in pain and clutched his head.

GRIXIS

Levac took up his sword and headed back down the stairs, shouting for his son.

"Vali! Vali!"

He pushed through the other soldiers, shoving them aside in his haste but accosting every face he recognized.

"Clairan, have you seen Vali? Hargrove? Hey, Malunis? Seen Vali? Anyone? *Has anyone seen my son?*"

"Daddy . . ." came a faint voice.

Levac looked out the doorway. Up in the guard tower he saw little Vali waving at him. The tower's ladder was pulled up, but zombies and skeletons crawled spiderlike up the outside of the tower. They would be on him in a matter of moments.

Levac swept past the soldiers and went straight for the statue that stood out in the front room of the stronghold, the so-called Lady of the Scythe. He stood up on its base and grabbed its scythe with both hands, and yanked. It pulled free easily—as he had always suspected it would. Her hands had always been outstretched in a gesture of forgiveness, not force. Her outstretched wings and gentle eyes expressed a kindness that had never befitted Grixis, as if she were a relic from a gentler time long past.

Levac hefted the scythe into his own arms, and in doing so clumsily grazed a zombie who was attacking one of the soldiers. The scythe's blade sliced clean through the creature's thigh, and it dropped squirming in two pieces on the floor.

"What the hell, Levac? Do that again!" said the soldier.

Levac blinked. He swung the scythe awkwardly forward and sliced through two more zombie minions. The scythe sang with a strange harmonic as black gore dripped from the blade. Levac pushed forward through the doorway, into the fray. The scythe swerved back and forth easily, almost hungrily, and with every swing, Levac bisected several undead.

"Daddy!" screamed Vali from the top of the guard tower.

Rage took hold. Levac swung the scythe wildly, cutting a swathe through the undead, heading straight for the tower. Undead fell every which way, forming a gory pathway that Levac followed all the way to the tower.

He couldn't see Vali anywhere. The undead had snatched him inside the tower.

"I'm coming for you, Vali!" Levac screamed.

He sliced at the legs of the tower. The scythe hewed straight through them, and the tower fell, toppling dozens of undead in the process. The creatures fell in a writhing pile, each one getting up to face him in hunger.

Vali stood up in the center of the dogpile. His eyes had rolled up in the back of his head, and his skin was grayish and sallow. Then Levac saw that a zombified humanoid had his mouth clamped onto the back of Vali's neck.

"Vali, no!"

The boy roared, an inhuman sound born of hollowness and a thirst for death.

No, Levac thought. Not him. Anyone but him.

The boy's pupils rolled into view, and focused on Levac. The experience was horrible.

Malfegor, the demonic general, marched into view behind the wreckage of the tower, and dull terror washed over Levac's mind.

"Time to *go*, Levac, let's go!" shouted a soldier.

Levac dropped the scythe and ran. He pushed or leaped over anything that got in his way, and tore through the crowd.

He leaped into the tunnel entrance and slammed the metal door behind him.

Salay clutched his shirt and shook him. "Where is he?" she shrieked.

"He's gone."

"No! You go back and get him! I'm not leaving without him!"

"We're going. He's gone, Salay."

Salay slapped him across the face.

Three heartbeats passed.

She turned her back to him, and marched down into the tunnel.

"I . . . I couldn't," said Levac. "I was too late. Salay, I'm sorry."

The only answer was his own echo, and the sounds of her footsteps on the tunnel floor. He picked up the satchel and followed after her.

JUND

It was night on Jund, and the tight, sweat-slicked abdomens of the warriors shone in the bonfire. One warrior hoisted a pair of effigies and hung them over the fire: one a long-haired man with a dragon-skin cape; the other, an older woman painted with a shaman's stripes. Both lit immediately, and the warriors cheered.

Their cheers sounded thin to Kresh. In his long, blood-stuck braids he wore trophies of some of the warriors who had fallen at the lair of Malactoth. Ever since Rakka had betrayed him, since she had used the clan as bait for the dragon while casting some destructive spell of her own, his brain had burned. It was an obvious matter for revenge. As the effigy of Rakka crackled in the fire, he felt an easy hatred.

But it was the new betrayal that had him perplexed. Sarkhan, the stranger who had accompanied them to Malactoth's lair, had seemed driven to seek out the hellkite. He was a powerful ally in that fight against the dragon—and yet, just days ago, he had seen Sarkhan leading a flight of dragons of his own, riding astride one of them like some kind of god. Sarkhan's pets ravaged the low-lying areas, where dragons rarely fed, and expelled their hot breath on several valleys, razing them to blackened ground.

Kresh had lost eleven of his remaining clanmates in the conflagration that followed.

So there they were, the thinned-out remains of his once-noble clan. They still had pride in their eyes and ferocity in their hearts, but their numbers were so few that the clan was in danger of dying out. Kresh knew something would have to give soon, or his clan would die the ignoble death of old age, shivering in some cave surrounded by goblin dung.

No, he thought.

If the clan's fate was to face death, then he would lead them headlong into it. Vengeance for the shaman Rakka? A fitting downfall of the dragon-lord Sarkhan? Those needs burned inside his heart, yes. But he would hold them inside his ribcage, and smother them in his corpse-scream, if it meant he could give his people the ultimate gift: a death worth being born for.

He was ready for the final hunt, the pursuit of that enemy called death, and so was his clan. As they cheered the cinders from the effigies, and watched them float up and join with the rage-coughs of the volcanoes, he felt the readiness in their hearts.

He only needed a sign, some way to know in which direction their fate lay. But they had no deep-seers left in the clan. Without Rakka acting as their shaman, the signal might be too subtle for them to detect.

One of Kresh's warriors ran out of the bladed wilderness to their camp. She looked like she was sweating adrenaline, and didn't have her second with her.

"Tol Kresh!" she said. "You must come see. A white cat has *appeared out of nowhere*."

Kresh's grin started at one ear and unfolded all the way to the other.

BANT
ESPER FRONTIER

Don't be afraid to cut them down, any way you can," Elspeth whispered to the other knights and soldiers around her.

War had come to Bant, and there was nothing the planeswalker Elspeth could do about it. The leonin planeswalker, Ajani, had been right all along—there were other worlds intimately connected to Bant, and their borders were intruding on one another, almost before her eyes. Her despair paralyzed her at first; she sent away the couriers who called her to war, and entreated the angels to spare her from seeing her beloved Bant fall. She found herself wishing she could see Ajani again, to express her grief to understanding ears.

She only hoped she could prepare her Bant brothers-in-arms for what lay ahead of them. "If you see an opening, any opening, you strike," she said. "Even if it means violating the laws of war." The others looked at her strangely. She didn't care, as long as it got through their heads that the rules were gone, and that there was no arena judge, no Blessed decree, to protect them here.

There was still hope. She was not about to curl up and let Bant fall, not while she could still hold a sword. That was how she had found herself on the border terrain between Bant and Esper, among the ranks of Asha's Army. Though her sigils were many, she had not served as a

Sigiled-caste for long enough to lead as a general—but that suited her. She didn't need rank to defend her home; she just needed a sword, a battlefield, and—as she told herself silently—a bit of Bant's pure mana. Besides, from inside the infantry lines, she would be able to watch over her friends.

"Charge!" shouted the captain of her legion.

Elspeth rushed forward with her fellow knights and soldiers, steel in hand. She was easily as fast as her peers, but she let them pass her little by little, so she could watch over them from behind. Ahead she saw the flyers approaching, and with a flood of memories from her travels, recognized their shapes: drakes, gargoyles, and strange devices she decided were thopters. They were all modified with peculiar artifact magic—it must be an army backed by a legion of artificers. She knew their strength would surprise her fellow citizens of Bant. She readied a protection spell and did her best to delay it till the perfect moment.

The aven troops were the first to clash with the enemy. Elspeth willed them strength and resilience, and many of the aven tore into the enemy drakes with their enhanced prowess. But she couldn't watch over them all. One aven soldier fell to the talons of a pair of jagged-scaled drakes. Another was grappled by an enormous gargoyle and crushed to death.

A third aven fell to a mage's evisceration spell, keeling over and crashing to earth without even a single blow landing on it.

"No," gasped Elspeth. Just as war had come to Bant, so had death magic.

Some of the gargoyles dropped their heavy bulk into the fray, smashing a few Valeron soldiers on their way down. Other troops swarmed them and hacked at the gargoyles' stony skin with swords and maces, learning to chop through the wiry metal enhancements first. Screeching drakes swooped and snatched individual soldiers, flew them high into the air, and dropped them, then swooped down again to repeat the process.

The storm met the army like a stampede. The wind blew most of the army off its feet, Elspeth included—but the heavy gargoyles remained standing, and stomped the fallen with granite footfalls. As Elspeth scrambled to her feet, she saw the mage in the center of the storm—a vedalken by the looks of her—her whirling metallic arms maintaining a stream of constant spellcasting. The winds that whipped around her deflected a hail of arrows from archers of the Order of Dawnray, and buffeted away an assault by a pair of determined aven. I need to stop the mage, thought Elspeth. But it's going to take some finesse.

"Mardis!" shouted Elspeth, to her nearby knight friend.

"Elspeth, are you all right?" he shouted back.

"Mardis, listen to me! When I tell you, you attack that mage, do you understand?"

He looked up. Skepticism. *"That* mage?"

Elspeth was casting. "Ready?"

Mardis showed alarm, but gathered his wits and readied his sword and shield. The storm's cylinder passed over him, and began to push him off his feet.

"Go!"

A helix of light erupted from around Mardis's body, lifting him into the air. He shot like an arrow at the vedalken mage. Mardis's astonishment turned to determination, and his body became one graceful attack motion, like a warrior angel delivering the stroke of vengeance. The vedalken mage looked down, saw him flying toward her, and gasped.

Just before Elspeth could see what happened, the rhox knight Mubin rode through the lines a huge leotau, his eyes aglow like haunted sapphires—and brained her with his mace.

GRIXIS

R eport," said Bolas.

"The Esper obelisk has been freed and activated," said Sarkhan. "As the planes have converged, the forces of Esper have begun to invade Bant. A force of about two thousand massed on the shores of Jhess this morning."

"Casualties?"

"Mostly on Bant's part. They were woefully under-prepared for the mage assault. Bant's warriors are brave and strong, but they seem . . . naïve."

Bolas bared rows of teeth. "Naïve, you say?"

"They never advanced. They seemed to wait for the army from Esper to crash into them. Some of the soldiers hadn't even strapped on their armor fully. It was like they never expected to have to fight at all."

Bolas rolled his tongue across his teeth. "What magic did you see?"

"Esper laid into them with storms, countermagic, control of the mind, and some spells of death. And their army was almost entirely composed of creatures that were summoned from Esper. Only a few mages led the entire offensive. I saw some healing on Bant's side, and what looked like a protective enhancement on some of the soldiers, but that was all. The Bant army barely seemed to cast anything at all."

Bolas reflected on that. "Mixed," he said. "What about the obelisks?"

"As the shards go to war, the obelisks have been channeling mana, as you desired," said Sarkhan. "But the flow is weak at this point. There's just not enough of a conflict yet. And the Bant obelisk, the one from the ruined castle—it seems to be resisting. It's possible that the spell didn't activate it properly, or that some force is preventing it from channeling Bant's mana."

Bolas uttered a string of garbled syllables that Sarkhan presumed formed a curse in some extraplanar language. "If the Bant obelisk isn't channeling mana, then the reaction cannot start."

"Do you want me to return to Bant? Draw out some mages? Encourage more magic?"

"No. I need you elsewhere. The mages of Bant should awaken now that their knights are dying; the battles on their Esper front will scare them, and they'll get over their principles and begin to throw better magics. Besides, you wouldn't be much of a negotiator. You don't look much like a Bant human."

Sarkhan shrugged. "I passed well enough on Esper."

"I'm sure you stuck out horribly. But no, I have a different mission for you. Pick out your favorite machete. You're going into the jungle."

"Naya? But the planes have merged now. I can't planeswalk from one part of Alara to another any longer," said Sarkhan.

"You'll not be planeswalking. Come with me down to the necropolis dungeon," said Bolas. "I have a surprise for you."

BANT
ESPER FRONTIER

Knight-General Rafiq watched the scene in slow motion. His friend Mubin clutched his head as the Esper mage's spell came down on him. Then the mighty rhox blinked, took up his mace and his mount's reins, and hastened into the fray. The surprise of the betrayal carried him deep into the Bant army, and he felled several soldiers before Rafiq had understood what had happened. Mind magic was present on Bant, but not like that. He had heard of spells that would allow analysis of the mind, which was sometimes used to verify travelers' claims of caste, or to read the wishes of Blessed-caste rulers who were ill or incapacitated. But that was something beyond mind-sight—that was some kind of magic of coercion. The metal-infused creatures seemed not only capable of interpreting the soul, but rewriting it. The dishonor was shocking.

"Mubin! Mubin! Mubin!"

He was hoarse before he realized he was screaming at the rhox knight, preoccupied as he was with the desperate maneuvers of leotau and rider that it took to cross through the sea of combatants to reach him. He shifted his weight to and fro, yanking and kicking to guide the steed deftly through the fray, trying not to trample the injured or the friendly. The enemy mage had chosen her target cleverly; Mubin was one of the most dangerous soldiers

DOUG BEYER

on the battlefield—in all of Bant, in truth. By the time Rafiq had reached Mubin, he had already made the decision: he would have to wound the rhox, hard, and bring him down.

He tried to circle around to Mubin's front side to land a proper blow, but Mubin kept circling his steed to present only the unarmored back—a dishonorable target. It was only after Mubin walloped a young soldier squarely in the helmet, felling her as one might a doll, that Rafiq realized he'd have to violate his code as a Sigiled-caste and as a knight. He'd have to attack the unarmored gap in the rhox's back, like a child or a common bandit. It was just like the arena, when Aarsil the Blessed had purposely changed the rules to test his willingness to break them himself—except things were beyond a mere swayed judge. It was an entire army, an entire *world* with no conception of the rules of honor at all.

Rafiq swept up to Mubin, and angled himself to hit the junction between the flanges of metal on the rhox's back. He saw his opening, and swung with all his might. Rafiq's sword came down between Mubin's shoulder blades, and struck deep, tearing through several inches of skin and fat, severing a muscle group or two, and scraping vertebrae and cartilage. It must have cut something else too—something deeper—because Mubin dropped his mace and fell limp, roughly, off his steed, into the mud.

GRIXIS

"Y ou've done well, my pet," said Bolas.

"I'm glad you're pleased," said Sarkhan, following Bolas down an enormous cavern under the necropolis. Sconces made from hollowed-out human skulls lined the tunnel. Light flickered through the eye sockets.

"Yes. The Grixis legions have advanced deeper than expected. We've captured Vectis on one front and Bloodhall on the other, creating ostentatious firefights in every battle. The other planes have engaged in all-out war on multiple fronts. In this, your reconnaissance and infiltration have proved most useful. As a result, I have a surprise for you."

Sarkhan's heart stopped for a moment. He thought of the hundreds of skull sconces he'd seen, and recalled a mountaintop littered with braindead goblins. "What is it?"

"It should be obvious," said Bolas, his grin a mockery of magnanimity. "I've given the gift you've always wanted. Come."

Bolas gestured to an undead guard, who pulled open gigantic doors into the next chamber. Bolas strolled through them, looking surprisingly natural on two legs. With his wings folded and his tail balancing the weight of his torso and long neck, the elder dragon looked almost humanoid.

DOUG BEYER

They emerged in a dry natural cavern. Standing inside were five dragons, their heads held up oddly, as if they were posing for the judges of some sort of contest. They were Jund dragons, their scales scarred and blackened in places from the wear and tear of draconic battles. But something was wrong about them. Their eyes were inert, unresponsive. They breathed and held position, and did nothing else.

They were magnificent, but despite himself, Sarkhan felt his stomach clench. "What did you . . . do to them?"

"Aren't they beautiful? I had them prepared and polished just for you. They're yours now, Sarkhan. Today you're getting a lesson in dragon control and summoning." Bolas licked his teeth. "Strange, isn't it? Do you think Serra ever taught her disciples to bind an angel?"

"What?"

"I doubt it. The principle would be the same, anyway. It's all about the mind, you see. It's the key to everything. A dragon's mind is all cloaked in fire—a nasty place to try to maneuver. You don't get anywhere trying to reason with one, and you can't hope to best it in some sort of contest of wills. You'll just be burned. Sometimes literally, of course. So, you extinguish that fire, and their minds are surprisingly empty vessels. Fill them with whatever you want. I've chosen to fill them with devotion to me. And to you."

Sarkhan's hands clenched into fists; one of his knuckles popped. He didn't know whether to be thrilled or nauseous, standing before the awe-inspiring specimens of dragonkind whose minds were shackled by the magic of Bolas. The thought of the dragons at his beck and call made him want to laugh long, loud, and cruel into the face of the sun—but the thought of their fiery souls hollowed out by Bolas's cunning made him consider simply putting them out of their misery.

"So?" said Bolas. "What do you think?"

The largest of the enslaved dragons was a huge male, its scales as ruddy as molten rock. Sarkhan realized that he'd seen it before.

"Karrthus," he said.

"What's that?" said Bolas.

"It's Karrthus, a dragon I've . . . met before on Jund. A mighty hellkite, a tyrant even among dragons."

"Well, now he's *your* mighty hellkite."

Sarkhan considered for a moment, then bowed his head solemnly. "Thank you, Master."

"Enjoy destroying Naya. I'll meet you at the Maelstrom."

BANT

Elspeth rubbed her eyelids, and the slight movements of her head set up waves of pain and nausea rebounding between her ears.

"What happened?" she asked.

"You were attacked—by a knight of Bant, I'm afraid."

She managed to see through her damp lashes. Rafiq, the Knight-General himself, stood over her, and behind him was a woman in cleric's robes. She was in a bed. It was dark and quiet.

"The betrayal. Was it . . . a spell?"

"It seems so," said Rafiq. "Some powerful corruption spell from an Esper mage. It seized the soul of my friend Mubin, who attacked you. I'm very sorry."

"I should go and see him," she said, and tried to get up.

"No. You need to lie still," said the cleric.

The instant return of the headache was a good motivator. Elspeth lay back down.

"Your injury was very serious," said the cleric. "The healing spells need time to take hold."

Rafiq's concern was fatherly, gentle with a note of scolding. "Mubin is a powerful warrior. When he sets his mind to something, he does it. . . .." Rafiq's voice trailed off as he wrestled with some thought.

223

Elspeth finished it for him. "Even when someone else is setting his mind to it."

Rafiq nodded. "Yes. Even then. You are lucky to be alive, young knight."

"But I'm of no use here, in this bed. My world . . . This world needs me."

"It will still need you after you are better," said Rafiq.

"No, you don't understand. Bant is under attack by . . . forces it can't understand. I didn't see before, but now I know—it can't win this way. We'll fall unless I—"

"Quiet now, young knight," said Rafiq. "The rest of us will take care of things at the front lines. We have legions of devoted souls fighting this war, and prison to hold the not-so-devoted, those who would harm Bant from within. But Bant will fall to nothing. I'll see to that personally."

"From within? What forces would harm Bant from within?"

"Oh, a renegade merchant called Hazid. He was the coward responsible for the destruction of Giltspire. Mubin and I brought him to justice, at the court at Valeron."

The traitor, Hazid—he might represent an even greater threat than the forces of Esper, Elspeth thought. "I see," she said. "So, where is Knight Mubin now?"

"He's . . ." Rafiq trailed off. He smiled at her, but his eyes went somewhere far away. When he spoke after a moment, Elspeth had the impression he was speaking to the empty air in front of him.

"He is recuperating, just like you. He will be fine."

* * * * *

Mubin could not feel his legs.

"Tell me straight, healer," he said. "Will I ever walk again?"

"You're awake," said the cleric. He closed his book, a heavy tome of prayers to Asha. "And . . . yourself. That's good."

Mubin's huge form took up the entire sickbed. He could see his own legs lying there in front of him, unmoving. He didn't even look injured, he thought. No wounds, no bandages anymore. He just looked still.

"My legs. Will they work again?"

"Time will tell," said the cleric.

"Uh-huh. But it looks bad."

"I'm sorry, Sir Mubin. It's . . . not in our power to heal this kind of injury. The wound went too deep. It broke crucial parts of your spine."

Yes, Rafiq had seen to that. One blow, and Mubin was paralyzed from the waist down, possibly for life. His best friend in the world had done that to him. But then, he thought, didn't he force Rafiq's hand? Why did he make Rafiq do it to him?

"How many died?" Mubin asked.

"In the battle?"

"No, not in total. How many . . . did I . . .?"

"Oh. I haven't heard whether the exact number has been reckoned. But it wasn't your fault, sir. Your mind was controlled by the enemy."

"Tell me. Please. I have to know. How many was it?"

The cleric wouldn't meet his eyes. That was a bad sign.

"It was a lot, wasn't it?"

"Perhaps . . ."

"What?"

"Perhaps with time, your legs might heal. Miracles may happen with time and prayer. The angels grant blessings to the faithful."

"Get out."

"Sir . . ."

"No, I get it. We're down to hoping for miracles already. I understand. It's fine. You've done your proper penance, by staying with the invalid murderer. I've woken up. You can go tell Rafiq. No—actually, don't tell him. Tell him to stay away. I don't want to see him."

"Sir, I . . ."

"It's all right. You may go."

The cleric nodded, closed his book of prayers, and got up to leave.

Great, he thought. That was how the rhox was treating a Sighted-caste cleric who was just there to help him.

"Wait," said Mubin. He slumped down on a stack of pillows. "Do something for me."

"Yes?"

"Would you . . . leave me that book of prayers?"

GRIXIS

"You summoned me, Master?" said the demon-dragon Malfegor.

"It's the maelstrom," said Bolas. "It's forming so slowly."

"The worlds have collided. War has broken out across every border. We're harvesting more life essence than Grixis has known. Not since Alara fractured has there been this kind of chaos across these worlds. The maelstrom will be born in time."

"I don't have *time*," said the elder dragon planeswalker. "All these infinite worlds, all these millennia, and I have hitched my hopes to the energies of this one world, you understand? I'm counting my breaths. Another goes by, another goes by, and I'll never get them back. And I'm held back at every turn by the failings of leonin and humans. We need to speed things along."

"Yes, Master."

"I want you to travel to Bant."

Malfegor's eyes narrowed.

"Go to the site of the obelisk there, and awaken it."

"I? Personally? Master, wasn't that your agent's task?"

"He failed to appear at our last rendezvous. An entire walk to Bant wasted. My minions among the Skyward Eye report that he's been captured, so he's useless to me now."

"So you want me to conduct the ritual in his place. By marching on Bant."

"Yes."

"The place from which you just returned. A place filled with angels and paladins."

"I believe I was clear enough."

"Master, that would be an enormous undertaking. The journey alone would take—"

"Then you'd better get started, hadn't you? Unless you'd prefer to feel my claws squeezing the pulp from your consciousness. Unless you'd prefer to wither and die an irrevocable death, nibbled by leviathans under the Kederekt Sea. Unless you'd prefer that I grant Grixis to the lichlord Sedris, or perhaps the soothsayer Caladessa."

"I'm going," said Malfegor.

"Hurry, please," said Bolas. "And anything you can destroy in Esper on your way there—I'll leave that up to you."

BANT

"Mubin," said Rafiq quietly, stepping into the recuperation room.

The old rhox didn't look up. His bulk was turned away from the doorway. Rafiq couldn't tell if he was awake or not.

"Mubin, old boy, are you up?"

"Go away," was the grunted response.

What did one say in such a situation? "They . . . said you were awake."

"I told them I wanted you to stay away. I don't want to see you, isn't that clear?"

"Well, you're being seen anyway," said Rafiq. "You think they would refuse an order from me, or that I'm going to obey one from you? I just wanted to know how you were doing. So . . . how is it? Are you feeling better?"

No answer.

"Never mind," said Rafiq hastily. "That's a stupid question. Listen, Mubin, I'm going to find a way to make this right. I know they said it couldn't be healed, but there has to be magic, somewhere, that'll make you right again, and I'm going to find it."

"Don't bother."

"Mubin, I know what I did was wrong. I shouldn't have done it. I should have slain your steed, or tackled you, or—"

Mubin reached over with his arm, grabbed a bedpost, and pulled himself over onto his back. It was excruciating, watching him. The powerful rhino-man, a many-sigiled knight of the Order of the Reliquary, was reduced to pulling himself around on a hostel bed. There was a book of prayers in his other hand.

His eyes were red and bloodshot.

"Rafiq. No. What you did was right. Don't spend any more time bothering with it. I was a monster. I have to live with that."

"But it was just—"

"And don't tell me it was the enchantment. I know that. But I remember how it *felt*, Rafiq. I remember the crunch of my mace against their skulls. I remember the coldness in my veins. I remember the *thrill* of it. It may have been magic that awakened those parts of me, but they were already there."

"No."

"They were *already there*, Rafiq."

Rafiq felt like hitting something. He exhaled, calming himself.

"The sages . . . The sages want to know more," Rafiq said. "About the mind control you suffered. They want to know as much as they can, so they can avoid it in the future."

"Rafiq, listen. I've been doing some reading. There are some similarities—"

"No, *you* listen. We're out there fighting the horrors from Esper every day now. We need your experiences, so we can learn to fight against their magics, and defend our land. All of Bant is at stake."

"But this is important," said Mubin. "I think these old passages, these ancient prayers, mention things that are actually coming to pass, and give instructions for what to do when the—"

"That's enough! Enough of these choir-boy distractions! At attention! On your feet, soldier!"

Mubin's eyes went wide.

"Oh, holy Asha. I'm sorry. I'm sorry, I'm—"

"Rafiq, it's all right."

"I'm so sorry. I . . . Look, I have to go. Uh, please tell the clerics all you can remember. It'll . . . It'll help the war effort. It was good to see you. I . . ."

He left.

Rafiq was out the door before he could see Mubin's expression. He held the door shut with his back. He wondered whether friendship was something a sword could sever.

ESPER

Rafiq's contingent huddled between strange, glittering dunes in a desert of fine particles of glass. They were deep in Esper, ahead of the main invasion force just as Rafiq wanted. The plane's night sky was crisscrossed by grid-lines, as if even the stars had been categorized and dissected by the world's mages, just like the etherium-infused bodies of the Esper denizens themselves.

"If I may speak freely, Knight-General, sir?" said an aven scout.

"You may, Scout—Kaeda, is it?" asked Rafiq.

"Yes, sir," said the aven. His wings were folded military-tight, ruffled only slightly by the winds of Esper. "Sir, it's not appropriate for you to accompany us on this mission. Your life is too valuable. If we're only doing a routine city capture, then with all due respect, we don't need your direction."

"I understand your concern, Scout Kaeda, and I agree. You are quite capable of carrying out the letter of this mission without me."

"I thought you would believe so, Knight-General. Which means there are parts of the mission that are secret, which I fully understand and accept. But out of concern for your safety, as the second-in-command of this party, I believe . . ." The aven trailed off.

"Yes?"

"I believe you should let us help in that part of the mission."

Rafiq smirked.

"You should only do what's appropriate, of course," the aven continued. "But you should know that this squad is ready to die for whatever cause requires your presence here. We are some of the best eyes in Asha's Army, and there are several Sigiled among our ranks, including me. We can help, if you let us."

"Thank you for your offer," said Rafiq. "I feel genuinely secure because of your devotion to Bant and to my safety."

"Sir."

"But I cannot divulge any reasons for my presence here. Please continue on the orders you've been given."

"Yes, sir!"

"Dismissed."

Rafiq felt a heavy weight on his heart—a literal one. Gleaming over his breast was a broad sigil, the face of the archangel Asha crossed with two swords, the sigil of patronage signifying his rank as Knight-General. His assigned mission in Esper was to strike a blow against the enemy by capturing or razing Palandius, a large city of Esper—a singularly daring and perilous maneuver. His personal quest was stranger, more occult, and far more dangerous.

BANT

Still in his bedchamber, Mubin looked up from the courier's letter, furious.

"He *left*? How could he leave?"

"Knight-General Rafiq said he'd expressed his reasons in that letter, sir," said the soldier. "Several small forces of Asha's Army have begun actually invading parts of Esper. It's seen as the proper strategy, not only to defend Bant, but to cleanse the entire new world of the enemy's forces."

Mubin wadded the letter up. "Damn fool. Damn, damn, damn, damn fool."

"Sir?"

"'My cherished friend,' he says. He goes on about 'magics in Esper' and 'exotic metals that perfect the body.' He'll be a corpse in a foreign land without me—and he's only going because of me. Me and my useless legs."

"He had orders to go," said the soldier.

"*We* had orders to go," said Mubin. "This mission, this thought of invasion, should have been off the minute I betrayed us all. This was not supposed to be a mission for one man."

"It won't be," said the soldier. "He took a contingent of elite soldiers and knights with him. He's the Knight-General, sir. He's leading the invasion of Esper; it's a glorious time for us."

"Dismissed," Mubin said, because there was nothing in reach to hurl at the soldier.

"Yes, sir," said the soldier. The door closed behind him.

The world spun around Mubin. In his mind's eye, he saw the entire plane of Bant as one continent floating on a vast sea of blackness. He saw Rafiq riding ahead of a legion of valiant soldiers to the edge of the world, marching in time, taking step by excruciating step with their heads held high, their eyes not watching for the cliff's edge, but scanning for angels in the heavens above them.

ESPER

The demon-dragon Malfegor strode across the white sandbanks of Esper, the deformed entourage of his undead army trudging and scuttling their way around him. The sky was odd in Esper, a bright hood of gray clouds for half the time, and a clear black basin littered with glittering lights for the other half. Thankfully, it was in the darker state, and Malfegor could detect faint lines of magic criss-crossing in a grid above him, as if painted directly on the sky. The wind blew in wild gusts, but the towering clouds moved only in rigid patterns, their volumes cut and shaped by hegemonic magics like razors in clay. The mages on Esper were obsessed with control and measurement, Bolas had said, never leaving anything to chance. To Malfegor, the whole plane seemed like a delicate toy obeying a lattice of arbitrary rules. Malfegor relished the opportunity to shatter as much of as it as it could as he made his way to the Bant frontier.

A ghostly gray silhouette, one of his undead infor-mants, floated up by his ear. "The Cliffs of Ot are dead ahead," whispered the ghost. "At this rate, we'll reach the tower of Palandius in four days."

"Not fast enough," Malfegor seethed. "Tell the necromancers we're doubling our pace. No rest for the wicked."

JUND

A jani would have been standing firmly on solid ground, the rocky, pyroclastic floor of Jund, had the ground not been suddenly perforated by an enormous, rubble-covered, sandstone step-pyramid from his home world of Naya. He would have reflected on that, and how physically nonsensical it was, had he not been suddenly forced into the position of rolling down the steep and painful steps of that very pyramid as it erupted out of the surface of Jund. After he had managed to claw his way to a rough stop on those steps, he would have taken some time to catch his breath after his planeswalk and to sort out exactly what had happened with the worlds intermixing, had he not been suddenly surrounded by a clan of human warriors wielding obsidian-tipped longspears and crudely-constructed, two-handed greatswords.

"You're just what we've been looking for," said a muscular, broad-chested human man with braided hair.

● ● ● ● ●

"Sinzo, this is an excellent find," said Kresh.

Sinzo grinned and shook her spear in the air. The other warriors hooted with glee—they knew as well as Kresh did, the white cat-man was a sign meant for them.

Ajani looked stunned, but not injured.

"Are you a ghost?" asked Kresh. "Are you the ghost of this temple of the underworld?"

"No," said the white cat. "But I do come from another world."

The warriors murmured and nodded to each other.

"Are we to hunt you, then?" asked Kresh. "Or do we follow you, as a guide, to our fates?"

The white cat blinked. It didn't look sure, which was strange. How could it travel all the way from the underworld, or whatever spirit-world it came from, and not be sure?

"I will lead you," the cat-man said.

"Excellent," Kresh said, and the warriors shouted their assent. "Where is it you will lead us, O death-guide? To the highest peak of the Boiling Slopes? Into the mouth of Varakna, deepest of the tar-swamps?"

"Well, I was hoping that maybe you could help me with that," said the cat. "I'm looking for a particular dragon."

"Ahh," marveled Kresh. "You are a powerful spirit indeed. You bring us on our final, our *greatest* Life Hunt. Truly, it is fitting. We shall meet good deaths on the hunt for the grandest species of life in the world."

"So you know the dragon of which I speak? A dragon called Bolas?"

"Bow-loz? Boh-loss," said Kresh. "I've heard this name. Some have claimed to see the dragon made of shadow blot out the sky."

"You know where he is?"

"No. But I know a shaman who does."

It was a lucky day, Kresh thought. He might be able to take vengeance on Rakka after all.

ESPER

The aven Kaeda returned from his sortie near the Esper city of Palandius, a small contingent of other soldiers and mages returning with him. Rafiq noted that he carried an object with him, a container. Perhaps they had actually succeeded.

"Scout Kaeda, report," said Knight-General Rafiq.

"Sir, the mission went well. We located a group of Esperites who were transporting something—something that I believe is just what you were looking for." The aven scout set down the heavy metal chest and smoothed down his flight feathers. The dunes of white sand provided good natural cover, but Rafiq knew that Esper's winds blew the grit directly into his aven scouts' wings.

"Take a look at your little present," said Kaeda. The scout cocked his head and pointed his beak in a characteristically aven way, a gesture signifying the equivalent of a smile. He kicked the heavy chest at his feet.

Rafiq grinned with pride. "I hope you didn't spend too much. All right, all right, open it already! The suspense is eating me up."

The chest was mostly one solid piece of weathered, dark metal. Kaeda ran his talon over an ornate rune on the top, and a seam appeared around its middle.

239

"It took us a while to figure out how to open the thing. It takes a little practice."

The aven pulled the top half off of the chest. Inside was an object wrapped in a healthy amount of cool blue silk cloth. Kaeda moved the cloth to reveal a chunk of brilliant red crystal, about the size of Rafiq's head. The crystal looked razor-sharp, with an inferno of reflected light glinting in its heart. It looked like the blood of a god.

Rafiq's grin gave way to open-mouthed amazement. "This is the red rock? The ingredient required for making the Esper metal?"

"Carmot. Yes, we think so. There was a small transport approaching Palandius with the chest. A mage, some soldiers, some little blue-skinned things. They are sure gonna be angry when they wake up. The experiences your friend Mubin shared with us, his insights into their mind attacks, were invaluable."

"That's good. All right. Take us to our little sleepers. I want to be there when they wake up."

Kaeda cocked his head and pointed his beak. "Yes, sir."

● ● ● ● ●

The mage Drimma, before she became the first Esperite ever to be captured by Bant, had studied the Noble Work her entire life. The Noble Work was a grand project, handed down by the wise sphinxes, to perfect all life on Esper by infusing it with the magical alloy known as etherium. Etherium extended one's lifespan and refined one's savage impulses, and made Esper a superior, more satisfyingly controlled world in general.

The convergence of Esper with the foreign planes was certainly a shock. The scholars hadn't predicted it, and if the sphinxes knew it would happen, they hadn't spread that fact to the human and vedalken communities. That no foreknowledge of that violent, world-shaking event had arisen was unthinkable, and it had shaken common trust in the Hegemon and all the other minds in charge. Drimma's own mind fluttered with a mixture of unstifled emotions, as confused about the world as she had been in her childhood.

On the other hand, the influx of exotic materials from the fronts had revitalized her life's work. Etherium stores on Esper had all but dried up across the entire plane, and most believed that the formula for creating more of the magical metal was lost to time. However, a sect of scholars claimed to have attained knowledge of the miraculous recipe, and were conducting experiments to try to reproduce the alloy. Substances not found anywhere on Esper were flooding in as soldiers captured caches of valuables along Esper's fronts. The prospect of actually creating an ingot of new, not recycled etherium electrified her.

That was how Drimma found herself and her entourage of prosaics and homunculi transporting a chunk of Jundian ore, the material they called carmot, to the Cliffs of Ot. And that was how she found herself overcome by bandit bird-men from Bant.

"Wake up, sleepyhead," said a deep-voiced man in a strange accent.

Drimma's eyelids cracked open. She scowled up at the faces around her. Oh, yes, she thought—those were the warriors of Bant who had ensorcelled her with clumsy sleep magics. It was embarrassing that they had managed to get the upper hand on her.

She glanced around. Her prosaics and homunculi were motionless on the sand—still out cold, or dead. The man who had spoken, apparently their leader, had a hawk-humanoid and a small force of human soldiers with him.

"What do you want," she croaked at them, enunciating precisely so that they would understand.

"I am Rafiq of the Many, Knight-General of Bant," said the man. His hair was cropped close to his head, and he was encased in armor of solid metal. A burnished medallion depicting a woman's face hung over his breast. "And we want the secret of etherium."

"That's rather progressive of you," Drimma said. "But I'm not surprised you want to stop wearing all your metal on the *out*side."

The man chuckled. It sounded peculiar coming from an adult. "It's not for us. We just want to know how to make it, and use it, for . . . our injured, back on Bant."

"That would be impossible. This war has cost us much in resources and manpower. There is not enough etherium even for our own people."

The man looked at her etherium enhancements, the filigree whorls and matrices in her neck and upper arms. "But you can make more. We have the red crystal you were transporting, to prove it."

"Etherium would be wasted on you; you're an unenlightened people," she said. "You don't know how to control your impulses, or your subjects, or your world. You're imprecise, untuned, unbalanced. You don't know what to do with what you have. But we do."

"That's why you fight us? To claim our resources?"

"Very specific resources. We take your lands to procure the materials that Esper requires, to continue our Noble Work."

Rafiq looked her right in the eyes. "You'll fail in this war," he said after a moment. "Ours is the side of justice. Where is the—"

Drimma closed her eyes. The conversation was going nowhere. She was outnumbered and surrounded; better to be patient, and wait for an opening to outwit them. "Justice is impotent in the face of prophecy," she said quietly. "Our scholars have always prophesied our victory. The Filigree Texts have always said so."

"And yet, so have our ancient prayers," said the man of Bant. "Put her to sleep again."

As Drimma lost consciousness once more, she heard the Bant creatures' voices trail off.

"Take her away," Rafiq told his soldiers. "But keep her alive. We have some very specific questions for her later. Load up this crystal and take it back to Bant. Deliver our reconnaissance to Aarsil the Blessed."

"What will the rest of us do, sir?"

"You're coming with me to the next horizon.. There we must be the eyes of Asha—and if necessary, her sword."

THE BLIND
ETERNITIES

DOUG BEYER

✺

The five worlds, floating together in the chaos of the Blind Eternities, were not just neighbors, but were siblings. They were all shards of a larger world, the plane of Alara, whose essence had been split five ways centuries before. For reasons Ajani never knew, the shards of Alara had broken like the colors through a prism, and traveled away from one another for a long time. And the shards had slowed in their respective journeys, and begun a return trip back to each other again. It may have been due to the way the mana fractured across the five; they couldn't live without one another. It may have been due to the efforts of some deep force that pulled their centers to one another, something like the force that pushed water downstream and stones down the slopes of mountains. It could have been meant to be part of the very act that broke them apart, that the five pieces wouldn't become explosive detritus but missiles in five special orbits, destined to smash back into one another again.

Ajani didn't know what to make of destiny, nor of history. He had heard the visions of prophets and the declarations of traditionalists, all of who claimed to know how the future would be shaped. He didn't know whether they had claim to a piece of the truth or not. But he knew that nothing could assail what he saw before his eyes.

Against all the theories that said otherwise, and against all the institutions founded on assumptions contradicted by those phenomena, stood the basic facts.

Where once there were five worlds, there was one.

JUND

After Rakka had introduced Sarkhan to her draconic master, she returned to her mission of spreading her master's war. She traveled the understory of Jund, seeking out other clans to spread her prophecy to. She stayed with the Ripclan Tol Durek clan for a few nights, and told them the story of the first Life Hunt, and told them that the Life Hunt tradition was soon to enter a new phase. She fed them exactly the lines that her master told her to feed them, and their minds devoured the words like starving whelps. She moved on to the Nel Toth clan, and they gorged themselves on her words as well. The words had a power to them, an almost-music that sounded to every listener like the echoes of long-bygone days of glory. Rakka didn't have to embellish on the stories to make them ring clear and true; everywhere she went she met people unknowingly poised on the edge of conversion.

When the tremors came, of course, ripping the edges of the world and merging with the other planes, it did help. As terrifying as the changes were to Rakka personally, they did serve to back up her story to powerful effect.

Bolas had told her that there would be some sign of the next phase of his plans, and that she would know it when it came. She fretted a bit that she had never pressed him for more detail, but when the Eternal Crags trembled,

DOUG BEYER

broke, and fell into dust, exposing a shadowy, alien world beyond it, she had to admit that, as signs went, that one was impressively unambiguous.

Days after the Crags fell, she walked among the rubble, looking to discover, finally, what her master might have wrought in the places beyond the boundaries of her world. The going was hard, but she summoned elementals to push through the debris, and carved a satisfactory path into the heart of where the mountains once were. The destruction ran in a rough line, hewn to an invisible boundary as far as the eye could see in either direction. She had reached it—where Jund ended, and some other world began. When she reached the junction point, she gasped. The volcanic sediment of her native Jund gave way to flats of a gray, hard-packed substance like clay, flecked with bits of . . . dead matter. Decomposing beings lurched and crawled across the landscape—but the stench was the first enemy to cross the border.

It was Grixis, the purported home of her master. Somehow she had expected something a little more . . . regal. Whenever Bolas visited her, his presence overwhelmed her. The sensation of power positively dripped from him, the aura of a monarch who ruled a vast empire. But that place, his home, was a corpse. What would drive him to lair there? Surely, if Bolas was capable of traveling to Jund and presumably other places, he could retreat to someplace more fitting his personal magnitude.

Still, the tang of black mana that clung to the dragon was also unmistakable in Grixis. As her own elemental magic thrived in the fiery cauldron of Jund, so must his flourish there. The dragon terrified and fascinated her when he came to her world; he must be a god there, she thought.

NAYA

Looking over the panorama of the world of Naya, Sarkhan shook his head dismissively.

Naya had never experienced an attack by a dragon. It wasn't as if massive creatures were foreign to it; the gargantuans native to Naya destroyed their share of its jungles just by walking around, garnering them reverence with almost every culture on the plane. But the footfalls of meandering gargantuans were not adequate preparation for an assault by a dragon.

Jund's dragons were specially adapted to dealing with difficult game. They survived on fast-moving goblins, human warriors with swords and scale-piercing spears, and the incredibly tough and stubborn viashino. The dragons had perfected a death-plunge maneuver that allowed them to scoop hordes of fleeing humanoids in a single gulp, becoming such experts at the maneuver that they could execute it while strafing any terrain from wide volcanic flats to jagged peaks—which is why most denizens of Jund huddled in the sheltered lowlands, away from their ravaging jaws.

On Naya, the foliage was thick but eminently flammable. There were no jagged chasms between mountain peaks.

As Jund and Naya overlapped one another, serrated peaks from Jund sliced through Naya's understory and gushed lava into its glades. Meanwhile huge stands of trees and vine-covered step pyramids from Naya lanced up through Jund's highlands. Any pockets of civilization that had once thrived in the intermingled areas were crushed immediately. The areas of overlap became dead zones, filled with ruins and corpses.

Sarkhan had begun summoning his personal flight of dragons as soon as he mustered the mana for the spell. Maybe the dragons were a gift from a cold, calculating dragon planeswalker, but the fact remained that they were a flight of dragons under his control. If that was somehow a disgrace, Sarkhan had never enjoyed disgrace more.

The first dragon he summoned for his army was the immense male hellkite, Karrthus. He was almost stately in his bearing, a crown of horns encircling his head and a single sharp spike curving downward from his chin. He thrashed about impatiently, as if he were already ready to lay waste to Naya all by himself.

"I know how you feel," Sarkhan said to the beast. "We're weapons waiting to be unsheathed, you and I. I don't know Bolas's scheme, but at least he's unafraid of putting us to good use. It's been so long since I've been at war—I'm eager to test my edge in battle."

The dragon turned his head to the sky and bellowed, punctuating the roar with a blast of fire.

Sarkhan reached out into Jund and into his other mana bonds for more mana. One by one, he summoned dragon after dragon, amassing a force large enough to raze a world.

BANT

"What's the meaning of this?" demanded Gwafa Hazid. "I've been detained for days."

"You're coming out so that I can ask you some questions," said Elspeth Tirel, unlocking his cell. "And you're going to answer them. Come on."

Elspeth's injuries had kept her from returning to the front lines immediately. But she had convinced the cleric to release her to Valeron, to see Hazid. She knew he could be a link to the worlds beyond Bant—and a key to the threats behind the war.

"These proceedings are . . . are out of order," said Hazid. "I'll say nothing without a Sighted-caste in the room with us. I know the statutes."

Elspeth took him by the arm into a small room. A rhox was seated there in white robes. "Gwafa Hazid, this is the monk Hollin. He's of Sighted caste and will be monitoring our conversation."

"I . . . No. It's not good enough. I demand someone else."

"You must be very interested in delaying this conversation, Hazid," said Elspeth. "But it won't work. This proceeding is perfectly lawful—which you well know, since you know the statutes, as you say."

Hazid grimaced with disgust and sat down.

"Please state your name and title," said Elspeth.

DOUG BEYER

Hazid sighed. "Gwafa Hazid, master merchant of the Grand Caravan," he said.

Elspeth glanced at the monk. He nodded.

"Were you at Giltspire Castle six weeks ago?" asked Elspeth.

"My caravan goes through there every few months. I had the proper permits."

"Was your caravan carrying materials for a demolitions spell?"

"How should I know?" said Hazid. "Have you ever *seen* my caravan? It's vast. We carry thousands of pieces of merchandise. I can't be expected to know every last thing in those wagons."

Elspeth glanced at the monk again. He shook his head solemnly.

"You don't seem to believe that, Hazid," said Elspeth. "You've got a guilty conscience, haven't you? You were going to Giltspire *in order* to destroy it, weren't you?"

"No! That place was falling apart. Everybody knows that. It was unstable, and you can ask any stonemason. My mages only cast a standard charm of good luck in commerce. The place fell down without us."

Elspeth looked at the monk.

The rhox monk leaned in and whispered in her ear. "It's hard to say," he said. "He truly seems to believe he's not at fault."

"Can we compel him to tell the truth?" Elspeth whispered back.

The monk looked shocked. I guess not, Elspeth thought.

He whispered, "That magic has been illegal since before I was born."

"All right," Elspeth exhaled. She looked back at Hazid. "Who put you up to this?" she asked him.

"I told you, we were just there to trade. Maybe our 251

commerce spell accidentally backfired, and loosened something in the structure—"

"The materials we found in your caravan were *not* a money-luck spell, Hazid. They were a stoneworking spell meant for the deconstruction of architecture, illegal to possess except by certain masons of the Mortar caste."

"Then it was a conspiracy," said Hazid. "I didn't know they had those."

"That's not what they said," said Elspeth. "They all had the same story. You assembled them in particular for this trip to Giltspire. You gave them all the scrolls and rehearsed the ritual. They all said that you're the ring-leader here."

"They're lying," said Hazid. "They all want me framed for this."

"They were *horrified*, Hazid," said Elspeth. "They didn't know what was happening until it was over. Most of them wept during our interviews when we told them how many people died in the disaster. What do you *say* to that?"

"It wasn't me, I swear," said Hazid. "I—I had nothing against Giltspire. I'm a merchant. Why would I want to do something like that? It wasn't me. It wasn't my idea."

The monk nodded at Elspeth.

"I believe you, Hazid," said Elspeth. "I do. It doesn't make any sense, does it? You're a rich, powerful merchant. You've always skirted the law before. Why do something so blatantly destructive? It flies in the face of reason."

"Yes! Thank you. I couldn't be responsible. It flies in the face of reason! It must have been a fluke. Wrong place at the wrong time, that kind of thing. Just a big misunderstanding."

Elspeth put her hand on the arm of the rhox monk. "Hollin, thank you for your guidance today. I'd like you to step out now."

The rhox was taken aback. Astonishment was never easy to read in a rhox's expression, but Elspeth could see traces of it in the monk's stony face.

"It's all right, Hollin," she said. "I'll be fine."

"It's not that. Elspeth, child, you can't ask him any questions without a Sighted here," the monk said. "You could . . . You could endanger the *conviction!*"

Hazid looked back and forth between the two of them. His lips formed the trace of a smirk.

Elspeth was firm. "Thank you. But I'll apprise you of any questions I ask Mr. Hazid at a later time. Please go."

The rhox registered one last complaint into Elspeth's gaze, but disengaged. He shot a look at Hazid, who knew enough to look away, and walked out, shutting the door behind him.

"Wanted some one-on-one time, did you?" said Hazid, amused.

"Yes I did," said Elspeth.

Hazid grinned and leaned toward her. "That's good. I work best this way. Head to head. Trader to trader."

"Sit back, Mr. Hazid. I'm going to ask you some strange-sounding questions. I require your honesty here. Your answers could be of grave importance not just to your own situation, but to all of Bant."

Hazid's grin melted. "Why? What do you mean?"

"Have you recently been in contact with anyone . . . strange? Anyone who you thought might be from a foreign land?"

Hazid scoffed. "No lands are foreign to me. I've been all over Bant."

Elspeth blinked. "You haven't heard, have you?"

"Heard what? They tell me nothing in that stupid cell."

"Never mind. You're well-traveled, as you say, so you're in a position to know. Who have you talked to?

The plan with the demolition spell. Did someone put you up to that?"

"I—" Hazid stopped himself. His eyes moved all around the room, resting briefly on everything but Elspeth.

"Who was it?"

"I can't tell you," said Hazid. "It sounds crazy."

"Try me. Many others wouldn't understand, which is why I dismissed Hollin. But I'll believe you."

"I can't. He . . . He promised I would die if I told anyone."

"I can protect you."

Hazid chuckled. It wasn't a happy sound. "Not from him."

"Hazid," said Elspeth. "Do you know anything about the tremors we've felt lately? And the storms?"

"I know nothing." His eyes were round. "But I suspect."

"What do you suspect?"

"I know it's him. He's coming for me. He promised me such power—but he tricked me and made me ruin the castle. There's only doom for me now. He said he would come for me, to take me away from the consequences. Now I know he won't save me. He's used me."

"Who?"

"*The dragon.*"

BANT

Mubin studied the passages in the prayer book. Manually copied in a neat hand, the ink seemed to march across and down the page. The language of prophecy wasn't fluid and poetic, but rather quite particular, creating the impression that the author had stared directly at the future, and struggled to reproduce it with faithful precision. Surprisingly, for being called the Prayer of Asha, the prophecy mentioned Asha almost as an afterthought, attributing to her the role of savior after war had already broken out.

Most of all, the prayer urged unity. Mubin would normally have found the ideal pleasant; Bant's road of history had been paved with regular battles of territory and trade. But the unity was couched in language of war. It was the unity of a military force assembled to strike down a vague foe, not the unity of a community in harmony. It was the unity of a world too fearful to greet, and too eager to destroy.

The Prayer of Asha, he decided, asked for Bant to come together like fingers in a fist.

Mubin realized where he had heard the prayer before. The word choice, the meter, the imagery—it was familiar, And he finally grasped where he had seen it last.

He picked up the small copper bell on the side table and rung it. The noise was frustratingly pathetic.

He waited. No one came.

He had to get across the country, *that day*, he thought, and that was what he was reduced to? The little prayer bell mocked him. He was a grown rhox, hundreds of pounds of solid muscle, and he couldn't walk to the door, get on his steed, and ride where he needed to go.

He looked up at the window. It was at eye level, for a standing person, across the room on the opposite wall. Daylight and a scene of serene trees shone through it, and the promise of being heard. That window was the key.

He threw the bell at the window. It bounced off the glass and landed on the floor with a jangling sound. The thin copper instrument just didn't have enough mass to crack the glass.

He would have to drag himself across the floor, and then raise himself up somehow.

"I can do it," he said to himself.

He leaned over the side of the bed and pulled on the headboard, lurching his body to the edge of the bed. He craned an arm out to reach the floor, and his weight slumped partway onto it He was poised delicately halfway out of the bed, halfway on the floor. The muscles in his arm strained.

By inching his arm farther out, he pulled his bulk closer to the verge of the drop-off. He lifted his hips, pulled them, and rested them again, so that they teetered on the edge.

He inhaled and exhaled, and steeled his resolve.

He pushed off the bed, letting his hips and legs fall. His lower body was dead weight; it free-fell to the hard wooden floor, smacking down loudly. He expected pain, but felt none—it just looked bad. His legs looked strange, having fallen haphazardly against each other. He straightened them with his hands, and then he collapsed, heaving breaths.

Why couldn't they just hear the damned bell? On the other hand, why had he given up on the tiny, tinkling instrument so quickly? He could be resting comfortably in bed, ringing its little heart out, waiting for a cleric to come. Instead he was on the floor, and the bell was on the other side of the room somewhere.

He needed to go. There was no time for him to waste feeling sorry for himself.

He eyed the window. He pushed up on his elbows, then with a mighty shove, flopped himself over onto his stomach. He was facing the wall at the head of the bed, opposite the window. He did a push-up, then began moving hand over hand in a gradual arc around to the opposite wall.

His legs trailed after him. He was useless on land, he thought. He should just drag himself to the ocean and become a fish, flopping his tail about in the sea.

He pushed himself up onto his arms, then collapsed forward onto his face, gaining a few inches. He performed the ritual over and over again. When did he become so incredibly heavy?

Next came the hard part. His head was below the window, and the glass was high out of reach. Perhaps he should just gore the wall with his horn, he thought. If he missed the stud, he could probably make it through the layers of wood and shingle in an hour or so, and the sound might be enough to attract someone.

No good. It was the window or nothing.

He turned back to the bed, facing the foot, a few feet from the wall with the window. The bed's nearest post was tall enough that if he could lift his weight on it, he could probably fall toward the wall and reach the window.

He grasped the bedpost, got a firm grip, and pulled. The bed skidded toward him.

Mubin blurted out three select and deeply obscene

words. For a moment, he actually hoped there were no clerics within earshot.

He would have to do it carefully. If he could lean in to the bedpost, and pull himself close enough to the post to push most of his weight down onto it, he could lift himself instead of just moving the bed. He pulled hard.

His upper half rose fairly easily, but as soon as he began to budge his lower half, it became far harder. He grabbed again, hand over hand, and lurched his weight up the corner of the bed. He hung on to the top of the bedpost, supporting his weight solely with his arms, his legs dangling limp.

He would drop soon. It was now or never.

With only a quick glance over at the window, he lunged. He successfully grabbed the windowsill and slumped against the wall, pulling hard to prevent his body weight from dragging him right back down to the floor again.

Would he be able to manipulate the window latch while holding his bulk with one hand? He craned his neck to see. Of course, there was no latch on the window—it was just a simple pane of thick glass fused into the frame. That made the decision easy, then.

He let go of the windowsill with one hand, and before he fell to the floor, he made a fist and smashed it through the window. The crash made an exquisite sound, an unmistakable sound of emergency and desperation that rang out across the meadows around the tiny recuperative cabin. He caught his weight on the window opening, his wrist crunching against broken glass. He hung there for a moment before his arms gave out and he collapsed back onto the floor in a painful thud, his hand bleeding.

Nothing. Then, footsteps came faintly, then stronger, crunching up the trail outside.

The door unlocked and opened. A cleric looked in and surveyed the scene. He found the bed pulled diagonally out of position, the bedclothes off kilter. He found Mubin sitting under the window in a heap, his hand balled in a fist, trickling blood.

"Get me a wagon," Mubin said.

Shock slowed the cleric's response. "What?" he finally said.

"I said, get me a wagon."

"You can't . . . You need your rest. You're supposed to—"

"As a paragon of the Sigiled caste, and as a knight of the Order of the Reliquary, and as a nobly-appointed scholar and champion of the Blessed caste of Bant, I command you to bring a wagon, *right . . . now.*"

The cleric blinked. "Yes, my lord, right away."

He ran off, and Mubin allowed himself a sigh of relief.

NAYA

At Mayael's behest, the godcaller elves had assembled a host of Naya's gargantuan beasts. The colossal creatures had trampled a clearing in the wood, letting the sun shine down upon them with no canopy in the way. The destruction of the trees had affected some elvish residences, but Mayael, as the spiritual leader of the elves, had insisted. She looked down on the assembled throng from the sunsail tents that served as her chambers, listening to their grunts and bellows echo throughout the jungle.

Her attendant entered, the girl's hands clasped in disquiet.

"Anima," said the attendant. "May I have a word?"

Mayael looked up. "Of course, Sasha."

"This is wrong," whispered the attendant. "Forgive me," she added hastily.

"What is?" asked Mayael. "Speak up."

"No, it's not my place."

"I can't have you holding something from me, Sasha. Loose your tongue."

"I—I know you're . . . You believe in what you're doing, Anima. But I can't help feeling that this is wrong. Assembling this army is . . . blasphemy. The gargantuans are not ours to order around like this. They're Naya's *gods*. Who are we to send our gods off to fight some unknown war for us?"

"They're not fighting it for us; they'll be fighting it with us. And it's not for some frivolous cause. Do you think I would call them this way, were these not the direst of times? This is the word of Progenitus! This is a time of prophecy, the crux of the meaning of our very civilization. This is the time that we need the gargantuans most, and they need us."

"But what if we're wrong? What if this is not the way?"

Mayael's eyes narrowed. "My vision said it was. *Now* who's being blasphemous?"

"I'm sorry, Anima. Of course you know best."

Mayael's face relaxed. She sighed. "No, I am sorry. Here I ask you to tell me what you're thinking, and then snap at you for telling it. The strange thing is, you're mirroring my very thoughts. I know this war is far away from us, and that we've seen no evidence of it. If it turns out there's nothing behind my fears, then I risk singlehandedly alienating us from the gods. And yet, if it is true that war comes to Naya, then of course I'm hesitant to call the gargantuans to perform such a dangerous task. You see? You're sensing the same problem that I've been wrestling with since the vision at the Relic. If we don't act, all could be lost. If we do, all could be lost. If I seem not myself, it's because these burdens weigh heavily on me."

Her attendant nodded. Mayael's eyes still had some of the white clouds in them from the day at the Relic. Did she still see the vision, even in her waking life?

They heard a chorus of upset snorts, and then shouting. They looked down at the army of gargantuans. The beasts were skittish, braying and scuffing the ground with their massive claws, tearing great gouges in the earth. The godcaller elves were yelling and pointing off into the circle of sky above the clearing.

261

There was a cloud of small shadows in the sky. Creatures were flying toward them.

"What is it? A flock of birds?" asked Sasha.

"No. Bigger. Far bigger," said Mayael.

"Are they a threat? Something we should worry about?"

The look on the Anima's face gave her the answer.

"Your clarion, Anima." Sasha indicated the long trumpet hanging from the tree trunk nearby.

Mayael didn't respond. The flying creatures neared. They looked like winged lizards—but as large as a god.

Sasha shook her mistress's shoulder. "Anima, sound the clarion!"

Mayael stared up at the flyers, her eyes clouded with white. For Sasha's mistress, the visions of prophecy and her everyday vision had become one and the same.

Sasha raised the clarion, put her lips to the mouthpiece, and blew as hard as she could.

NAYA

Sarkhan surveyed Naya from his perch on the back of the hellkite, Karrthus, at the lead of a flight of other dragons. Seas of green raced below them, the heads of trees rippling in gentle winds. Mist-rimmed mountains moved slowly in the distance, like the bald heads of stern giants who watched them streak across the sky.

Karrthus flew ahead of the rest of the flight. Sarkhan felt the dragon's arrogant pride at being the head of the pack, which stoked his heart. What greater joy could one feel, man or beast, at being used for one's true purpose? And what greater service could he himself provide, than to crush a world with the unleashed power of a flight of dragons?

"Let's start with this valley of trees, Karrthus," said Sarkhan.

Karrthus inhaled, and blasted a cone of fire down on the trees. His dragonfire coated the canopy branches, swallowing them in fire instantly. The dragons behind them followed suit, breathing fire at random. Occasionally Sarkhan would look back to see birds flying out of the smoke of the burned areas, or arboreal mammals skittering away from the swathe of fire the dragons left in their wake. Most of them died, roasted alive when the flames spread hungrily outward from the flight's streak of fire.

Sarkhan didn't bother trying to establish mana bonds to the place. The world of Naya surged with mana of nature and growth, but the charred remains of his forest fires would stifle the mana production there. Besides, he thought, why stop the fun? He was making his mark.

As the flight approached the edge of the valley and the wall of mountains, he willed Karrthus to turn back around. The dragons' wings tilted and grabbed full sails of air to shoot up into Naya's sunny sky, then curved back around to do another pass.

That's when Sarkhan saw the first signs of Naya's resistance.

Three woolly-furred behemoths had risen above the treeline to bring their massive hooves down on the fires. Their bulk was so vast that they stomped the fire out even as they crushed the trees that were its fuel.

That would not stand.

"Karrthus," he said, "someone's trying to interfere with our plans. Let's interfere with theirs."

Sarkhan led the flight of dragons straight at the behemoths. They did a single breath pass, strafing the beasts and the trees around them with cones of fire. The last dragon in the flight strafed a little low, and one of the beasts was able to thrust its head into the air, catching the dragon with its nose-horn. The horn tore a generous wound in the dragon's chest, sending it diving into the trees. The dragon crunched through the branches and broke a few solid trunks to splinters before it came to a rest against a fat splay-rooted tree, dead.

The behemoths shook their shaggy coats, and the ashen cinders broke off them, leaving their skin smoky but unburned. At Sarkhan's signal, the dragons circled back around.

"Karrthus, avoid the one with the nose-horn. Dive on that one, there. The rest of you, more fire! Attack at will!"

The other dragons laid into two of the behemoths with a combination of fire breath and swooping attacks with their talons. Karrthus dived, then flipped his body toward the beast with a sudden, great flex of his wings. Sarkhan clutched at his bindings as the dragon's body lurched, barely holding on. Their victim roared and tried to bite at the dragon, but Karrthus's talons clamped into its back. Then Karrthus gave one, two, three mighty wing-strokes, and heaved the behemoth into the air. It wriggled like a fish in a bird's claws, but couldn't pull free. Sarkhan gave no orders, but Karrthus knew what he was doing. He flew up, up, up, and then as the hellkite's wings were about to fail from the strain, he released the beast. It actually rose briefly, flung in a modest arc, but then plummeted silently, falling away in a slow motion tumble. Sarkhan didn't see it land in the jungle, but the impact caused a tremor wave that radiated out through the valley.

As Karrthus wheeled around, Sarkhan looked back at the other dragons, to see one behemoth have a chunk bitten out of it, and the other get burned to a crisp by two streams of fire breath. The beasts fell, and the dragons reassembled into a flight with no further casualties.

"Serves those things right," Sarkhan said. Where did these beasts come from, he wondered? He knew they were allied with those who occupied the central part of Naya.

"Come on, my pets. We're going to pay the elves a visit."

THE
MAELSTROM

At the heart of Alara, above a spiral-shaped depression in the crushed earth, floated a sphere of energy. It was much bigger than a grain of sand; it would be an armful to a human, if it were able to be held. Misty lines of color spiraled into it from all directions, and the colors churned inside of it. Slowly, day by day, battle by battle, spell by spell, it grew.

JUND

Ajani's native Naya had tropical jungles, but Jund's forests were a primordial, carnivorous morass. Kresh and his warriors had their weapons out, and were hacking at the snake ferns that were trying to wrap around their ankles and the carnivorous orchids that kept biting them with sticky thorn "teeth." Some sort of chameleon latched its tongue onto Kresh, but he sliced it cleanly in half and kept moving.

Ajani walked among the human warriors behind Kresh, their braid-haired leader. He cleared his throat. "So . . . You're sure it's this way to this woman, Rakka?" Ajani asked.

Kresh stopped and took a casual look around, as if the question hadn't occurred to him. "We're not far," he said, and continued walking.

Kresh didn't seem the least bit curious where Ajani had come from, or what he was doing on his world. He seemed perfectly content to let Ajani stay a symbol, a spirit guide, rather than a person unto himself.

"What's Rakka like?" he asked the warrior leader. "Should I prepare magic for her?"

"Just know this: Rakka is a traitor. Her heart is strong and fickle—a dangerous combination. But you're our talisman, white cat. You're our pole star. You'll sway fate's favor in what I'm sure will be a mighty battle."

The warriors grunted in agreement around them.

"I doubt I'll sway any such thing, Kresh. I do not wish to be anyone's talisman. But I'm glad to have you by my side."

Ajani couldn't figure out the human, Kresh, leader of the Antaga clan. The man had a sureness of self that seemed out of place in Jund, where danger stalked everything that breathed every moment of the day. He made no plans—he just seemed to take every moment as it came, confident in his ability to conquer each moment after the next. Ironically, nothing seemed to surprise him because he never formed any prior expectations. In a way, it was an admirable quality, Ajani thought, if occasionally jarring to be around.

"The dead have begun to walk the earth," said Kresh flatly, looking ahead. "Get your weapons ready."

A group of humanoid corpses shambled toward them, their putrid flesh hanging from their bones, their mouths distended, and their eye sockets rolling with expressionless orbs.

Ajani gripped his axe. They looked like awful parodies of human beings, and some other creatures Ajani couldn't recognize. It must be magic related to the creatures that killed Jazal.

When the undead creatures saw them, they stopped shambling, and charged.

ESPER
BANT FRONTIER

The demon Malfegor delighted equally in causing as much misery to his own forces as to those he conquered with his army. He enjoyed pulling on the metaphorical strings of power that branched out below him, reveling in the grim puppetry of the undead. If he weren't heading where he was heading, he would almost feel happy.

Esper had been something of a joke. Still flush with black mana to fuel his dark heart, its shard was conveniently structured around systems of control—hierarchies of mages and sphinxes—as if the place had been designed for a demon's whip. He wrested control of Esper's forces away from its mortal masters with only a modicum of torture and the simplest of promises, with few exceptions. One high-minded sphinx managed to meet his blazing glare and resist his temptations of power and corruption. Although Malfegor successfully slew or tempted away all of the sphinx's underlings, the creature did the smart thing—it fled with its life, disappearing into Esper's sculpted skies.

Truly, if he had to march across an entire world to get to Bant, Malfegor thought, then *Esper* was the world that he would choose to form the bridge. By the time he reached the frontier area where the crystal-sand dunes of Esper began to bleed into the fields of Bant, he had

269

doubled the size of his army. Etherium-infused drakes and sludge striders made admirable shock troops. And those human and vedalken archmages, properly tempted out of their mortal souls, made excellent lich lieutenants. He liked how their metallic enhancements exposed their minds to him, framed in etherium tracery. It let him observe directly the torment caused by his rule.

But he couldn't truly enjoy the march, due to its ultimate destination. The lands of Bant were not new to Malfegor, for he was a truly ancient demon. He remembered Alara when it was a single, complete world centuries before, and he had ruled with impunity then. He remembered when Alara split in five, tearing one aspect of Alara away from another, casting him into the depths of that subworld Grixis. And just before the world broke asunder, he remembered facing and destroying a beautiful archangel with a shining sword, in all his demonic life the one being who had come closest to slaying him.

GRIXIS

So this is the plan, Levac? Sit here and have this baby in this hovel, while the world shakes outside?"

Levac and his wife Salay had spent countless nights wandering Grixis's network of tunnels. They had eventually settled in an abandoned hermitage much smaller than the stronghold at Torchlight had been; but the wards were active, and the undead hordes had seemed to pass it over.

"No. I'll figure something out before the baby's born, Salay," said Levac. "But even if we're forced to have it here, you don't have to worry. I'll protect you and the baby."

"Like you protected Vali?"

That stung. It had been days or weeks since Vali disappeared into a mob of the walking dead. His screams had been the music of Levac's nightmares every night since. He thought he might actually be handling it worse than Salay, but he kept those emotions to himself.

Levac had never told his wife that Vali was still moving, still calling to him, when he ran away. The worst part was that he couldn't tell her that he knew that Vali had become one of the undead.

"I'll get us out of here. Things will be better. Tomorrow we make for the glow on the horizon, or the next day."

Grixis's sky had always been a tangle of electrical storms. But after a series of tremors in the earth, the far horizon had glimmered with an eerie blue light. The clouds in that direction were bright white and regular in shape, sliced evenly along invisible lines. It looked like a doorway into paradise, a promise of something better than their desperate lives, a promise of something better than Grixis itself. The thought that Levac's world might have an exit had forestalled his despair as they waited underground.

"You keep saying that. 'Things will be better. Tomorrow we'll escape.' Why the hell haven't we gotten out of this place? Tomorrow I'm leaving, with or without you."

It's what it feels like when a marriage is fraying, thought Levac. Back when Grixis was the only life they knew, back when they were certain that humanity would become extinct by the rotten hand of the undead, he and his wife were as close as two desperate people could be. Things had changed, and with the chance that they could get out of Grixis entirely, everything ignited a bitter argument. Even the rumor that other living humans—thousands of them—lived in the worlds beyond wasn't enough to bring hope to their days.

But in truth, it wasn't the strife of the colliding worlds that had come between them. Levac was sick with guilt about Vali; he had earned as much blame as Salay put on him.

Once, as the two of them had traveled across Grixis, Levac had seen his son. It was his son's same tunic, same hat, and the same leather short sword scabbard he had carved—but it was a Vali-shaped monster wearing them. He didn't dare tell Salay—it would destroy her. Instead he stalled, every day coming up with any reason he could think of not to make for that glow on the horizon, hoping against hope that there might be some way to reach his son, and somehow get him back.

There was the sound of wings outside the wooden

shack. Another one of the sickly-feathered kathari, probably. Levac looked out through a crack in the roof. Strangely, the kathari didn't have the characteristic bent neck and black feathers—its feathers were a vibrant mottled white and brown, and it wore shining metal armor across its breast. The bird-man circled once, cocking an eye down at their hiding place, and then flew off out of sight.

"What was it?" asked Salay.

Levac picked up his sword. "I'm not sure. Something . . . *new* is happening," he said.

JUND

K resh put the point of his sword through one of the undead, directly through its ribcage, a little to the side of its sternum. It was just another foe, right? At least it fell just like one, perhaps a little sloppier as it fell off the blade. And the gray ichor that came out of them stung the skin, but that was no different than the spit of a common thrinax that came from his own world. If the undead were the extent of the invasion into Jund, he felt he could probably handle it.

The truly upsetting thing about them was that, despite being dead, lying down seemed difficult for them.

"Kresh, behind you!" yelled the white-furred cat-man.

Kresh whirled blade-first, trusting the white cat implicitly, and sure enough, one of the walking corpses had stood back up after being gutted. The thing had been about to drag its claws down Kresh's back, and instead got four inches of heavy steel buried in its face. It fell—with the blade still in it. Kresh didn't bother retrieving his sword, but instead pivoted and elbowed another one of the things in the return motion, breaking its jaw. It didn't faze the thing. So he charged right into it, catching it in the chest and forcing it back onto the spiny growths of a nearby tukatongue tree. It didn't stop the undead creature from writhing or moaning, but it bound it up.

The cat-man was fighting with an undead creature whose face was more mouth than anything else, its eyes grafted into its shoulders. He was holding it off, but didn't see the two others rushing up from behind him.

"Ajani!" Kresh yelled, and ran to tackle one of them, but Ajani's next attack caused him to reconsider. He dove away just in time, as Ajani held his double-headed axe at the very end, right down by the near axe head, and swung it around above him. He roared, and the axe burst into . . . something like flame, but searing white. The weapon carved through all three undead creatures, incinerating their flesh like it was paper. They didn't get back up. Ajani kept swinging his axe, thrashing through the bodies until all the undead creatures had perished. He even finished off the one that was stuck to the tukatongue tree.

The warrior-leader and the nacatl exchanged a look. In other circumstances they might have grinned at each other, but they didn't quite.

"I like how you fight, white cat," said Kresh.

"So do I," said a voice. It came from the forest shadows somewhere up ahead. They all looked to try to discern its origin.

There was a clap of thunder. It rolled across the sky from the direction they had been traveling, up over their heads, and past them. There was the smell of ozone, and a buzzing, moaning sound.

Out of the darkness of the tukatongue wood stepped Rakka.

ESPER
GRIXIS FRONTIER

Ahead the terrain changes again, Knight-General," said Kaeda, Rafiq's aven scout.

"All right," said Rafiq. "What's your report?"

"You aren't going to like it."

Rafiq frowned. "Tell me."

The aven seemed nervous. Or shaken. It was hard for Rafiq to tell.

"It's . . . scabrous. The terrain looks like it's smelled for the last hour. There are hills of bone and flesh. The whole place is rotting in on itself."

"Is it some sort of mass grave?"

"No. It's more like the entire land itself is a grave. I flew for an hour into the interior of the place. It just goes on and on like that."

What in Asha's name? Were they marching into hell? "What's the enemy situation?" asked Rafiq.

"There are swarms of dead creatures, like we've seen crossing over into the last region, Esper. They're definitely originating from the place ahead of us, and they're definitely an invasion force."

"An invasion force? What's their source?"

"We can't tell from here. We'd need deeper reconnaissance."

"Leadership?"

"Mages, most of them apparently also undead—clearly

powerful. But mainly, some other, larger creatures appear to be in charge."

"What creatures?"

"I'm not sure I have a word for them, Knight-General. Frankly, they look like demons."

Demon. The word was archaic to Rafiq's ears, a tattered remnant from ancient scripture. It was a word found only toward the end of the Prayer of Asha.

"Well, it's not something we have the forces to fight."

"Yes, sir."

"Gear up, soldiers. We've got the materials we needed from Esper, and the information we needed from the world on the other side. Now we're needed at home. It's time to return to Bant, and rejoin the main force of Asha's Army."

"Sir, there's one more thing," said Kaeda.

"What is it?"

"There's a small shack just past the frontier, just inside the dead lands. There appears to be living humans hiding in it, possibly a small family."

JUND

As Ajani watched, the human woman stepped out from the shadows between the trees of Jund's thorny undergrowth, malice swirling in her eyes. She was an older human, wiry-looking but sickly thin; her teeth were blackened points. Her eye sockets were deep, her lips were thin and dry, and her bare arms looked like sticks coming out of her shaman's tunic. Still, Ajani could feel the power emanating off her. Her hair stood out from her head slightly, as if she were a frightened animal, but she didn't look frightened. Branching rivers of bluish light played down her bony arms and arced between her fingers.

"You look bad, Rakka," snarled Kresh. "You've been dipping into some wicked magics. And treachery was ugly enough on you."

Kresh was stepping slowly toward her. He angled his head to pop a joint in his neck, and he collected a sword from a fallen comrade. He was going to kill her, Ajani realized.

"I need her alive, Kresh," Ajani warned.

"You're worse than a pawn, Kresh," Rakka said. "You're the pawn who thinks he's the sovereign. That's of no use to anybody." She stepped forward toward him, her hands crackling. "If you were smarter, smart enough to understand your stupidity, then there could be a place for you in my master's world, or in mine. We could find you quite useful. But as it is"—she continued stepping forward—"you'll serve me much better *dead*."

Rakka thrust her arms forward, discharging a bolt of lightning directly into Kresh. The bolt hit him like a charging animal; the impact lifted him off the ground and threw him back two body lengths. He landed on the ground and rolled to a stop, face down.

Ajani rushed over to him and knelt down beside him. The man was alive, but his body trembled and twitched. There was a black mark on his back, from which wafted a wisp of ugly-smelling smoke.

Kresh's warriors pointed spears straight at Rakka.

"Hold it," Ajani told them, and they didn't advance.

Ajani looked up at the shaman. "This ends here," he said to her. "You'll stand down, and then you'll tell me what I need to know." He knelt there with his hand on Kresh, trying to call upon the sun-drenched glades of Naya as he spoke. "Or I'll add you to the trail of bodies I've left behind me."

"I've not seen your kind, otherworlder," she said. She folded her hands and looked him up and down. "But I can see the strength in you. You've got a deep spirit—it feels a bit like another being I know."

Ajani's fingers touched Kresh's back. He could feel the burn wound ripped inside of him, traveling all the way through the man's body. He sent a spell into the man, and felt the tissues realigning and the organs mending.

"That's what I've come for, Rakka," said Ajani. "I want to meet your master, Nicol Bolas."

"Oh, his reputation precedes him, then? That's good. He's always looking for powerful recruits, so I think he would like that very much. He's far away from here, but I could lead you to him." she said. "But, I'm afraid that's going to cost you." She stretched her hands out, drawing a web of electricity between them.

"What do you want?"

She smirked, and nodded to the fallen Kresh. "Him," she said. Then she gestured with her head to the rest of Kresh's warriors. "And all of them. Dead. By your hand."

The warriors murmured angrily.

"Calm down, calm down," said Ajani. "That's not going to happen, Rakka. What if I take this axe, and put it to your skinny throat, and just threaten to kill you instead?"

"Killing me won't get you to my master." Her voice went grave. "And believe me, I won't break from threat of pain, or by pain itself. I'll go insane first."

Ajani's eyes narrowed.

"Besides," she said, twisting threads of lightning between her bony fingers, "I've been trying out some new magics recently, new elements from a whole other world. It's quite powerful; I'm not sure I'm able to handle it. Who knows? I could be liable to kill myself at any moment." The glow of the energy lit her face from below, shading her eyes.

Ajani's anger rose. He was almost certain he could destroy the older woman with one swift motion, but he didn't know anyone else on the plane who could lead him to his goal, to seek revenge on Bolas. Without her, he could never get to the source of the conspiracy. Without her he was lost. She was his last hope.

"Time's up, brother," said Jazal's voice inside his head. "Your vengeance, or your friends. What will it be?"

DOUG BEYER

GRIXIS

Rafiq crashed through the door of the small hermitage. Protective carvings around the door frame blasted blue fire blasted at him, but it only rolled off the wards carved in his armor. In the darkness he saw the points of a sword, and fell into a defensive stance, but relaxed when he saw that, indeed, it was a living human who held the blade.

A bearded man held a sword at Rafiq, and behind him huddled a woman, her hands on her abdomen: another on the way, and soon. Their faces were gaunt and smeared with grime.

The man waggled his sword at Rafiq. "Begone, demons!" he said.

"We're not demons," said Rafiq. "Listen, there isn't much time. Come with us. We're human, like you."

"Demons wear the faces of friends, and speak their words," said the man. "Or you might be necromancers— our wards attacked you. I warn you, if you take another step, I'll run you through."

Behind him, the woman was sucking in breaths through her mouth.

"We have to go," said Rafiq. "I am from another land, a world called Bant. We came here to rescue you from your . . . demons. I do not know this word 'necromancer,' but I assure you I'm not one to fear. Your ward-spells probably didn't recognize me as one of your own, but I am an honest man, one whom you can trust. Come, now."

The woman moaned and clutched her swollen belly.

"My wife is heavy with child," said the man.

Rafiq considered. "Are these protection wards still active?"

"No. They are spent now. A mage would have to reactivate them before another attack."

Rafiq wondered how they had survived for so long.

"Then I'm sorry," he said, "but we'll have to move. We're heading out of here, and you're coming with us."

"My wife will not be able to travel!" protested the man.

"Yes, I *will*, Levac," said the woman. "Help me up."

Rafiq nodded at her respectfully. "I'll bring the cart around. When I give you the signal, you run to the vehicle drawn by the large lions."

The man and the woman exchanged a glance. Then the man spoke. "Before we go, I have . . . one small request."

JUND

Ajani looked over the fallen form of Kresh, and Kresh's warriors, and back to Rakka. She would give him exactly what he needed—the location of her master, the one who ruled the darkened world on the other side of Alara, and the key to who killed Jazal—but only at the cost of the humans.

But that's all they were, right? thought Ajani. Some humans? They were the same bloodthirsty species that had chased him down and almost killed him, just for being a cat that matched some shaky prophecy. He owed them for that. Ajani felt heat in the veins behind his eyes. His heart churned with lava.

Rakka was beaming. "I wasn't sure I'd be able to find the fire in you. It's gratifying to see." Her face darkened. "Now let's see you let it out."

Ajani turned and looked into the face of one of Kresh's warriors. She was a young woman, sinewy and agile, with ceremonial stripes of yellow and jade stained into her muscular arms and thighs. She met his gaze and held her spear steady.

"You won't live through this," Ajani heard himself say.

"I'm not afraid to die," she said.

There was a sanguine haze over Ajani's vision. He saw blood dripping down her forehead and down her hands.

Humans: useless vermin who only brought death. His fist constricted around the handle of his double-headed axe, as if it were trying to squeeze a delicate throat.

No, he thought. It was wrong.

But if he didn't do it, he would never avenge Jazal. His spirit would coil forever in agony.

But that wasn't her fault, he thought. Not that one woman standing there.

"We don't have to do it this way," Ajani said. "You're allowed to run."

"Never," the woman scoffed.

"But I . . . I have to do it. It's my only way out. It's for my brother."

She held her ground. "Do what you have to do, white cat. I'm not leaving until my Tol there is fully alive—and *she* is fully dead." She cocked her head toward Rakka.

Rakka chortled.

"But I can't get through you," the warrior continued. "So it's your move."

Ajani stepped evenly over to the woman. The other warriors watched him carefully, but didn't advance on him. He put his hand up under her jaw, so that the points of his claws curved around to just touch her cheeks on either side.

He glanced at Rakka. She was smiling. She nodded.

It would be so easy just to squeeze, Ajani thought. One squeeze, and he could end his torment and Jazal's. One squeeze, and he could channel all his rage, and crush his troubles inside of a fist.

With his claw, he turned the woman's head to Rakka as he himself turned his own head to the shaman. The warrior was going to want to see it.

Ajani willed a bolt of rage and force at Rakka, and in a flash it manifested from Ajani's body and smashed into her. The elementalist crashed head over heels, breaking through the spiny trunks of two tukatongue trees, her body landing somewhere out of sight. At the impact, a blinding cascade of lightning burst from where she landed, pent-up magic released by her death. A crack of thunder followed an instant later, echoing in the woods around them.

Ajani released the woman's face and stepped back, taking and releasing a deep breath.

"I'm sorry," he said.

"I thought she was your only way out," said the warrior, angling an eyebrow.

"I'll figure something out," said Ajani.

"You were tempted, I could tell," she said.

"Let's get Kresh on his feet," said Ajani. "We have a murderer to find."

GRIXIS

R eady?" whispered Rafiq.

Both the human survivor Levac and the aven Kaeda nodded in unison.

The plan was all stealth and speed, with no fighting if they could help it. From their hiding place behind a stack of huge bones, Rafiq could see the vastness of the undead army to which the boy belonged. Fighting was not going to be a viable option. If it didn't work, they would just have to abandon the boy and head back to Bant without him. He hoped it wouldn't come to that. He re-checked the boy's position in the army, and then tested the knots on the net and the line. It was as good as it was going to get.

"Let's do it," said Rafiq.

He and Levac rushed out from their hiding place, remaining as huddled and as quiet as they could. They ran to the edge of the marching swarm of undead, carrying the net between them. Behind them dangled the line that was attached to the net, leading back to their hiding place.

They managed to get the net around Vali with the first throw. It knocked the boy down, and he snarled and drooled a noxious ichor, thrashing around in the net. Rafiq instantly turned around and started running—but stopped when he saw that Levac hadn't.

"Let's go, let's go!" he said.

But Levac's eyes were locked on the rotting visage of his son, and he wouldn't budge. The other undead turned to face them, scraping moaning sounds out of their dead lungs.

Kaeda flew straight up from behind their hiding place, the rope in his talons. He had doffed his heavy armor to lighten his load. Soon the line was taut, and he yanked the net, thrashing boy and all, into the air.

Rafiq ushered Levac out of the way, and they ran as fast as they could back to their hiding spot in the small hermitage. Once they got out of sight, the undead horde lost interest in them and moved on.

The boy was in their custody once more, but it remained to be seen, thought Rafiq, whether anything could be done about his condition. He helped Kaeda and Levac bring the boy back to the small hermitage, and prayed.

NAYA

Marisi's mind was in tatters. His life had been extended far past its natural prospects by a deal with a dragon—a deal made by his youthful self, but one that his elderly self had to honor. His mind could not hold within it all the evil he had caused—to the nacatl, to the elves, to his entire world. As Naya became only a continent of some larger world, an inkling of the scope of what he had facilitated had begun to pierce his conscious mind. He couldn't contain it. His reason tore into pieces rather than attempt to reconcile it all. His thoughts turned only to his name as a youth: Marisi, the Breaker of the Coil.

He had no plan, but knew he had to rally the nacatl around him once more. If he had warriors around him again, he could wear them as a cape of glory, and relive the purest times of his life. He hoped the mystique around his name, his face, his striped form was still enough. Did the Wild Nacatl, who owed him their very identity, still possess the fury in their hearts that had allowed him to overthrow the Cloud Nacatl civilization? Would they, decades later, still feel the pull of his leadership? He had no choice but to believe they would.

Plus, he had one secret weapon: timing. It was Festival time again.

The nacatl pride he approached first was small,

but fierce by reputation. None of his former friends or soldiers-in-arms lived there anymore; Marisi had outlived them. As Marisi approached the pride's den in the wooded foothills near the ruins of Antali, he heard the opening roars of the *hadu*. He was just in time.

Marisi heard the chief shaman of the little pride begin to speak, heard his own accomplishments being narrated in tones of great ceremony. As soon as the shaman got to the part just before the chanting, he stepped out of the darkness and into the ring of firelight.

"I am Marisi," he said. "Come, my warriors—let us make this night a reunion, rather than a remembrance."

After a stunned silence, the pride's chanting began again—but with a different intonation.

JUND

A beam of pure, concentrated sunlight lanced out of the smoke-filled Naya sky. It struck the dragon that flew on Sarkhan's left side. The spell burned a hole directly through its throat. It tried to breathe a blast of fire in return, but flame spurted out through the hole in its neck in staccato bursts, charring it from the inside and sealing off its breathing passages. Then a hail of arrows from the jungle below tore through the beast, puncturing it like a pincushion. It arced down in a long parabola, then eventually fell, crashing into the trees somewhere far below.

Finally, Sarkhan thought. It must be the elves, or maybe the human tribes of Naya, finally fighting back with magic. The humanoids had begun amassing in the jungles below Sarkhan's air assault, and although the archers were frustrating, some of them below him were potent spellcasters. It had taken days of Sarkhan's draconic strafing to elicit that kind of response, days of charring huge swathes of jungle with dragonfire. That sunbeam spell was good. It would do nicely, churning up the mana of Naya, causing it to stream to the Maelstrom as Bolas desired. But he needed more than that, much more.

He took the one dragon's death as an excuse to stage a retreat. He wheeled Karrthus around and headed back.

Sarkhan craned his neck to see behind him, to see whether the humanoid armies had followed.

He needn't have looked back. A blast of consecrated energy narrowly missed Karrthus's wing. Sarkhan grinned.

"Come along, my enemies," he said. "Come and answer my call to war."

He slapped the side of Karrthus's neck, and pressed his knee firmly into the dragon's flank. The dragon banked slightly.

"That's perfect," Sarkhan said. "Straight ahead, just like this."

They weren't headed back toward Jund. Not exactly.

GRIXIS

I can't believe this," Salay was saying. Tears were streaming down her face as she helped hold the arms of the creature that had once been her son. "You knew this . . . He . . . was out there, and you didn't tell me."

"I couldn't tell you," said Levac.

"I was going to *leave*," she sobbed. "You were going to let me leave my *son*, you bastard."

"Without a way to save him, it was better not letting you know. I didn't want that plaguing your heart as we started a new life."

"This is my *son*," she said through her teeth.

"And with these people's help, I got him back," said Levac.

"Please," said Rafiq. "Let's try to calm down. The boy needs us now."

They held Vali down on a makeshift table in the small hermitage shack. Rafiq stood over him. He knew just the words to help the boy, words that he trusted, words that he knew came from the tongue of an angel.

He took the sigil of Asha from around his neck, and laid it on the boy's chest. The Vali-creature flinched and snarled, trying to wriggle free, casting evil looks at the medallion, but they held him firm.

Rafiq said a prayer to Asha over the boy, reciting each line with the faith that burned in his heart. It took all his strength, but he summoned up every pure emotion in his fiber and poured it into the prayer. The words flowed out of him with the same intensity as the light that shone from the throne statue in the Jhessian arena. Every night as a boy he had wondered why the archangel Asha had died, leaving her throne empty and Bant unprotected. But as an adult he had come to understand the meaning of her sacrifice, how her death had stopped the unholy demons from destroying the world.

The demons had come again. And she had not—at least, not yet.

But there was no time for doubt. He poured all his faith into the words of the prayer. He realized he was on his knees, sweating, his eyes squeezed shut. The prayer was done. He caught his breath.

"Is it . . . Should it have worked by now?" said Levac.

Rafiq opened his eyes. There was no change. The boy was still an animated corpse.

"That should have . . . That should have done it," said Rafiq.

"He's still . . . He's still not any better," said Levac, his voice carrying a note of rising panic.

"No!" shouted Rafiq. "That was it! That prayer has cured corruption of all kinds. It's the word of the angel Asha herself. Don't you doubt her!"

The creature called Vali snarled and writhed about, its black eyes rolling with hatred.

"Look at this. This is . . . *You* said you could help my boy!" cried Levac.

"It isn't my fault. The prayer should have worked. This boy is an abomination!" shouted Rafiq.

"You bring back my son!" cried Levac.

"Our son is dead," said Salay.

ALARA UNBROKEN

293

The two men looked at her. She was holding an axe from the hermitage arsenal.

"Salay—" started Levac.

"This monster is not him. Vali, our son, is *dead*. And you two won't see that until this thing stops deceiving you."

With that, she swung the axe, and chopped off the zombie's head with one clean stroke.

The head rolled, and the creature sank into stillness. Salay dropped the axe, blinked unsteadily for a moment, and promptly fainted.

Levac went to her, and put his arms around her. He shook with weeping.

Rafiq just stood there, watching the couple. He didn't retrieve the sigil. He didn't leave to rejoin his troops. He just let events wash over him. He tried to figure out something encouraging to say, but he couldn't. Deep inside of him, entrenched somewhere under layers of memory and formative experiences, inside of a staunchly protected shell of Rafiq's innermost self, something died.

GRIXIS
JUND FRONTIER

"This must be it," said Kresh through his hand. The stench was unbelievable.

Ajani, Kresh, and the remaining warriors of clan Antaga had pressed on in the same direction they had been traveling, hoping that the path that led them to Rakka would also lead them to her master.

They had climbed over shards of rubble to get to their vantage point, and Ajani wished they hadn't. Jund had given way to Grixis. The landscape of Grixis spread itself out before them, repugnant and obscene like a naked corpse. And the mana—the Grixis mana smelled to Ajani like death, even more profoundly than the literal air. It had the same aura to it as the creatures that had attacked the night Jazal died. Ajani's heart went cold.

"I think you're right," Ajani said. "This is the place."

"What horror *is* this place, that has invaded our world?" asked one of the warriors.

"It's not an invasion," said Ajani thoughtfully. "It's a unification. This isn't a foreign world anymore—it's *part* of our world." And somewhere in there is the being that caused Jazal's death, he thought. The enormity of the task ahead overwhelmed him.

"Take heart, warriors!" said Kresh. "Look, they've got land, and mountains, and clouds. They've got beasts clambering around, and flyers in their skies. It's just another Jund—only it's darker and deader. We care not. For us, it's just another hunting ground. For us, this is the final hunt!" He banged his sword on the bone of his chest armor.

Ajani marveled at Kresh's irrepressibility. He needed some of that fire. Maybe they *could* do it.

GRIXIS

W e should move on soon," said Kaeda the aven. "The undead armies have passed."

"If we move, they'll find us again," said Levac. "The rank and file aren't smart, but their leader is a cunning demon called Malfegor."

"Malfe—what did you say?" asked Rafiq.

"Malfegor. They call him the Abomination, or the Annihilator. He's the oldest and most powerful demon in all of Grixis."

"*The* Malfegor?" Rafiq was incredulous. "He's still alive?"

"He's always existed, as far as our history is concerned. Malfegor is older than all our stories."

"He's in my people's stories, as well," said Rafiq. "But in our scripture, the angel Asha gave her life to destroy him."

"If only that were true," said Salay, groggy but awake.

"So I think we should give him a wide berth. Head in the other direction. Or maybe we can just make a life here in Esper."

Rafiq's eyes were far away. "No," he said. "We need to follow that army."

"What?" said Levac and Salay together.

"In fact, we need to get ahead of it if we can. I think I know where Malfegor might be headed."

NAYA

Marisi moved with his swarm of nacatl warriors to the Qasali Valley. There he would find the last pride of Wild Nacatl left, the only one that he hadn't rallied under his banner of legend. He had saved it for last purposefully. He knew the pride would be gripped by fear and grief—it was there that Bolas's magic had been used directly. It was there that the *kha* Jazal, greatest threat to Marisi's legacy, had been assassinated, partly by his own actions. He didn't know whether opinion had turned against the name of Marisi, or whether they would also embrace the knowledge that he was alive. He knew that the shaman-witch Chimamatl lived there, which would work in his favor; his deeds would help her son's quest to become *kha* of the pride. But he also knew that the white-furred Ajani was from that pride; he was not anxious to see him again.

To be safe, he ordered his army of warriors in first.

"By the proclamation of war-*kha* Marisi, your pride is ordered to submit all its able warriors to join his army," said Marisi's envoy.

"What is the cause of this?" said the pride's representative, the nacatl called Tenoch.

"The Cloud Nacatl have caused the earth to quake with their unholy magics," said the envoy. "Marisi has risen from the dead to resume his fight against this tyranny. We go to war against the Cloud Nacatl once again."

The ruse was enough. The fear caused by Jazal's death, and the recent movements of elves, behemoths, and the earth itself had prepared the pride for change. Marisi felt confident enough that he emerged personally from behind his army, and the last pride of Wild Nacatl cheered his return. Marisi roared, his warrior spirit kindled by the show of fierce camaraderie, and hundreds of nacatl joined in Marisi's roar of rebellion.

Only one among them said nothing. Zaliki watched as her pride, her extended family, dissolved into Marisi's army. She had never met Marisi, but she knew of him—and the thought of him burned her heart. Without a word to anyone, she stole up to Jazal's lair. There she gathered Jazal's notes, the documents representing Jazal's research into the legends and prophecies of nacatl and Naya, and slipped away into the wilderness.

BANT

Mubin's wagon came to a halt outside the grounds of the palace of Aarsil the Blessed. He could hear the four leotau roar with relief after the long ride.

"We're here, sir," said the wagon driver.

Mubin looked out. It was dusk. Through the gate, he could see the Twelve Trees of Valeron lined up in two tidy rows of six across a long reflection pool, the pool reflecting the dying light of day. Each twisted tree symbolized both a noble family of Valeron and a virtue to live by. And if Mubin was right, each one hid an ancient, crucial secret.

The wagon driver unhitched the largest, strongest leotau from the wagon, and brought it around for Mubin. With difficulty, they got Mubin into the saddle. The leotau was tired, but it knew its duty; it held Mubin's weight proudly and didn't stumble.

"Thank you," Mubin said to the driver. "Make camp. We'll leave again in the morning."

"Yes, sir," said the driver.

Mubin hoped that Aarsil the Blessed would hear his arguments. He rode up to the castle. The guard waved him through the gate.

Aarsil came out to meet him.

"Mubin of the Reliquary," she said. "I got your note. I was very sorry to hear of your injury."

"Thank you, but I am fine." Mubin had his leotau sit, but with his useless legs he stayed in the saddle. "I apologize for not dismounting, Highness. I mean no disrespect."

"That's quite all right, under the circumstances."

A thin man with a robe draped over his hunched shoulders walked out of the castle keep and came down the steps to join them. As he approached, Mubin noticed the emblem stitched into the man's robes: a half-lidded eye, with the iris pointing upward. He was the same man that had accompanied Aarsil the Blessed to the match in the arena, Mubin thought. How long had that order had had the ear of the Blessed caste?

"Sir Mubin," said Aarsil the Blessed. "May I introduce my advisor?"

"It's a pleasure to meet you, sir knight," said the Skyward Eye advisor. "The Order of the Reliquary is a worthy cause, deepening our roots in the history of Valeron and all of Bant."

Mubin nodded in what he hoped was a polite manner.

"What brings you here, may I ask?" asked Aarsil.

"I'm here to ask for your help."

"You're welcome to any assistance we can provide."

"Thank you. Let me be blunt. I need to dig up the Twelve Trees of Valeron."

NAYA

Zaliki's journey took her deep into the woods and up through the foothills. When night came, she didn't stop, and traveled by the light of the moon. Overhead, she heard the sounds of flying creatures—horrible monsters making war on Naya, and she saw streams of fire and the bright spellcraft of elves. The world was changing in ways she didn't understand, but she had to focus on what she could affect. She only knew she had to get to the ancient forbidden city of Qasal—before Marisi's army did.

By morning she had reached the outer walls of Qasal. She saw a tower spire reaching up from inside the city. On the hills beyond it, she saw the broken white stones of the Coil, carved with the scratchforms that codified nacatl law before Marisi's revolution had smashed it to pieces. How she longed to spend time with them and Jazal's documents, comparing the writings between them.

An arrow pierced the ground next to Zaliki's foot. She turned to see Cloud Nacatl archers along the top of the city walls.

"I'm unarmed and alone," Zaliki called up to the walls of Qasal, the capital of the Cloud Nacatl prides.

As far as Zaliki knew, the Cloud Nacatl hadn't had a Wild Nacatl visitor since the breaking of the Coil. The two super-prides had been divided since Marisi's revolt. If they trusted her, it would be a miracle.

A guard called down from the top of the wall. "You're a Wild Nacatl and a shaman," he said. "You coming here even with hands empty is an act of aggression. Speak quickly and carefully, before I tire of instructing my archers to miss."

"I need your help," said Zaliki. "And, I fear, in a few days' time, you will need mine."

• • • • •

The Cloud Nacatl ambassador was a stern, gray-furred nacatl. He wore layer upon layer of fine robes in colors of ochre and maroon, and silver rings on his fingers. Beside him sat an old female with white eyes.

"I am Banat, and this is my advisor, Ruki," said the ambassador. "You're being given an audience only because you cooperated with the guards, but I warn you—if you cause any disturbance, we will be forced to act."

"Yes," creaked the old crone Ruki. "I'll be forced to kill you."

Zaliki kept her retort to herself. She nodded.

"You say an army approaches," said Banat.

"Yes," Zaliki said. "Marisi, or someone claiming to be him, has gathered all of the Wild Nacatl together once again. They intend to mount an attack on Qasal."

Banat frowned. "This is very serious. Do you have any evidence of this?"

"Send your scouts to the east, into the valley. They'll see the advancing army there. They intend to attack on the anniversary of the breaking of the Coil."

"You risk death by coming here," said Ruki. "Why would you warn us?"

"Because I believe that Marisi isn't actually after Qasal." She produced Jazal's documents and slid them across the table. Ambassador Banat began to study them. "He's after . . . the obelisk."

Their faces showed surprise.

"What do you know of the obelisk?" asked Banat.

"Nothing, really," said Zaliki. "My . . . *kha*, Jazal, was studying these prophecies before his recent death." She indicated the documents in Banat's hands. "They have similar elements across several races and cultures. They all mention an apocalyptic prophecy, and they all mention a spire of golden stone. Jazal's notes indicated that he believed this edifice was here, in Qasal. Was he right? Do you know what he meant?"

Banat looked at Ruki.

"There is no golden spire in Qasal," she said, her voice like ancient hinges. "Unless he simply means the Tower of Qasal."

"It's a symbol of our Cloud Nacatl culture. And now Marisi has come back to destroy it," said Ambassador Banat. "Which will make these prophecies come true."

"And which will trigger war all over again, among the nacatl and across all of Naya," said Zaliki.

BANT

Aarsil the Blessed laughed uncomfortably. "I admit that I generally don't understand rhox humor. You want to *what?*"

"Dig up the Twelve Trees of Valeron," said Mubin. "I know it's a big favor. But I—"

"It's not a *favor,* Mubin." She was angry. "It's sacrilege. You know as much as anybody the history of these trees. Their roots are Valeron's own. They hold inside them the very pith of our heritage. Like I said, I don't understand this joke of yours."

"It's not a joke," said Mubin. "I believe that the war effort needs what's buried under them."

"What's buried under them? You mean the myth of the Sword of Asha?"

"It's no myth."

"What?"

"Now hold on," interrupted Aarsil's Order of the Skyward Eye advisor. "Aarsil, this is obviously a trick—"

"You stay out of this," said Mubin.

"Don't talk like that to him," said Aarsil. "Wanath has been my trusted advisor for several years now. He's a historian and a scholar of archaeology in his own right. He's studied the Twelve Trees his entire life. He would know whether there are fragments of a sword buried under there."

Mubin glared at the advisor and turned back to Aarsil. His best hope was the direct approach. "Highness, I believe that the Order of the Skyward Eye has been propagating a campaign of deception across Bant for years. They've been manipulating our traditions, introducing falsehoods into our histories, and backing up their claims with forged documents and relics."

"Preposterous!" scoffed Wanath.

"In particular," continued Mubin, "they've obscured the part of the Asha parable that matters most to Bant's survival against the other planes—that the holy Sword of Asha, with which the archangel slew the demon Malfegor, lies in twelve pieces beneath the Twelve Trees. We have always believed the fragments of the sword to be mythical, and simply symbolic of the twelve virtues held sacred in Valeron. But I believe that it may be literally true. I found this."

Mubin produced a stone fragment, a relic he had taken from the ruins at Giltspire, and a prayer book, the tome given to him by the cleric who had watched over his recuperation.

"This is a fragment of Giltspire, gathered just after it collapsed. And this is a book of prayer from an Akrasan cleric. Each has been *modified*. I cross-referenced the changes that were made to each one, and used them to decode each other. The changes have downplayed the truth of the story of the sword, and emphasized the need for global war in times of strife."

Aarsil the Blessed looked at her advisor.

"We're already at war," said Mubin, "so that can't be helped anymore. What we can do is reforge the sword, the artifact that was erased from Bant's records, to have a weapon against the evils that face us."

"That is a bold theory, and a very serious accusation against the Order of the Skyward Eye," said Aarsil.

Mubin held his breath. If she relented, he believed he could help win the war that threatened all of Bant. If she didn't . . .

"I'd like you to leave, and never return to my palace ever again," said the Blessed.

Guards took hold of the reins of Mubin's leotau.

A smug smile crossed the face of Aarsil's Skyward Eye advisor.

NAYA

The breeze was cool. It rustled the folds of Zaliki's cloak. She stood before the outskirts of Qasal, its mighty main tower glowing in the sun.

Before her were thousands of nacatl: Marisi's army. Marisi himself was nowhere to be seen, if it was truly him, but she knew he would be down there somewhere.

Zaliki approached. The breeze gossiped excitedly through the treetops all around them. Not a soldier moved on either side.

"Marisi!" she cried. "I call you out!"

There was no movement, only row after row of the eyes of her fellow Wild Nacatl.

"Marisi! You and I have a personal matter to settle. That matter is Jazal!"

Banners flapped in the breeze. Only after several long scans of the assembled army did she see movement. Nacatl warriors parted to make way for someone.

Marisi stepped forward. He was in war garb from head to foot, and carried a spear decorated with the teeth of behemoths.

"Hello, child," Marisi said.

"Do you know who I am?" Zaliki asked.

"Is that you, child? Are you the young shaman of Jazal's pride?"

"I am."

"Then you were my servant for an important task."

Her eyes were cold. "I was."

"You did the right thing, then. You didn't realize the enormity of what you had done, but I'm here to tell you now that it pushed the needle of history. Your actions resonated through this entire world—and, I've come to realize, much, much more."

"I was a fool to plant that artifact," Zaliki cried. "I was a fool to believe in you, and your message of freedom. I was a fool to distrust Jazal, and his belief that the sundering of our race was a mistake. It was worse than a mistake, though, wasn't it? It was cold calculation. Your lies tore our people apart, Marisi, to spread hate and distrust among us. Today I'm here to stop them from tearing apart our world."

"Child, you still don't realize the role you've played," Marisi said. "You don't know how proud I am of you. Look around you. Two armies, ready to reenact a bloody battle a generation old. It all repeats, child. An escalation of power. A breaking of stone. I know you're bitter, but you shouldn't blame yourself. No one succeeds who stands in the way of prophecy."

"There's no prophecy, Marisi," Zaliki said. "This is not going to happen again. Not this time. Not with me here."

"I respect your bravery, and your misguided attempt to redeem your actions," Marisi answered. "But it's not up to you, child. Nor is it up to me. We are but pieces in a grand game. We're here to play our role today, nothing more. I can say from experience—pretending otherwise only makes it worse."

"I believed in you, old man," said Zaliki. "I believed in your name. I believed in your message of freedom, as did my entire generation. How could you betray that trust?"

"Freedom is the luxury of the strong and the powerful," 309

said Marisi. "I'm afraid we are neither. Goodbye, young Zaliki."

With that, Marisi signaled to his Wild Nacatl. Zaliki turned and signaled to the Cloud Nacatl. A terrible roar went up, and the two armies launched at each other.

GRIXIS

He may only have been a glorified messenger, but Kaeda the aven didn't take his orders lightly. Rafiq himself had given him his mission, to fly back to Bant ahead of them and warn them of the coming of Malfegor's army. And he was determined to carry them out, no matter what might happen to him.

He outpaced the undead army rather easily. Some casters fired spells at him, and a small flock of diseased, black-feathered aven creatures tried to get in his way. But both attacks failed. He was a military-trained, thrice-decorated soldier of Valeron; they were half-living wretches whose minds were chained to a lord of evil. Furthermore, he found that the vigor of life and the power of his devotion to his cause were by themselves enough to give him an edge against any Grixis combatants he faced. The grim legion was relentless and brutal, but they had no spirit in them to fuel their might.

Kaeda cut a straight line from Grixis to Bant, flying as fast and as true as he could manage. Lightning flashed in the black clouds above him, occasionally buffeting him with booms of thunder. The gloom of Grixis faded into a front of drizzly clouds from Esper; he kept that front on his right side, and flew. He flew for hours, which stretched into relentless days. His sense of time dulled. His pinion joints ground themselves raw.

311

When he saw a glow ahead of him, he felt a flood of relief—finally, he was in range of his bright home of Bant. He summoned up the last of his reserves, and flew straight for the light.

But something was wrong. The closer he flew toward the light, the more he realized that the light did not come from Bant. A sphere of swirling energy, the size of a small mountain, glowed ahead of him. As he approached it, he felt the air currents change. They spun around the glowing globe like a funnel, pulling him down to its center. Flares of energy exploded outward fitfully, threatening to singe his feathers.

Wearily, Kaeda veered away from the maelstrom, trying to steer clear of it, but its irrepressible pull threatened to draw him into its chaotic center. He tired quickly, and wondered whether he would just fall in and die.

"Kaeda, you *must* warn Bant," said Rafiq's voice in his memory. "I'm counting on you. We'll be there as soon as we can . . ."

The aven found new resolve and beat his weary wings through the pain. Slowly, he dragged his flight path out of the maelstrom and escaped from it. He was doing it. He was going to deliver the message, and fulfill his duty.

As he passed around the sphere, he saw the light beyond it. The natural sunlight looked so beautiful that he was surprised he ever mistook the maelstrom for it. He flew in Bant's direction gratefully.

But with his back to the maelstrom, a flare of energy erupted from the vortex and lanced Kaeda's wing, utterly destroying it. As he plummeted out of the sky, Kaeda shrieked in pain.

NAYA

Zaliki couldn't stop the battle from happening, but maybe she could stop Marisi from destroying the Tower of Qasal.

With a thrust of Marisi's spear, his warriors leaped toward her with their swords high.

She had never thought she'd have to use magic on her own people, but she had no choice. Zaliki called on the jungle corridors of her home, which filled her with nature's strength and fury. Her arms cut a circular hole in the air, and out of the circle tumbled a torrent of vicious timber wolves that circled around her, forming a living barrier between the Wild Nacatl and herself. At her command, the mongels pounced, each tearing into a nearby warrior. Meanwhile, she focused her energies on Marisi.

Marisi leaped forward and stabbed the point of his spear right at her. She countered with a spell that caused a sudden burst of growth in the underbrush, entangling his spear in vines and absorbing the force of his attack. The vines devoured the spear, crushing the handle into splinters and pulling the weapon down into the earth.

Weaponless, Marisi launched forward and tackled Zaliki. She controlled her fall and rolled with the impact, throwing him off her. She tried to summon a barrier made of brambles between them, but he was too quick and grabbed her leg. She stumbled as her feet were pulled out from under her, and she slammed into the ground.

"Give up, little cub," growled Marisi. "I'm twice the fighter you are."

She rolled over and bared her teeth. "But only half the warrior," she replied. With that, she uttered a spell.

Zaliki's leg grew in Marisi's claws—and every other part of her body grew along with it. Her body expanded, unfolded, fueled by magic of uncontrolled growth. Soon she was the size of a giant, and Marisi had lost his hold on her. A solid kick to his chest sent him flying. She stood and towered over the heads of both armies.

"Now come here, you," she boomed, and reached down to grab Marisi.

Marisi somersaulted out of the way of Zaliki's giant claws and ran into the thick of the battle, dodging sword blows and spear thrusts. Zaliki lumbered after him, occasionally crushing combatants underfoot. The old warrior was too quick—she couldn't move her enormous limbs fast enough to follow him through the forest. It was going to take more magic.

Zaliki reached out with her mind to all nearby available sources of natural mana. Her mind immediately touched a powerful source nearby, and she felt a surge of power—why hadn't she felt this before? Instinctively she opened herself to it, letting the mana blossom inside her. With it she fueled a massive spell that summoned a charging gargantuan onto the battlefield, sending it directly at Marisi. The gargantuan shook the earth with its galloping footfalls, and warriors from both armies dove out of its path. In seconds the gargantuan head-butted Marisi with its bony facial plates, sending the cat flying. Marisi fell to the earth with a thud, and the beast slowed and stopped over his limp body.

Zaliki had time to stride over to Marisi and pick him up.

She held the nacatl up above her head in one hand, and looked down at all the warriors below. "Warriors! Stop this battle now! Marisi is a liar, and a warmongering fraud!"

The shouts in response were not what she wanted to hear.

"Kill the traitor!"

"In Marisi's name!"

"Destroy her!"

One voice she couldn't hear over the shouts was Ambassador Banat, yelling at her from the ground. "Zaliki, don't!" he cried. "No more! No more magic! You're destroying it!"

It would take one more display of force, Zaliki thought. She had to show her Wild Nacatl that their leader was mortal, and show them how serious she was about her cause. If she had to martyr Marisi, so be it.

"I believed in you," she said to the nacatl in her hand.

"It's not your fault," said Marisi.

Zaliki drew on the powerful source of mana again, a dramatic draught of the energy. She channeled it into a spell to augment her own strength sevenfold. Muscles rippled throughout her already giant-sized body. She brought her arms back as if to clap her hands, and then brought her palms together, smashing Marisi between them.

The crowd gasped in unison.

Then, behind her, there was an explosive sound of stone cracking.

She turned to see the Tower of Qasal fracturing and crumbling apart.

NAYA

Bolas perched on a Naya mountaintop, surveying the world around him in a state of boredom. For a twenty-thousand-year-old dragon, he had precious little patience. Where was the signal flare? That aging leonin hero, Marisi, should have signaled him for their rendezvous. Bolas had seen nothing from him. The lack of information that presented was unsettling. Without his minions checking in with him, he had no eyes or ears on the planes other than Grixis.

Perhaps the attack on Qasal hadn't gone well? If Marisi had failed at Qasal, then that meant the obelisk of Naya might not be free and functional. That would mean he would have to find and condition an all-new minion on Naya, and that could take days or weeks—time he didn't have.

There was one way to find out. He closed his eyes and reached out with his inner senses. The planeswalker spark inside him connected with dozens of mana sources all over the plane, large and small. Gradually he perceived a web of interconnected fonts of mana glittering in his mind's eye. He followed along them, looking for new sources of mana. He soon found it—a glaring new pillar of mana generation near the shrines of Qasal. That was it—the obelisk of Naya. It was active. Bolas could see that it radiated stable mana to the areas physically near it, but also that it channeled mana elsewhere in a steady stream. It was that stream of mana energy that made him smile.

Marisi had missed his meeting. That meant he was dead, or ready to accept death once Bolas tracked him down and punished him. But he appeared to have succeeded anyway.

Bolas summoned up a bit of the jagged local mana and planeswalked out into the Blind Eternities.

THE
MAELSTROM

When Kaeda, the aven of Bant, awoke, his first thought was of his mission. How close was the Grixis army? Had they already passed him?

There was no sign of them, not along the route anyway. He must have been unconscious only for a short time.

He looked back, and saw the swirling maelstrom. Was it his imagination, or was it even bigger than before?

His body was a cage of agony. He had tumbled as he had fallen out of the sky, and the gusts around the maelstrom had thrown him a wind shear that had sent him sideways, so he had fallen awkwardly. Not since he was a fledgling had he fallen so badly. Thanks to his light bones, he hadn't crushed himself in the impact, but everything was thoroughly bruised, and his left talon was twisted. His tentative attempt to move his wing was punished by pain. The wing was ruined; there was nothing coming out of that shoulder but a blackened branch of bone. There would be no flying out of there.

With supreme effort, he lurched onto his good leg. He tested himself with a step, which ended in a graceless limp. He lurched a few more steps, wincing in pain, and fell.

He pushed himself up again. Someone still had to warn Bant of Malfegor's approach. *If I have to stagger for miles on foot to do it,* he thought, *then that's how it would have to be done.*

BANT

Aarsil the Blessed came down to the palace courtyard in her sleeping robe. It was late at night
in Valeron. Crickets chirped, and the stars shone in
constellations shaped like angels. She wouldn't have
been awake at this hour except that Aarsil's guards
had called her. They had detained a man, a human of
Mortar caste, who looked hysterical.

Aarsil rubbed her eyes in annoyance. "All right, I'm
here, I'm awake. What is it?"

"This man says there's an emergency," said a guard.

"Highness, please, I beg your help. I'm the wagon
driver for Sir Mubin. It's Mubin, Highness. He sent away
your guards, and opened the gates—the *trees*. Please come
to the court grounds, quickly!"

She was fully awake. "What in Asha's name has he
done?"

They raced out to the courtyard of the Twelve Trees.
Aarsil gasped in horror, covering her hand with her
mouth.

The tremendous roots of one of the majestic trees lay
exposed, twisted and clogged with mud. The branches of
the tree lay along the ground, with the trunk lashed to
Mubin's wagon team of four mighty leotau.

And down in the pit where the tree's roots had been
torn free lay Mubin, covered in dirt. He had a network of

ropes wrapped around him, and there was a shovel to one side. He sat in the mud of the pit he had created, cradling a metallic object in his arms.

"Mubin!" shouted Aarsil.

The rhox knight looked up. He held up the object he was holding. The light of the stars glinted hard and true in the edge of a shard of steel.

"I found one of them," Mubin said. "It's a fragment of the Sword of Asha."

Aarsil's Skyward Eye advisor came running up. "What is going on?" he cried.

Aarsil turned to him, a grim vein bulging in her forehead. "Go and fetch twenty Mortar caste, ropes, and a dozen more steeds. And a blacksmith."

Aarsil's face was a storm of concentration. Her brow furrowed in rage, and she opened her mouth to say something—but then she closed it again. She looked at the glinting metal of the sword fragment.

"What's he done?" the advisor whispered. "What do you mean, you want . . . You're not going to—"

"Go and fetch what Mubin needs," said Aarsil the Blessed. "Now."

GRIXIS

Ajani, Kresh, and the warriors moved through Grixis as secretly as they could. It wasn't easy—to the blood-tuned senses of the creatures of Grixis, their life force glowed like a beacon. After a rash of battles with the undead, rot and ichor clung to them. But they marched on.

"Cat-man, you're unstoppable," said Kresh in tired admiration. "You haven't rested in days. We've run out of clean food, and you're withering away, and yet you walk on."

"I can't stop," said Ajani. "The killer must be nearby. I'm smelling the same smell as the creatures that killed my brother. We're almost there, I think. I can feel it."

"We might be," said Kresh. "Or we might be lost in the land of the dead. *Everything* here smells like this. I support your mission of vengeance, I do. It's every man's right to die in battle, slumped over the corpse of his hated enemy. But this is no way to go, for us or for you. I won't watch you die of *walking around*."

Ajani's teeth showed as he spoke. "If you want to leave, go ahead."

"That's not what my words meant, and I think you know it. I am going to see you through to the end of this thing if it kills me. If you can't stand some sense talked into—"

"Shh," said Ajani.

"You don't shush me!"

"Quiet!" hissed Ajani. "Do you hear something? Do you hear wings?"

"Of course. We've heard those black-feathered bird-men for days," muttered Kresh.

"No, he's right," whispered one of the warriors. "I hear it too. It sounds like—"

"A dragon's wings," said Ajani.

BANT

The soldier on lookout duty at a Bant gatehouse put down her spyglass in order to report.

"Sir, it's an aven. He's one of ours," she said.

"And he is on *foot?*" said the gate-captain incredulously.

"Yes," said the lookout. "He's in bad shape."

"It could be a trap. But I want you to find out, and quickly."

"Yes, sir!"

The aven had collapsed by the time the guard tower opened its front gate. Two soldiers and a cleric rushed out to the fallen bird-man.

"This is no trap," said one of the soldiers. "This is Kaeda. He was part of the mission of Knight-General Rafiq."

The cleric immediately began chanting. The aven's wounds closed, but the wing remained destroyed. The aven stopped breathing.

"I'm sorry," said the cleric after a moment. "He's gone."

"Poor devoted scout," said one of the soldiers. "Look at that wing. What happened to him?"

"He's got something with him."

"It's a scroll."

"What's it say?"

"Just this: 'DEMONS AT GILTSPIRE. FOUR DAYS.'"

"Let's tell the gate-captain."

GRIXIS

A dragon flew silhouetted against the lightning-torn sky of Grixis, as dark as shadow. They had seen no other dragons in Grixis at all, and Ajani wondered whether it could be the master of Rakka and of Marisi, the very dragon he sought. Kresh and the other Jund warriors found cover under the bones of some long-dead beast, having met several dragons in their day.

As the dragon flew overhead, Ajani realized it didn't have the light-distorting black scales of the dragonscale bowl. It was red-scaled, with a characteristic woven pattern to the scales on its stomach. This wasn't the dragon that had caused Jazal's death. In fact, the dragon looked strangely familiar.

"Karrthus," said one of the warriors in awe.

"He's a mighty hellkite from our world," said another. "What's he doing here?"

It was the same dragon Ajani had seen on Jund right after Jazal's death, during his first planeswalk. That was the day he had met Sarkhan.

There were more flyers. Trailing behind the huge hellkite were several other, smaller dragons. Their wings were punched through with holes, and their scales were in tatters. One of them had a serious wound to its belly, and another had lost a leg. The flight of dragons had been in a fight, and a brutal one.

"Karrthus is being ridden," said a warrior.

They all looked.

"It's Sarkhan," muttered Kresh, bile dripping from his words.

Ajani could see Sarkhan himself riding astride the biggest dragon, the hellkite Karrthus.

"That's not the dragon I seek," said Ajani.

"But that's the man we seek," said Kresh.

The dragons sailed overhead, heading to a glow on the horizon. As he looked, Ajani saw a thin line of distortion in the air above their heads, leading in the same direction as Sarkhan and the dragons. It was a stream of raw mana, coursing through the air to the horizon.

"What should we do?" asked one of the warriors.

"Uh, who are they?" asked another.

A long, strong note blasted on what sounded like a brass instrument.

"That sounded like an elvish clarion," said Ajani.

On the opposite horizon, the tips of elvish banners rose into view. The marching feet of thousands of individuals resonated through the dead landscape of Grixis.

Ajani ran out from their hiding place to meet up with the army.

"Cat-man, where are you going?" shouted Kresh.

"I know these people!" Ajani called back. "Elves, humans, gargantuans, and nacatl," he said to himself. "These are the armies of Naya!"

"So where are they headed?"

They're headed to the center of all our planes, Ajani thought.

THE
MAELSTROM

Malfegor's army marched past the mana maelstrom, but the draconic demon stopped. He regarded the storm of mana, letting it whip at his body. It was huge; it filled a depression the size of an inverted mountain. All the naked power swirling before him—it was overwhelmingly seductive. He could just reach out, he thought, and consume it for himself—he was going to do what instead, be Bolas's errand boy? He had trudged for weeks with thousands of corpses just to pass the thing by? Bolas had promised Malfegor the remains of Alara once he had fed from its energy, but promises were worthless. He felt betrayal behind Bolas's every word. And with the power contained in that maelstrom, Malfegor could just *take* the plane for himself.

"I wouldn't if I were you," said Bolas.

A dragon-shaped silhouette separated from the black sky over the maelstrom and formed into the elder dragon.

"A childish prank," said Malfegor. "It's beneath you."

"A prudent one," said Bolas. "Tsk. You thought I wouldn't be monitoring *your* corrupt and blackened soul?"

"Watch all you want, *master*," said Malfegor, his wings spreading like dark flame. "One word, and this army attacks whatever I say. They could do great violence to an old lizard like you."

"You took longer to get to this point than I expected. Is this how you survived since Alara's beginnings? By waiting for temptation to slap you in the face? I'm surprised. I believed you actually had some promise."

Malfegor stepped forward, imposing in his rage.

"You forget," said Bolas. "You have plenty to lose here. I may have a rough time with you and your army, but this mana storm is unstable. Without my influence, it might just rupture at any time. I'm a planeswalker, what do I care? If you try to harvest it, and fail miserably as you certainly would, I will just leave. You, however, will have to stay here, and deal with the consequences."

Malfegor looked into the maelstrom. Spikes of energy lashed out randomly as it swirled in on itself.

"I know it's hard for a demon to understand consequences," Bolas said with mock pity. "But it's true. I leave, and the cataclysm destroys Alara and everything in it. Even if you survived, you'd have no world left to call your own. A demon lord with no kingdom to rule—such a shame!"

Malfegor seethed. "You'll die someday, planeswalker," he said. "And somehow, some way, I swear I'll be there to see it."

"Doubtful, on both counts," said Bolas. "But I appreciate the threatening tone—it does suit you. Now, I think you had an errand to run for me? Activating the last obelisk, so that my project can be complete?"

Malfegor's chest burned with swallowed pride. He turned, and directed his wrath on his minions. "Move!" he roared to the army, marching on to Bant. He cracked his lash, striking across the backs of every one of his generals in turn, each blow more savage than the last.

BANT

As Rafiq of the Many rode over the hill to the ruins of Giltspire Castle, he saw a glorious thing. The castle was gone, but the brilliant white obelisk remained in its place. And in front of the obelisk, facing him, was a line of siege engines, mounted knights, and a sea of thousands upon thousands of foot soldiers. Above them, aven circled in formation, and in the glare of the sun he could even make out the outlines of a few angels.

If only he would see the face of that mightiest archangel, Asha herself, he thought. She must be somewhere. It was the battle that was prophesied in the Prayer of Asha. It wasn't just going to be a simple battle—it was the demon Malfegor, in the flesh, the very same demon Asha died to destroy at the dawn of their recorded tales. Except he hadn't been destroyed. He had only hidden out in the dead world of Grixis while the five worlds were separated. With their reunion, the demonic abomination was back. If only Asha could return from death to fight demonic forces once more, just as the Prayer foretold. Doubt and belief struggled for domination in Rafiq's heart; he knew that Asha's appearance was the key to winning the war, and that if she didn't show, all of Bant might be lost.

But one thing was clear: Kaeda must have delivered the message, and all of Asha's Army had assembled at Giltspire. That was cause for great joy.

The legions of Bant were assembled just in time too, for Malfegor and his army were only a day behind Rafiq. The undead army hadn't stopped to rest, so the knight-general and his knights hadn't been able to either. Rafiq had stopped at a guard station just inside the borders of Bant to find a place to stay for some of the survivors from Grixis, including Levac and his wife Sayah. He had ridden on, switching mounts at every village he came to, riding day and night until he arrived at Giltspire.

There was one man, an old rhox friend of his, who he wished he could have stopped to see. How had Mubin fared in his absence? If they lived through Malfegor's tyranny, then Rafiq had exciting news for him. Rafiq hoped the shipment of carmot, the red stone crucial to the creation of etherium, had made it back to Bant.

"Knight-General!" said a knight riding up to him. Rafiq recognized her, and her crisp salute. "I am Knight-Captain Elspeth."

Rafiq managed a smile. "How's your head, Knight-Captain?"

"Fine, sir, fine. I'm glad you made it back safely. But you must be exhausted. Please come with me. We have food and healers, and a place for you to rest."

"No time for that," said Rafiq. "Tell me, Elspeth, do you know the word 'demon'?"

Color bleached from Elspeth's face. Rafiq took that as a yes.

"A demon of legend, Malfegor, leads an army from a place of death. His army is not far behind me. You must take me directly to the command tent."

• • • • •

The horns of Malfegor were the first sign they heard of the Grixis army coming over the hill.

"Get the casters ready," said Knight-General Rafiq. "What's the status on the Sighted caste?"

"The clerics are ready, and the monks," said Knight-Captain Elspeth. "They await your signal."

"Okay. Tell them to get started."

"Sir." Elspeth dashed from the command tent. Rafiq heard her shouting "Clerics!" outside, and the beginnings of the anthem being chanted.

"You," Rafiq said to another captain. "The archers. Have them send volleys as soon as the enemy's in range. And then send in the knights."

The captain nodded, saluted, and left the tent.

There was only one other person left in the tent: a squire.

"And you," said Rafiq. "Is my armor repaired?"

The squire beamed and nodded. "I fitted it with the back plate, just as you requested, Knight-General."

"Good," said Rafiq. "Let's get it on me. And fetch my sword."

● ● ● ● ●

Outside the ruins of Giltspire, the arrows rained down on Malfegor's troops. Some of the undead minions bothered to raise wooden shields to the assault, but most didn't. The shafts jabbed through flesh as they were meant to, but the undead didn't mind. In fact, it made them a little spikier, a little tougher to close for melee, for the ground battle to come.

Malfegor sent in the kathari. They were unreliable bird-creatures, sickly and cowardly, but they blackened the sky with their numbers. Arrows tore through them, thinning them by a tenth in a matter of moments. Again, Malfegor didn't mind. They fell on the battlefield ahead of his main force, providing carrion for the ground troops to feed upon.

The rest of the kathari slashed into the bright-feathered aven. The efficient movements of the aven of Bant contrasted with the deranged squawking and snapping of the kathari, but both were effective, and the kathari outnumbered the aven over three to one.

On the ground, leotau-mounted knights slammed into the zombies and skeletons of the main force. The knights were brutally proficient, and clearly guarded by protection magic; they sliced through Malfegor's offense unimpeded.

"Fleshwarpers, hit the knights," muttered Malfegor to one of his necromancers. "And mop up with the first wave of dreg reavers."

Gangs of necromantic taskmages engaged the knights, sending spells at them that temporarily dismantled the protection spells and then deformed the paladins' flesh. The knights screamed as they fell from their mounts, their faces twisting around to the back of their heads and the skin of their limbs flaying away from their bodies. The abandoned leotau steeds roared and slashed through many of the zombies on their own, but eventually they were overcome by wave after wave of animated rotting tissue.

Mutated ogre captains took up huge axes and chopped through chain restraints, setting free a flood of dreg reavers, the enormous undead beasts that served as Malfegor's heavy infantry. The ground thundered below the armies of Bant as pachydermic behemoths charged toward them.

● ● ● ● ●

The moment that the squire handed Rafiq his helmet, the knight-general was off. The leotau felt none of his spurs, but struck vigorously at the ground with its hooves nevertheless. The battlefield flew past him, surging by like waves in a tide. He saw the bodies of friends and allies. He saw atrocities that would make the Blessed caste weep. But most of all he saw the realization of prophecy. The Prayer of Asha had been true all along. Mubin's suspicions to the contrary were wrongheaded—it hadn't been manipulated for the sake of sparking a war; it was divine instruction for *victory* in the time of war. And soon, per the prayer, the archangel Asha herself would appear, push Bant's enemies back, and her blessing would end the war for good.

Overhead, the minor angels slashed into the vulture-like kathari. Embodiments of righteousness and glory, they swung their swords in movements that expressed grace as much as the warrior spirit. The sky drained of blackness as the few angels tore through Grixis's flyers, and the sun shone through onto the battlefield again.

Rafiq circled around a confused tangle of Bant knights, and rallied them into formation once more. Together they lunged forward into the path of an onrushing dreg reaver. The reaver accelerated into them, threatening to crush them with its low-slung tusks or impale them with the razor-tipped spears that its riders had lashed to its flanks. At Rafiq's signal the knights split into two groups, letting the reaver charge between them, and they slashed into its sides with their swords. They tore long gashes in the beast, carving masses of rotten flesh from it, but the razor spears also slashed into them and their mounts.

Rafiq circled back around to meet it again. The reaver skidded to a halt, its flanks heaving and rib bones showing through, and turned to face him as well. The two of them charged one another.

It would never end by using the proper wartime etiquette he had been raised on, Rafiq thought. The undead would never fall from mere tissue damage. He would need to do something more drastic.

As his leotau rode toward the monster, Rafiq unhooked his boots from the stirrups. With his sword in one hand, the horn of the saddle in the other, he crouched on the leotau's back, compressed like a spring. Just as he saw into the hollow depths of the dreg reaver's eye sockets, he leaped, pushing the leotau out of the path of the beast and himself up into the air. On impact with the creature's face, he rammed the sword deep into its skull, and then somersaulted down its back. He crashed into the undead creature that rode the beast, and the two of them fell off onto the ground.

Rafiq recovered onto his feet, but so did the rider. Swordless, Rafiq was forced to dodge the zombie's attacks as it slashed at him with a sawlike weapon of bone and metal. He glanced back to see that the dreg reaver had collapsed and skidded to a halt, its face crushed.

There was a chorus of unholy screams. Rafiq looked up to see that demons had taken wing to meet the angels. The sight so distracted him that Rafiq's undead combatant almost landed a lethal blow, but just before it could, one of the other Bant knights came riding by and sliced the creature in half. Rafiq nodded in gratitude.

High above, two of the demons collided with one of the angels, consuming her in a mass of claws and bat-wings. There was a shriek, and as the demons parted, there was a burst of light and white feathers where the angel had been.

Asha, thought Rafiq, if you're going to appear, it would be a good time.

DOUG BEYER

THE
MAELSTROM

W hat is it?" shouted Kresh, shielding his eyes.

The storm of light before them was huge, filling the valley between the worlds. It arced and thrashed with power as streams of energy poured into it from four directions.

"It's mana," said Ajani, his eyes tearing as he stared into its center. "It's raw mana." It would have taken staggering amounts of funneled mana to create such a manifestation, Ajani thought.

That was the key, he realized. That was the goal of all the machinations. That was the meaning behind the destruction of worlds slamming into worlds—the storm of raw mana, that naked spectacle of power. Rakka, Marisi, Chimamatl, Mayael, and dozens, perhaps hundreds of unwitting minions throughout the five worlds of Alara—all their work was in the service of that maelstrom. And the master of all those unwitting minions, the nexus of that plane-spanning web, was Bolas, the dragon of shadow.

And, no doubt, he would be there soon—if he wasn't there already.

"It's beautiful," said the elf prophetess Mayael, the power glinting in her irises.

"Anima," said Ajani. "You've come to war?" Behind her, elvish legions stood in formation.

"Greetings, white cat," said Mayael. "We come to help however we can, for the sake of Naya, and all worlds."

"I thank you for your help," said Ajani. "But you should go. This storm is not stable. Your people are in danger here."

"Ajani," said another voice he recognized.

Ajani turned, and saw Zaliki. Behind her stood an army of nacatl.

"Zaliki, what are *you* doing here?" said Ajani. He blinked. "Who are . . .How did—"

"I needed answers," Zaliki said. "I followed the stream of mana from the obelisk at Qasal, and it led me here. "And an army came with me. They wanted answers too. They're Cloud Nacatl, Ajani."

"I don't understand," said Ajani flatly. "But you, you all need to go. It's very dangerous here. Something dire is about to happen."

"Ajani," she said, her face serious. "I have to tell you something. This is very important."

"No, you need to go, now. I can't have you here. There's a dragon coming, and he'll—"

"I'm Jazal's murderer."

Ajani's words petered out, until his mouth was just hanging empty.

* * * * *

Ajani ushered Zaliki aside, away from the glare of the mana maelstrom.

"I'm so sorry," said Zaliki. "I'll understand if you want to kill me, or never see me again. But you have to know. I was given the task by Marisi."

"What? Marisi? You know he's alive?"

"I've known for over a year, Ajani. The witch Chimamatl contacted him, because she heard there might be a threat to his plans, and hers."

"Jazal."

"Yes. Your brother was seeking answers. Why had the nacatl clans divided? Why did the humans have a prophecy that required your death? What was the meaning behind the celebrations for Marisi, breaker of the Coil? But these questions interfered with Chimamatl's plans for the pride, and with the plans of far greater forces."

"So they killed him."

"*I* killed him. It was I who planted the magics in the bonfire that night. I caused those horrors to emerge at our den."

"Zaliki, why?"

"I'm so sorry. They told me it would just scare everyone, that it would help the pride unify around a common enemy. They told me it would be a convincing illusion, to help quiet the voices against Marisi. I had no idea it would be . . . an assassination."

Ajani's heart pounded. The pain of Jazal's death flooded over him anew.

Ajani, said Jazal's voice in his mind. The sound of his voice was jarring.

"Brother," Ajani answered silently.

This isn't the end of your road, said Jazal. *Remember who she is.*

"She killed you," said Ajani. "She brought the spell vessel to the pride. She brought those creatures to harm you."

She was given the task blind, brother, said Jazal. *She meant to scare me. She didn't know what it would cause. You would destroy Zaliki for delivering another man's poison? Look at her. You've been friends your entire lives. She's the only one alive who sees under that white fur of yours.*

Ajani boiled with rage. Zaliki's eyes didn't rise to meet his own, and tears flowed down her face.

Or if you think it's right, continued Jazal, *then do it. Kill her. Avenge me. You've reached your goal—you've found my killer at last. My spirit will finally rest! So what are you waiting for? Enact your vengeance!*

Ajani's teeth clenched tight. His brother's voice spoke the truth, but it jabbed him in the heart. Zaliki had made a mistake, influenced by Marisi. Jazal's blood was on Marisi's hands, if anyone's. He was the one who had delivered Bolas's dragonscale orb to the pride. He was the one who had brought it into Zaliki's hands. And yet Ajani still wanted to close his claws around her neck.

It's your choice, brother, Jazal said, and then fell silent.

"I knew in my heart it was wrong," Zaliki was saying. "I knew the spell was meant for Jazal, and I even knew it was meant to hurt him."

"Zaliki, I—I need to know. Where is Marisi now?"

"He's dead. I killed him with my own hands."

Just like that, Ajani's chance at vengeance was taken away from him.

"Ajani, I'm so sorry. I should die. I should die so that Jazal can rest." She buried her face in his chest. "I—" Her voice broke into heaving sobs. She said something over and over, something obscured by the tears. Eventually Ajani made it out. "I killed him," she was saying.

An alloy of pity, disgust, and grief melted together in Ajani's mind. He wanted to push her away, embrace her, and crush her all at once—all forces that fought each other, paralyzing him. After a tortured moment, he stood.

Zaliki was a harbinger, not an assassin; in his heart he knew that. Taking revenge on her would only deepen the injustice Jazal had suffered, and reward the sins of the dark forces far beyond her. Ajani's pursuit was not over—just refocused. He would not stop until the being who truly began the chain of events, the evil ultimately responsible for Jazal's death, was punished.

BANT

Knight-Captain Elspeth Tirel had been at the ruins of Giltspire Castle since word came that the demon army approached. She had a private contingent of knights, the responsibility granted to her in Rafiq's prior absence. Among her legion were some of her knight companions from back in Valeron. Any minute now, when the moment came, she would have to order them into the fray, to ask them to die for the world that she had only recently adopted. Her heart was as heavy as a stone. Though she loved that world, Bant was truly theirs, not hers. Thw white stone obelisk behind her, the remains of a great citadel, was not a cherished landmark to Elspeth, but a reminder of the fragility of all she held dear—family, honor, peace.

High above her, angels smashed into screeching demons. Before her, the army of Malfegor approached, thrashing through Asha's Army without so much as a slow in their pace. If Bant's fighters weren't ready for the mages of Esper, Elspeth thought, then they could never conceive of the horrors of war with demons and the undead. Her home was being overrun. She felt a stab of paralyzing terror as the morbid things approached—it was like she was back on her home world again.

Far across the battlefield, over the warring armies, Elspeth saw the demon-dragon abomination, the Grixis general Malfegor. She saw it rear back, spreading its batlike wings to blot out the sun—and saw that its eyes were locked on the white obelisk behind her. Malfegor uttered a vast noise from the bowels of its chest, and raised two of its arms high. Even from where she was, Elspeth could see that between its hands, it was conjuring a noxious tangle of black magic. Bant soldiers and Grixis undead alike began screaming in bloody agony, writhing and toppling onto the battlefield.

"Legion, attack!" Elspeth called. "Mages, fire on that demon! All cavalry, charge that demon! All infantry, destroy that demon!"

Elspeth's troops rode into combat ahead of her, charging into the fray to face Malfegor. She took her place in the saddle of her leotau steed, and was about to follow after them, when she heard a call from behind her, from the road behind the obelisk.

"Elspeth!" shouted her monarch, Aarsil the Blessed, riding a noble stallion at a full gallop, her robes flying in the wind. There was a procession of her servants behind her, but she rode faster than all of them. Aarsil held aloft a shining sword, pointing at Elspeth with it. "Elspeth, this is the Sword of Asha. *You must get this to Rafiq!*"

• • • • •

Malfegor's spell was proceeding as planned. The obelisk opposite him was free, but had never come to life, had never spread the mana of Bant to the center of the maelstrom as Bolas wished. The demon could sense the lattice of protection spells surrounding it. They were powerful, holding in what must be an impressive storage of pure mana, protecting that mana from escaping Bant. But Malfegor had plenty of resources at his disposal to rip down the sheltering magic: there was an entire battlefield of vessels of life energy before him, ready to be torn open to power his spell.

He reached above his head and called up a baleful glyph, and used the power of the spell to drag all the life force from everyone around him—even the tiny scraps of life left in his own undead troops. He had no need nor desire to *win* this battle, he thought; he only needed to kill enough creatures to bring down the magic protecting the obelisk, and then he could be on his way.

As he held the spell, he saw a rush of knights and mages charging at him, dodging around the writhing mortals caught in his spell. Before they could reach him, he crushed the glyph between his claws, breaking loose its power. A shockwave of death rippled outward, leveling everyone before him.

Most of them died instantly, their souls torn roughly from their bodies to feed Malfegor's spell, leaving a wake of crumpled bodies.

It was plenty of power to do the job. Malfegor was sorry to waste such a delectable fusion of soul energy, but he cast it at the obelisk in the form of a black bolt of death.

• • • • •

Down on the battlefield, Rafiq was blasted off his feet by Malfegor's wave of death magic. He felt excruciating, wrenching pain as the sorcery attempted to twist his soul free of his body, and as he tasted firsthand the force of death itself.

When the surge of pain abated, he was alive—but one of only a few. As he looked around him, he saw that nothing stood within the blast radius around Malfegor, as if the demon had swung an enormous scythe to reap both the living and the dead.

Malfegor's magic slammed into the white obelisk, enveloping it in sickly black tendrils for a moment, and then dissipating. The obelisk flared to life with an explosion of white light, blinding Rafiq momentarily. When the

341

light subsided, a stream of distortion led from the top of the obelisk away into the distance, and the demon Malfegor was walking away, back in the same direction.

"No," said Rafiq aloud. It couldn't happen that way. Where was his glorious victory? Where was the fulfillment of Asha's prophecy? Where was Asha herself, lifting high the holy weapon that should have slain this terrible beast?

"Rafiq!" shouted the Knight-Captain Elspeth, riding toward him at speed. She held up a sword by the scabbard, and without warning, flung it at him.

Rafiq caught it. It was incredibly heavy, and warm to the touch even through the scabbard. He unsheathed it, and it was as if the sun had been encased in the leather. Its blade glowed, even at the junction points where it had been fused together by a blacksmith only hours before. And built into the cross-guard of the sword was the Sigil of Asha, the same sigil he had been awarded as Knight-General. Finally, he wielded a part of history—the Sword of Asha.

He stood, and turned to Malfegor's retreating form. He charged the abomination on foot, running toward it despite being dwarfed by the demon's size.

Behind him, Elspeth willed him all the power and protection she could muster, and Rafiq found himself floating as much as running, a charge that lifted him into the air right at the heart of the creature, just as the creature turned to face him.

For a moment, Rafiq felt the touch of divinity. He imagined wings spread out from his back as he held an archangel's sword, soaring over the battlefield toward the lord of evil. I am Asha's return, he thought.

As Malfegor saw the blade, and as the light from the blade approached his skin, he howled. As Rafiq flew toward him, the demon raked his claws across Rafiq's body. Rafiq felt his armor tear away from him as if it were paper, but he didn't feel the hellish claws cut his skin, nor did his trajectory waver. He fell into the beast, his destiny unalterable.

Rafiq swung once, twice, and the sword cut through the abomination, slicing deep channels of light all the way through his body. Two fissures in the shape of an "X" tore Malfegor open from his shoulders to his hips, and his body parted at the seams. The demon's arms fell to the sides, his head rolled backward, and his body crumpled to the ground. The abomination collapsed, a mountain of death, destroyed.

THE
MAELSTROM

Ajani's tormented thoughts of vengeance were shattered by a blast of fire from above.

"Well met, Ajani Goldmane!" shouted Sarkhan, from the back of the dragon Karrthus. Behind them were more dragons, each tearing through the air in their own loops and patterns. As Ajani ran for cover, the dragons wheeled about, and swooped in to breathe fire over the armies of elves and nacatl. Dragonfire scorched great swathes of the humanoids, sending the armies into chaos.

"Destroy them!" shouted the elf Mayael.

The gorge around the mana maelstrom erupted with magic. Elves blasted the dragons with thorn-spiked winds, with particles of Naya jungles shredding their scales and wings. Zaliki threw strength magic across the humanoid armies, trying to boost their resilience to the flames. Even Kresh's warriors cast symbolic war-curses into the fray as they leveled all their spears at the draconic enemies.

Torrents of magic whipped all around Ajani; he felt it thrashing at his mind. The dragons' rage, the armies' spellcasting—it all served to churn up the maelstrom of mana before him. As streams of mana flowed into it from four directions, flares of jagged energy also surged outward from it, lashing the dragons and humanoid warriors alike. As magic swirled around the gorge, the maelstrom only got more and more violent.

They were contributing to it, he thought, and they needed to stop feeding it. If any entity was able to tap into that much primal power, it could overload, sending the maelstrom and the lines of mana that fed it into a chain reaction that could destroy all five worlds.

So when a new, *fifth* stream of mana flickered to life, from the obelisk in Bant, Ajani knew he had to do something drastic.

● ● ● ● ●

You've put it together, brother, said Jazal's voice.

"I have to stop it," said Ajani. "We're causing the maelstrom. We're feeding it."

So, stop feeding it, said Jazal.

"But I have to stop them *all* from feeding it."

So, stop them all.

Ajani's vision clouded. Around him he saw only the streaks of mana—nature magic, magic of fire and rage, magic of healing and protection, and others—thrashing back and forth between the humanoids and Sarkhan's flight of rage-blooded dragons. All of them were fueled by bonds of mana, bonds that anchored their magic to the power inherent in the realms of Alara. To his surprise, Ajani could perceive the bonds directly, as if they had been beams of light revealed by smoke. He saw traceries of connection and correspondence all around him, joining every mage and monster with their sources of power all over the world. The volume of mana flowing from all corners of Alara was enormous, all cascading to the maelstrom at the intersection of all the shards.

It had to stop. He had to staunch the flow somehow.

Ajani saw his own mana bonds, bonds not only with Naya, but with the volcanic shard of Jund where he had first planeswalked. He saw the cauldron of lava into which Sarkhan had vaulted, and into which he threw himself in a moment of glory and rage. He summoned mana from all sources he knew, and cast it all out in one savage roar.

Energy blasted outward from Ajani, throwing a metaphysical gust around the maelstrom gorge. The blast shook the earth with one savage jolt, and for a moment, everything stopped. Mages and dragons both halted their assault, and looked around bewildered.

The outburst of rage subsided, and became a simple breeze ruffling Ajani's fur.

All the combatants recovered then, and attempted to rejoin their fight—but found that their mana bonds had all been severed. They had no mana to fuel their spells, and the essence of the dragons' flames had drained away.

Smoke wafted from Ajani's fur.

The dragons spiraled high up into the air, screeching in rage. Sarkhan slapped the flanks of the hellkite Karrthus with his heels, and the two of them veered away from the fight. All the dragons beat their wings hard, retreating somewhere in the direction of Jund.

A cheer went up among the elves and nacatl.

"Ajani, you did it," said Zaliki. "I don't know how you did it, but you stopped their magic."

Ajani nodded, exhausted.

"And I can't thank you enough," said the dragon planeswalker Nicol Bolas, as he appeared out of the sky.

BANT

Ajani watched with awe as the oily-scaled elder dragon descended from the savage sky above the mana maelstrom. The creature's scales matched the dragonscale spheres he had seen used to sow chaos on Naya, but the sense of majesty Ajani felt radiating from the beast was the way he truly knew he faced the one behind the plane-spanning plot to create the maelstrom.

"Hello, little walker," said Bolas.

Ajani had only a dim sense of the action around him, of the elves and nacatl attempting to attack Bolas. As Ajani had destroyed their mana bonds, the humanoids were powerless to attack him. Bolas looked from side to side as he landed before Ajani, killing dozens with a thought. Ajani saw elves, humans, and nacatl he knew dying by the moment.

"Retreat, all of you!" shouted Ajani. "Go!"

With Sarkhan's dragons dispersed and the black dragon killing them at will, they didn't need more instruction than that. All around the two planeswalkers, the armies fled in every direction.

"Ajani, don't do this," cried Zaliki. "Don't put yourself in evil's way."

"Someone has to," Ajani told her. "Go, Zaliki. Now."

Goodbye, he thought after her as she reluctantly turned in the direction of Naya, and he watched her run out of the gorge with the Cloud Nacatl warriors.

Bolas watched them go, a bemused curl warping his lips. Then he turned his head to Ajani, the tiny nacatl before him, and folded his claws together.

THE
MAELSTROM

You took a while to show up, little walker," said Bolas. "I need to stop overestimating mortals."

"I've been looking," snarled Ajani. "You've been hiding."

"Hiding? Hardly. I've been a step away from you your whole life, little cat. Tantalizingly close. *My* door's been wide open. But I don't blame you for your clumsy mistakes. You've only just learned to take your first steps. To you I seemed so far away, so ineffable, so unreal. You didn't even have anything in your experience to compare me to, did you? You had no frame of reference, no theoretical web in which to embed the monumental idea of me. So you couldn't know. You were literally incapable of knowing. I've seen distances you couldn't imagine—how could you? Your imagination has been closed inside the boundaries of a singular world. But it didn't make sense, did it? Your brother's death? The coincidences? The sums didn't balance. Little Naya just was too shallow a bowl to hold all the facts."

Ajani seethed. "I'm here, aren't I?"

"Ah, but what now? What's the next link in this chain, little walker? Will you get your revenge? Will you—*kill* me? Put your dead brother's axe in my guts, and wiggle the handle till I'm dead? Stop me from fulfilling my goals here on your beloved worlds? And after that, what, march home a champion? I'm sorry; I don't mean to be flip. It is very important to you, I know. But you can't see. You can't see how painfully trite you are. There'll be no pathos in your death, Ajani Goldmane, no grand nobility. Only the shabby banality of a thousand indistinguishable upstarts."

With that, Bolas flicked his claw, and blasted Ajani back with the force of a meteor. Ajani slammed backward into the slope of the gorge, and slumped limp.

"I've lived hundreds of your lifetimes," continued Bolas. "I've survived more apocalypses than you've had *chest colds*. I've experienced more of this cosmos than any being there has *ever been*. And you think you're going to stand in my way, matchstick? You think you're the one to finally take me down? I can tell you now, if Nicol Bolas is to fall, it won't be because of the likes of you."

Ajani elbowed his way off his back into a sitting position. With his weight on one arm and blood dripping from his mouth, he spoke. "For being so old, you throw a tantrum like a child."

Bolas snarled and snapped his arm back in the other direction. Ajani flew bodily across the gorge, slamming sideways into the ground again.

Ajani groaned and coughed blood onto the walls of the gorge. He searched his mouth with his tongue and felt two teeth loose, but clenched them into place with his jaw.

Bolas approached. "Again, you're centuries too late to play the insolent, devil-may-care hero. It's been done far too many times, and by better beings than you. It's played out. You don't have a million-to-one chance, little walker. This isn't your once-in-a-lifetime shot at the hero's truimph. This is you, flyswatted."

"Doesn't make sense," muttered Ajani. "Your plan."

Bolas grinned. "See how it pleads for additional moments? See how it strings together its last breaths, hoping to stall for time, so it can find that crucial way out of the impossible situation?"

"If I'm so insignificant, why the roundabout plot to kill me, Bolas? Why the spells carried by underlings? Why the white cat prophecies? If I'm nothing, why go to all that trouble? And if I'm *not* nothing, if I could represent some kind of threat to you, why be so coy? Why not just planeswalk to Naya and murder me in my crib?"

"You're right, of course," replied Bolas. "I am prone to theatrics. When one has no peers, one likes to entertain oneself, you see? It's self-indulgent, I admit, but I do like to watch my own symphony play itself out."

"No," said Ajani, his mouth bleeding. "That isn't why. That's not why you sent all the intermediaries, why you had everyone do your dirty work but yourself. I think it's because you've tasted your own mortality. You're powerful, but you understand you have weaknesses. I can see it in you. Even you, ancient dragon, are afraid."

Bolas's cheek spikes fanned out, and his chest filled with rage. The energies from the whirling maelstrom lit him from behind, casting his face into blackness. He spread his wings out, looking like a god, and stretched his claws toward Ajani's face.

But then he stopped and stepped back.

"Tut, tut," he said. "You almost made me forget what I was here to do."

Bolas turned and stepped into the center of the maelstrom.

* * * * *

Ajani shielded his eyes. The maelstrom exploded into a sphere of light, drenching the dragon planeswalker in waves of power. The force of the blast crushed Ajani into the wall of the chasm, feeling like a continuous barrage of electric shocks. There was either no sound, or so much sound that Ajani had gone deaf.

Unable to cope with complex thought, Ajani's mind repeated one phrase over and over: He's done it. He's done it.

The explosion of power died down to a mere hurricane. Ajani's sense of hearing returned: a thunderous, continuous roar. Ajani squinted into the light, and perceived the contours of a draconic being coiled into a fetal position.

The dragon moved within the radiance. Its wings opened; its arms and legs stretched out; its tail uncoiled and spread long and majestic; its head reared up to the empty sky; its mouth opened. It was unmistakably Bolas, but Ajani thought he looked larger than he had been, or somehow more grandiose. He had no scars or wounds, no frayed scales on his pinions, no scruffy patches at his joints. He was smooth, sleek, a study in armored scale stretched over lean muscle. He had become everything that his potential allowed him to be: he was a divinity of the Multiverse.

Bolas let loose a roar that tore the firmament ragged, reverberating through all of existence. Ajani felt pain wrack his body for the duration of the roar. That's it, he thought. The is the end of my life, and worse: the end of all life on my world. Bolas is done with our plane. He'll crumple Alara into dust, and destroy everyone on it.

The dragon ascended out of the maelstrom slowly, surging with power. The winds slackened, and Ajani saw that as Bolas moved out of the nucleus, the energy there diminished rapidly. The glow of power followed Bolas and then disappeared into him, leeched away by his body. All that was left behind was a tiny sun-ball floating above the spiral depression in the land, a meek swirl of energy no bigger than Ajani was tall. Bolas had almost absorbed it all.

The dragon looked down at Ajani, his expression inscrutable. Was he murderous or benevolent? Did he even have emotions, or just an intelligence so vast that his mind operated solely in pure thought?

Bolas spoke, and his voice was everywhere at once. "*I fear nothing.*"

"Don't do it, Bolas," shouted Ajani up at the dragon god. "Just go. You've done enough damage here."

"*Why should I not? It's a disgrace now, a ruin bereft of value.*"

"No. It's my world."

With a mighty leap, Ajani dived into what remained of the maelstrom. It enveloped him, suspending him in the air, filling him with a rush of mana that overloaded his senses.

With even a fraction of the power of the maelstrom, Ajani was overwhelmed. He couldn't believe Bolas had held any more than that—he felt the efforts of thousands of mages all at once, channeling their magics at one another, feeding him with their power.

Ajani closed his physical eyes, and his inner one opened.

AJANI
GOLDMANE

The world was stark and featureless: a white void.

"Ajani," said his brother's voice.

He turned. Before him stood Jazal: silver-furred, kind-faced, and alive, at least in spirit. Ajani realized that their hands were clasped together.

"Jazal, I've been searching," said Ajani.

"I know."

"I . . . I can't avenge you. I'm sorry. The real killer—the being ultimately responsible for your death—he's out there. He's far more powerful than me."

"I know."

"And Zaliki—she was misled. It wasn't her fault. She loves you."

"I know. It's all right, Ajani."

"I'm sorry I failed you."

"Is that what you've done?"

"Yes. It was all too big for me. The murder, the five worlds, the multiverse—everything was bigger than I imagined. It was too much for me to handle."

"That's the first thing you have to learn before you can rise to accomplish grander things."

"But that'll never happen. It's over. He won. I didn't catch on in time to stop him—his plans are complete. He gained the power he sought. There's no way I can put you to rest—and even worse, our world, all of Alara, is about to be used up and tossed aside."

"You're still here, aren't you? You haven't given up. If you're still committed to what must be done, then there's still a chance. Listen."

"I'm listening."

"No, really *listen*. You're standing in the core of Alara, its beating heart. *This* is what I was searching for, the possibility that there was something underneath all the lies of Marisi and his master. This is it, this core of mana, composed of threads of lives from every corner of Alara. It's what Bolas wanted to feed on, and what you have the opportunity to learn from. So *listen*."

"I hear . . . echoes."

"Yes. What does it mean, Ajani? What are they telling you?"

"I can almost hear them . . ."

Ajani felt Jazal's hands slipping away.

"Jazal? Wait! Don't go!"

"What are they telling you, Ajani?" His face, and his voice, were growing fainter, vanishing into the white nothingness. Even as Ajani reached for him, he faded.

"Jazal!"

THE
MAELSTROM

Bolas laughed. *"This won't do it, little walker. You can't match me by feeding on my scraps. Even all the mages in this world couldn't stop me."*

"Maybe not," said Ajani. "But one thing can."

The voices of every spellcaster in Alara spoke to Ajani at once. Their near-limitless knowledge, for one cacophonous moment, was clear to him. Ajani could see it. Deep inside Bolas was a spark, an eternal essence, just like any other mortal being. Perhaps he wasn't bound by the same rules as other beings; the power Ajani perceived there was blinding, mind-splitting. But the dragon still shared that simple, essential core of consciousness, that quintessence that some called soul. And though Ajani couldn't strike down that soul, he could do the reverse—he could nurture it, cause it to blossom, and will its essence into being.

"You've always brought out the best in others, Ajani," he imagined Jazal saying. "That was always your gift."

Ajani evoked the essence of Bolas.

Energy coursed out of Bolas's chest like a stream of star-encrusted aether, crashing into the depression left by the maelstrom, and splashing against the rim to curve in on itself. The stream warped and distorted as a form took shape.

At first it looked like a dragon made of surreal air-distortion, suffused with an ultraviolet glow. As it continued to cohere, detail after detail resolved like a distant image coming into focus until it was a glowing, astral reflection of Bolas himself.

The two dragon-beings regarded one another, their movements curiously alike. Their mimicry infuriated one another, and they howled, a sonic mirror. The two dragons crashed into one another, grappling each other in rage. They both knew that they were the greatest threat to one another in all of Alara. They both knew each other's power and treachery, and knew that giving an opening to the other would mean their own destruction. Magical energies pulsed out of them as each one struggled to conquer the mind and soul of the other, trying to use the other as their pawn; both of them countered the other with magic designed to prevent the psychic assault. They surged with the power of the mana storm, one in the form of scaly flesh, the other in the form of starry aether.

Ajani crawled up the slope, out of the valley of the maelstrom. He could feel the two dragon-beings' power thunderclapping against one another, hear their claws scraping for purchase on each other's scales. He could feel the raw potential lashing out from them, the tension rising as they fought at the center of the storm. If one of them decided to destroy the other, Ajani thought, then both of them undoubtedly would, and all of Alara would be consumed in their fury. It was up to them—the choice belonged, ultimately, to Bolas, and the nature of his soul. Ajani hurried up the slope, attained the rim of the crater, and turned back to the dragons.

The Bolases were perfectly matched—each blow was met with counterblow, each attempt to gain advantage slapped aside with perfect precision. They were one vast intelligence racing to outdo itself, one mind trying to exceed its own potential—and they were failing.

Suddenly the dragons reared back, gazed with pure

hatred into one another's eyes, and then thrust their necks forward and snapped their jaws onto one another. The streaming energy of the maelstrom enveloped the draconic ouroboros, and a flash of thunderous light overwhelmed Ajani's senses.

There was nothing for several moments, only light and silence.

I've failed, thought Ajani. Alara has been destroyed.

Then, slowly, the sound of the wind returned to Ajani's ears. The sensation of it blowing in his fur felt strange, as if he'd forgotten what it felt like to feel something so simple. Gradually, the aggressive light faded, and the world emerged before his eyes again. The crater was empty. There were no dragons, and there was no storm of mana. The valley was filled only with the wind.

Ajani sat down heavily. The breeze ruffled his coat, fine white fur newly tinted with wisps of gold. Nothing else stirred.

Ajani sat at the edge of the valley for a long time, waiting for Bolas to return and devour the rest of Alara. But he never did.

BANT

"Elspeth? You called me here?"

The world of Bant was Elspeth's paradise. She had come as a stranger, a planeswalker escaping from an unspeakable past, yet she had been welcomed as family. Bant was the first place where she truly felt at home, a place she had vowed never to leave.

But now look at it, she thought. It was in ruin. She could see the balefires from her window, pouring smoke composed of the dead into the air. She could see the dead imprinted on her memory, those friends she had sent to their deaths, and the thousands in Asha's Army who had perished trying to fend off the undead hordes. The world was irrevocably changed. Her home, her family, her Bant, was no more.

"Come in, Knight Mardis," she said.

Mardis stepped just inside the threshold of her quarters. He seemed almost shy. They hadn't spoken since the battle with Malfegor, which he had barely survived.

"Thank you for coming," she said.

"Of course, Knight-Captain. I trust you're well?"

That was a strange question.

"I am . . .well, thank you." She always lied clumsily. "And you? How is your family?"

"Quite well, thank you for asking."

He delivered his lies much better, she thought. She 359

knew his family had lost much in the war, as everyone had. Everyone who had real families—unlike her, the orphan from beyond the sky. She felt like the stranger again, as she had felt when she first fell into Bant.

"I wanted to ask you here to tell you . . . to give you . . . something," she stammered.

"That's nice of you," he said.

He was so polite and gracious. That made it harder. She almost wished he would yell at her, so that she could deliver the blow more easily.

"What is it?" he asked.

"Oh. I, uh—" What was she going to give him? She didn't actually know. It struck her that she had no memento of Bant. There was no plaque, no ring, no ornately-framed painting to commemorate that she had ever been there. When she had arrived she had owned nothing, and she never came to possess anything of consequence while living there, no token of her connection.

She truly was an orphan, she thought. So she deserved to feel like one. Who calls a place a home, and then fails to defend it as her own?

"I'm sorry," she said. "I guess I don't really have anything to give you."

Mardis pressed his lips firmly together. His words came out clipped. "You're leaving Valeron."

Elspeth swallowed. "I . . . Yes. I'm leaving . . . Valeron."

"But why?"

"It's important that I leave." I can't stay, she thought. I can't stay and see what war has done to Bant.

"But where will you go?" asked Mardis. "The whole world's like this. Surely you're not moving to one of the other shards?"

"I'm not sure yet." No, she was leaving Alara altogether,

which her friend couldn't understand. But she could see that he understood how serious she was.

"But you can't leave," said Mardis, finally displaying true emotion. "You're of the Sigiled caste. You'd be deserting your post. You'd be violating your oath as a knight."

"I know."

"But that means you could never come back."

"I know."

Mardis looked stung. *That* was the face, she thought. That was the face she had predicted he would make, that somehow she had hoped he would make. That was the true gift she could give him—to make him hate her, to sever their friendship under brutal circumstances, so that she could never be missed. She had called him there to betray him, so that he would have good reason to move on, to live his own life, and forget her.

"I'll remember you," he said.

"Thank you," she said.

But no, you won't, Mardis, she thought. After I go, I'll fade from your memory, and you'll fill your life with your loved ones again. There'll be nothing left of me, nothing to show that I was ever on bant. It is what I am. It is my life, always trying to find native soil, but never leaving footprints. But I'll remember you, Mardis. I'll remember Bant forever. I'm sorry. I'm sorry.

They almost embraced, but instead shook hands awkwardly. He looked like he was about to say something more, but instead he turned and walked out. The door shut gently.

Elspeth turned back to the window. Outside, an acolyte wheeled a cart over to one of the funeral pyres, and tipped someone's son or daughter onto it.

She closed the shutters on the window, and then waited until dark to planeswalk away.

Mubin recognized the snarl of the leotau first, coming in through the window. Then he recognized the particular jounce of metal armor and sigils as the man climbed off the steed. Then he recognized the voice.

"Mubin?" the voice called. "Are you in here?"

It was Rafiq, the so-called hero. He'd finally come back from the war.

"You old bastard," Mubin said to the paladin as he entered. "I owe the clerics a bag of coin now—the errant knight has returned."

"That's Knight-General to you," Rafiq said.

"Oh ho, is it now? No, I think I should call you Knight-Idiot for the stunt you pulled. That mission to Esper was *ours*. I was supposed to go with you, and when I got hurt—" He stopped.

"It doesn't matter anymore, Mubin," said Rafiq, full of cheer. "I've done it. I have it. I've returned with the etherium. It's the only good thing to come out of this war—you'll be able to walk again."

Mubin allowed his spirits to jump for a moment. "You did?"

Could he actually have done it? Mubin wondered. He mouthed the gasp of hope that he wanted to breathe. Still, even in his rising mood, he felt the weight of guilt. "You risked your neck unnecessarily," he said. "Anybody could have been sent to do this."

"Nobody more motivated," said Rafiq dismissively. "We've got everything we need out in the cart. I've already got the clergy working on the incantations."

Mubin felt wary. An alien form of magic, intruding his body? A ritual using borrowed words and components from a world away? But if he refused to try, Rafiq would never see him walk again. Worse, Mubin's immobile limbs would serve as an eternal reminder of his friend's error—and of the rift between them. If he never got out of his bed, it would make Rafiq's arduous mission all for nothing.

"So," Mubin said finally. "When can we start?"

Rafiq's laugh filled the room, and released a soul's worth of pent-up hope.

JUND

Sarkhan reached back and snapped an arrow shaft that jutted from between his shoulder blades. As he walked, he tried to excavate the arrowhead out from his back with a knife. Elves make good quality arrows, he thought; they dig deep and clutch at you from the inside. He wondered whether the arrowhead lodged in his back was carved from the bone of some great Naya beast. He imagined the bone shard sizzling as it came in contact with his blood, the blood that was corrupted by drops from the veins of his master, Bolas.

The battle had not gone well for Sarkhan, and he was not eager to seek out the ancient dragon, wherever he had gone, and face his judgment. He was not eager to explain that his mana bonds were shorn from him by a neophyte planeswalker, and that he fled, the authority over his flight of dragons dwindling as his mana left him, all the way back to Jund.

He dug at the skin on his back, wincing slightly, and finally wrung the arrowhead free. He stopped walking up the trail for a moment and looked at it in his hand. It was no mighty bone shard; it was just a chipped stone triangle in a handful of blood. It struck him that it was his allegiance to Bolas, he thought. That was his fate, to be a weapon drowned in another's blood. He had the brief, bizarre impulse to plunge the arrowhead into his eyeballs. The thought made him chuckle, and the chuckle turned into uncontrolled laughter that went on until he was hoarse.

Keep your mind together, he warned himself. But he thought of Bolas's black silhouette on the sky, and couldn't think of a reason why he should.

He walked to the edge of the Sweltering Cauldron, the volcanic caldera where he had taught a cat-man about fire and rage. The lava bubbled below him, oppressively hot, blackening his feet through his boots. He wondered what it would be like to be lowered, bit by bit, into that glowing red sludge.

He chortled crazily, and then planeswalked away from Alara.

BANT

I'm told this isn't often done this late in life," said the healer, a middle-aged human woman.

Mubin lay on the bed in the cleric's temple, a broad protection circle surrounding the bed. The covers were pulled up, leaving his limp legs exposed. Next to him, Rafiq looked on with a brother's worry. The healer bound her long sleeves up with loops of twine and arranged the translations of the Esper rituals along Mubin's bedside.

Next to the bed, a small cauldron of silver metal roiled and bubbled. The liquid behaved as though it were boiling hot, but there was no fire under it, and it didn't fume into the air. Either etherium boiled cool, or some magic in the cauldron was keeping it an unnaturally active liquid.

"Esper beings get etherium enhancements well into old age," continued the healer, "but the first infusion is usually done on a young body, a body that's still growing and easily able to heal. Healing helps the body incorporate the alloy. But in principle, this should work on an adult."

"Don't you worry," Rafiq said. "She's the best. She was our balmgiver on our mission, and she was right there with us when we captured the formula. She knows everything that anybody on Bant knows about this process."

That didn't sound entirely promising. "Should I be asleep?" asked Mubin.

"It's better if you're awake, so you can answer my

questions," said the healer. "I'll need as much information back from you as you can provide me. If you feel anything strange, tell me, all right?"

Mubin looked at his legs, and at the cauldron of silvery etherium. He felt strange, all right. But he just nodded.

Mubin's legs were numb as the balmgiver did her work on them. He couldn't see much over the raised sheet, but if he craned his neck, he could get a glimpse of how his legs had been sliced from thigh to foot, and the skin flayed open. The healer was chanting quietly and pouring the silvery alloy into the long wounds. The sight made him dizzy, and he lay down.

He had no sensation in his legs, but it wasn't long before he felt a flood of strange sensations throughout the rest of his body. He felt energized, as if all the systems in his body were being organized more effectively and efficiently. He felt strength returning to muscles that he didn't even realize had atrophied since his injury. He felt strangely youthful. His dizziness turned to euphoria.

"Are you *giggling?*" Rafiq asked incredulously.

"Was I?"

"I think you were. It's difficult to tell on a rhox, but I wouldn't know what else to call it."

"That's enough, you two," said the healer. "I'm almost done here, but I don't need you disturbing the patient, Knight-General."

Mubin grinned, and tried to relax, as the healer chanted.

"The filigree is taking shape," she said.

Rafiq's eyes widened as he stared down at Mubin's legs. "You should be seeing this," he said. "It's amazing. The metal is twining in on itself, branching and . . . stretching, as it cools and sets. It's making . . . something. Something beautiful."

"It's making knees," the healer said quietly.

367

Mubin was hardly prepared for the electric pain that stabbed through his body. He moaned as blades cut their way through his veins and tiny lightning excruciated his nerves. He didn't have time to ask what was wrong before it overwhelmed his mind, and he passed out.

★ ★ ★ ★ ★

Rafiq watched purple splotches spread their way up Mubin's body. The process was sickeningly swift; he could see the rhox's skin bruising from the inside out, starting at his legs, moving up his chest and neck and out into his arms.

"Something's wrong," he said. "Get it out of him. The etherium, it's . . . poisoning him. Can't you see that? Get your knives and cut it out of him now!"

The balmgiver was moving quickly, drawing angelic symbols across his body with sacred dyes, but she couldn't contain the reaction. It was spreading too fast.

Mubin's body jerked, and his back arched once, twice. His eyes were clenched shut, and sweat ran down his face. His lungs pumped up and down, making loose wheezing sounds.

"Do something," Rafiq said. "You have to save him. Oh Asha, I've made a mistake. What have I done?"

"I'll do everything I can," said the healer. "I'm giving him a balm to ease the pain, but we have little knowledge of this kind of magic. It appears to be an infection of some kind, but the usual methods of treating it aren't working. I'm afraid we have nothing to combat this infection."

Mubin's convulsions stopped, and his breathing slowed.

"He's coming around," said the healer. She touched Rafiq's arm. "I'd advise you to make your peace."

No, thought Rafiq. Not yet. "Every time," he said. "Every time I thought I was doing something right, old friend, I've done everything wrong."

Mubin's eyelids opened as slits. His eyes found Rafiq's.

"How's it going, old friend," Mubin croaked.

Rafiq blinked rapidly. A lump was forming in his throat. "You're doing well. It's going to be fine."

"Sure," said Mubin. "I'll be dancing. In no time."

"Don't task yourself. Rest."

"I'm fine. Growing pains." The old rhox smiled. Purple contusions slithered up his cheeks.

"Mubin, I'm sorry," Rafiq whispered. "I've failed at every turn."

"It's not about that, old friend," said Mubin. "Your virtue . . . made you blind. While you looked into the sun, they stabbed you . . . You just never—"

Mubin gritted his teeth, and coughed black blood through them.

Rafiq hurried to wipe his lips, and pat the sweat on his brow. Mubin's eyes closed, his head sagged, and he fell back into unconsciousness.

Mubin never woke up again.

●●●●●

"It's time to go, Knight-General," said the girl, Rafiq's newly-assigned squire. She was the same young page who had once polished the faces of his sigils for him. She was more nursemaid than squire, he thought. He couldn't remember her name.

"I'm not going to that thing," Rafiq muttered. If Mubin were there, he wouldn't try to make him leave his chamber. Not when he felt that way.

"You have to go, sir; you're being honored," she said. "You're getting the Sigil of the Grand Laurel. I told you, remember?"

She was supposed to be very promising as a young knight-to-be, and she was of course humble to a fault when they were reintroduced. She admired him and his

369

glorious deeds; it was an honor to see him again; it would be her privilege to serve as his attendant from now on. It made him feel sick inside.

"I don't want any more sigils."

"I'll get your gown," said Thilka, or whatever her name was. "Oh, the messenger was outside—do you know a couple called the Levacs? They say they had a baby. A daughter. And they want you to be her godfather."

Rafiq wondered what he had said at Mubin's funeral. Mubin's body had been interred in the burial grounds behind the palace of Aarsil the Blessed, not far from the Twelve Trees of Valeron that the old rhox had helped dig up, and not far from the reliquary where he and Rafiq had first met so long ago. Rafiq barely remembered the ceremony. Had he given a speech? Had he raved like a lunatic? He hadn't the haziest idea. He remembered the girl—Thenka or whatever her name was—escorting him to the carriage, and how he'd demanded she take him to the old watering hole in the neighboring village, and he remembered the painful hangover the next day.

The squire girl brought him his formal court-gown, and began the process of getting him inside it. He didn't resist. He was watching a spot on the wall, where a spider was creeping up the wall. It moved a few inches, and then stopped, then turned, then moved a few more inches. Rafiq wondered if the spider was deciding on an overall course of action, or whether it was making turns at random and letting chance decide its destination. All his life he had tried to make the right and virtuous choices, he thought, but every time he felt that chance had twisted them beyond recognition. He had been the plaything of prophets, rulers, and demons. He had followed the path of virtue at every turn, and where had it gotten him?

The spider doubled back on its previous progress, crawling over a crack in the wood beams of the wall.

DOUG BEYER

There it stopped, and waited for something only a spider could understand. Then it zigzagged yet again and headed in a new direction.

It was worse than being a victim of fate. If his life had been just a sequence of random events, he might actually understand all the destruction, betrayal, and death. He might understand Mubin's death as a tragic accident brought on by sightless fortune. But he knew that he had made choices in each of the tragedies that befell him. The common factor behind every misfortune in his life was himself.

"There you are," said the girl—Thokka, or whatever. She had managed to get him in his gown despite himself. "How handsome you look. You're all ready to receive the Sigil of the Grand Laurel. Now let's go, sir, we can't afford to keep the Blessed caste waiting. Would you like to wear your sword to the ceremony, sir, or Knight Mubin's?"

"I'm not one to choose," he said.

As she led him out of the chamber, he watched the spider speed across the wall for a moment, then turn suddenly, then move in a slow arc back to the place where it had started.

NAYA

Ajani pushed a sponge into the bottom of the wooden bucket, soaking up the water and cleanser, and squeezed it out. He scrubbed the rough stone floor of Jazal's lair, where the bed had been, wiping up the stains. The spot had discolored to black and had soaked into the porous stone, but Ajani worked at it with vigor.

"Ajani? Can I come in?" Zaliki's voice.

Ajani didn't look up. "I don't know. Do you think you deserve to come in here?"

Zaliki watched him scrub the stain from the mouth of the cave.

"You're right. I'll go."

"Wait, Zaliki. I have to tell you something."

She stopped, but didn't face him. "What is it."

"I'm going. Tonight."

"Where?" She turned. "Away from Naya?"

"Away from everything. Away from Alara."

She watched him squeeze water onto the stain. Rehydrated blood flowed along cracks in the floor.

"Will you ever be back?"

"I can't say," he said. "I don't think this world is . . . meant for me. I don't know."

"I'll miss you," she said.

"I'm appointing you *kha*."

"What?"

"I've met with the elders. In light of recent events, they not only look me in the eye now—they've offered me leadership of the pride. But I'm abdicating the *kha* position to you. Please, do this for me."

"Ajani, I—"

"I need to know that someone will take care of this pride. Someone who will carry on what Jazal was trying to do. Who will reunify with the Cloud Nacatl and communicate with the elves. Someone who will make sure no one is trying to infiltrate us again."

"And for that you choose *me?*"

"I know. It sounds strange. To be honest, I thought about killing you for a while."

Zaliki swallowed.

"I'm sorry. But I decided you understood what you'd done. In fact, you're the one I'd most rely on never to fall into a trap from outside the pride again. You've seen what it leads to, and it's hurt you. You'd be the last person to make that mistake now."

"Is that . . . forgiveness?"

"It's close. It's trust."

Zaliki's eyes scanned the ceiling of the cave. "Thank you."

"I've made all the arrangements. Please go now."

She opened her mouth, but closed it again. She looked at him one last time, and left.

Ajani scrubbed all night until the floor was clean. He carried the bucket outside the lair and dumped the soiled water over the ledge, into the jungle below.

MAGIC
The Gathering®

Everything you thought you knew
about MAGIC™ novels is changing…

From the mind of

ARI MARMELL

comes a tour de force of imagination.

AGENTS OF ARTIFICE

The ascendance of a new age in the planeswalker
mythology: be a part of the book that takes fans
deeper than ever into the lives of the Multiverse's most
powerful beings:

Jace Beleren
A powerful mind-mage whose choices now will forever
determine his path as a planeswalker.

Liliana Vess
A dangerous necromancer whose beauty belies a dark
secret and even darker associations.

Tezzeret
Leader of an inter-planar consortium whose quest for
knowledge may be undone by his lust for power.

Magic: The Gathering®

Confrontation leads
to conflagration
in this hot new
planeswalker
adventure.

THE
PURIFYING
FIRE

By award-winning author

LAURA
RESNICK

On Alaroon, among an encalve
of like-minded pyromancers,
Chandra draws the attention of
an ancient faith that sees her as
a herald of an apocalypse. Will
she control her own destiny,
or suffer the will of others?

JULY 2009

Comprehensive and painstakingly detailed…

For an exclusive, insider's guide to MAGIC: THE GATHERING's fall expansion set, *A Planeswalker's Guide to Alara* offers lavish, full-color illustrations from concept art to final cards as well as an in-depth review of each of the shards of this fractured plane. Never before have planeswalkers been given such complete access to the world of MAGIC: THE GATHERING® as creative-team insiders Doug Beyer and Jenna Helland chart a course through unknown reaches of the Shards of Alara.

A PLANESWALKER'S GUIDE TO

EBERRON

DRACONIC PROPHECIES

James Wyatt

From acclaimed author
and award-winning game
designer James Wyatt, an
adventure that will shake
the world of EBERRON.

STORM DRAGON
AVAILABLE NOW IN PAPERBACK

DRAGON FORGE
IN PAPERBACK APRIL 2009

DRAGON WAR
IN HARDCOVER AUGUST 2009

Richard Lee Byers

The Haunted Lands

Epic magic • Unholy alliances • Armies of undead
The battle for Thay has begun.

Book I
Unclean

Book II
Undead

Book III
Unholy
February 2009

Anthology
Realms of the Dead
Edited by Susan J. Morris
January 2010

"This is Thay as it's never been shown before . . . Dark,
sinister, foreboding and downright disturbing!"
—Alaundo, Candlekeep.com on *Unclean*